STARS AND BONES BOOK II

Mage in the Undercity

BEATRICE B. MORGAN

AUTHORS 4 AUTHORS PUBLISHING
Marysville, WA, USA

Published by Authors 4 Authors Publishing
1214 6th St
Marysville, WA 98275
www.authors4authorspublishing.com

Library of Congress Control Number: 2020936734

E-book ISBN: 978-1-64477-106-8
Paperback ISBN: 978-1-64477-107-5
Audiobook ISBN: 978-1-64477-057-3

Edited by Rebecca Milkkelson
Copyedited by Brandi Spencer

Cover design ©2021 Brandi Spencer. All rights reserved. Interior layout and designs by Brandi Spencer.

Authors 4 Authors branding is set in Bavire. Book title is set in Allura and Bilbo Swash Caps. Series title and other headers are set in Cinzel. Juniper's handwriting in Bilbo. All other text is set in Garamond.

STARS AND BONES BOOK II

Mage
in the
Undercity

BEATRICE B. MORGAN

AUTHORS 4 AUTHORS CONTENT RATING

This title has been rated 17+, appropriate for older teens and adults, and contains:

- Intense implied sex
- Intense violence
- Moderate language
- Mild alcohol use
- Child slavery

Please, keep the following in mind when using our rating system:

1. A content rating is not a measure of quality.

Great stories can be found for every audience. One book with many content warnings and another with none at all may be of equal depth and sophistication. Our ratings can work both ways: to avoid content or to find it.

2. Ratings are merely a tool.

For our young adult (YA) and children's titles, age ratings are generalized suggestions. For parents, our descriptive ratings can help you make informed decisions, but at the end of the day, only you know what kinds of content are appropriate for your individual child. This is why we provide details in addition to the general age rating.

For more information on our rating system, please, visit our Content Guide at: www.authors4authorspublishing.com/books/ratings

DEDICATION

To Laurel, for being there through
every season and every storm.

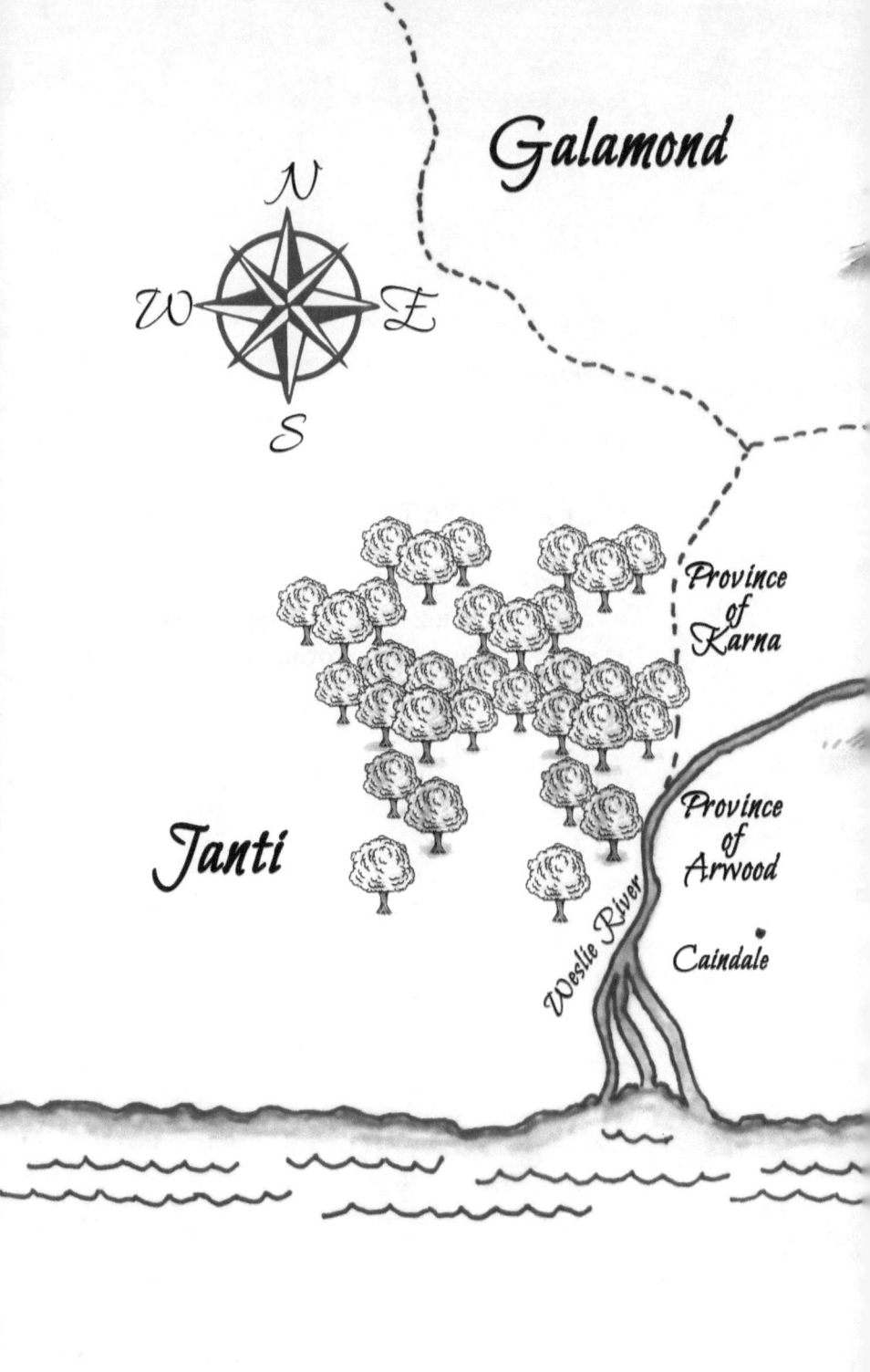

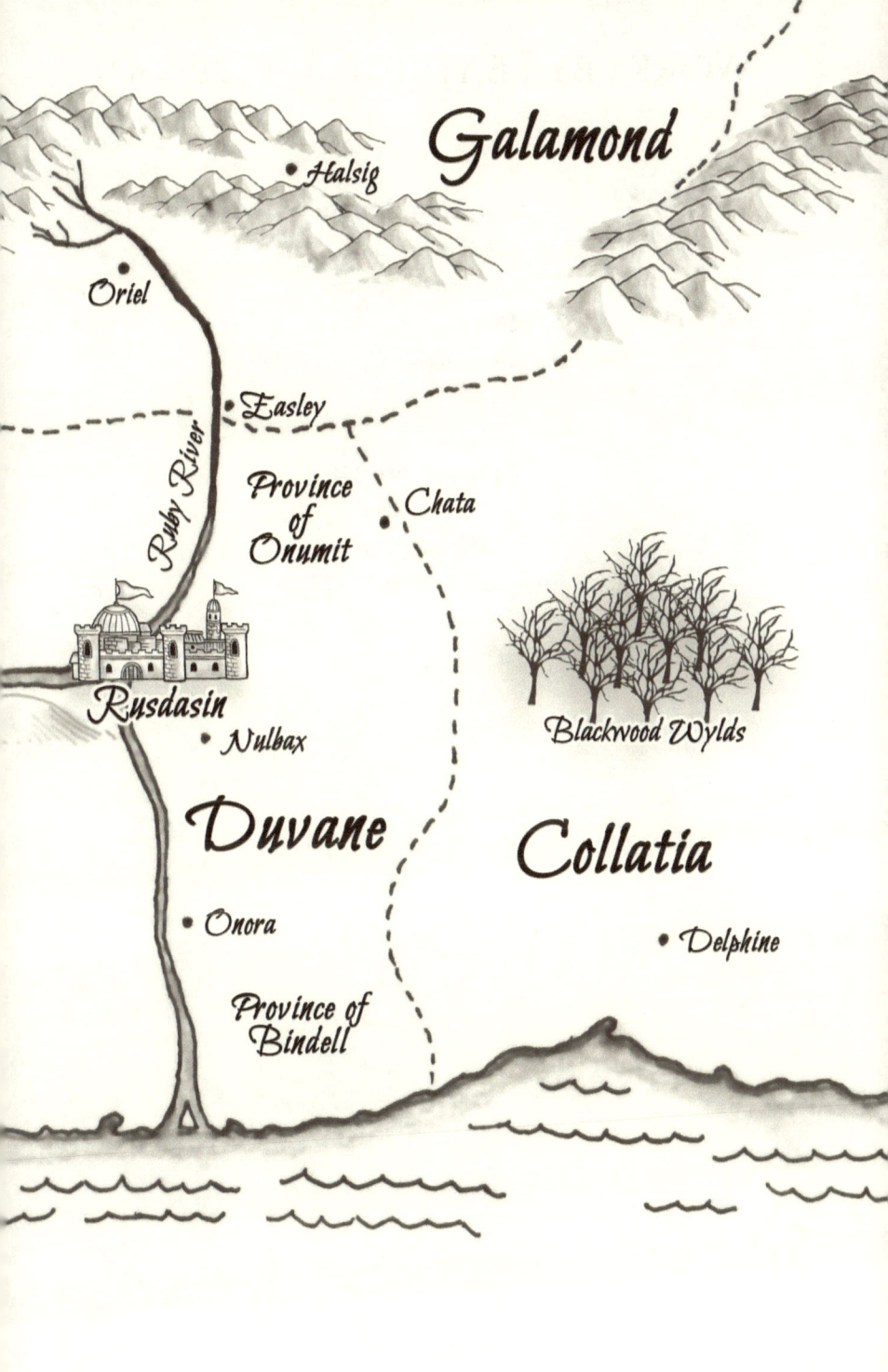

Works by Beatrice B. Morgan

Stars and Bones:

Thief in the Castle

Mage in the Undercity

Dreams in the Snow

Nightmares in the Ice (Spring 2023)

Hard as Stone:

Hard as Stone

Thick as Blood

Strong as Steel (October 2022)

TABLE OF CONTENTS

TABLE OF CONTENTS

CHAPTER ONE

Fresh blood ran between the ancient stones. It glimmered in the bluish light as it flowed along the deep grooves in the stone, filling one after the other. He watched it from the side, careful not to interrupt. The master had warned him about interrupting the blood flow.

The source of the fresh blood blurred, all wide eyes and torn skin, but the screams persisted. He could look away from the body but not the screams. He focused on the blood instead. It began to slow. Not enough to fill the rune. More. He needed more.

The body in the middle of the transformation circle stopped screaming. The blood stopped flowing.

Two more, said the voice of the master. *Two more, and the transformation will be complete.*

"Ison?"

Ison Rolin jumped at the sound of his name—he'd fallen asleep again. He blinked, and the workroom reappeared. The boiling mixture before him had nearly burned, but Mason Hobbs had reduced the magic flame underneath the flask to a simmer.

The mixture in the flask cooled quickly, the crushed polar hare bones at work. The glass slowly frosted, and the bright green mixture turned aqua blue.

"It appears that you have not ruined the tonic," said Mason sternly.

Ison straightened and wiped his sweaty palms on his robes, then held his hands under the worktable so Mason wouldn't see how they trembled. Swallowing hard against his dry throat, Ison met the eyes of the old man.

Mason did not look at him with anger. He looked at Ison with pity, which felt worse. Did he know what Ison dreamed? Mason noticed everything—one did not become the Court Magician of Duvane without being observant and clever. He studied Ison for a long moment, his severe face suggesting nothing of his thoughts—of course, Ison had never been the best at reading faces.

Ison swallowed and glanced back at the tonic he had been working on. Using the tongs, he moved the flask of Polar Potion onto a leather-padded cradle above a small woodstove. If left alone, the Polar Potion would freeze

1

and be ruined. Ison tucked his hand into a heat-resistant glove and unlocked the iron door on the woodstove. He added a handful of wooden cubes to the smoldering fire and shut the door.

When he stood, Mason was standing in the same spot, wearing the same expression.

"I-I'm sorry for sleeping on the job," Ison said, his voice small. He turned his gaze away from the court magician and onto his list of chores. He was running behind.

Mason let out a deep sigh. The wrinkles at the corners of his eyes deepened. When he spoke next, his stern tone softened. "Ison, step into my study."

Ison's heart fell. Mason never asked him into the study to talk.

Knees quivering, Ison walked a step ahead of Mason into the grand study that took up the majority of space in the court magician's chambers. Ison sank into one of the armchairs angled in front of the ancient rosewood desk. The wood had been carved with whorls, runes, and ageless symbols. According to castle lore, each court magician had left a mark on it for his or her successor.

Mason walked around the desk to the matching high-backed rosewood chair. His billowing purple robes floated out around him as he sat. With a wave of his bony hand, the leather-bound tomes sitting on his desk shut themselves and then flew onto the shelves. The books arranged themselves in perfect order. The scattered paperwork arranged itself neatly into two stacks on the end of his desk.

Mason leaned forward, elbows on the desk, and laced his fingers together. He set his gaze on Ison, bushy white eyebrows together, and Ison tried his best not to look as horrible as he felt.

He knew this day would come. He had messed up one too many times, and the court magician would dismiss him from his apprenticeship. Mason would find another mage who would cause less trouble and be better at spellwork. Ison would be cast out of Castle Bradburn and back into the jaws of the Marca—the school for mages controlled strictly by the Knights of the Order. He'd never find another job like this one, let alone a job outside the Marca. No one would look twice at a dishonored mage.

"I'm sorry," Ison blurted. He wrung his fingers together. "I-I didn't sleep well last night. I know how expensive the polar hare bones are. It was foolish to start the potion as tired as I was." Ison focused on his hands. He couldn't bring himself to look at the court magician. He didn't want to see the disappointment that surely turned his mouth downward. "I-I should've paid better attention."

A moment passed in silence, and Ison chanced a glance at the old man. He sat still, eyes on Ison, expression unreadable. "Ison," Mason said at last, his tone strong and even but exasperated. He closed his eyes and took a long breath. "I know what bothers you."

Ison swallowed—his throat had gone dry.

"You are remembering."

Ison released a shuddering breath and hung his head in his hands. Each time he blinked, he could see it, the blood, the bodies. He could hear the screams. "Yes," Ison said, his voice small and weak. "I am."

It had been two weeks since the wechun had been slain, but each day felt like a month. Ison remembered that night—he had been in his chamber, in bed with a terrible headache. He hadn't heard the chaos spread as demons attacked Bala's Ball. He had felt a severing, a sudden and inexplicable snap somewhere in his mind. A fog had been lifted.

Ison hadn't said a word to anyone about it. He had slowly gained his memories. An apostate—a rogue mage outside the Marca's authority—had used Ison as a puppet. Under the apostate's control, Ison had subdued servants in the castle and taken them into its bowels.

The wechun had done the dark ritual, but Ison had killed them. Every one.

Every night for the past two weeks, Ison remembered a little more. Each time he blinked, he saw their mangled flesh. Silence only brought their tortured, frightened screams. When he looked at his hands, he saw their blood. If he thought too long on it, he could feel it, warm and sticky on his fingers.

The world swayed. Ison leaned forward, head in his hands, and focused on the scuffed toes of his boots.

"I can't imagine what it feels like to remember such things." Mason's voice dropped to a whisper. "You were forced to commit atrocities against your fellow humans, and unlike those who perished, you must live with the memories."

Ison let out a weak groan of agreement.

Mason continued, "There isn't any potion or spell that will make those feelings go away." He cleared his throat. "In my experience, talking helps the most."

A beat of silence passed.

Ison pulled his head out of his hands and looked at the court magician. "Talking?" he repeated.

"Yes." Mason motioned to Ison. "Talk to me, son. Getting the worry off your shoulders will do you good."

Ison tried to swallow again.

What are you? Mason had asked the thing inside him—the apostate. Mason hadn't understood what was happening to Ison either. He had subdued Ison by magic, fed him Mad Weed Potion, and warded him inside his bedchamber.

Ison tried to reason that Mason acted out of concern for his wellbeing, but as he sat under the older mage's clinical gaze, the words he asked for wouldn't come. Ison tore his stare off Mason. He still didn't entirely trust him. He knew too much and had told Ison too little.

Mason leaned back in his chair and set his folded hands in his lap. "Of course, mine are not the only ears in the castle." He nodded toward the open doors of the study that led out into the sitting room, through which the main doors of the court magician's chambers could be seen. "Perhaps there is another pair of ears you would rather speak to?"

One name came immediately to mind. Reluctantly, Ison nodded.

Mason glanced at the grandfather clock on the far side of the study, carved from the same rosewood as the desk and chair. The clock, however, had not been carved with whorls and runes. Its face held two dozen hands, each a different metal and pattern and length. How Mason read the time from it, Ison didn't know. The short bronze hand moved too quickly, and the twisted iron hand hadn't moved since Ison had been there.

"She should be between breakfast and lunch," said Mason. "If you would like to pay her a visit, now would be best, I think."

"What about my work?" Ison asked.

Mason waved his hand dismissively. "It will not go anywhere." His old, thin lips curved into a rare smile. "And I know how to crush herbs. I may be old, but I know my way around my own workroom." His smile vanished. "Right now, the health of your mind is more important. Go."

Ison stood on shaky legs. "Thank you, sir."

Mason's white brows furrowed. "We've talked about formalities, Ison. There's no need."

He nodded. "Thank you...Mason."

The court magician nodded and waved his hand toward the bookshelf. One of the books he'd previously magicked aside lifted itself from the shelf and landed in his hand. Its title had long since worn from the leather on both the front and the broken spine. Mason began to read, and Ison let himself out.

The cooler air of the corridor seeped through his robes and sent a chill along his neck; Mason kept the temperature of his chambers magically controlled, and the balmy spring air that fluted through the drafty corridors took him by surprise. Sunlight was streaming in from the window at the end of the corridor. Its bright, welcoming light made the rest of the castle look dreary and hopeless.

Ison walked to the iron-lattice window at the end of the corridor. Spring had unfurled across the Royal Grounds and the many rooftop courtyards of the castle. The breeze carried the scent of blooming wildflowers, grass, and weeds. He would soon be busy with harvesting the herbs from the gardens and ordering and receiving shipments from the Royal Greenhouses.

He should be in his workroom. Working.

Ison closed his eyes and let the breeze brush against his face. In the darkness behind his eyelids, he saw stone grooves running thick with fresh blood, shining in the blue light of the flames. Blood that he had spilled. Carved from the source by a knife he had held.

And the screaming—it filled his ears with startling clarity.

Someone in the corridor was screaming!

Ison collapsed to the stone floor. His shoulder smacked hard against the stone, knocking the vision out of his mind. The screaming stopped. Ison rolled onto his back, chest heaving. The corridor was empty. No one had screamed.

Gods, why him? What had he done to deserve this?

Ison rubbed his face vigorously. He could feel the bruise on his shoulder. Mason was right. He needed to take care of himself before he ruined any expensive tonics or potions.

Talking. He could talk.

Just not to Mason.

Ison pushed himself to his feet and started away from the window. He passed countless servants carrying baskets of linen, trays of tea and snacks, and clean laundry. Royal guards stood at every intersection and doorway, their black and gold doublets pristine, their faces passive and alert. The royal seal, a curved double-headed ax, had been embroidered on their sleeves in gold.

Despite the wechun's defeat, knights still patrolled the castle corridors. He passed several of them, their silver armor gleaming. Ison kept his eyes averted in case one of the knights recognized him from the Marca.

The Order had formed the Marca nearly a thousand years ago and called it a safe place for mages to learn and practice magic, but anyone inside it knew what it was—a prison. A way to control those born with magic. Most people hated mages or feared them, and if anyone discovered what Ison—a mage—had done, he would be a dead man.

But maybe that was what he deserved.

CHAPTER TWO

A two-note knock sounded.

"Enter," Juniper Thimble said listlessly.

The bedroom door opened, and Juniper glanced up from her book. Sir Isaac Pinul stepped over the threshold but came no further. He leaned casually against the doorframe.

"Have you been reading all morning?" he asked.

"Reading may be a bit of an overstatement," she said.

Isaac walked into the bedroom with the easy grace of a trained knight. In the couple weeks he had been appointed as her guardian, he'd never entered her bedroom without her permission or awareness. She had told him his chivalry was unnecessary, but he refused to budge. Rather than the silver armor of the Order, Isaac wore a simple tunic the shade of fresh pineapple. The years in the sun had aged him beyond his forty-five years and left his skin tanned and his hair pale. He wore a thick leather sword belt. His Mage's Bane sword hung from one hip, and a dagger on the other.

Juniper tried not to stare at the Mage's Bane sword. Knights carried special blades crafted with a secret formula of minerals; they turned the sword a dark blue feathered with crimson. One cut from a Mage's Bane sword, even a shallow one, and a mage's magic would turn against them, killing them slowly from the inside out.

Like most in the castle, Isaac did not know that she was a mage. An apostate.

Isaac came to stand at the foot of her bed. He gestured to the book propped up against her legs. "Then what have you been doing all morning?"

"Trying to read," she said.

Isaac's brows rose. He nodded, took a small step closer to the bedpost, and leaned against it. "I see," he said in his pleasant, casual cadence.

Did he see it? Juniper doubted it. She'd woken up before dawn, laid awake until the daylight was bright enough to see by, and she had been reading the same page for...she didn't know how long. Time didn't feel the same as it once had. She had no desire to find out what happened next. Her fingers barely had the strength to turn the page.

"You have a meeting with His Majesty this afternoon." Isaac gave her a warm smile that reached into his eyes and stretched the fine lines around his mouth. "It would be in your best interest to...look your best."

Juniper blinked at him. Was that pity in his gaze? She glanced at her hands, and as she did so, locks of unwashed, greasy black hair fell over her shoulder.

"When was the last time you washed?" Isaac asked. Pity—no mistaking it.

She shrugged.

"Combed your hair?"

She tossed her dirty hair back over her shoulder.

"Gotten out of bed?" Isaac asked with a raised brow.

"This morning," she said. "To use the bathing room." And she hadn't given her reflection a single glance. She had been avoiding it as much as possible.

Isaac let out a small hum. He tapped his fingers against the bedpost.

Juniper sighed through her nose. "Gods, I must look horrible. Like I live in a rat-infested hovel." Not that anyone in the castle thought any better of her.

"Nothing a good scrub won't clean up," Isaac said with a smile. He straightened and folded his hands behind his back. A soldier's stance. "Shall I call a servant to ready your bath?"

"No, I can do it myself." Juniper shut her book and pushed it aside. She hadn't marked her page, but it didn't matter. She barely remembered what she had managed to read. She would have to start over anyway.

She scooted to the edge of the bed and set her bare feet on the floor. She stood—the weight of her body settled on her knees, and they gave out. Isaac rushed to her side and grabbed her arms before she hit the floor. He lifted her back onto her feet as though she weighed nothing.

"Are you all right?" he asked, quickly scanning her for injuries.

"I'm fine," she said, though it came out faint. Her feet didn't feel like her own; neither did her hands. They felt ages away from the rest of her. Gods, when had she gotten so weak? So...pitiful? Of course, she hadn't moved much in the past two weeks.

Isaac hesitantly lifted his hands from her arms. As she walked to the bathing room, he walked a step behind her. He stood in the doorway as she lit the candles.

"I will get the staff to bring more candles," Isaac said, eyeing one that had maybe an hour left in it.

Juniper didn't respond. The dark didn't bother her. She turned the brass tap. Water gurgled through the pipes and splat into the clawfoot tub. The tub, like most of the bathing room, was white marble. The candlelight shaded it golden, glinting off tiny flecks of silver within the white. While the water rose, she rolled her head over her shoulders. Her entire body felt stiff from disuse. When *had* she bathed last? Not that it mattered.

A few months ago, Juniper had been caught trying to steal the king's crown. He gave her the choice of execution or servitude, and at the time, she thought more highly of her life and chose the latter. She signed her life away in blood and became Prince Adrian's royal protector. The binding spell between them made it so any wounds he sustained would transfer to her, and later, an apostate had sabotaged the spell so her wounds also transferred to the prince, thus the need to keep her alive.

A hand touched her shoulder, and Juniper jumped.

It was Isaac—the tub had filled, and he had turned off the faucet. "Are you positive you are all right?" His pale green eyes wore fatherly concern.

Juniper nodded. Isaac lingered, giving her time to reconsider. She didn't.

"If you need anything, just shout. I will be within earshot." The knight left, closing the bathing room door behind him.

Juniper heaved a sigh, inhaling the steam rising from the water. She searched through the cabinets for the fine oils and salts that remained. She had used the majority of them, and the staff had not restocked. Perhaps she could ask Isaac to ask for those along with the candles. She found the remains of a jar of blue salts and dumped them into the water. They hit the surface and sizzled, turning the water pale blue and scenting the entire room with moon lilies and jasmine.

It smelled wonderful, especially compared to her.

With her back to the large mirror, she peeled away her dirty pajamas. Gods, she smelled like she lived in a rat-infested hovel. Felt like it too. She wiggled her fingers through her dirty hair. Black locks fell around her face, frazzled from being uncombed. Disgusting.

Her hair had been dyed black to better resemble Lady Roslyn Derean, the young woman Juniper was pretending to be. She barely remembered what color her hair used to be. The dye had been magically imbued to not fade, and Juniper hadn't even seen her roots. Her hair had grown black too.

Juniper climbed into the bath and released a sigh as she sank into the warm, scented water.

Before this, before the binding spell, she'd been an unrivaled thief. Her name had conjured fear in the Undercity. Everyone in Duvane's capital city of Rusdasin knew of Juniper Thimble. She had been gone for months. Her guild master, Maddox, would think her dead.

Even if being the royal protector didn't kill her, the king would never let her walk out. It would be foolish of him to. He would want to keep the news of the wechun silent, and he wouldn't want her to sell any maps of the castle to potential thieves or assassins.

She took a deep breath of the steaming, scented air and let it out slowly. The steam made thinking easier.

And then there was Reid Sandpiper. At the thought of him, her chest squeezed, making each subsequent breath feel like it might be her last.

She hadn't seen him since the aftermath of Bala's Ball. Isaac and Squire Penet Berwick had taken his responsibilities as her guardian.

There was no mistaking it now; she had fallen in love with him. Shame on her. She had fallen in love with a squire, a future knight, while holding back the secret of her nature as a mage. The moment he had discovered her magic, the moment she had used her magic to save his life and Adrian's, his love for her turned to ash.

She thought—a foolish part of her had thought—Reid would accept her regardless of any secret she kept, but she had been wrong. A squire like him would never be able to love an apostate like her. She should have known. She shouldn't have let him get close. She'd done it to herself.

Juniper pushed all thoughts of Reid aside. She found it easier not to think about him when she thought about nothing at all. Thinking always led back to him, his twisted anger at her when she had saved him, the way he had spat her name like a curse—she would rather feel nothing than the miserable, squeezing pain that made her want to hold her head underwater until she drowned.

She kept her chin above the water and scrubbed the grime from her scalp. She thought about the hole in her chest, the nothingness, the blackness. It grew and grew until it made her fingers limp and her legs numb, but it was easier than feeling the pain.

CHAPTER THREE

Juniper soaked until her skin pruned. Reluctantly, she pulled the drain and toweled herself dry. She combed out her hair—a struggle with the tangles—with the bejeweled bone comb that had come with the bathing room. The comb would fetch enough gold in the Undercity to feed a dozen people for a month.

She pulled her favorite pink silk dressing gown around herself. She returned to the bedroom to find it empty, but a shuffle of feet told her that Isaac had taken up a guard's position in the sitting room, right outside her bedroom door.

He hadn't gone far. Just like he had said. A knot in her chest unwound.

Juniper walked across her spacious bedroom and into the dressing room full of fine dresses and clothes they had allowed her to better look the part of a lady. She collapsed into the cushioned chair and eyed the full racks. She hadn't worn anything but her pajamas since the ball. She hadn't been allowed to leave her room, she wasn't allowed visitors, and the only people who saw her knew exactly who she was—she hadn't had the need to wear anything nice or be clean.

But for a meeting with King Bentley Bradburn? She would have to wear something decent. Isaac was right. The king held her fate in his hands. He could send her to the gallows with a wave of his hand or have her killed on the spot just as quick.

The thought gave her a shiver. If not for the altered binding spell, he might have already sent her to her death.

After eyeing the dresses for what felt like hours, she chose a dark blue gown with black and silver accents.

Reid had told her once that he liked her in blue. It brought out her dark blue eyes.

Pins impaled her heart at the thought, and she pushed it down, down, down. No thought, no pain.

With hands that felt apart from herself, she pulled a soft chemise over her head, tied up her corset, and stepped into the fine blue gown. She braided her damp hair into a crown—she had learned how by watching the servants—and returned to the bedroom. Her bare feet slapped against the floor; the air felt too warm for house boots. She reached for the discarded book. Might as well try to read a bit more.

Her fingers had just brushed the leather cover when someone knocked on her chamber door. Her heart thudded, and Isaac's sure footsteps crossed the sitting room to answer it.

Who would be calling on her? Servants, most likely, but she hadn't gotten up for breakfast, and it didn't feel time for lunch. How long had she been in the bath?

Isaac's voice drifted from the sitting room: "Ah, Ison. Glad to see you."

Juniper's heart lurched for a different reason. She hadn't seen Ison since he had accused her of being a mage. He had been agitated, not himself. And then the ball had happened.

"Is the lady busy?" Ison asked, his somber voice soft.

Juniper let herself into the sitting room. Isaac held one of the mahogany doors open, and Ison stepped through. At once, his steel eyes fixed on Juniper. His grimace flickered into a ghost of a smile—a greeting full of guilt. He wore robes of sage green, and his brown hair had grown enough for soft curls to form.

"Ison," Juniper said in greeting. "It's nice to see you well this morning."

Ison gave her a quick, curt nod. "And you, my lady."

Isaac's curious gaze flickered between Juniper and Ison. His fingers twitched on the brass door handle. After a moment, he cleared his throat and said, "Squire Berwick will be here later to escort you to your meeting. I shall wait for him in the corridor."

Juniper nodded. "Thank you, Sir."

"It is my pleasure, my lady," Isaac said, knowing she was no lady. He stepped out of the room and into the corridor, gently shutting the door behind him.

For a moment, Juniper and Ison stared at each other. Ison's gaze traveled along her dress, and he asked, "Are you busy?"

"No more than usual," she admitted. "I have a meeting with the king, but it's not until the afternoon."

Another beat of awkward staring.

Ison cleared his throat. "Can I speak with you?"

"You already are."

Ison nodded. "I...I want to apologize for my behavior the last time we met. I wasn't myself. I was... I don't know how to explain. I haven't been myself." He looked up at her with sleepless, weary eyes. "I don't know who else to turn to about it all."

Juniper motioned to the armchairs angled around the sitting room hearth. The hearths in her chambers had gone cold, but with the spring showing signs of summer, she didn't need a fire. The sun kept the castle warm enough, and the stillness brought her a strange sense of peace. Logs had been stacked by each hearth, just in case she changed her mind.

Ison sat, and Juniper sat beside him. He stared into the hearth, cold and distant. "I'm not all right," Ison whispered. He lowered his head into his hands. His trembling fingers snaked through his hair.

She felt a pang of sympathy for the poor mage. Softer, she asked, "Ison?"

His worried, bloodshot gaze met hers. "First, I must confess something, but you must promise to never tell another soul."

A tremor started somewhere in her gut and worked its way through her ribs. Ison's gaze bore into hers.

After a beat, she nodded. "Okay. I promise."

He glanced at the chamber door, to where Isaac stood guard on the other side. Ison whispered, "The apostate, the one controlling the demons, the wechun...he used me. He controlled me, got into my head and forced me to do his will." Ison's voice cracked. "I-I didn't want to do any of it. He made me."

Juniper said nothing; she had no words. The apostate had controlled Ison? The wechun had said *they—they* had done it all. She thought it had meant itself and its master, but it had meant Ison and itself. It felt like a fist had squeezed the breath from her lungs. And if anyone found out that Ison had assisted, he would be executed. Immediately, likely with Mage's Bane.

Ison shut his eyes and knotted his shaking fingers together. "I've been remembering things," he whispered. "More every day. Things I did, things he forced me to do."

Whoever *he* was. Juniper didn't raise that question. Not the time.

"It's not just bits and pieces anymore." Tears lined Ison's eyes. "It's like I'm back there...and..." He shuddered. "I killed them. I killed all of them."

Juniper remained silent. When she didn't respond, Ison turned his teary eyes to her. Fear and panic and unfathomable guilt looked back at her. "Ison..."

"I-I didn't do it on purpose," he pleaded. "I didn't want to. I..."

"I understand," she whispered.

He blinked; he didn't believe her.

"You were not yourself, like you said."

Those words—she saw their effect on him. Something she couldn't see lifted from his spirit.

"And it is bothering you." Juniper held her hand out to him, palm up. "It would bother anyone. I'm here for you. Whatever you need."

Ison blinked, smearing tears across his dark lashes. He clasped his fingers around hers. A single tear fell from the corner of his eye and traced a wet line down his cheek. "Thank you..." A crease formed between his brows. For that small moment, he looked like himself, like the kind, shameless, studious mage she had met weeks ago. "You never told me your real name."

She half laughed. "I didn't. Do you have any guesses?"

Ison's fragile smile shattered. He clearly wasn't in the mood for her humor.

She cleared her throat. "Juniper Thimble."

Ison gaped, looking her over, disbelief settling. It gave her a small jolt of pride, but she hid it as best she could. Not the time for that either.

She recounted the king's plan to protect his son. Ison didn't seem that surprised.

"If I hadn't been otherwise occupied, I might have figured it out myself," Ison said, his voice dampened by what had occupied him. "But, it doesn't matter. Thank you, Juniper."

"Now, you wanted to talk to me?"

Ison told her about the things he remembered. Blood on an old stone floor, daggers, runes, butchered bodies, and the screams. With every word, his voice shook a little more. He gripped her hand a little harder. "I killed them," Ison said, his voice shaking terribly. "I killed them, and the wechun transformed them into those...monsters."

Abominations. Everyone had thought them to be demons, but they were not. They were, in Juniper's opinion, worse.

"There was a rune carved into the stone that needed to be filled with blood. It took a dozen people to fill it. Just to make a single transformation." Ison gripped Juniper's hand. He let out a laugh, but it held no humor. "I've started calling it the Death Chamber."

He told her about the chamber, how he had led the subdued servants into the deepest bowels of the castle through the doorways the master provided—doorways in the stone that appeared and vanished at his will. Ison couldn't bring himself to speak of their deaths. His voice shook so badly, he could barely speak at all.

"They were silent until they realized what was happening," Ison whispered. "That they were going to die. They pleaded"—his voice faded—"and cried and screamed."

She felt foolish for feeling like she did about her problems. Shame and guilt layered in her stomach, building like bile. Here she was wallowing over a broken heart while Ison had been dealing with having been forced to murder people.

"What you've been through would haunt anyone," Juniper said. "It's no wonder you can't focus. I wouldn't be able to either."

Ison gave her a small smile that quickly faded. "I can't help but think that everything that happened, all those people, the injuries you sustained, none of it would have happened if I hadn't...if I had been stronger."

Juniper pulled his hand closer to herself. "Nonsense," she told him firmly. "Their deaths are not your fault. They are the fault of the monster behind it all. If the apostate hadn't taken you, he would have stolen someone else. He wanted to kill those people, and he would have, regardless of who he used. It is his fault, not yours or anyone else's."

Ison drank in her words, though he did not look convinced. "What if... What's stopping him from using me again? Or someone else? Who's to say he's not controlling someone else right now?"

Juniper bit her lip. She didn't have an answer. The thought of someone else in the castle being mind-controlled by a murderous, vengeful apostate made her glad to be locked in a guarded room. But she said, "Nothing has happened since the wechun died. There's a chance we frightened him away."

"I-I don't think so," Ison said, eyes dark.

She whispered, "Can you still hear him?"

"No. I haven't heard him since before the ball." Ison's hand trembled. "I came to your room that day because I thought that you might be the apostate controlling me. I know you're not, now, but at the time... I was so angry, and tired, and confused, and—"

"And not yourself," Juniper finished for him. She bent forward to look him in the eye. "You were right about me, you know."

He raised a brow.

"Being a mage," she whispered. She offered him a small smile, but he did not return it.

"I take it that Reid doesn't know?" Ison half laughed.

Juniper's small smile vanished.

"He does?" Ison's brows rose. "And you're still alive?"

She released a fragile breath. The sound of his name reopened a hole in her chest. It must have shown, for Ison's gaze narrowed in concern. She said, "It's stupid in comparison."

Ison tugged on their joined hands. "Talk to me."

So she did. She told Ison exactly what had happened in the bowels of the castle, how she had used her magic to slay the wechun. "I haven't seen Reid since the day after the ball. He hates me. I know he does. All he said, all I felt...it doesn't matter."

She didn't know how to tell Ison about the hole she felt, the darkness, and how she would rather not feel anything at all. She didn't have the words.

Ison reached for her cheek and stroked his thumb along her cheekbone. "You'll find someone better than him. Someone who treats you like you deserve."

Reid did treat her like she deserved, like the scum she was. Better, even.

She offered Ison a small smile anyway.

Juniper talked Ison into saying for lunch. Isaac joined them but said little. Ison and Juniper talked mostly about books—she told him about the book she had been trying to read. Ison smiled; he had read it, and he promised her it would be well worth the restart. Isaac finished his meal first and resumed his post in the corridor, leaving Juniper and Ison to talk over tea.

A lull came over the conversation. She stared into the dregs of her tea. Ison had never stayed so long in her chambers before. It felt like ages since anyone had stayed or talked to her. It felt good. The darkness didn't beckon as much.

Ison set his tea down and folded his hands together over the table. He looked at her with a renewed determination—like his old self. He had needed this talk as much as she had.

"Jun," Ison started, "Can I ask something of you?"

She set her tea down. "Yes, Ison, ask me anything."

His steel eyes bore into hers. "I want to return to the Death Chamber."

CHAPTER FOUR

Juniper blinked several times. Had she misheard? "You want to go back there? Why?"

"I need to see it for real, not just in my memories," he said. He inhaled, closed his eyes, and let the breath out slowly. "I think it will help me deal with it, make it less intimidating. When I was little, I was afraid of this room in the Marca. We used it for storage near the end of our corridor. I hated it. In the dark, it looked like the giant maw of some beast ready to snatch me away. The stories the older mages told about monsters in the basement didn't help either. Finally one day, I went inside and cast light on the shadows. The maw became an old hearth. Seeing it like that, my fear vanished. I think it will be the same with the Death Chamber. I just need to shed light on the nightmare for it to go away."

Juniper nodded. It made sense. "Okay. But why ask my permission?"

His fierce steely gaze held hers. "I want you to go with me."

She blinked—she hesitated a moment too long.

Ison threw up his hands between them. "I know, I know, but I don't know if I can do it alone." His voice softened. "I can't think of anyone else I'd rather have go with me. It would be nice to have you there as moral support or a sword arm if there are lingering monsters there."

She gave him a small, genuine smile. His words struck the old pride she had at her abilities. "Can't have you gallivanting face-first into danger, can we? Of course, I'll go." And, despite it all, the idea of leaving her room sounded marvelous.

His face brightened, and a light returned to his gray eyes.

"Besides, what are friends for? But—" She paused.

Ison's determination faltered.

"I want you to do something for me in return."

He frowned. Doubt crept into his eyes. "What?"

She steeled herself and then said, "Teach me how to use my magic."

He deflated—his shoulders slumped, his head fell forward, and he let out a woeful groan. "I'm not a good teacher."

"But"—she struggled for excuses—"you know more than me, and no other mage in the castle knows that I'm a mage too. You're the only one!"

Ison considered her, his steel eyes working through the ifs and maybes. She feared he would say no, but then after a long moment, he said, "Are you sure you want to learn?"

"Yes." She clenched her hands in her skirt. "When I needed my magic most, it failed me. I failed because I couldn't control it, because I didn't know how. I nearly died because of it." Not that her control of it had mattered. Even if she had been able to control her magic and defeat the wechun and the demon gracefully rather than sloppily, she still would have exposed herself as a mage.

"Okay," Ison started. "Well, uh, to start, can you manifest your magic?"

"What does that mean?"

"Uh..." Ison swallowed. That was not the answer he wanted. "Can you summon your magic?"

Ison brought his hands together in front of him, cupping his palms. A ball of grayish wind appeared there like a tiny, spherical tornado. Juniper could feel the magic, the tingle in the air, the slight metallic scent—like freshly polished silver and wildflowers.

Juniper had never seen Ison's magic before. Somehow, the color suited him. She brought her own hands out like his, but nothing happened.

"Concentrate," Ison said, his voice soft and soothing. "Feel the magic in your body, your spirit. It's there, waiting to be called upon, waiting for your command. It follows the will of your spirit, your mind."

She concentrated, feeling down deep where she thought her magic had been kept all these years, the place her apostate tutor had told her younger self to lock it away. She had been taught to lock it away too well, for nothing happened in her hands.

Ison instructed her form and her focus. After an hour of trying, she managed to summon a few flurries—even that small amount of magic drained her. She felt sweat along the back of her neck, her spine, underneath her hair. Her limbs felt exhausted, worse than she had been that morning but different somehow. Earned. The exhaustion went deeper, further than her bones, and would make her stronger.

Stronger. The word did little, but that feeling of exhaustion in her bones somehow instilled the meaning of it—that she would get stronger. Giving in to that exhaustion, Juniper slumped back into her chair. The soft material welcomed her, beckoning her to sleep for a while.

"I don't understand," she said. "I froze the first demon solid. Everything was covered in ice, the walls, the ceiling—everything. I tried to do the same to the wechun but couldn't. Why couldn't I do it then? Why can't I do it now?"

Ison leaned forward, elbows on his knees. His eyes were alert, clear. He didn't look remotely as tired as he had when he'd first arrived. "You've spent your entire life hiding your magic. You're going to have to relearn how to not hide it. It's easier to teach young mages because they are more in step with their magic. They're...freer with it. And, from your story, you acted to save Adrian and Reid. It might have been your primal instincts to protect taking over, and your magic responded to attack the first demon. Because you have pushed your magic down, your well is likely shallow."

"So I just used it all?"

"Sounds like it."

She gave him a tilted grin. "Does that mean it would work better if we put you in mortal danger?"

He returned her smile. "I'd rather not. And it will take practice. It took me a while. We'll practice again tomorrow when you've rejuvenated your stamina." He smoothed wrinkles from his robes. "And eat something hearty for lunch. Magic takes a lot of energy."

She frowned. He'd seen what she had eaten for lunch; he'd been sitting across the table. "I had a decent lunch today."

"Yes," he said hesitantly. "But double that."

"You want me to gain weight?"

He chuckled. "You'll be using plenty of energy in your magic. You'll need the extra."

She mirrored his smile, and it felt foreign on her cheeks. "Okay. I'll make sure to add a double helping of everything. What about you? When would you like to return to the Death Chamber?"

His smile vanished; determination took its place. "Tonight. The sooner the better. I want to get it over with."

A little sooner than she would have liked, but maybe he was right with getting it over with as soon as possible. "Tonight it is."

A set of armored footsteps stalked toward her chambers. Juniper met Ison's curious stare. The Royal Guard did not wear their bronze armor inside the castle—they wore doublets—which meant a knight or a squire approached.

It took her a heartbeat to realize— "Penet," Juniper whispered.

Armored footsteps marched toward her chamber door, assured and calm. She blew out her next breath in relief, willing her heartbeat to slow.

"Oh," came Isaac's surprised tone. "I was expecting Penet."

She froze—not Penet Berwick? Then who—

The armored footsteps halted. "The king asked me to escort her to the meeting," came a clear, articulate, and confident male voice.

Every bone in her body turned to molten steel at the sound of his voice, white-hot and slippery. Ison turned to her, his eyes wide. She tried to look confident, but by Ison's continued concern, she failed.

His voice sounded the same as it always had. Where it had once filled her with warmth, it filled her with cold dread.

"As His Majesty requests," said Isaac, though strained.

Juniper wanted to rush out to Isaac and beg him to take her to the meeting instead, but she couldn't move. Her feet, her arms, her thoughts—everything halted at the sound of that voice.

Reid Sandpiper let himself into her chambers. He wore the silver armor of the Order, though his breastplate remained unadorned with the owl signet to identify him as a squire. He had gotten sun in the past two weeks; his bronze skin appeared a shade or two darker. He wore his usual scowl, and his chestnut hair remained immaculate, cut short in the no-nonsense style that most of the knights wore.

His honey-brown eyes settled on Juniper, and her heart jumped into her throat. He looked at her with cold indifference. His gaze shifted to Ison, and his scowl deepened. His fingers twitched toward his blade.

Reid turned his gaze back on her and said flatly, "You have a meeting with the king. You were supposed to be ready."

The bitterness in his tone brought some of the feeling back into her limbs. "I am mostly ready," she argued.

"Then hurry up and finish," Reid said. "The king doesn't like to be kept waiting."

"Allow me to fetch my shoes." Heaving a dramatic sigh, Juniper stood and brushed off her dress. Her legs felt like wood. She had imagined the day she would see Reid again several times, but she hadn't pictured it like this. No, in all those thoughts, she had something clever to say that would disarm him and leave her feeling victorious. Currently, she felt as though she had been squished beneath his gaze.

Juniper held her head high and strutted into her bedroom. She slipped on a pair of simple leather shoes with golden adornments. She had worn them enough that the soles had molded to her feet. *Hers.* She checked her hair in the mirror, deemed it worthy of the king's presence, and wrapped a thin shawl over her shoulders.

"Don't you have duties to attend to, mage?" came Reid's brute voice from the sitting room.

"No." Ison spoke firmly and with a cool indifference that made Juniper a bit jealous. "Mason gave me the afternoon off."

Juniper returned to the sitting room to find the two men glaring daggers at one another. She fought for something clever to say, but no words came to mind. She said instead, "I'm ready. We shouldn't keep His Majesty waiting."

Reid cast one last suspicious glare at Ison, who glared back. Juniper walked between the two—she caught a whiff of Reid's scent as she passed him: sandalwood, leather, and metal. It twisted her stomach into knots. Though the linens had been changed since he had shared her bed, every once in a while, usually while trying to fall asleep, she thought she smelled it.

The night after the ball, she had woken up from a dream and in reflex reached for Reid. As her hand roamed over cool, empty sheets, her panic had risen only to be doused with shame as realization struck. She had cried herself back to sleep that night.

Reid held the door open for Juniper, and she walked through without looking at him. She couldn't. Just having him so close made her knees weak and her stomach turn over. Damn her for being so foolish.

Ison started to follow her into the corridor, but she stopped him, saying, "This meeting shouldn't take too long. Feel free to stay here."

Reid shifted. His hand on the door handle tensed.

"If you're sure it's all right," Ison said.

Reid inhaled to speak—

"Of course it is," Juniper said before Reid could say differently.

Ison returned to the armchairs and sat.

Reid shut the door a bit harder than he should have and started down the corridor. Juniper held her shoulders straight and fell into step a short distance behind him.

After a few steps, Reid spat lowly, "What the hell were you two doing?"

"Talking."

"About what?"

"Nothing that concerns you." Her voice came out weaker than she would have liked.

He didn't press her for details. He glanced over his shoulder at her, but she looked away before their eyes met. She couldn't handle his eyes looking at her so coldly.

Reid hated mages. He hated them for murdering his family when he was a boy. He'd joined the Order to hunt down apostates, to either kill them outright or imprison them in the Marca. Apostates just like her.

"You will get yourself into trouble if you keep talking with Ison," Reid said. He put an emphasis on *talking* that made her stomach curl—he didn't believe her.

Anger bubbled up in the emptiness inside her. She spat, "Why warn me? Why not let me get into trouble? That way, you can be rid of me."

He glanced over his shoulder, and she dared meet his cold anger with her own.

She added lowly, "Because two mages could only be talking about how many people we can kill, is that it?"

Reid clenched his fists and forced his gaze ahead of him. He sighed through his nose.

Apologize, said a voice in her mind. She knew she should, but she didn't. Not until Reid apologized for all the pain he'd caused her.

They passed a young guard who looked bored out of his mind, but at the sight of Reid, he straightened and fixed his too-wide gaze on the opposite wall. Reid walked by without a word, but Juniper winked at the guard.

Reid led her up a spiraling staircase whose only light came from a hanging candelabra. It flickered pitiful light over the bare stone steps. Reid's armor clinked as he climbed, and Juniper held her dress to avoid tripping.

Reid whispered, "People might get suspicious of you spending so much time with him. There are those who suspect his involvement in the Demon Crisis. It would be in your best interest to avoid unwanted attention." Reid let out a short sigh. "If anyone discovered that you are an apostate, you would be blamed."

"I know," she whispered. She wanted to argue for Ison's innocence, but she didn't. He *had* been involved, but she couldn't tell Reid that. His stiff justice would have Ison executed before sundown.

Reid gazed at her, and the accusation she found there made her angrier still.

She whispered, "Why? Thinking of turning us both in? Making yourself the hero while tossing two mages to the gallows? That way, you wouldn't have to follow me around. You could be the proud knight you've always wanted."

"That is not my decision," Reid said, each word clipped and strained.

"But it's what you want, isn't it?" Juniper glared at his unadorned breastplate. Even in the dim light, the silver gleamed. "To get rid of me once and for all? To be free of the job you've resented since the beginning? To have something worth your precious time?" To speak the words aloud felt liberating. It loosened something in her chest. "To throw me to the wolves and be done with it?"

Reid tightened his hands into fists but didn't retort.

Her entire chest twisted. He truly thought those things?

They reached the landing and a set of mahogany doors like the rest in the Royal Chambers. He closed his hand around the brass handle but hesitated.

Juniper stepped onto the landing and, before she could stop herself, spat, "Or is it because you've heard how good the Marca mages are in bed?"

That did it. Reid's grip turned white-knuckled. He turned toward her, rage pulsing through his stare, burning through his skin, radiating.

For a terrifying moment, she feared his reaction, that she had pushed him too far.

"You're wasting time," he spat. He yanked the door open and started into the sunny corridor beyond. Compared to the stairwell, it was too bright. "Best not keep His Majesty waiting."

CHAPTER FIVE

Reid escorted Juniper into a corridor of ancient suits of armor and portraits of past Bradburn kings, dukes, queens, and magistrates; she felt a chill run down her spine as they passed a sour-looking woman with dark, downcast eyes. She knew this corridor. She had snuck into this very corridor the night she planned to steal the crown.

Her heart skipped a beat. Then another. And another. Reid turned down a corridor, and she followed—and stopped dead.

A royal guard stood outside the very lounge that she had used to gain entrance into the Royal Chambers. Was this a joke on her? They knew; they had to know. Why else would the king choose this lounge?

Her knees shook, her hands trembled, and her heart felt as though it had stopped entirely.

When Reid realized she didn't follow, he stopped. He glanced back. "You're pale," he said, a hint of concern in his voice.

She forced herself to take a step, then another, until she caught up with Reid. He fell into step beside her, matching her pace. She swayed, and she spotted the twitch in his arm—ready to grab her should she start to fall.

Her heart squeezed. Always the diligent knight. Even for a girl he hated.

Under his breath, he whispered, "Are you all right?"

Words failed her again. She nodded instead.

What did meeting in this lounge mean? Would her entry point also be her exit? Would they toss her body from the tower's courtyard and call it an accident?

Reid opened the mahogany doors of the lounge for her. She stepped through, and at once, all eyes inside turned to her. They had arrived last, it seemed. The eyes she met first belonged to the king.

King Bentley Bradburn stood by the doors that led to the rooftop courtyard, his hands folded behind his back. He wore simple but elegant clothes. He did not wear his sword belt, but he didn't need to be armed to be intimidating. He stood like a soldier, solid and strong, like the strongest wind in the world wouldn't make him budge. The sunlight dappled his dark blond hair. He did not wear his crown.

Reid closed the lounge door, and the sound of it jarred Juniper out of her stupor. Reid gingerly touched her elbow and led her to one of the armchairs angled around the cold hearth. Like her own, logs had been stacked beside it. Reid took a guard's position behind her. Out of her view, thankfully.

Tea had been served on the low coffee table with enough cups for each person in the room. The thought of tea made her stomach twist.

"Juniper?"

She looked over at the speaker. It was Prince Adrian. Unlike his father, his hazel eyes looked at her with friendly concern. He shared his father's dark blond hair. He reclined in his chair, his long legs stretched out in front of him. He did not have the presence of a soldier like the king; he instead radiated with regal grace and intelligence. Adrian had always been welcoming to Juniper, and seeing his disarming smile again brought a warmth through her chest.

"I'm glad to see you are well," Adrian said.

"As I am to see you," Juniper replied, trying to mirror his kind smile.

Across the sitting area, Mason Hobbs regarded her with an unfeeling gaze. The ancient man wore dark purple robes to signify him as a master mage and court magician. His bony fingers were draped on his lap. His short, silver-white hair was half-hidden beneath the hood of his robe.

Behind the court magician stood Reid's uncle, Captain Sandpiper of the Royal Guard. He shared his nephew's impassive expression, rich bronze complexion, and dislike of mages. The captain, unlike Reid, had green eyes. He did not look enthused at her presence.

On the far side of the room, just outside the sunlight streaming in from the glass courtyard doors, Isaac stood beside Sir Destry, the knight tasked with protecting Adrian at all times.

Juniper felt a pang—if Isaac planned on being in the meeting, why couldn't he have escorted her?

King Bradburn cleared his throat. "Now that we are all gathered, let us get this meeting underway as quickly as possible." He looked around the room at each person, and his stare landed finally on Juniper. "It has been two weeks since the wechun's defeat"—he glanced at Reid and pride flashed in his eyes—"slain by our own Squire Sandpiper."

Captain Sandpiper swelled with pride.

Adrian caught Juniper's eye and winked.

Juniper swallowed. Only Reid, Adrian, and Ison knew what had truly happened to the wechun. As far as anyone else knew, Reid had slain the monsters.

The king continued, "And we have yet to have a demon attack or a hint of the apostate's presence. However, we should not treat this as the end of our trouble. The apostate responsible for controlling the wechun and the demons is still out there, possibly lurking among us." The king turned to the court magician. "Mason?"

The court magician stood. Juniper felt Reid shift behind her, and she saw Captain Sandpiper's hand twitch to the pommel of his blade. She had no doubt Reid had mirrored his uncle's actions.

A mage-hater, raised by a mage-hater.

If Mason noticed, he did not show it. He said in a calm, ancient voice, "I have been researching binding spells. My original aim was to undo the first spell and create a new one so that the wounds would only transfer one way." Mason's eyes lingered on Juniper, and she tensed; a glimpse of accusation blinked back at her. He shifted his gaze back to the king. "But I cannot dispel the altered binding spell without uncertainty for both Adrian and Juniper's wellbeing.

The king nodded. "I see."

Mason continued, "I then attempted to fix the alteration; however, I am again unsure of how to do so without possibly harming it or them."

Juniper was sure that if it were only her life on the line, he would not feel inclined to hesitate.

"And," the king said reluctantly, "because we are unable, at this time, to undo the binding spell, it will remain like it is." His gaze fell onto Juniper. "We must keep the thief here, protected, where she will not be used to harm my son."

She felt a shiver of cold and shifted her gaze to her knees. *The thief.* No more than a thing, an obstacle. The emptiness widened in her chest, a great blackness to swallow her whole, and when the king spoke again, his voice sounded ages away.

"We cannot continue to pretend that Roslyn Derean is visiting. Tomorrow morning, she will embark on the long journey home to Galamond."

From behind her, Reid asked, "What does that mean for her?"

"It means," Adrian said simply, "she will no longer be paraded about as an impostor."

26

Juniper met Adrian's gaze; he didn't look happy.

King Bradburn glanced only once at his son—had they been arguing? He stepped closer, stopping on the other side of the couch. "She will be a *guest* of the castle. Until the matter of the binding spell is resolved, she will stay here. Under guard." He looked over her shoulder. "Squire Sandpiper, you are to resume your duty as her guardian. Understood?"

Reid paused only a moment. "Understood."

"Good."

Juniper swallowed. The king knew. How many others knew what had happened between Reid and her? Gods, she might as well be standing naked in front of them all.

"You get to keep your chambers," came Adrian's charming voice. "Someone voted to throw you into the dungeons, but luckily, someone else"—he pointed at himself—"mentioned how important it would be to keep you happy. Wouldn't want you to throw yourself out of a window, would we?"

She found her voice, but it came out hoarse. "Thank you."

He gave her that winning smile of his, genuine and calming. "This way," Adrian continued, "we will still get to have tea together from time to time."

King Bradburn cleared his throat. He did not share his son's sentiment toward Juniper. "From here, your actions will determine your path once the binding spell is nullified. Should you give me or anyone in this castle a reason, you will meet your end at the gallows. Understand?"

Behave, or she would never see Rusdasin, the Undercity, Maddox, Amery, or anyone outside the castle again.

The king glared at her. Waiting.

She swallowed against her dry throat. "Yes, Your Majesty. I understand."

CHAPTER SIX

Juniper didn't speak on the walk back to her chambers—her prison cell.

Neither did Reid.

A guest, the king had said. Laughable. She was no more a guest of the castle than the apostate. King Bradburn hadn't given her a choice in the matter; he had decided it for her. She had served her purpose as Adrian's royal protector, and now she was an object to them, a possession—a means to protect Adrian.

How long would it take the court magician to break the binding spell? Days? Months? Years? How long would she be imprisoned in the castle?

A part of her already knew. She would live out the remainder of her life as an extra life for Adrian. She would never see Rusdasin again. She would never see the Undercity again. She would never get to explain to Amery what had happened the night they tried to steal the crown. Maddox would never know what truly happened to his best thief.

They returned to her chambers, and Juniper headed straight for the bedroom. She wanted to sleep until the world righted itself again or, at least, until it stopped spinning. She marched through her bedroom door, yanked her shawl off her shoulders, and tossed it onto the bed. As she kicked off her shoes, someone cleared his throat.

Juniper jumped; Ison sat at the small table in her bedroom. At the sight of him, she released a breath. Three books she had never seen before sat in front of him. From their covers, they looked like magical texts.

"Good thing I didn't start to undress," Juniper said halfheartedly.

Ison gave her a small smile. "Please, don't feel imposed by my presence."

"Ah, he is still here." Reid stood in the bedroom doorway, his armored shoulders taking the entire width. His eyes fell onto the books, and he frowned. "What are those?"

"Books," Ison said coolly. "A few that I thought Jun would enjoy."

Reid let out a short huff.

Juniper strolled to the table and touched the pale leather cover of the first volume. It had seen better days; the leather was worn at the edges, and the title had faded. She would rather not tell Reid about the magic lessons. "You could borrow one. I know how much you enjoy the smutty ones."

Whether he blushed or not, she didn't know. He stalked back into the sitting room; then the main door opened and closed.

"He left?" Ison blinked. "I didn't realize he offended so easily."

Juniper sank into the chair beside Ison. "He posted himself outside. Better to ignore me out there."

She pulled the pale volume closer. It had been well used. *Mergermite's Guide to Magic* had once been written across the cover in black. The letters had faded into barely-there gray.

"I'm sorry about what happened between you," Ison said softly.

Juniper pulled her bottom lip between her teeth. She'd rather not talk about her failed love life. "I should have seen it coming. A knight and a mage. It could never have worked out. He'd never see past his animosity for mages and magic and see me."

"Did you..." Ison waved his hand toward her bed.

"Just once. The night before the ball." The emptiness widened at the memory of his body against hers, all corded muscle. "I thought—I hoped—he wouldn't care about my magic." Her stomach squeezed, threatening to chuck her lunch back up. "I was wrong."

Ison's lips parted with a soft breath of pity.

She looked away. Her eyes fell onto the bed, and memories of Reid swarmed—of nights spent in his arms, his mouth on her neck, of the sculpted body he hid underneath his armor.

She shoved those memories away as best she could and pulled *Mergermite's Guide to Magic* toward her.

"Jun," Ison started.

She opened the book to the introduction. "I am not the first to experience the marvels of heartbreak. Nor will I be the last."

Ison hesitated—his breath hitched. "I understand. I can't say I loved Clara," as her name left his lips, his small voice became a whisper. "But I understand losing someone."

Her heart squeezed. Clara had been Juniper's servant, and she and Ison had connected. She had been among the last he'd taken to the Death Chamber.

"I'd rather not speak of this anymore," Juniper said. "It's unpleasant."

Ison cleared his throat and tapped the book she held in front of her. "I brought you a few basic texts. *"Mergermite's* is foundational to learning magic. I suggest reading it first. It gives more background and understanding on how magic works and the way mages use it. The history is also interesting. This one"—he held up a slightly newer tome entitled *Corella and Sona's Basic Elements: Water*—"is for water magic."

Juniper glanced down at her hands. "Mine is ice."

"Yes, but that stems from the water element. It's better explained in here." Ison motioned to *Mergermite's Guide to Magic*. He held up the last book, a brown volume, *Magic for Water Elements*. "This one will give a deeper understanding of the magic best suited for a water mage." He stacked them in the order he had presented. "Read them in this order for the best understanding."

"How many times have you read them?" She ran her finger down the worn spine of *Mergermite's Guide to Magic*.

"I've read that one more times than I can count. It's useful, straightforward, and"—he blushed—"I've written notes in it. I'll warn you now, some of them date back to my awkward adolescent days. Don't mind any strange notes or pictures you find."

"Oh?" She flipped through the well-worn pages with more interest. He had indeed drawn a few archaic symbols here and there, underlined passages, and added a few boy-centric drawings that looked like people. Ison did not have a skill for art, thank the gods. She gave him a smile. "Are there naughty pictures in here?"

"There might be in the later chapters." He chuckled and gave her a sheepish smile. "You'll know the chapters we went over when I discovered the carnal side of humanity. But it gives you something to look forward to between the history and the definitions. Each page is a surprise."

Her smile stretched farther, and the sensation felt odd on her cheeks. How long had it been since she had last smiled? "I've got time before dinner. Would you like to stay, or do you have duties to return to?"

Ison let out a short sigh, and she saw his answer on his face before he spoke. The rejection stung, though she knew it shouldn't.

She reasoned, "It's all right. I've kept you plenty today. I'm sure Mason misses you."

His expression softened. "Thank you, Jun. I mean it. This, today, I needed this. I needed you." Those words brought a warmth to her cheeks. Ison stood. "I'm glad that I have you here to talk to."

"And I feel the same, Ison." And she meant it. She reached across the table and touched his hand. "You are welcome back anytime, day or night. As long as you don't mind the grumpy squire standing outside."

He smiled; then it faded. His eyes hardened. "Jun, tonight. Do you still want to go with me?"

It took a moment to remember what she had agreed to do. Nodding, she said, "Yes. I said I would go, and I will."

"How will you get away from your guard?"

She blinked, once, twice, and then ran through the options she had. A plan quickly formed, a simple plan. "Come to my room after dinner. Penet will be here for the night. I'll tell him I fancy a walk. I will happen to meet you. We will walk together."

Ison frowned.

"Penet is more trusting than Reid or Isaac." And bashful. She gathered it came from his lack of experience with women, for in the first few days he stood as her guard, he had blushed every time he looked at her.

"What if Reid doesn't leave for the night?"

She bit her lip. That would ruin her simple plan to sneak past naïve Penet. "Then I will think of another excuse in the meantime." Though, she knew Reid wouldn't let the two of them out of his sight. Not for all the gold in the castle would he shirk his duty. She admired and abhorred that about him. "We could wait until he passes out from exhaustion," she said, waving her hand dismissively toward the door where Reid currently stood. "He won't know we've gone until the morning, and then he can yell all he wants."

"Are you sure you want to risk angering him?"

She shrugged. "He'll never *not* be angry at me."

Something close to pity came into Ison's eyes, but she didn't linger on it.

She stood and walked him to the door. "I mean it when I say you are welcome here anytime." Juniper reached out to his hand and closed her fingers around it.

He gave her hand a light squeeze. "Thank you, Jun."

He moved first—he wrapped his arms around her middle and hugged her to his chest. The contact took her by surprise, but she laid her arms around his shoulders. Ison was not as tall or as wide as Reid, but his lithe form had been built with lean muscle. She felt his heartbeat, and being so close to another human being, one who understood the pain she felt, warmed something in her chest that made her want to hold onto him as long as she could.

The door swung open, and when Juniper lifted her head from Ison's shoulder, she met Reid's very angry, mildly shocked glare. Behind him, a servant held dinner.

Dinner for two.

Dinner for her and Reid.

Ison's embrace had not warmed her cheeks, but being between Ison and Reid and being caught in the arms of another did. Her entire face burned like fire. She and Ison quickly let go of one another. Ison cleared his throat, muttered a goodbye to Reid, and ducked into the corridor without looking back.

The servant arranged dinner on the table while Juniper stood back. She felt Reid's glare, but she refused to look at him. She didn't want him to see the blush on her cheeks.

Table set, the servant bowed himself out.

Reid shut the door behind him and said grimly, "No doubt that will make the gossip rounds in the kitchens."

"Do you require an embrace too, Squire?" Juniper asked calmly, but the thought of holding Reid in her arms once more made her knees quiver. She had never been more glad to be wearing a dress.

Reid started toward the table with his shoulders squared. "No, I do not."

The malice in those few words chilled her to the bone.

❄

Dinner passed in awkward silence. Juniper kept her gaze on her meal, pushing her food around her plate. Reid sat across from her. Neither spoke.

No, I do not.

Cold words, spoken bitterly. The more she repeated them in her mind, the more bitter they became. Certainly, Reid no longer thought about her *that* way. She had been a convenient body for him, nothing more. He had known she would one day leave, despite the promises he made to keep her. Lies. It had all been lies.

Reid finished his meal first. "I'll be outside." He started toward the door, his armor clinking. "Penet will be here for the night."

A twinge of hope surged through the hole in her chest. That would make her plan of sneaking out much easier.

Reid let himself into the corridor.

Juniper didn't attempt to eat anything more. She drank a glass of water and retreated into her bedroom, where the magical texts waited. She washed her hands and face and changed into a clean set of pajamas. She grabbed

Mergermite's Guide to Magic and crawled into bed. Someone had changed the linens while she'd been gone, and the human stink had been replaced with fresh cotton and citrus.

Setting the book against her thighs, she began to read. She read the introduction, but she learned nothing that she didn't already know about magic. It came from within a person; users of magic were called mages; mages could summon their magic and command it to their will; natural magic took on the form of one of five basic elements.

Ison hadn't joked when he called the text basic.

She skipped past the chapters on magical theory and the Iluvin—ancient mages who had vanished since the Great War a thousand years ago—and stopped on the introduction to the elements. A chart of tiny, delicate script and overlapping circles showed the elements: fire, earth, water, air, and energy. Bold lines divided the chart into five main sections, one for each element, with energy in the middle.

On the top of the chart, "light" was written. On the bottom, "dark" was written. On the far right side, "light" appeared again, and on the far left, "dark." A spectrum—one of several that divided the chart into a dozen slivers.

She turned the page to find an explanation: "Magic is measured on a scale of light and dark." She turned back to the chart. Fire was in the light-light sliver of the chart. Air, below fire, was light-dark. Water, opposite fire in the bottom left, was dark-dark.

What did that mean?

In the fire section, in the far upper right corner, "healing" had been written. Healing was good; she understood how it would be considered light-light. In the far corner of the water section, as far dark-dark as it could be, "ice" was written.

Her heart felt cold. What did it mean that her magic was on the darkest end of the spectrum? She turned the page, but she found no immediate explanation. She swallowed, but her throat had gone dry. Juniper closed the book and pushed it away. Dark-dark. Bad. Evil.

She released a breath. Learning about magic did not have the effect she thought it would. She pushed the magical text aside and reached instead for the fiction book she hadn't been able to read that morning. She started over, but she found the words no more appealing than she had before.

CHAPTER SEVEN

Juniper watched the moonlight drift into her bedroom. She hadn't gotten much further into the book. Too many troubling things plagued her thoughts, pulling her in every direction except into the story. Every sound in the corridor stole her attention. She listened for Penet's arrival and Reid's departure.

Finally, she heard Penet's calm voice. "Evening, Reid. Any trouble?"

"None at all," Reid said, his voice low. "She hasn't been feeling well."

Hasn't been feeling well? She inhaled but held in the retort. She didn't need Reid's attention right now.

Then, another thought struck, and her simple plan transformed. Reid's comment could work in her favor.

"I'll keep my eye on her," said Penet.

With a quiet goodbye, Penet took up the post outside her chamber door, and Reid departed. She waited for the moonlight to reach farther into the room, then pulled her dressing gown over her pajamas and tucked her feet into her leather boots—the boots she had come to adore. They were of better make and quality than the pricey Undercity boots she'd had before. Like her others, they had molded to her feet.

Juniper stood in the moonlight, letting it soak into her skin.

Dark-dark.

She had always felt at home in the shadows, like she belonged there. All this time, that feeling was rooted in her magic. Her magic felt at home in the dark. Maybe the dark was where she belonged. Hidden away. Locked up.

When the ticking brass hands of the clock upon her mantel read nine, she took a deep breath, as though the moonlight could be breathed, and started toward the main doors of her chamber. She was not looking forward to the Death Chamber, but she had promised Ison. As horrible of a person as she was, she wouldn't break a promise to one of her only friends.

She gently opened the door.

"My lady?" Penet's brown eyes widened, his eyebrows rose nearly to his hairline, and he quickly straightened. A pale blush warmed his sun-stained cheeks.

He looked guilty. Juniper looked him up and down, and then she spotted the thing he clutched behind his back. It looked like a book.

Penet tensed, then cleared his throat. "Are you—I mean, is there a problem, my lady?"

"What is that you're reading, Squire?"

His entire face reddened. He swallowed. "Nothing," he said quickly. "My lady."

She raised a brow at him and sauntered a step closer. He inhaled sharply, then sighed. His shoulders slumped. He showed her the book, *Full Moon at Fort Nessie.*

Her curious smile grew wider. "Ah. I didn't think you the romance sort."

His face burned hotter still. He looked like he would rather melt through the floor than be having this talk with her.

She set her hand on his armored shoulder. "Don't worry, Squire. Your secret is safe with me." She gave him a warm smile, one that he halfheartedly returned. He looked only mildly relieved. "I don't know how you would survive the night. It sounds dreadfully boring."

He didn't confirm, but the subtle shift of his eyes told her he agreed. He cleared his throat again. "Is there something that you need, my lady?"

"Yes." She turned her gaze downcast. "I came to ask you to send for Ison." She set a hand over her stomach. "My dinner didn't settle well."

Penet nodded, and her small request instilled a glimmer of determination in his dark brown eyes that she had so often seen in Reid's. Without further question, Penet summoned a servant to deliver the message. Juniper retreated into the sitting room to wait, and a minute before the clock read nine twenty, Ison appeared in her doorway with a stomach tonic. The tall glass rested on a silver tray, not unlike the tonics he had brought her during the Demon Crisis.

He looked only mildly confused, but as he and Penet stood in the sitting room while she drank the tonic, he listed the things that might have turned her stomach against her, including wine and a handful of foods. The tonic tasted much better than the others, like sweet cream and strawberries. When she finished the tonic, she leaned back in the chair.

"Thank you, Ison." Sighing, she put a hand over her chest. "I think I drank it too fast."

Understanding drifted across his face. "A walk will help settle it."

"That sounds agreeable." Juniper stood. Keeping a hand on her stomach, she turned to Penet. "Squire, I require a walk. Ison will escort me."

Penet glanced at Ison, but his gaze was more curious than cautious. He nodded. "Of course, my lady."

Juniper snaked her arm through Ison's. "Don't worry about me, Penet. Ison will keep me safe and sound."

Penet didn't look confident about it. Meekly, he said, "I will be here." He held the door for her and Ison, then took up his post outside.

She and Ison had taken a handful of steps when she heard the distinct ruffle of pages. She smiled to herself; she hadn't asked his permission, which did not give Penet an easy option to refuse her. Reid would have simply refused, but Penet was too shy.

Juniper and Ison strolled down the corridor, then down another. She kept their pace leisurely, just in case a guard should spot them. She'd memorized the guards' positions by now; they had already been seen by at least three.

She felt a bubble rise in her throat—too quickly to avoid it. She covered her mouth, but the bubble escaped.

Ison grinned. "Very ladylike."

She tapped his arm playfully. "What was in that tonic? It feels like there's a bubble in my chest."

"That might be the fog essence," Ison said. "It can have that effect on people. I'll make a note not to add it to anything I bring you."

"Fog essence?"

"It's a complicated, smoky substance that resembles fog. It's not actual fog. It is an ingredient in most stomach tonics." Ison cleared his throat. "It's also known to have...uh, flatulent side effects." He motioned to her as another bubble rose in her throat.

"Thank you for keeping this evening lighthearted," she said.

Ison chuckled, then his eyes darkened with the reminder of their destination.

Juniper guided them down another corridor, toward the edge of the Royal Chambers. Through the windows, the sky above the Royal Grounds was dotted with stars and sparse, inky clouds. Spring scents filtered in through the same drafts that had allowed Blugo's winter chills to seep through. She paused at one window—the air teemed with chirping frogs and crickets. In the distance, on the other side of the Royal Grounds, the Royal Greenhouses were a pale green glow.

"It's so different than the sounds in the city," she said woefully. If the map in her mind was correct, a guard stood in an alcove down the corridor, within earshot.

"I'm sure it smells better, too," Ison said.

She gave him a small smile, and they walked on. She guided them down a short, unremarkable corridor with a set of mahogany doors at the end. The doors were smaller than most in the Royal Chambers, and to someone who did not know any better, they might lead into a broom or linen closet. Juniper knew better. She eased one of the doors open and motioned Ison inside. With one last look down either corridor to make sure they remained unseen and unfollowed, she shut the door.

Light spilled in from a single narrow window high on the wall. It cast moonlight over the stacked barrels, buckets, boxes, and a large portrait hanging on the opposite wall.

Ison glanced about the room, then lifted an eyebrow at Juniper. "What's this? If you want to have a tryst, you could just ask."

Juniper chuckled and dismissed the idea with a lady-like wave of her hand. She walked to the portrait and ran her hands along the rosewood frame, over the elegant bumps and whorls, until she found the hidden handle on the left side. The portrait swung open and revealed a hidden staircase that descended into the darkness.

"This is how we are getting into the bowels," Juniper said.

"Ah." Ison's brows rose. "Interesting. I was going to suggest a servant's passage."

Juniper started, "How's your light magic? Is there some spell—"

Ison summoned a blue flame in the palm of his hand.

Juniper smiled. "That's better."

It took her a heartbeat to catch the scent—like wet metal.

They climbed through the portrait hole. Juniper closed the door behind them, plunging them into semi-darkness. Ison's magic flame became their only light.

Ison whispered, "Do you think Penet knows we're up to something?"

"He knows I am not Roslyn Derean, but I'm not sure if he suspects who I really am. He's never asked." Juniper hadn't had the thought to ask Isaac if they'd told Penet anything about her. "But, if he suspects who I am, then he most likely will think we're off to a midnight tryst."

Ison half laughed. "Why does everyone assume that about me?"

"Because rumor has it that you're fantastic in bed."

Ison chuckled, but not a spec of blush warmed his cheeks. "Well, I suppose that's a better assumption than others."

Juniper would much rather everyone assume she and Ison were exploring each other than a Death Chamber underneath the castle. It would be far easier to explain.

CHAPTER EIGHT

The bowels of Castle Bradburn were no more welcoming than they had been before. Juniper walked a step behind Ison, who held his flame in front of him. She didn't need it to see; she had always had good night vision. They walked for a while in silence, down, down, down into the bowels, through narrow halls and rough-hewn passages. She had a decent sense of direction, but she struggled to keep herself centered with Ison's weaving and wandering. He seemed to know where he was going, though Juniper didn't ask.

She didn't like the sound of the echo. It reminded her of how deep they had gone and how alone they were.

"Wait," Ison finally whispered. He paused at an intersection between two halls. He flattened his hand against a cracked stone. The two cracks made a crude triangle. A marker. He turned down one of the passages. "It's this way."

They turned down a wider tunnel that didn't look familiar. The far end of the tunnel ended in darkness. A few side passages veered from it, each as empty and dark as the next. Somewhere, water dripped.

She didn't like the silence of the bowels. She'd heard the servants gossip about what sort of monsters lurked in the shadows, ancient and clever creatures, none of which she wanted to meet. Dragonlings. Snakes thick as wagons. Bats with fangs longer than her fingers. Imps.

"Ison?" she whispered.

"Yes?"

"I looked at the first book."

A beat, then he nodded. "How was it?"

She bit her lip, then asked, "What does it mean for ice to be in the dark-dark corner of the spectrum?"

Ison glanced back at her, his neutral expression not giving any indication into his thoughts. The flames exaggerated the shadows on his face and made his gray eyes appear blue.

She asked, "Does it mean that ice is evil magic?"

His lips fell into a frown. "You didn't read the book," he said flatly.

"I read it...parts of it."

Ison sighed and turned his attention back to the tunnel in front of him. She had the distinct feeling of having been reprimanded. Ison said, "If you had read it from the beginning, you would have read the explanation of the light-dark spectrum and the reason why each element is where it is on the map."

"So...I'm not evil?"

"No," he said. "The light-dark spectrum doesn't correlate with a good-evil spectrum. It's a measure of how the magic works, where it works best, and in what conditions it thrives. It's a gauge of magic as we understand it. Since your magic is in the dark-dark corner of the spectrum, the talents rooted in the light-light corner, like healing, will be harder for your magic to perform."

A small relief went through her chest. Not evil by birth. "I won't be able to heal?"

"All mages can heal to some extent, but you won't be able to stitch wounds together like the royal healer." Ison glanced down another dark passage, and his voice drifted as he said, "She is a fire mage. I'd bet a year's salary on it." When nothing appeared down the passage, he glanced at her. "I highly suggest you start over in *Mergermite's*. There's a lot of information like that in the first part, before it gets into the technical charts and those types of things."

Feeling a bit foolish, she said, "I'll start over. I'm sorry I didn't heed your advice in the first place."

He let out a soft chuckle. "Magic doesn't work like some people believe. It's not a list of spells we're casting. It's more of a...force we can harness and control. That's how one of my professors put it. Each mage has a different form of magic than the next, which makes teaching mages harder than other students."

"Do I really have to read about all that magical theory and history?"

"There is some interesting information about the Iluvin in there. Their magic, they say, was more powerful than mages today, considerably so." He glanced down another passage. "There is also the legend that all mages are descended from the Iluvin, that the magic was gifted to the five Iluvin clans by the gods or something, I forget the details. But that's where the elements are supposed to have come from."

She asked, "What is the energy element?"

"It's non-elemental. It's rare too. I'd say that out of every twenty mages who come to the Marca, one of them is an energy mage. They're right in the middle of the light-dark spectrum, but it's the least understood of the elements."

Juniper looked at the flame in his palm, effortlessly kept alive. "How does it work? To keep it going?"

"Hm?"

"The flame."

"It takes magic." Ison made the flame smaller, then larger again. "The bigger the flame, the more magic it takes. I can keep this flame for a while, several hours, before I'll grow tired."

"But you're an air mage?"

"Yes." Ison nodded. "Fire mages can use natural magic to produce a flame, whereas everyone else has to use unnatural magic."

She looked down at her hands and tried her best to summon her magic, but all she managed were a few flurries, which quickly evaporated in the light of his flame.

"Save your strength," Ison warned.

She tucked her hands into the deep pockets of her dressing gown.

They reached the end of the long corridor. It ended in stone. Two side passages branched off from it, and after a moment of indecision, Ison chose left. Juniper followed.

Ison began to speak, if only to cut through the silence. "Earth mages are better for enchanting or runesmithing. Because air and earth oppose each other, I would be a poor enchanter or runesmith. It doesn't mean I can't. It means I would find the magic involved more difficult than an earth mage."

She nodded but doubted that Ison saw. He was looking at the walls of the tunnel, running his hands over the carved walls, nudging debris with his boot. Remembering.

Were they getting close?

"It works the same with water and fire," he said absently. "You, being a water mage, wouldn't be as good at healing or burning things. Likewise, a fire mage wouldn't be good at freezing things. Can you see in the dark?"

"I can."

"It's a trait of water magic. To have your raw magic in the dark-dark corner implies that you're more powerful at night. Given your previous occupation as a thief, that's not surprising. Fire is more powerful in the day. Earth and air are indifferent to the daytimes. A bonus of being in the middle of the spectrum. Same goes for energy."

"I've spent most of my life in the dark."

"Being able to see in the dark is often referred to as Night Sight, or Night Vision. I've heard people in Janti call it Night Eyes."

"What is raw magic?"

Ison started to walk a little faster, and he spoke faster. "Raw magic is the magic in its raw form; yours is ice. The magic within you is your raw magic. The Order calls it natural magic. The Marca teaches that raw magic is unstable and dangerous, and so we're taught to manipulate the magic in the air, not raw magic. It's safer, they say, easier for spellwork. Apostates who learn to use their magic on their own use more raw, natural magic and less spellwork." He came to an intersection and started down the right passage without hesitation. "That's how the knights find apostates. When a mage uses raw magic, it taints the air. Knights can sense that taint. It's another way they can tell the apostates from the Marca mages."

Which is how she had kept her magic hidden all this time. She hadn't used her magic.

Ison turned down another passage. As he turned, the light shone on his angular face. He wore a grave expression. He muttered, eyes on the passage, "I'm not a very good teacher."

"Nonsense," she said. "I've learned more from you in this short time that I did the entire time I was attempting to sort out that chart."

A ghost of a smile flickered across his lips.

"And I've got plenty of time in my near future to read all three books, start to finish."

Ison stopped and turned, his grim expression better lit now that he faced her—she nearly ran into him. "What do you mean?" he asked.

She quickly recounted the meeting with the king that afternoon.

Ison's frown deepened. He continued down the passage without the urgency of before. "They're keeping you here as a prisoner? That's not fair."

"I agree, but there's nothing else that can be done until the binding spell is broken, and the court magician said he didn't know how to do it without harming me or Adrian. More so Adrian, though. I doubt the king would think twice if the risk was only to me."

Juniper thought she heard a gurgle from behind them, but when she turned, she saw only darkness. She stepped closer to Ison.

They came to another intersection, and Ison glanced down each passage before he chose one. He whispered, "Mason is keeping secrets."

She didn't doubt that. The old man had that look about him. Maddox had it too, like he knew much more than he let on or admitted.

"He knows what happened to me," Ison said, his voice hard. "He locked me in my room. He knew someone or something was controlling me. He knows that I'm remembering the terrible things that I did, but I never told him about it. He just knows. Whenever I ask him about it, he starts talking in riddles or pretends that I'm not in the room." Ison paused to look down a passage. After a heartbeat, he started to walk down it. "He's been reading in the old Iluvin texts more and more. He brought several back from the Order's library, even."

The Iluvin. Another chapter in *Mergermite's* that she had skipped.

"What does that mean?" she asked.

"The Iluvin supposedly had magic like we wouldn't believe, old rituals, and powerful magic. They used natural magic, not the spellwork like the Marca teaches, which is why most things concerning Iluvin magic is forbidden. Most of the magic they did would be impossible for a mage like me. I'm not strong enough. But Mason? He's different."

"You think he had something to do with the Demon Crisis?" She did, but she wouldn't openly accuse him.

"He knows more than he's telling. He leaves details out when the king or the captain is listening. He only tells them part. I've heard him do it."

"But what could he be leaving out?"

Ison paused. He looked down the tunnel and back the way they'd come as if he expected someone—or something—to be lurking in the shadows. He whispered, "I think he knows who did it, but he's covering the tracks."

Her heart flip-flopped. All the pieces led to Mason. "Why would he help the apostate?"

Ison shook his head. "I don't know. He's given me evidence that he's working with the apostate, and he's given me evidence that he's working against him." His frown deepened. "Still, he never warrants the king's suspicion, which I find suspicious."

"Unless the king knows," Juniper said darkly.

Ison tilted his head toward her.

"What if the king knew that Mason was summoning demons? What if he used it as an excuse for the binding spell?"

"But...to what end?"

She shrugged. Her entire body deflated. "I don't know. It doesn't make sense, I know. Nothing about this demon mess has made sense."

They continued down the tunnel, then another, and another. Juniper didn't mind the drop in conversation. A part of her wished she hadn't started it in the first place; all the unanswered questions and reminders had left her stomach in knots. So did knowing that an apostate who could control other people lurked in the castle, and that the apostate had used other people to kill. It all unnerved her to the point that she thought she needed to empty her stomach.

Ison led them down a narrow staircase with uneven stone steps. The stairs led them into a domed chamber that looked to have once held stone benches. A few were still standing, though most had crumbled to the floor. Dents in the walls held the remains of candles long burned out.

Unease crawled over her skin, like breath on the back of her neck. She turned but saw no one. Only darkness, only shadows for things to lurk unseen, to slither on the edge of awareness.

"I don't like this place," Juniper whispered.

Ison had gone pale and his lips, thin.

They had reached the ancient ruins of whatever came before Castle Bradburn, before the founding of Duvane, maybe even before that. Tunnels branched off the chamber, but Ison led them to the far end. A stone podium stood at the head of the room on a small dais. The stone had been elaborately carved with runes—a few looked strikingly similar to those on the court magician's desk.

Her skin prickled. "How good are you with runes?"

He didn't answer. He lifted his flame to better see the podium. He made a lap around it, and the flame's shadows stretched and weaved through the chamber. Juniper could almost picture the shadows of people sitting on the benches, wide enough for four or five people, and it gave her the worst chills down her spine.

"I don't recognize many of these." Ison pointed to a smaller rune cut with lines that never intersected. "This one is for knowledge. This one"—he pointed to a wide rune with few lines—"is for protection." Some of them were winding lines and whorls, curving around the smaller runes. Some were straight angles and corners. No rune intersected another. "Whoever built this place," Ison said, lifting his flame higher to cast the room into better light, "they were mages."

Ison started down a passage behind the podium, and Juniper followed without a word. She didn't like these ruins at all. Why had the first Bradburn king built his castle on top of them rather than destroying them? He might not have known about them, but why make secret doors leading into the ruins? Or—a sinister voice suggested—he couldn't destroy them, so he built over them.

She followed Ison down a side passage, then another, through what appeared to be an ancient kitchen and eating area. Old ovens stood at the far side of the room, crumbling and gaping. Ison led her through a passage, then another, all dark doors and doorways, and Juniper tried her best not to look too long at the shadows.

She was focusing on not looking into the rooms, and when Ison turned a corner and then stopped, she nearly ran into him. She held onto his arm and peeked around his shoulder. They stood in a long hall. At the end, an old wooden door was set into the stone. Light seeped through the cracks in the wood, between the boards and around the handle. The seeping light appeared to be the same bluish-white as Ison's flame.

Magic flame.

Ison let his light go out, dousing them in near total darkness.

"Is someone inside?" Juniper whispered.

Ison shook his head. He'd gone very pale. "No." He started walking, and Juniper held onto his elbow. They reached the door, and he closed his fingers around the handle. "It's forever flame. It only goes out when the mage who summoned it wills it to go out."

"But..." she started. She gripped his arm a little tighter.

His hand tightened on the handle. "They won't go out," he said, his eyes focused on the door. "Because I put them there."

CHAPTER NINE

A shiver ran up Juniper's spine, and every hair on her body stood on end. The Death Chamber. She'd known their destination from the start, but standing so close to it made her want to run the other way. And if she dreaded it so, she couldn't imagine what Ison felt. She tightened her fingers around his arm, and said softly, "Ison?"

He took several deep breaths.

She slid her hand into his. "I'm with you."

He nodded. "I'm ready."

He pulled open the old door. The hinges squeaked viciously but held. The bluish-white of forever flame dotted the walls of the passage in conveniently spaced indentations in the stone, perfectly shaped for cradling a magical flame. Ison took the first step into the passageway, and Juniper followed. The walls of the passage hadn't been carved; they were constructed of stone blocks.

Juniper reached out and placed her hand against the stone. Smooth as glass.

"This cavern was created by magic," Ison said darkly. "Can you feel that? The residual magic in the air, even after all this time, it's still here."

She felt it: old magic, powerful magic. It made the air feel thick, stifled, tainted with evil magic, with wrongness. She realized with a sickening feeling that she had felt it before—when she and Reid had chased that monster into the sewers and when she had encountered the wechun after the ball.

She withdrew her hand from the stone as Ison started forward. Did he feel the same sense of foreboding as she did? It told her to run as fast as she could the other way. Instead, she walked beside Ison.

At the end of the passage, the walls widened. The ceiling rose. The passage became a large chamber. The stones of the walls moved effortlessly with the curve of the chamber. No simple mason could have made such a structure. Magic-made. Juniper felt the lingering magic enter her nose and mouth with each breath, into her lungs, into her blood. Ison let out a shuddering gasp beside her, and his grip on her hand turned shaky.

In the center of the chamber, carved into the stone floor, was a rune the size of her bedroom. The whorls and circles and connecting symbols laced together in the most complicated fashion she had ever seen. The pattern of the rune had been etched into the stone, leaving a trench deeper than her finger. The insides of the trench were stained red. Gray and white bones were strewn all around the chamber.

Ison's breath hitched. He began to tremble. He squeezed Juniper's hand and brought it up to his chest. He pressed it against his heart. Underneath her hand, it beat erratically.

"Ison?"

"I know." His shaking voice came out several pitches too high. "I thought I could...maybe I would... I thought I was ready to see this. But I-I..." His voice cracked. "I'm not." He shuddered. "For every monster, the trench had to be filled. With blood."

Juniper glanced at the trench. It would have taken a lot of blood.

His knees gave out. He collapsed, teary eyes on the rune. Juniper collapsed with him and wrapped her arms around his shoulders. His entire body shook. His voice came out barely more than a whisper. "When the rune was full, whoever came next...became the monster."

"Gods," Juniper breathed.

Ison had seen it all, witnessed such death, such horror. She felt sick thinking about it.

"Ison," she pleaded, "let's go back upstairs."

He didn't move. He continued on as if she hadn't spoken, "I remember the ones who transformed." A tear slid down his cheek; then another carved a second path, illuminated in the forever flame. "They screamed. And screamed. And *screamed.*" He choked on a sob. "The voices...changed. They merged together, the voices from the blood, the bodies...twisting and..." He sobbed, tears falling freely down both cheeks.

"He made you do it, Ison," she told him, "It's not your fault."

"But the blood is on my hands." His wet voice quivered. "I can hear them. I can see them. I can still hear her screaming for me."

Juniper felt the floor fall out from under her feet. She knew whom he meant. Clara.

Ison sobbed, and Juniper held him tighter. His trembling hands fisted in her robe.

She felt utterly foolish. She had been moping about a broken heart for a man who would never love her, while Ison had been reliving murders that he had been forced to commit. In comparison, she had no right to complain. She would move on from this, but Ison would never forget the horrors that he had done, that he had witnessed. He had lost a love too, not because she had cast him aside, but because someone had entered his body by magic and forced him to murder her.

She held him tight and whispered into his hair, "I'm sorry."

When the worst of the fit had passed, Ison cast his bloodshot eyes at the dark empty rune, then at Juniper. "She didn't understand what I'd done, that I'd done it to her. She trusted me." Ison wiped his face on his sleeve. "Her screams..." Ison shook his head. "I don't want to hear them anymore. I..." *I'd rather be dead*, is what he didn't say.

Juniper hugged him close. "I'm sorry."

After a moment, Ison let Juniper help him to his feet. They made their way back through the ruins and dark passageways. Ison held his flame, but it did not burn as brightly as before.

❄

Juniper and Ison returned to her chambers in silence. Penet, while his brows rose at their approach, didn't ask any questions. He held his book open in front of him, but his eyes were on them. Gods, they must have looked pathetic.

She started inside, but Ison hesitated. Before he could speak, Juniper pulled him over the threshold.

"Jun," he started.

"Stay here." She shut the door behind him. "I don't want you to be alone right now."

She didn't care what Penet would think or what he would tell Reid or what Reid would think. Right now, Ison needed her the most. She couldn't push him away, not as he was, not right now. She pulled him into the bedroom, to the bed large enough for several people. Ison didn't argue.

She shed her dressing gown and boots; he removed his robes and dropped them to the floor. Juniper picked them up and draped them over a chair instead. With shaky hands, Ison removed his boots and crawled into the bed, wearing only his undershirt and shorts. Juniper blew out the candles, leaving them in blue-black darkness. She climbed into the bed, opposite Ison.

Ison's presence beside her reminded her of when Reid had shared her bed, of those few nights she slept soundly in his arms. She'd not feel Reid's warmth again, she told herself firmly, and moping about it wouldn't change a damn thing.

She didn't fall asleep immediately. Ison's breath evened out, but every few breaths hitched. He turned onto one side, then the other, and then his back.

After a while, Ison whispered, "Jun?"

"Yes?"

He rolled onto his side, facing her. In the darkness, all she saw were two blinking eyes. She could easily imagine a brown-eyed squire there.

"Can I..." He shuddered. "Can I ask something of you?"

"Of course."

"I-I can't sleep. All I hear..." A tired desperation shook his voice. "Please, I need to hear something else, someone else."

To cleanse those horrible screams out of his ears.

"Would you like me to sing to you?" She didn't know any lullabies, and she doubted he wanted to hear a bar song.

His breath hitched. "No. I need to hear you."

"Hear me?"

"You can say no. I understand."

"Ison, what do you need to hear? If I know it, I'll say it."

Then, she felt it. A gentle touch along the side of her stomach. But Ison hadn't moved. Magic, she realized. Ison touched her with his magic. The magic touch snaked along her skin, along the curve of her hipbone, and hesitated at the beginning of her underthings. At the same time, the magic snaked another path up her ribs and divided in two. Those two ropes of wind traced mirrored paths along the underside of her breasts. For a tiny moment, the winds that touched her were Reid's fingertips.

She knew what Ison wanted to hear. "I can't say I'm very good at those sounds."

In the dark, she thought she saw his lips twitch upward.

"But I'll try if you need me to."

"You don't have to," he whispered. The wind-fingers retreated down her ribs.

"Ison," she nearly gasped. "Touch me."

The wind-fingers moved, and Juniper didn't need to pretend—a gasp left her throat as one slipped underneath her underthings and the two encircled her breasts. She gripped the sheets. Ison knew exactly what he was doing. He drank in the sounds she made as his magic worked every sensitive part of her, and she knew exactly what those smutty mage books had been talking about.

CHAPTER TEN

Reid knew something was wrong the moment he turned the corner. Penet looked dead ahead, avoiding Reid altogether. Penet, while a talented squire, had a nervous habit of twitching his fingers, which he was currently doing.

"Penet?" Reid asked casually.

"Morning, Reid," Penet said quickly.

"Is something wrong?" Reid set his hands on the pommel of his sword. He'd caught Penet reading on the job before, but he hadn't said anything. He knew how boring the job could be.

Penet opened his mouth but shut it quickly. He briefly glanced at the doors behind him.

Reid felt a shiver of panic. Juniper? "What is it?"

He didn't answer, and Reid's panic rose. What had she done this time? Or—Reid clenched his fists—that mage!

Reid let himself into her chambers. Penet tried to stop him. He reached for Reid's arm, but his grip didn't hold. Penet called Reid's name, but he barely heard it. He reached the bedroom door and let himself through.

His panic burst into too many emotions for him to notice just one.

Juniper lay asleep, but she didn't sleep alone. The other side of the bed—*his* side of the bed—was taken by Ison.

Penet had known. He'd tried to stop him from seeing.

He had been replaced. By a mage. By Ison, no less. Reid curled his fists. He wanted to throw the mage out of the window and let that settle it, but the windows had been sealed.

Reid couldn't take his eyes off the space between Juniper and Ison, space enough for another person. From his angle, they both looked clothed, but he couldn't be sure. He didn't want to know. Had she?

He tore his eyes from them and walked back into the sitting room. Penet stood in the doorway, eyes wide and worried.

"Thank you," Reid said, louder than normal. Movement stirred in the bedroom. The bed creaked. Clothing swished. "I will see you tonight, Penet."

"Until then," Penet said with an apologetic nod and left.

Reid lingered in the open door. She had replaced him so quickly. Perhaps she had never truly been his to begin with. Or, if he had just—

Ison hurried through the bedroom door. At the sight of Reid, the mage froze. He paled with guilt. His robes were slightly wrinkled. Through the door to the bedroom, Reid heard water running in the bathing room.

Ison cleared his throat. "Morning, Squire Sandpiper."

"Ison."

Eyes on his feet, Ison walked toward the main door. He reached for the handle but paused. He turned his steel eyes to Reid; he wore a defiant look that Reid did not like. Ison started to speak but changed his mind. Without another word, he left.

Reid curled his fists. Had Ison meant to brag? What would he have done if Ison had? Hit him? Gods, he wanted to. Hard enough to shatter his skull.

"Oh, I wondered who was talking so loud so early." Juniper stood in the bedroom doorway. Her pajamas were skewed, showing more of her collarbone on one side than the other. His eyes snagged on the beginning of the pale scar that snaked down her front, left by a demon.

No sense in avoiding it. "Ison spent the night?" Reid asked with more bite than he'd meant to.

Juniper's midnight eyes narrowed, then with a sigh, her features relaxed. She leaned her head against the doorframe, tilting her gaze. She looked more like the arrogant thief he'd met months ago, clever and cunning. Her old self. "Yes, he did. We went for a walk last night and returned later than expected. We'd been talking, and Ison talked himself into a bit of an emotional corner. I didn't think he should be alone like that."

"That's kind of you," Reid said, his voice low.

Juniper shifted her weight to the other foot. She yawned, then asked, "Is there something you need, or did you just feel like barging in?"

He straightened. "The Royal Seamstress is coming by this morning."

She frowned, and her black brows came together. "Why? Do I need to be fitted for my execution gown?"

"She will take the dye out of your hair," Reid explained flatly.

Her gaze met his; her eyes sent shivers down his back—phantoms of her nails.

He glanced quickly about the room. He couldn't think about those things. Not anymore. His gaze settled on a stack of books on the shelves that hadn't been there the last time. "Also, the king asked me to remind you that Roslyn went home early this morning."

A beat passed, and Reid risked looking at her. She stared absentmindedly out the window, her nails tracing slow lines on the wood. He had half a mind to ask her about her thoughts, but he stopped himself.

"It has been decided," Reid said, "that while you are a guest here, you are to introduce yourself as Ursula Genton."

"Ursula?" She laughed. "Why do I need yet another fake name? No one comes to see me, and I rarely leave the Royal Chambers." She released a short sigh and added darkly, "I'm locked in this room, and no one beyond a handful of guards knows about me."

"It was suggested, again, that you be thrown into a dungeon cell," Reid said. His uncle seemed adamant about the cell, although Reid suspected that his own falling out with Juniper had something to do with it. "Adrian advocated on your behalf." As had Reid, but he didn't have the motivation to admit it to her.

"He's sweet." Juniper crossed her arms. "At least someone in this castle doesn't want me beheaded."

Reid opened his mouth to argue, but a knock sounded on the door. The seamstress didn't hesitate; she let herself in. This time, she came alone. Miss Flox Jenson was a larger woman of middle age, with a sharp eye for fabric, thread, and all things fashion. She ran her eyes over Juniper.

"Miss Jenson," Juniper said in greeting, though she didn't look enthused to see her. She regarded the older woman with indifference.

"You've lost weight," said Miss Jenson. "No matter. Good thing about corsets is that they're adjustable. I suggest adding more bread to your diet. Maybe some milk. Add some layers to those bones."

Juniper blinked; a pink blush came over her cheeks. Her eyes briefly met Reid's. She had lost weight. Her cheekbones were sharper, her collarbones clearer, as were the bones on her hands. As if sensing his stare, she pulled her pajama shirt over her collarbone.

"Come on, let's get you back to your former glory." Miss Jenson ushered Juniper into the bathing room.

Reid meandered about the sitting room, eyeing the new books—mostly adventure novels and romances. The seamstress would be a while. Reid sat down before the dark hearth. His thoughts drifted to the thief in the next room. He had a pitting feeling in his chest that he had a hand in her current state—her indifference, her coldness, her weight loss.

A knock sounded against the door, jarring him from his thoughts.

Servants brought in breakfast for two. The sunlight had brightened, and feminine voices drifted from the bedroom, along with the stench of whatever magical concoction the seamstress had used.

He buttered four pieces of toast, two for him, two for Juniper. The seamstress was right. She needed more bread in her diet. While he added food to his own plate, he did the same to hers.

He had eaten half a piece of toast when the bathing room door opened. Footsteps sounded across the bedroom, and Juniper Thimble appeared in the doorway. Juniper, not Roslyn. The raven black had been removed from her wavy auburn hair and eyebrows.

Her eyes met his. A beat passed, and she cast her eyes elsewhere. She sat down at the table and started to eat. Miss Jenson left with a hurried goodbye.

Juniper halfheartedly nibbled on the end of a piece of toast, eyeing her full plate. "I won't be able to eat all of this."

"Miss Jenson's right." Reid motioned to her plate with his fork. "You need to eat more."

She glanced at him, then quickly returned her eyes to her plate.

No retort? No smart comment? What in Bala's name had she and Ison been talking about to put her in such a mood?

They ate in silence. Reid ate slower to make sure that she ate. She ate, but not much. A knock sounded on the door, and before Reid could answer it, Adrian let himself into the room. Sir Destry followed a step behind, looking attentive and irritated as usual.

"There she is," Adrian said to Juniper.

She twisted in her seat to see him, and her entire face lit up. Adrian sat on the bench beside Juniper and ran a hand through her loose hair. She didn't look remotely shocked by the touch.

"I'd forgotten what color your hair had been," Adrian mused.

"Less exciting than black," Juniper said.

"Nonsense." Adrian wound a lock around his finger and gave it a gentle tug, a strangely intimate gesture that set a fire underneath Reid's ribcage. "I like this color. Like a newly minted bronze piece. Reid, what do you think?"

They turned to him, Adrian's hazel gaze playful and mischievous, Juniper's wide and unsure.

"It's nice."

Adrian laughed. "*Nice.* You woo me with your command of language, Reid."

Juniper stole her midnight gaze from Reid.

"Did you hear what my father wants to name you?" Adrian asked her.

She frowned. "Ursula."

He smiled wider. "I told him it was a horrid idea. I wanted to give you a much more common name, like Jen or Coni, but my father rarely listens to me."

In that moment, Reid felt glad to have Adrian between him and Juniper. With Adrian, Juniper spoke, she laughed, and life returned to her eyes, a glimmer of the girl he'd fallen in love with, a glimmer of the girl he had pushed away.

CHAPTER ELEVEN

Adrian arrived early for the meeting. His father hated when he arrived late, and Adrian didn't feel like sitting through another lecture on kingly duties and responsibilities. He sat to the right of the empty king's chair at the head of the meeting hall. Without his father to fill it, the king's chair seemed less grand. Just a wooden chair. Built identical to the other dozen that circled the table. Identical to the chair Adrian sat in.

He released a slow breath. Sir Destry stood in the corridor, and for the first time in months, Adrian had a moment of solitude.

It didn't last long, as two sets of footsteps approached down the corridor. Before Adrian could guess their owners, the door opened. His father and Sir Isaac Pinul entered, and whatever hushed conversation they had been having ended at the sight of Adrian.

"We will conclude our discussion later," said his father to Pinul.

"Your Majesty." Pinul bowed his head. He gave Adrian a friendly nod and vanished into the corridor.

King Bradburn took his seat at the head of the table. He wore no crown, but he didn't need to. No one would question his judgments. The sword at his waist would end any argument. Would the council take Adrian as seriously as king? He wore no sword. Not that he could use one with much skill.

To Adrian, King Bradburn said, "You're early."

"I didn't want to be late." Adrian glanced at the closed door, then added, "You've been speaking more to Sir Isaac."

The king folded his hands together over the table. "Yes. There are matters that I have entrusted to him and him alone."

"Do they involve her?"

The thief, as his father would say.

His father gave no answer; his hazel eyes bore into Adrian, implying that those matters did indeed involve Juniper and did not involve Adrian.

Adrian released a heavy sigh. How many times would they have this argument? "She doesn't need all the guards. She won't try anything."

"It isn't just that," his father whispered. "If anyone discovers the binding spell, she would be a target. With her unprotected, your life is in much more danger than if you were unprotected."

Adrian agreed in that aspect, though he saw no need to lock her up as a prisoner.

A flurry of feet and voices came from the corridor—the royal advisors. Adrian straightened; his father did the same. They shared a short glance of unspoken understanding between one ruler and the next that ended as the door to the chamber opened.

Rourke Hendle entered first. The middle-aged man with tied-back ash-blond hair and a matching beard held himself like a commander, a posture learned from his years in the Royal Army. Destin Ulgan followed, a man with thinning brown hair and a round waist. Neither appeared the least bit happy about whatever they'd been discussing.

Ulgan opened his mouth, but a vicious cough captured his breath. He leaned on the chair in front of him and held his bent arm over his mouth until the hacking fit had passed.

"Ulgan?" the king asked. "You sound ill."

The advisor stood up straight and waved off the concern. His usually peachy skin looked pasty, sickly. "It's been a recurring sickness these past few weeks. I daresay I caught it from the market; I heard several people coughing. I have been on a routine of tonics from the court magician."

"Good, good," said the king. "Don't push yourself too hard, Ulgan."

"Nonsense." Ulgan motioned toward Hendle. "Hendle's boy has been kind enough to assist me these past few weeks. Boy's got a mind for politics."

Hendle's frown deepened, and Adrian fought hard not to smile. Four of Hendle's five sons had followed in his footsteps into the Royal Army. The youngest, Ronald, had found his talents with his mind, not his sword, and Adrian had always liked him best.

The two advisors glared at one another, and Adrian suspected that their argument had been over Ronald Hendle. No doubt, Hendle wanted his son to go into the Royal Army.

Ulgan coughed, though not as violently as before. He sank into a chair on the king's left but kept two chairs between them. Hendle sat within view of them all, with one eye on Ulgan.

Adrian began to relax, expecting another meeting of trade routes, bandit problems, and—

"There have been confirmations that rebel Collatian mages have made it into Rusdasin," said Hendle grimly.

Ulgan glared sideways at Hendle, not at all surprised.

"The City Watch has connections, as Captain Tinnly called them, who report foreigners in the Undercity. An increasing number of them these past few weeks."

"Apostates," Ulgan agreed, voice croaky. "My eyes have told me as much."

"Captain Tinnly has mages in the Undercity who report to him," Hendle said. "According to him, there is a band of rebel mages recruiting any and all mages they can."

"For what purpose," Ulgan started, a cough on his tongue, "we don't know for certain, but it can be assumed they are recruiting for something dastardly."

"Possibly a force against Duvane," Hendle said grimly. "We do not need a force of rebel mages in our basement. They must be stomped out before they can cause trouble."

"How?" Ulgan croaked. "The entrances to the Undercity are hidden and guarded. The moment we send men down there, they will be slaughtered." Ulgan cleared his throat. "While they are in the Undercity, they might as well be untouchable."

"Are you suggesting we wait until they come to us?" Hendle raised a brow. "By that time, they will have prepared themselves for a fight."

"If Captain Tinnly has contacts in the Undercity, he would be the one to ask," Ulgan said, frowning. "Your thoughts, Your Majesty?"

The king was silent for a moment, then said, "I dislike having a band of rebel mages so close, but there isn't a clean way to be rid of them. If we wait for them to show themselves, there will be casualties. If we charge into the Undercity looking for them, there will be casualties."

Adrian inhaled to suggest they ask Juniper but then realized that Hendle and Ulgan had not been let in on the secret of her presence. He bit down on his tongue, which thankfully went unnoticed by either advisor.

"But I will speak with Captain Tinnly about these mages," said the king.

"I will send word to the captain at meeting's end." Hendle nodded.

The king nodded in return.

Ulgan straightened in his chair. "It is possible, Your Majesty, that these mages are connected to the Demon Crisis. Our mysterious apostate might be one of them." He glanced at Adrian, then turned his attention back to the king. "Given that no threat seems to remain in the castle, I would bet gold that our apostate came from them and has returned to them."

Hendle considered that, then nodded. "I agree. It is a fair assumption to make. However, I don't think we should assume that the apostate has left the castle."

The familiar bubbling tremor started in Adrian's stomach and worked its way down to his toes and up to his ears. He felt it whenever someone mentioned the Demon Crisis and sometimes when he found himself alone in a space, which, thanks to Destry, wasn't that often.

Ulgan adjusted himself, hand on his chest. He winced. The man looked terribly ill. His lips paled to a worrying white. He leaned back in his chair, and the color slowly came back to his face, though not much. When he spoke, his voice came out hoarse. "I hate to be the one to suggest this, Your Majesty, but if the apostate behind the Demon Crisis is here or with the mages, then there—" A cough stole his breath.

"There is a chance for a resurgence of attacks," finished Hendle.

Ulgan nodded grimly, holding a handkerchief to his mouth.

The room fell silent.

"I see," said the king.

The tremor in Adrian's gut turned into a wave of nausea. No one else looked surprised by this suggestion, and Adrian realized they had already assumed as much. Had he been foolish enough to believe himself safe, to believe the ordeal over? If the apostate yet lived, he understood his father's hesitancy on letting Juniper go. Adrian still needed her protection. And if the apostate found her outside the castle...

"On the lines of suggestion and suspicion," said Hendle, his tone near awkward and unsure, "I hear there is another guest staying in Lady Derean's chambers."

Adrian's heart clenched. Neither advisor lived in the Royal Chambers; however, they had eyes and ears all over the castle. Bala only knew what they had learned through their network of spies.

The king answered swiftly, "Yes. A guest arrived, one who asked for a low profile while staying here, and since Lady Roslyn's chambers were cleaned and fit for a guest, we let our guest have them."

"May I inquire as to the identity of this guest?" asked Hendle. Both he and Ulgan wore the hungry eyes of a mosscat.

"You may inquire, but I will not tell. It is the request of our visitor that her presence be kept quiet." The king met the gaze of each man without flinching. "And I highly suggest that the two of you keep that information to yourselves."

Or he would know who had let the information slip, and he would find a punishment fitting.

Ulgan and Hendle cast each other a wary gaze; the king had outright refused them information. They would assume the visitor to be one of great importance, someone whose presence would cause a stir. Adrian saw the mirrored question between them: *Who?*

Hendle opened his mouth, but the king spoke first. "We will not discuss this further."

Ulgan cleared his throat, gave a hoarse cough into his sleeve, and then said, "Speaking of the Demon Crisis, Ison Rolin has been rather ill of late. I find it suspicious that, immediately after the wechun is slain, he becomes ill-tempered and withdrawn. Mason is aware, but he is refusing to answer any questions about the boy."

Hendle nodded. "It is a strange set of circumstances. I believe that Ison knows more about the Demon Crisis and the apostate than he is admitting."

Ulgan hummed in agreement.

The king took these statements in, keeping his face neutral all the while. Adrian never understood how he and Reid could school their features so readily. The king said, "I have spoken to Mason about Ison, and he believes the young mage innocent."

Ulgan scoffed. "That old man is no good. You trust him too much, Your Majesty."

"I have my reasons why I trust Mason," the king said dismissively.

"It is not Mason I am concerned most with," Ulgan said, his voice gravel-filled. He cleared his throat and placed a hand over his mouth like he might cough, but he didn't.

Hendle continued for him, "It is Ison."

Ulgan motioned toward Hendle and nodded.

They had discussed it before, Adrian assumed. For the two men to be in such agreement, they had to have discussed it considerably.

"Ison is being watched by the Order," the king said flatly. "They have not found reason to suspect him."

Neither Ulgan or Hendle retorted, but neither looked happy.

Adrian released a slow sigh. Again, demons and apostates. When would it end? When would he be allowed to walk the halls of his home without an armed escort? Destry had been giving him lessons on self-defense and swordsmanship, and he had gotten better. He would never level with Reid's skill, but he would learn to defend himself. He refused to allow himself to be defenseless again.

The meeting turned to the happenings in the city, of market losses and complaints, the Marca, of associations and organizations arguing between themselves, to names of possible council members should Councilman Bron finally die in his sleep after seventy years of service.

Adrian let his attention wander to the unfinished letter to the real Roslyn Derean on his desk, to all the things he wanted to say but didn't have the words.

CHAPTER TWELVE

Juniper read into the night. Ison had been right; after the first few chapters, she found herself drawn into the story. The adventure swept her away, and she forgot about Reid, Ison, and the Death Chamber. When she felt sleep tugging, she set the book aside and snuggled back into the pillow.

She didn't fall asleep. She laid there, blinking at the frame of her canopied bed, on the whorls and knots in the finely polished cherrywood. Her mind refused to settle.

The other side of the bed felt terribly empty.

She clenched her fists in her pajama shirt. Had Ison been a mistake? He had left so quickly that morning, without a word to her. Did he regret it? Did she?

Reid knew, or he suspected. He had been short with her, more so than before. She felt the need to explain—Ison hadn't touched her. His magic had. She had offered herself to him after, but he had declined. He had rolled onto his other side and gone to sleep. The idea that Reid thought she and Ison had gone further twisted her stomach into knots, but gave her a spiteful satisfaction at the same time.

Clara had been right: Ison's magic had known exactly how to touch her and where, and even thinking about it made her squirm. Maybe growing up in the Marca wouldn't have been so terrible, what with the orgies in the dormitories.

She rolled onto her back and sighed. With her thoughts roiling between Ison's magic touch and Reid's indifference, she wasn't tired. Admitting defeat to finding sleep, Juniper got out of bed. She wandered to one of the sealed windows. The starry sky blinked overhead. The torches of the castle flickered. Guards patrolled along the battlements. She wished she could open the window and feel the night breeze on her face.

Of course, she didn't have to go far to be outside. The Royal Chambers had several rooftop courtyards.

She made her decision in a heartbeat and pulled her dressing gown over her pajamas. She shoved her feet into her leather boots. Penet wasn't overjoyed to see her this late, but with a promise to stay within the Royal

Chambers and a kiss on his cheek, which brought a mad blush to his face, he let her leave.

She started to walk, and he didn't follow.

She knew exactly where she wanted to go. She went to the smaller of the courtyards within the Royal Chambers. It was a patch of green lined with blooming pear trees. Her boots sank into the thick spring grass, ripe with blossoms and pollen. The night air kissed her skin like an old friend.

She meandered to the far side of the courtyard, to a spread of grass between new shoots of blazing star, patches of honeysuckle, and sprigs of lavender. She closed her eyes and inhaled the lavender and honeysuckle. It smelled like home, but the castle added other scents, and it didn't quite smell the same. She could almost see her old bedroom, the off-white walls, the wooden shutters, the yellow rug. She remembered the smell the most, the lavender and honeysuckle that grew just outside her window.

She opened her eyes, and the illusion shattered. Sighing, she fell backward into the grass. The stars glittered above her. Oh, how she had missed the night and the freedom it brought! She lay there a long moment, letting the night settle her bones, and for the first time in a long time, peace settled in her chest. She felt at home in the shadows, in the moonlight, under a sky full of stars. She ran her hand along the soft grass. They didn't have grass like this anywhere else in the city, not where she could go freely, at least. The parks were observed by the Watch, and the temple courtyards were watched by equally fierce monks and priestesses.

How many nights had she stayed out until dawn, just looking at the sky? It wasn't just the familiarity or the peace; something stirred in that deep down place inside of her, the place where she had shoved her magic. She had spent so long pretending not to be a mage, she had never thought of how it felt at night.

Now, she focused on the fluttering deep in her chest.

She glanced up at the castle. This time of night, most of the windows were dark. The pear trees blocked most of the view, and no one but the moon could easily see her. Juniper sat up and cupped her hands.

And she focused.

Flurries appeared in her hands, glinting in the moonlight. She focused on those flurries as they tumbled about her cupped hands. Her skin cooled but not unpleasantly. She focused, concentrated harder. A few more flurries appeared. Dozens of them glinted like little metal discs. She concentrated harder still. She felt the strain in her body, the energy being sponged out of her, tighter and tighter, until—she gasped with a sudden twist of pain. The flurries vanished, and she bent forward, hands flat on the grass, gasping for the warm breaths of spring. Slowly, her breath returned, and that seizing sensation in her body relaxed.

She took a deep breath and collapsed back into the grass. What she wouldn't give for a tankard of ale and a few hours to sit on the rooftops of Rusdasin with Amery. She would find the entire situation laughable.

When Juniper got out—if she got out—she would have to take something to prove that her story was true. Should she start stockpiling her pilfered things in her closet?

She let out a laugh. She had eyes on her at all times, and no one would allow her anywhere near the jewel room.

She felt a tug of exhaustion, and before she fell asleep in the grass, Juniper rose and started back toward her chambers. That small bit of magic had left her exhausted, and if she practiced a while longer, she would tire herself out enough to sleep without dreaming.

She plucked a sprig of honeysuckle as she left. Oh, it smelled of spring! She twirled the stem as she strolled through the corridor, the yellow petals catching the torchlight. She rounded a corner, eyes on her honeysuckle, when movement ahead caught her attention. She blinked. Once. Twice.

The wall was moving.

She blinked again, but the illusion didn't dissolve. The stones of the wall were *moving*.

Juniper ducked into the heavy shadows of a suit of armor, and from between its legs, she watched the moving wall. The stones slowly retracted from their original positions, rolling into the wall like a scroll until an archway appeared.

The torchlight did not penetrate the archway; beyond was inky black, as heavy as if someone had painted the stones. Then, a shadow stepped out of the darkness. A man, by the shoulders. A dark cloak hid his face and hands. He looked both ways down the corridor and started to walk toward Juniper.

She held her breath as he passed. The shadow of his hood hid his features. Only the pale tip of a chin could be seen. He walked past the suit of armor without even a glance in her direction. He rounded the corner where she had just come from.

She released her held breath. Her heart thumped, thumped, thumped.

That man had walked through a solid wall. Magic, no question. She started to get up to follow, then stumbled as another thought raced through her mind—*a man who walked through doors that were not there.*

64

Like Ison had said.

The apostate.

Juniper slid out from her hiding spot and down the corridor, slick as a shadow. Something cold steeled her bones, a determination she hadn't felt in a long while. She spotted the cloaked figure at the end of the next corridor. The apostate had chosen a route between the view of the guards—he had known exactly where to go without being seen.

He paused at the end of the corridor, and then the wall between two paintings began to move. They unrolled inward, forming an archway, and the cloaked figure stepped through. The stone began to fit together again, coming together seamlessly. Juniper started toward the archway, but the stones moved too quickly. She paused on the other side. There—her heart thudded—movement in the darkness. The cloaked figure stood just on the other side. A heartbeat—then, the blink of an otherwise invisible eye through the darkness. The stones fitted seamlessly back together.

Juniper stood there a moment longer, waiting for the stones to move again. They did not. Then, the reality of it sank in. She slumped against the opposite wall, knees shaking and hands trembling.

The apostate was still in the castle.

CHAPTER THIRTEEN

Juniper went straight to her chambers.

"My lady?" came Penet's worried voice. He gripped the hilt of his sword. "Are you all right? You're pale."

She jumped at Penet's hand on her arm. She nodded, though her thoughts were moving too quickly to form words. Penet guided her into her chambers, to her bedroom. She sat on the edge of the bed.

"Do you need anything? The healer? A drink?" Penet's voice did not carry the steadiness that Reid's held, the confidence of a knight.

Juniper shook her head. "I-I got lightheaded," she lied. "Nothing to worry about."

She tugged off her boots and her robe; her fingers trembled. She snuggled into the blankets, but Penet hadn't moved. Disbelief creased his brow.

"A drink," she said. "Something warm. Herbal tea."

Penet marched into the sitting room. Juniper leaned forward, head on her knees. Sleep felt leagues away. The apostate. Here, in the castle.

She hadn't been able to see beyond the archway, but how? She had always been able to see well in the dark, even before she had accepted her magic. Yet her magic-aided sight hadn't been able to penetrate the archway.

The only answer she could think of was magic.

And the apostate, had he seen her? Would he send his minions to find her before she could speak of his return? Would this spark a new wave of missing servants and demon attacks?

Her heart raced.

But...if the apostate knew of the binding spell, why hadn't he tried to harm her? If he truly wanted to harm Adrian, he would have known that the best way to do so would be to harm her first. And she had given him the perfect opportunity.

Unless he didn't know of the binding spell. Unless someone else had sabotaged it.

But who? Who would have gained from it? Mason Hobbs came to mind—but the cloaked figure hadn't been tall or thin enough.

But if the apostate could walk through walls, what stopped him from walking right into her bedroom? Penet stood outside the door, not inside, and she couldn't rightly ask him to stand inside her bedroom.

She gripped the sheets. She would feel safer if Reid still slept on the other side of the bed, within reach.

Her chamber door opened. A quick exchanging of words, then Penet appeared in the bedroom doorway with a tea tray in his hands. He set it on the table.

Juniper climbed out of bed and set her bare feet on the stone floor. Penet moved to the bedside with his squire's grace, hands extended toward her should she fall.

"I'm all right. A hot cup of tea is just what I need." She sat down at the table and poured steaming tea into the delicate china cup.

Penet lingered, and for once, she didn't mind his presence. As she stirred honey into her second cup, Penet came around the table, into her view. He wore worry on his youthful face.

"My lady." He swallowed—he looked terrified. "I was asked to watch over you and report anything odd or out of the ordinary. I-I'm not sure what to think."

"I apologize," Juniper said, and she meant it. "I didn't mean to cause you worry. I didn't think a walk would bother me so." If only she could confess what she had seen. Had it been Reid, she would have. "I should have asked you to come with me or maybe eaten more for dinner."

A timid smile came over his lips. Juniper offered him some of the tea—the kitchens had sent two teacups.

"No, thank you," Penet said. A beat passed, and he added, "My lady."

She half laughed. "We both know I'm no lady, Squire. You don't have to keep up the formalities."

A relief came over his features. "I had guessed as much." He shifted his feet. "They said you were Roslyn Derean, but then they said she went home, and now you're Ursula. And your hair is red, not black."

"I told them the plan was stupid, but they didn't listen to me," she said with a small chuckle. The tea had helped; her chest felt looser and not so twisted up. Herbs, no doubt. Penet's steadfast presence likely had something to do with it too. "What do you think is going on?"

Penet's fingers twitched toward his palm, then out again, a nervous gesture. "You were brought in as a decoy because of the threats against Prince Adrian."

"See?" Juniper tipped her tea toward him. "It's not a hard plan to figure out. Half the staff has probably guessed as much. Serves them right for parading me about, trying to entice the assassin out of hiding."

She took a gulp of tea. She couldn't quite place the herbal taste.

"I know who you are," Penet said quietly.

She looked over her teacup at him. He looked terrified at what his admission might bring, but he held her gaze.

"And who do you think I am?" Juniper raised a brow. Her lips quirked into a half-smile.

Penet pulled his bottom lip inward.

"I could just tell you," she said, pouring a third cup of tea. "But that would defeat the purpose of your deductive skills. I'm sure that, as a knight, they would come in handy."

"They wanted to keep you secret," Penet said. "I've an uncle in the City Watch, and I hear all about what's happening in the city. The same night that Roslyn Derean arrived at the castle, Juniper Thimble went missing. Thimble hasn't been seen in the city since."

Juniper sipped her tea, holding her stare on Penet's.

"I've seen your wanted posters," he whispered. "I've heard my uncle describe you. You're her."

"And how do you feel about having to guard someone as deplorable as myself?" When he didn't answer, Juniper added, "I wouldn't hold it against you if you hated me. You would not be alone. In the first week I was here, Reid threatened to kill me at least twice a day."

At Reid's name, Penet shifted on his feet. "Reid swore to keep it a secret, he said."

"And you see how crabby it's made him. Poor boy would have been better off if he'd not met me."

Penet gave a short laugh.

"You don't think so? Have you met Reid lately?" It might have been the herbs that loosened her tongue or her desperation to keep Penet in the bedroom as long as possible, just in case the walls began to move.

"I..." Penet stopped himself. He looked at his hands, then at the window. "I don't mean to speak outside of my position, but when Reid was guarding you, I can't say I've seen him as happy."

Juniper downed the rest of her tea in a single gulp.

"My lady?" Penet's brows rose—he knew he had said the wrong thing.

"It doesn't matter." She stood—the floor wobbled.

Penet caught her—she hadn't been aware of falling. He helped her back to her feet and to the bed. She collapsed onto the pillows. Penet made to leave, and she muttered, "You don't have to call me that."

Penet hesitated, then pulled the blankets to her shoulders. "I will keep this event between us. Goodnight...Juniper."

Juniper closed her eyes, and the herbal concoction pulled her under.

If only it had lasted.

Sleep came and went. She tossed and turned to find pockets of sleep, her fitful dreams full of opening walls, shifting shadows, and eyes in the dark. Each time she woke, she scanned the walls of her bedroom to make sure none were moving.

Finally, she yanked her bed-curtains closed. She knew it would do nothing against an apostate who wanted to kill her, but it made her feel better. It made her immediate area smaller, easier to defend. She sat in the middle of the bed and worked on her magic, summoning a few more flurries each time, until she wore herself out and the sleep returned.

CHAPTER FOURTEEN

"You look sick," Reid told her first thing the next morning.

Juniper rolled onto her other side, away from the sunlight pouring in from the bed-curtains that Reid had so unceremoniously whisked aside.

"Get up," Reid barked. "Breakfast is on the table."

Juniper begrudgingly got out of bed. She didn't bother fixing her hair or washing up. She trudged into the sitting room where the aromatic breakfast beckoned. She sat opposite Reid, and the two of them began to eat in silence. She waited for him to say something about the night before, but it would appear that Penet kept his word.

She pushed eggs around her plate. Reid needed to know about the apostate; the Order needed to know. But before she spread panic, she wanted to talk to Ison. It might not have been the apostate, and he knew more about the moving walls than she did.

She forced down a bite of buttered toast. It turned to ash on her tongue, but she swallowed. She chased it with a gulp of tea. She took another bite—she would need the energy if she intended to practice her magic.

Reid's hand appeared against her cheek, and she jumped. She hadn't seen him move, yet he stood beside her.

"You're not feverish." Reid flattened the back of his hand against her cheek. At his touch, her skin went clammy.

Reid walked back to the other side of the table. His golden brown eyes looked at her with indifference but also with a clinical concern that reminded her of the royal healer. She felt the ghost of his hand against her cheek, and between it and his stare, her stomach fell into her ankles.

The bread in her hands felt like lead. It tasted like it too.

"Are you feeling all right?" Reid asked. "You've barely eaten."

She didn't want to talk about it, not right now. Instead, she asked, "Would sickness transfer?"

"I don't know." Reid hadn't taken his eyes from her face. "I will confer with Adrian this morning to see if he felt anything of the sort." He looked back down at his plate of ham and eggs. "He might have had a touch of something, and before he felt it, it transferred to you."

She nodded. It made sense, and she didn't want to give him a reason to doubt her.

"Eat what you can," Reid said after a moment. The softer tone of his words prickled her skin.

When the servants came to clean the table, Juniper retreated into her bedroom. Reid stood in the doorway, making sure none of the servants tried to sneak a peek at the supposedly "high priority" guest. Although, if any one of them were as clever as Penet, they would have figured it out by now.

"You might need a tonic," Reid said, though his voice hardened on *tonic.*

She was about to decline when the idea clicked into place.

"It might be for the best," Juniper whispered as to not be overheard. "I could use a walk as well. Don't send for anyone, I'll walk to the court magician's chambers."

Reid's neutral expression at once turned a shade darker. His brows came together. His lips twisted in disapproval. Then Juniper realized—Ison. Reid knew he had stayed in her chambers, and she had never requested to visit him before.

"Unless you would prefer to call for him," Juniper added, her voice small. It didn't matter where. She just needed to talk to Ison.

"We will take a walk," Reid said lowly. He turned his attention back to the servants.

Juniper thought about thanking him, but she held her tongue. She shouldn't have to thank him for allowing her a small freedom. She could go anywhere in the castle she wished, with or without his allowance! She was Juniper Thimble for gods' sake, the most notorious thief in Rusdasin. In Duvane!

And for the first time in a long time, she felt like it.

*

Juniper walked a step behind Reid. Because no one knew who she was and because they were leaving the Royal Chambers, Reid suggested she wear a veil. The one she found in the dressing room looked like something to be worn at a funeral, not for a walk through the castle. The dark silky gossamer hid her face and hair but made seeing difficult.

She fought to tug at the gossamer that obstructed her vision. She could see the blurry shapes of the corridor and the outline of Reid's armor, but her vision had been stunted. She didn't like it; her sense of walking relied on Reid, and she hated the lack of control.

A short time ago, she would have followed him anywhere.

Despite the veil, Reid avoided the main corridors. He led her through servant passages between floors. It took twice as long to reach the court magician's chambers.

Reid knocked on the door, and after a moment, Ison answered.

"Morning," Reid said flatly.

Ison blinked several times at Reid, then at the strange woman in the veil.

"Do you need something?" Ison asked pleasantly, ever the professional apprentice.

"Ison," Juniper whispered. "It's me."

A smile came over Ison's face. He looked to be fighting back a laugh. He stepped aside and said, "Do come in."

Juniper stepped inside, and Reid followed her. Once the door shut, she ripped the veil from her head. "Gods, that's uncomfortable," she said, shaking her fingers through her hair.

"What do I owe the pleasure?" Ison asked, looking between Juniper and Reid.

Reid didn't take his eyes off the mage, but his neutral expression didn't change. "Juniper is feeling ill this morning."

"I can handle it from here." Juniper set her eyes on Reid.

He closed his mouth, although he didn't look happy about it. "I will be in the corridor." Reid turned swiftly and let himself out.

"Is there something you need?" Ison asked lower. "Are you feeling all right?"

"I might...could use a tonic." Juniper glanced at the door. Reid would be standing on the other side. Listening. "I didn't sleep well. I was a bit faint this morning, and Reid thinks I'm turning ill."

"You do look a bit on the ill side." Ison looked her over. "Mason isn't here. Come into the workroom. I'll start a tonic for you."

Juniper followed Ison through the sitting room, through a spacious and grand study, and into the sunny workroom. Two long tables ran the length of it, cluttered with vials, brewing equipment, burners, flasks, and tubes of glass and different kinds of metal. One wall of shelves held nothing but glass jars, metal containers, and wooden boxes—more herbs and minerals than she had ever seen.

"Sorry," Ison said as he removed a stack of books from a stool. "I'm usually working alone."

Juniper sat, and while Ison started a tonic with adept hands, she started to tell him about her previous evening. The tonic smelled fantastic, and the smell changed as the tonic went through different tubes, flasks, and flames, as did the color. She'd never seen Ison work before and found herself transfixed by it. He crushed the herbs with gentle, precise fingers and never faltered or slowed.

He turned the flame low and added what smelled like blueberry extract. It made the entire workroom smell like freshly picked berries. Ison went to the cabinet and selected a glass, and as he brought it to the tonic station, she told him about the cloaked figure and the moving stones.

The glass fell from his grip and shattered.

She jumped.

Ison stared at her, gray eyes wide, as though she had plunged a dagger into his side. "You saw him?" His voice was barely audible.

Juniper nodded. "I think so. You told me the apostate could make doors where no doors were, and that is just what this man did. A doorway appeared in the solid stone, then vanished."

"What about the light?"

"The light?"

"Light." Ison started to shake. "Did light enter the passage he made?"

She shook her head. "No. It looked like the doorway had been painted, but much darker than any black paint I have ever seen. I couldn't even see into it."

"Gods." Ison leaned against the desk. "I thought it was over." His fingers shook. He looked like he needed a tonic more than she did. "I thought it would be over when you killed the wechun."

"I thought so too." She bit her lip. The tonic turned a shade bluer. "What do we do about it?"

"First, I suggest you pour your tonic before it burns."

Both Ison and Juniper jumped. The glass underneath Ison's feet crunched.

The court magician stood in the doorway to the workroom, his old hands folded in front of him. With a flick of his hand, the glass Ison had dropped picked itself up, the shards stitched themselves together, and the glass appeared on the counter as though it had never been broken.

Ison poured the tonic into the renewed glass.

The court magician magicked a second glass beside the first. "Split it between the two of you. You both look pale."

Ison did as he'd been told.

"Second," said Mason Hobbs, "I want both of you in my study."

CHAPTER FIFTEEN

After she finished her half of the tonic, Juniper did feel better. Ison looked like he felt better too. She followed Ison into the study, a room worthy of a master mage with towering rosewood shelves packed with ageless tomes, delicate figurines, and hundreds of bound scrolls. A red and purple rug adorned most of the floor, whorls and runes stitched into the material. She sat in one of the large armchairs angled in front of the rosewood desk.

The desk had been carved and engraved with hundreds of whorls, runes, and archaic symbols. She recognized a few of them from carvings all over the city, for health, for protection against intruders, for a number of things. Her heart sank when she spotted a few that looked like those she had seen on the podium in the ruins underneath the castle.

Could one of those runes be for intimidation? Her nerves shook. What would Mason know about the ruins and runes carved on them? A wicked voice in her mind hissed, *He probably carved them.*

The court magician sat in his rosewood chair, adorned with its own carvings, and folded his hands together. His piercing gaze moved between Juniper and Ison. "So," Mason said, his wizened voice sure and strong. "Tell me about the wechun."

Juniper steeled herself; Ison flinched.

What did Mason already know? The court magician held her gaze. She managed to say, "What do you mean?"

"You were there when it was slain," he said simply. "I'd like to hear your story. Without others peering down at you."

His tone... Did he already know? She glanced at Ison, but he had firmly fixed his gaze on his boots. She brought her gaze back to the court magician. He held his hands in front of him, patiently waiting.

"It's okay," Ison said, his voice small.

With Ison's encouragement, Juniper told the old mage the truth of what had happened in the tunnel after Bala's Ball. The court magician didn't speak. His gaze remained on her, never flinching, as she told how she froze the first demon and fought the second, finally impaling it with steel. She confessed that Reid and Adrian had lied to protect her.

When she finished her story, Juniper lowered her gaze to the whorls on the desk, to a rune that ran along the front panel. It looked older than the others. Among the whorls were what looked like stars intertwined with human bones.

Reliving the story had left her with a harsh feeling of guilt. She heard Reid's voice shouting at her, her name a curse on his tongue.

"I see," Mason said at last. "You *are* a mage."

The way he had said it...

"You knew?"

"I suspected." The court magician's stare had softened the tiniest bit. "I detected magic in the cavern where the wechun had been killed. I knew that Squire Sandpiper hadn't done it alone. The magic was raw magic, not the unnatural magic of the Order, and not the tainted magic of the wechun," he said, more to himself. "I had previously guessed it to be ice magic." A small twitch of his lips. "I am glad to know I haven't lost my keen senses."

Her heart somersaulted. "You could tell that just from the cavern?"

"The Order attributed the magic to the beast, not to a mage. You don't have to worry about them bursting down your door in the middle of the night." Mason's smile grew a little wider and stretched the wrinkles on either side of his mouth. "Ison also borrowed books from my library specific to ice magic."

Ison blushed. "I apologize. I thought myself sneakier than that."

Mason's gaze sharpened. "Tell me, did you have a part in the Demon Crisis? Did you hear anyone speak to you? Any blackouts in your memory?"

Beside her, Ison shrank into himself.

"No," she said.

The court magician leaned back in his chair. "Then it is plausible that the apostate did not sense your magic, just as I had failed to sense it." His gaze flickered with curiosity. "You've never been to the Marca, I take it."

She shook her head. "My parents hired an apostate to teach me to hide it. I've been hiding since."

"There are mages who would rather not be mages at all, but we have no control over who we are, only what we become." Mason released a sigh, and for the first time since she had met him, he looked his age. "Tell me about the apostate you saw last night. Please, do not leave out a single detail, either of you."

Juniper's gut trembled. She and Reid, and she and Ison, had spent time discussing how Mason could have been the apostate or helping. The king trusted Mason, but it didn't alleviate her distrust of him.

Mason raised a bushy white eyebrow. "You don't trust me?"

She sucked in the breath that had been about to leave her. "No, it's not that—"

He chuckled. "I see. There is a powerful apostate wandering about the halls. There is a powerful mage sitting in front of you. You would not be the first to suspect that I and the apostate were one and the same."

"How do I know you aren't?"

"Because if I wanted you and the prince dead, you would have died months ago." Mason's tone sent a shiver down her spine, and she knew he meant it. "This apostate is playing games, and he is the very reason mages are distrusted. He needs to be stopped, and his demise needs to be supported by the magical community to show that we do not condone such behavior."

Why did it feel like she had just been scolded? Beside her, Ison looked like he felt the same.

She nodded, and she told Mason everything.

Mason's white eyebrows rose nearly to his hair. "The wall moved?"

Juniper and Ison nodded in unison.

"How?" Mason leaned forward. "How did the wall move? Did it shimmer as though turning to water or did a shadow appear over the stones?"

Ison didn't speak, and Juniper took the lead. "No, the stones themselves moved."

Mason blinked. He repeated, "The stones themselves."

Juniper tried harder to describe the way the stones moved and rearranged themselves. The court magician listened to every word, his attention never faltering.

Finally, he said, "That is interesting."

"Does it mean anything?" Ison asked.

"Nothing you need to worry over," Mason said, waving away the question. He turned his gaze to Ison. "Tell me, are you attempting to teach her magic?"

Juniper fought the urge to argue at his sudden subject change. It *did* mean something.

Ison nodded.

"How is it going?"

Ison frowned, and his body slumped.

"We've only had a few short lessons," Juniper said, trying to boost Ison's spirit.

"Learning magic at an older age is harder than learning when you are young." The court magician glanced between them to the small library on the other side of the study. "If you are interested, I could teach you the basics when I have time."

Juniper blinked. To learn magic from the court magician himself. She said, "I'm sure you have more important things to do." Like find out what the moving stones meant.

He gave a small shrug. "An unlearned mage can be as dangerous, if not more so, than a learned mage. The power required to freeze a monster solid is considerable, even for an apostate without formal teachings. I would rather spend the time to make sure you are comfortable in your power than send you on your way."

Juniper turned over the offer. She did want to control her magic. She wanted to be able to freeze things at will. Having magic meant she would never be defenseless again. "I would like to learn."

"Does anyone else know of your magic?"

"Only you, Ison, Reid, and Adrian."

He nodded. "The fewer, the better. I ask that you come here three times a week, in the evening, under the guise of eating dinner with Ison. I will teach you the basics of magic during those evenings."

She nodded.

The court magician stood. "I will inform the squire. He will not glare so at me."

She gave him a small smile of thanks, although she knew what Reid would think of it. Mason walked out of his study and started across the sitting room to where Reid stood in the corridor.

Ison sighed and leaned forward on his knees. "I'm sorry I couldn't teach you more, but Mason is a much better teacher. He knows more. He's seen more."

Juniper nodded, although learning from the most powerful mage in Duvane sent a wave of nervousness down her back, and the voice in the back of her mind whispered, *He wants to keep an eye on you.*

Good, Juniper said back. She wanted to keep an eye on him too.

CHAPTER SIXTEEN

"It is a horrible idea," Reid said once the doors to her chambers were closed.

Juniper yanked the veil off her head. Her auburn hair fell from its restraints and flounced about her shoulders. Frowning, she said, "What's horrible about it? I won't be a danger if I know what I'm doing."

Reid crossed his arms. Did she not understand all the things that could go wrong? He didn't trust the court magician. For all they knew, he was the apostate behind the Demon Crisis and wanted to get closer to Juniper for revenge or to recruit her into his circle of apostates. Gods, the man knew about the binding spell! He could *accidentally* kill Juniper while teaching her magic. He could blame her for the Demon Crisis and use her as a scapegoat to save himself.

And he didn't want her to spend any more time with Ison than she had to, but he knew it stemmed from a different feeling. He knew what they had done, what they would likely do again if they had the chance. The idea of another man—a mage—with her like *that* sent a fire through his blood. It had him envisioning Ison's death in a hundred different ways.

"Besides," Juniper said as she started to her bedroom, "I'll be out of your hair for a few more hours a week. You can go do whatever it is you do when you're not waiting for a chance to run me through."

If only he could.

Reid let himself out and took up a guard's position in the corridor. Damn her. Why did she have to be so cold? Why did he have to return it?

They could not be together, not now. He could never be with a mage without wondering, without suspecting.

He had been so full of rage that night—at himself for failing to protect Juniper and Adrian. She had thrown herself in front of them, saved them with her ice magic, defeated the demons, but the very sight of her magic had stirred the old hatred in his heart. He had failed and been saved by magic. And when she had started toward him, he had thrown his anger and hatred at her.

Fear. It had been fear on her face in the moment before she ran. Fear of him, of what she had done, of what she had revealed.

If only he hadn't. She would still be sleeping in his arms, not Ison's.

Reid would rather have her be dragged to the Marca than live like this, with her coldness and indifference, while watching her spend time with someone else.

Why did this keep happening? First Nanette, now Juniper. Both took him by the heart and let go as soon as someone else came into the picture. Something dark squeezed his lungs, bitterness born of jealousy and hatred.

No, he told himself. He took a deep breath and steadied his shoulders. Knights could face any threat, and he would not let a girl defeat him.

Let her go, he told himself.

He inhaled, exhaled. If only letting Juniper go was as easy.

❊

Footsteps in the corridor stirred Reid's attention. They were the quick footsteps of a guard but unarmored. Reid squared his shoulders and set his face in neutrality. Around the corner came Ronald Hendle, the advisor's youngest son. His sandy hair had grown out enough that Ron had tied it behind his head. He had his mother's handsome face and warm blue eyes. Ron was Reid's age; they had joined the Royal Guard together and had trained together until Reid became a pledge to the Order and Ron found work in politics.

"Ah, Reid, a friendly face." Ron made quick steps to where Reid stood.

"Ron," Reid said in greeting. Ron outstretched his hand, and Reid shook it. "What brings you to this side of the castle? The last I knew, you were recording council meetings."

He laughed, a charming sound that would give Adrian steep competition. Ron pulled a missive from his jacket pocket. "I'm on an errand to deliver this to the king. It's from Advisor Ulgan. He's taken ill and seems to think that I make a better nursemaid than his nursemaid. He has one of those too, lovely little servant girl, but he's got me running his errands for him."

"How does your father feel about it?" From what Reid knew of the advisors, they did not get along.

"Oh, he hates it," Ron said with devilish glee. "He's been asking about Ulgan every chance he gets. He thinks Ulgan is using me to get information on him or slipping me information purposefully hoping I'll tell my father."

Reid chuckled. "You wanted to go into politics. I'm sure the captain will take you back if you ask nicely. Maybe bring him a batch of gingersnaps."

"Not a chance. I liked the Royal Guard, but this stuff,"—Ron motioned to the missive—"is like reading a novel: people trying to slip past others, betrayal, sneaking. It's more fun than I thought it would be."

Reid shrugged. He would hate Ron's job. "If you say so."

Ron looked about the corridor. "So, Reid, my friend, could you direct me to the king's chambers? I'm lost."

Laughing, Reid gave him directions. The king would have guards outside his chambers, and Ron would know the doors. He set off down the corridor, stepping with a guard's grace and a messenger's determination.

❄

Reid stood watch with nothing but his thoughts to keep him company until Isaac came around the corner, hand on his Mage's Bane sword.

"Sir?" Reid blinked. "Where is Penet?"

"His mother is in the city and has taken ill, and I offered to take his post tonight."

"That is kind of you."

Isaac nodded. "He should spend as much time as he can with his family. I spent too much time trying to be a knight. I lost my mother to a sickness one winter, and I couldn't get home for the snow. I've carried that guilt since, and I don't wish it upon anyone else."

"I understand," Reid said. "I find myself spending little time with my uncle, even though he's a few corridors away."

"You've got a lucky lot to have your aunt and uncle so close," Isaac said. "Most squires and knights will only see their family a few times a year, if that, until they retire."

Reid nodded. "If my parents were alive, it would be the same for me."

"Where were you born?"

"To the south, in the Bindell Province. A small town called Onora."

"I've never been to Onora, but I've passed through Bindell on a few occasions. Lovely country." Isaac laced his fingers together and set them on the pommel of his sword. "Your father and your uncle are from there as well?"

"When my grandfather died, my father and uncle came to Rusdasin. Neither wanted to be a farmer. My uncle joined the Royal Guard." Reid motioned toward the barracks. Isaac could infer the rest of that story for himself. "My father soon met my mother. She didn't care for the city, and they returned to Onora."

"Hmm," Isaac said.

Reid waited for the next question, the one that would require him to recount their murders by apostates, but it didn't come. Isaac knew about it, then.

"Tell me, Reid," Isaac asked, his voice low, "given your history, given who you now stand guard for, are you holding up all right?"

Reid blinked at the older man. Did he mean standing guard for a criminal, ex-lover, or a mage? Isaac did not give away the answer—he was fishing then.

"I don't consider it in that way," Reid said. "Regardless of what she's done, the king asked me to guard her. And I will do so to the best of my ability."

Isaac looked hard at Reid; then a smile came over his face. He laughed and slapped Reid on the shoulder. "Spoken like a knight. Your uncle is right about you, son. You have a bright future ahead of you in the Order. If you ever decide to become the knight commander, you will have my vote. Of course, that is counting on Fowler dying eventually. Knowing how stubborn he is, the old man will outlive us all."

Reid smiled, feeling a mixture of pride at the statement and nervousness at the conversation. "Thank you, Sir."

Isaac took a stance beside him. "But I am here to relieve you."

Reid stepped away from the door. "Thank you again. I will see you come morning."

Reid started toward his chambers. He would warn Juniper of Isaac the following morning. The knight knew more than he said. Given how quickly the king had brought him into the secrecy of Juniper's situation, there had to be more to it. The king obviously trusted Isaac, but Reid didn't. Nor did he trust the court magician.

But, if Juniper wanted to learn magic, there was little he could do about it.

Reid arrived at his chambers and removed his armor. Arranging it on the stand, he absentmindedly cleaned it, although it didn't need it. He needed the action to clear his mind. Finished, he readied for bed and then came to sit on the bedside. Rolling his head along his shoulders, his eyes fell to the cabinet of his bedside table. Inside the cabinet was a box, and inside that box was the only thing of his parents he had: his mother's ring. It had been passed down from mother to daughter for generations, but his mother hadn't had a daughter.

If Reid had a daughter, it would be hers.

He opened the cabinet and took out the box. He held the ring between his thumb and forefinger. It was a masterwork of silver. Pale aquamarines encircled a lovely white moonstone. His mother had loved the ring more than anything else she owned. When the apostates had first come to their cottage, she had taken it off so they wouldn't see. When those apostates had returned, she had thrust the ring into Reid's hands and told him to hide—*Never lose it*, she had whispered—and like the child he had been, he had hid.

He had been hiding under his parents' bed when those apostates murdered his father, his mother, and his brother. He had clutched the moonstone ring hard enough to cut his palm. A small sliver of a scar remained. He looked to that scar, the reminder of what he had done—what he hadn't done.

He had fantasized about sliding the ring onto Juniper's finger, but he had hesitated. Then, the night before the ball, the night she had pulled him into her bed, he had known. He had planned on giving her the ring the night after the ball. He would ask her to stay with him, forever—but then everything had gone wrong. That dream of his future had been shattered along with the wechun.

The trouble was, he couldn't imagine another finger wearing the ring.

He returned the ring to the box. Another time.

CHAPTER SEVENTEEN

Juniper spent the next day looking forward to her dinner with Ison and her magic lesson with Mason Hobbs, though a small amount of dread of her inexperience kept her anxious. Mason was a master mage, and she could barely summon her own magic. During lunch, she forced herself to clean her plate and felt sick afterward. Reid chided her about eating so much but didn't say anything when she spent the next hour in bed letting the food settle.

Later that day, she and Reid left her chambers for the court magician's rooms. She wore the veil, and Reid walked a step in front of her. The servants they passed did their best not to stare at her. She did not let it bother her. The dread and excitement at attending her first magic lesson stole too much of her attention.

They arrived at the court magician's chambers, and the four of them ate dinner in moderate silence.

"I hear the servants are whispering about the Veiled Lady," mused Mason Hobbs. "No one knows who she is or why she is here, but I've heard them whisper that she might be a Janti ambassador, Collatian royalty, or even a bastard child."

Juniper snorted her laughter. She didn't know which she'd rather be. Reid did not share her humor. He glared at his plate, eating in silence. She tried to ignore him, but she felt his presence as readily as she felt sunlight on her skin. After the meal, Reid stood by the main door in the sitting room—as to not draw attention to himself by standing outside. Ison vanished into one workroom, and Juniper followed Mason Hobbs through the library and into another, more private workroom. He sat down in a simple wooden chair, and he motioned for her to sit across from him.

"Ison tells me you are not able to summon your magic at will." Mason motioned toward her. "Show me."

Something told her, even if she schooled her face into one of confidence, he would see through it. So she didn't. She cupped her hands and focused. A few flurries appeared in her hands. They swirled together in a faintly spherical shape.

"Hmm," hummed Mason, neither approval nor disapproval. He stood, walked to the single narrow window and released the hatch. He pushed the shutters open, and a warm breeze fluttered inside. It brushed against her hands, her arms, her cheeks. Summer. "Does it feel warmer than it should?"

She let her magic fade. "It feels warm."

"Your raw magic is ice," said Mason. "Did you notice the temperature drop?"

"No."

"You lack control, not magic." He stepped away from the window, leaving the shutters open. "The breeze is cool. Feel it. Tell me if you can feel the difference after a moment."

The warm breeze fluttered against her cheek, and gradually, that warmth became a chill.

"When you release your magic, you are not aware of it enough to focus it solely in your palm. You are letting it seep from every part of you." With a wave of his bony hand, the shutters magically closed and latched. "Tell me, when you fought the wechun, did your magic listen to you without problem?"

She thought back to that disastrous night. Her ice snaking up the walls, along the ceiling, across the floor. "No, it went everywhere," she admitted.

Mason nodded. "You lack control and focus. They are not the easiest to learn, but not impossible. Once you master them, your magic will come easier."

He returned to the chair across from her, and the lesson began. He walked her through basic control, the feeling of magic—the crawling sensation underneath the skin as the magic worked—and how to feel focus. By the end of her first lesson, she could summon no more flurries than she could at the start, but when Mason opened the window, the breeze felt cool.

"Small steps, Juniper." Mason folded his fingers together. "No mage masters his or her magic within a single night. It takes years to fully master, sometimes decades."

Decades. Would it take her decades? If the binding spell remained in its altered state, she would have plenty of time.

Mason seemed to read her thoughts, for he said, "Better to learn from me in a leisurely manner than from whoever you may find in the Undercity. Hm?"

She blushed but nodded. He was right. She knew mages in the Undercity; there were a few smaller guilds, but she didn't know whether she trusted them enough to teach her magic without a steep price. Most of them were still learning too.

Sheepishly, she asked, "How long did it take you?"

He let out a small, thoughtful chuckle. "Longer than I can remember. That period of my life has blurred together with the years. One of the non-magical lessons I can offer is how the past few years are always the most memorable, and those beyond blur. The farther away the past is, the blurrier it becomes."

She repeated those words to herself. There was wisdom there, but she didn't want to dwell on it yet. "May I ask another question of you?"

He nodded. "One may always ask; however, I reserve my right to answer or to decline."

"What form does your magic take?"

He blinked. He hadn't expected that question.

Juniper clarified, "Ison's told me about the basic elements."

He considered her for a moment, then held his hands out before her. A bright yellow sphere of magic formed. At first, she thought it to be lightning. It appeared to be light, churning within itself, light given color and strength.

Her confusion must have shown, for Mason answered, "It is energy."

"I've never seen magic like that," Juniper said, eyes caught on the yellow magic. "Ison told me that energy is rarer than the others."

He shrugged. "They say it is because, unlike the other elemental magics, energy is harder to spot. We cannot shoot lightning or ice from our fingertips." He gave her a small smile. "Now, I think that is enough for today. You look exhausted. Remember to eat a hearty breakfast to replenish the energy lost tonight. I also should warn you that you will sleep deeply. Another part of the magic replenishing itself."

"Thank you again," she said, bowing.

He chuckled. His look became one of interest. "I am continuously surprised by you, Juniper Thimble. Tell me, when you are released from your time here, will you return to a life of crime?"

In truth, she had no answer. She thought briefly of the future promised by Reid, the future she had ruined. Without Reid, without a home here, she would have no choice but to return to the only other home she'd known, the Undercity, Maddox's keep. But she said, "I don't know."

Mason hummed, his lips turning downward slightly. "If you haven't anywhere else to go, I will arrange something for you. I know plenty of people within the Marca." He hesitated, and at the mention, she bristled. He added softly, "and outside it." He gave her a mischievous smile.

She held in her surprise at the admission. "You know apostates?"

He beheld her with an unreadable expression. "A man of my standing and age? It would be far stranger for me not to." And he trusted her with that information while withholding it from the knights.

She bowed again. "Thank you."

He spared her a small smile. "You should be on your way." He started toward the door and held it open for her. "Your squire is getting irritated with how long you've been inside."

She followed him back into the sitting room, where Reid leaned against the wall. At the sight of Juniper, he straightened and uncrossed his arms. She walked across the sitting room while Mason sat down in his study.

"About time," Reid muttered as Juniper donned her veil.

She said nothing as she followed a step behind Reid. This time, she paid attention to the servants and guards they passed, wondering what they thought of the Veiled Lady. It sounded like something from a novel, a mystery, a ghost story.

She hadn't anticipated the magic lesson improving her mood like it had, and that night when she collapsed into bed, her dreams were of the Veiled Lady and her haunted castle in the mountains, guarded by twin dragons.

❈

The following week, Juniper found herself looking forward to her evenings with Ison and Mason. Between her magic lessons, she read in *Mergermite's Guide to Magic*. After four lessons with Mason, she could summon a few more flurries in her hands, and she could feel the magic under her skin, in her bones, and everywhere inside of her. It didn't quite listen to her, but she could feel it.

She spent her nights laying on her bed, feeling the magic. She couldn't describe it. It felt like millions of flurries under her skin, only they did not move like they did when she summoned her magic. They flowed like water, charged and powerful, like the air before a lightning strike. It was a force of its own, and each night, she fell asleep while listening to it, feeling it.

Ison came by in the mornings or early afternoon for tea, and they talked about magic, about the apostate, and the strangeness of the court magician.

"I haven't seen the apostate since that night," Juniper whispered. "I haven't been looking for him..." Her thoughts slammed to a halt.

Ison raised a brow. "Juniper?"

"I haven't been looking for the apostate," she said, her voice a pitch higher. "Because I've been busy with learning magic."

Ison's brow furrowed. Continuing her thoughts, he said, "Mason is distracting you from looking further into the apostate." He shut his eyes and rubbed his temples. "He's got me making more potions than usual too."

"Mason told me he knew people inside the Marca and outside it," she whispered. Ison hung on every word. "He knows apostates."

Ison nodded, face grim. "He might not be our apostate, but he knows more about him than he claims to."

❄

Despite her suspicions of Mason Hobbs, he gave her little reason to think him responsible for the demons or the wechun. Their magic lessons were focused on her skill, and he spoke of little else. At the end of her sixth lesson, she decided to test the waters.

"Mason, may I ask you a question?"

He nodded. She'd not asked one that he hadn't given her an answer to.

"What was the wechun?"

He didn't speak for a while. Then, he said, "Is. What *is* the wechun."

Her skin prickled. Her hands fisted in her skirt. "It's not dead?"

"A wechun cannot die, not like humans do. They are magical beasts of ancient origins. They are few in number. They cannot easily die. They are not easily born." His gaze drifted to the window. "A very long time ago, before the Great War, the wechun were servants to the Iluvin. According to legends, a wechun was bound to the archmage of each family. It is said that the wechun could not defy an order given from the archmage, which made them the perfect servant."

"Each family had one?" She imagined a wechun for each family in Rusdasin. It would be madness.

"Each Iluvin family," Mason corrected. His brows furrowed; then he realized she did not understand his meaning. "The Iluvin were divided into five families, one for each element. There could have been several families within the family, but the larger family is what I'm referring to. For example, had we been born into the Iluvin era, I would have been a part of the energy family, and you would have belonged to the water family. They had proper names, but no one remembers them.

"Each family had a faithful wechun who listened to the archmage, the matriarch or patriarch of the family, the mage who held the most power. It is said that the gods themselves gifted the elements to five humans, who then became the first archmages. It is that magic that the wechun respond to."

"But..." Juniper tried to wrap her mind around it all. "The archmages would have been dead long before now, right?"

"The Iluvin lifespan is far different than a human's," Mason said. "I have spent many years studying the long dead people and their ways, and it was not uncommon for an Iluvin to live beyond five hundred years. The archmages lived longer. They were not immortal; a dagger to the heart would kill an Iluvin just as sure as it would kill a human. Iluvin magic, particularly the archmage's magic, was said to be inherited. When one archmage died, the magic would choose the next archmage within the family."

"How?"

He shrugged. "Iluvin magic worked in its own ways. There is little research done and few books that even mention the inheritance laws."

He set his gaze on her, and all of his words wound together in her mind. Then, she understood. Her heart flip-flopped. "If only an archmage could control the wechun..." She recalled that day when she and Reid chased the wounded demon into the sewers. They encountered the wechun within a cavern, and before it could do them harm, it was called back. By its master. By the archmage.

The breath burst from her throat in a shaking gasp.

The court magician leaned forward and took one of her shaking hands between both of his. He had surprising strength for a man of his age. "Juniper, I know what I am about to ask you won't sound ideal, but you must listen."

She nodded.

"I do not know what grip the apostate has on my apprentice. I fear that he is a spy, whether he is aware of it or not. Please, leave this conversation solely between us. I do not want the apostate to know what I suspect of him."

And if she mentioned something to Ison, Mason would know.

She nodded, but he didn't release her hand. She swallowed—her throat felt dry. She nodded again and managed to say, "Okay."

"It would be best to watch what you say to him as well," he warned.

She nodded, though the floor felt very unstable. If she could not trust Ison, who could she trust? Her heart responded without missing a beat—Reid. She could trust Reid, whether he hated her or not.

❋

The next day, Ison came to her room for tea. He looked as though he had slept better than he had in a while. Reid stepped into the corridor, and she felt the urge to call out to him, to make him stay within the room.

Then, she reminded herself shrewdly that Ison was not the apostate.

Her heart squeezed. First, Mason had distracted her from thinking of the apostate; then he drove a wedge between her and Ison. What game was he playing?

Despite that, when Ison asked about her magic lessons, she didn't tell him about the Iluvin or the archmage.

"I can summon it better." She cupped her hands and showed him. Sure enough, flurries whipped around her hands, accompanied by a soft, pale blue aura.

Ison grinned. "See? I told you Mason was a far better teacher than me. If we were having secret lessons in your room, you'd still be where you were."

"You have other talents," she said.

He chuckled, though he looked doubtful. "It's strange. When I mentioned the apostate to him this morning, he kept brushing me off. He said he had looked into it, but he hadn't found anything of note. No more moving walls or missing people."

Juniper tensed. She didn't want him to ask her about it. If what Mason suspected was true, and the apostate was using Ison to listen in on their conversations, then she indeed needed to be careful. She didn't want to have to lie to Ison—or be caught lying to him. She hovered her hand over her steaming tea, feeling her magic pulse through her palm. The steam gradually faded, and then the surface of the amber tea started to glisten. A drop of sweat trailed down her temple, and she felt her insides start to seize. She let her arm fall to her side. Her breaths came in short pants.

Ison's grin returned. "See? You're getting better."

The frost on the surface of her tea quickly dissolved.

"And one day, you'll be able to move the water too," Ison said, eyes on the tea. "I've seen water mages move entire pools."

"Your magic," she said to Ison, mostly to keep him off the subject of Mason or the apostate, "It felt like something physical." She felt the residual touch of those magic tendrils, and her skin prickled. A blush came over her cheeks.

Ison blinked; then understanding came into his steel eyes. "You will be able to do the same, but it will take a while to use your raw magic like that. Air is different in that it doesn't burn or freeze. It's all around us, easily manipulated with little effort."

She felt it again, as gentle as a finger—a tendril of wind magic trailed down her cheek. Ison hadn't moved, but she saw the fierce focus in his eyes. That tendril drew a line down her cheek, along her jaw, and down to her collarbone. Her knees twitched. A heat grew in her stomach, and she drew a sharp breath.

Ison smiled, and a soft laugh escaped his lips. The tendril ran over her collarbone, back and forth. "I didn't realize it had such an effect on you. I'm not a woman, so I wouldn't know for certain."

Her cheeks flooded with warmth. "Maybe when I am able, I could practice on you."

"I'd rather not have ice snaking over those parts of me," Ison said, smiling wider.

She had a retort on her tongue, but the tendril of his wind magic dipped below the neckline of her dress. It split into two snaking fingers and each wiggled underneath her chemise as though she wore nothing; she let out a small gasp when those tendrils encircled her breasts, sending shocks of heat down into her toes.

Ison watched her, eyes focused, hungry. She'd once seen that look on Reid.

"Perhaps this isn't the best place," she whispered.

The tendrils retreated.

Juniper pulled Ison into the bathing room and kicked the door shut. He didn't argue. She ran the water hot, filling the air with steam. Ison's magic slid underneath her dress, and his mouth crashed onto hers, needy and urgent. Yanking and pulling, their clothes ended up on the floor. She hooked her legs around his middle and pulled him closer. She tightened her hand in his curls. She gave herself to the white-hot abyss, and sooner than she would have liked, Ison collapsed onto the bathroom floor beside her, chest heaving.

Then, without looking at her, Ison stood and shut the water off. "I'll have a contraceptive tonic ready for you for tomorrow," he said, his tone distant.

She heard his words, but the residual bliss numbed her limbs and mind. Climbing onto wobbly feet, she felt as though something had been set free, something undone. She snaked her arms around Ison's middle. The water rippled their faint, candlelit reflections.

"We should bathe before Reid comes looking for you," Ison said shortly. He stepped out of her arms and into the bath. His indifferent tone tightened a knot in her stomach.

Ison was right, and the thought of Reid standing within shouting distance made her stomach tighten and churn at the same time. She joined Ison in the spacious tub. They washed without speaking, and with every passing moment, the knot in her stomach tightened until she felt like she might be sick.

CHAPTER EIGHTEEN

The following day, when Juniper went to attend her lesson with Mason, Ison had a tonic ready for her. She drank it without question and away from where Reid could question her about it. She didn't want to explain it.

A baby would complicate things more than she wished. She hadn't told Reid, or anyone, but she had never seen herself as a mother. In her line of work, children were not welcome. It would do no good to think on things that would never happen.

Ison remained in the workroom, while she and Mason sat across from one another in the library. He walked her through summoning ice, not just flurries. She cupped her hands and used the focus she had learned, and those flurries became thicker, less snow and more ice. With Mason's guidance, those ice crystals formed together into a solid sphere of ice. Solid, uneven, and glittering like a diamond. Frost floated from the surface.

She let out a shout of delight, and in that excitement, she lost her focus. The ice shattered into flurries that quickly vanished in the warmer air.

"I did it," she whispered in the cool air left in the wake of her magic.

Mason chuckled and opened the window with a wave of his hand. The shutters eased open, sucking out the cool air and letting the spring air rush in. "You have made excellent progress. You have talent, and with practice and shaping, that talent could make you a master mage one day. Had you gone to the Marca as a child, I have no doubt you would be well on your way to being my successor."

And she wouldn't have been sold, taught to cheat, steal, and kill. And her life wouldn't be indebted to Maddox. And she would have had a normal life with friends and something of a future. For the first time, the Marca sounded like the better option, but it didn't matter. She couldn't change the past.

❄

When Juniper wasn't learning with Mason, she studied the books Ison had brought her and practiced magic on her own. She had given herself the task of freezing a glass of water. On a sunny afternoon that made her wish she could open the windows, she sat at the table in her bedroom with a glass of water. She had moved the books to the bed just in case.

She focused—her magic responded. The water turned colder but did not freeze. Frost appeared on the surface, slowly working through the water, the icy tendrils creeping through the water.

According to *Corella and Sona's Basic Elements: Water*, she would be able to freeze the water completely and also heat it to boiling. Mason told her to focus on freezing first, as it would come easier to her, and once she had mastered it, focus on the other.

"Look at you!"

She jumped. Her knee knocked into the underside of the table, and the thin sheet of ice that had formed on its surface broke. She grasped the glass of water before it could spill.

Adrian stood beside her, eyes on the glass. His hazel eyes met hers, and his grand smile diminished. "I'm sorry, I thought you heard us walk in."

Us. She whipped her head about, but only she and Adrian were in the bedroom.

"Destry is in the sitting room, talking with Reid," Adrian whispered. He winked. "And don't be sorry, love. You've not done anything wrong."

Low male voices drifted in from the sitting room.

Juniper heaved a sigh. "I'm lucky he didn't follow you in," she whispered.

Adrian took the seat across from her. "Considering they both know you can't hurt me without hurting yourself, neither of them are worried about leaving us in a room together." Adrian slouched, draping his arms over the sides of the chair.

"To what do I owe the pleasure of your visit, my dear prince?"

"Nothing more than a few moments of your time. Despite everything that's happened, I do enjoy my time spent with you," Adrian said, a calm smile turning up the corners of his mouth.

"You are among the few."

"I mean it." A soft pity formed in his eyes. "You demand nothing of me, you are not feeding me specific information to further some future goal of your own, and you're not trying to talk about some lord's daughter that you met and how smart, beautiful, and witty she is."

"Your mother, I take it?"

He chuckled darkly. "She is getting more persistent. I'm avoiding her as much as I can. My father assures me she has my best interests at heart, but I don't believe him when she wants me to marry her best friend's daughter or some conniving damsel with connections." He sighed and placed a hand over his breast pocket. "I sent a letter to Roslyn this morning. I've only returned from the trader."

"You trust a trader to deliver it?"

"We use a specific caravan, a Galamondian man and his brother. If Roslyn trusts them, then I do as well." His absentminded stare fell on the glass of water. "If I could convince her to come to me, we could marry without my mother's consent, and then there would be no more talk of marriage."

"You'd elope?"

"With Roslyn? Of course I would. If I could steal away from here without notice and marry her, I would have done so by now." He blinked, and a weariness came over his handsome features. It reminded Juniper so much of his father. "But taking a fully armed guard of a dozen men would draw attention."

"The more heavily guarded a caravan, the more wealth there is in robbing it." She winked.

He laughed, not asking her how she knew. "This is why I come here, to you, to relax and not be a prince for a few moments and to make sure that everything is all right for you." He motioned toward the glass. "No one told me about this."

"It's a secret," she whispered. "The court magician is giving me magic lessons. I don't want to be caught defenseless again. If I'd been able to control it, I could have done something sooner."

Adrian's gaze softened. "Juniper," he whispered, "there is nothing you can do to change what's happened. What is done is done."

She nodded, though guilt weighed on her shoulders.

"One of the scholars from the library told me years ago that we are exactly where we are supposed to be, and all that happens is meant to happen," Adrian said, eyes on Juniper.

"I'm supposed to be here, drowning in misery and learning magic in secret?"

He frowned. "You are drowning in misery?"

Her thoughts first went to Reid, but she held her tongue. It didn't matter; Adrian's gaze drifted to the bedroom door. Nodding, the prince sighed. "I am sorry it happened the way it did. He's noble and honorable to a fault, but he can be a stubborn ass."

She gave him a small smile.

Adrian started, "Do you wish for someone else to—"

"No," she said, and Adrian lifted a brow. "Despite all that happened, I trust Reid with my life."

"As do I. And, if you need someone to speak to, a shoulder to cry on, or someone to remind you that you're wanted in this castle, come see me." He glanced at the clock on the mantel and sighed. Standing, he motioned for her to do the same. He took her into an embrace and kissed her temple. "I am sorry, but I must go be a prince again."

"If you decide you don't want to be a prince anymore, I'm sure I could find you work in the Undercity," she said. "You'd make a pricy courtesan. A few clients, and you'd be set for the rest of your life."

He laughed, a genuine laugh. "I will keep that in my options. Until we speak again, Juniper."

"My dear prince," she said, curtsying low in a dramatic impression of the court ladies. It brought a warm smile to Adrian's face.

She listened as Adrian and Destry left her chambers, and Reid took up his silent vigil in the corridor. She focused on the glass of water. She saw the water, only the water. The surface barely rippled as frost began to form, as needles of ice eased through the water.

Her magic seized; she gasped and collapsed back into her chair.

Despite her panting and lingering tension in her body, she smiled. Ice had formed an inch thick in the water.

❄

Juniper snapped her fingers just like Ison had showed her, but nothing happened. When he had snapped, a small flame had appeared on the tip of his thumb, no bigger than a candle's flame. She tried again, but nothing happened.

"Harnessing the unnatural magic of the world is different than using your natural magic," Ison explained. "It will also be harder for you because you are a water mage. Air and fire are neighbors on the chart, so it comes a little easier to me."

They sat in front of the hearth in her bedroom. The hearth was dark, the sun shone through the windows, and the day promised to be lovely. She longed to walk about the castle and visit a courtyard or two, to feel the summer on the breeze, but she would have to go with Reid, and she would rather stay inside than punish herself with his cold stares.

The farther away the past is, the blurrier it becomes.

She repeated those words to herself whenever the thought of Reid caused her pain. If she could put him and her feelings for him in the past, it would be easier to get on with the nothingness that would be her future.

"It's something about the friction that makes it easier for non-fire mages to produce a small flame," Ison explained, eyebrows furrowed at his thumb's spark. "I'm not sure I can explain it better."

"Could Mason explain it?" She didn't want to admit it, but Mason often explained the workings of magic better than Ison. Not that she thought less of him for it. He'd warned her about his inabilities.

Ison paled. "Uh, he doesn't know I'm teaching you these things. He told me not to, actually. He wants you to learn slower."

She groaned and rolled her eyes. Mason had given her a speech about patience and learning to control her magic slowly. "I don't care about learning slow or better; I want to learn useful magic, like conjuring a flame when there isn't flint around. You know how useful it would be?"

Ison nodded, guilt on his face.

She focused on her hand, on her fingers, on the small amount of heat that was created when her thumb moved over her other fingers. Again. Again. Again. Until her fingers hurt.

"You don't have to get it on your first day," Ison said. He doused his flame. "It will be harder for you—"

"Because I'm a water mage," she finished, having heard it countless times in the last several weeks.

"And because you're an *ice* mage," Ison said, a bit irritably.

She ran her thumb along the soft material of her dress, feeling ashamed. "I'm sorry," she said, looking down. "I didn't mean to say it like that."

He mumbled, "It's fine." He walked to the window and touched the sealed glass, looking through with longing. He'd been distant the last few weeks.

"Ison?"

He didn't speak. He leaned forward and rested his forehead against the glass. His breath fogged the surface.

"I'm sorry for nagging you about all this," she said. He had been short, but she had been impatient. "You're right. I shouldn't expect to make a flame on the first try. I couldn't summon my own magic at first either."

Ison let out a sigh that clouded the window. "It's not that." He knotted his fingers together and met her gaze. "Jun, about what happened that day in the bathing room... I just... I think we should talk about it."

Her heart squeezed so tight, she lost her breath. Had she done something wrong? Crossed a line? She folded her arms loosely over her chest. Underneath Ison's stony gaze, she felt as vulnerable as if she stood naked in front of him. They hadn't talked about it, not once.

"Of course," she said, her voice a pitch too high. "Whatever is on your mind."

He started to speak several times. His eyes shifted about the room, from her, to the mantel, to the hearth, to the window. "I'm not... I mean, I don't..." He sighed and ran his hands through his hair, then hooked a hand on the back of his neck.

I don't want to be with you, is what her mind filled into his silence. Her heart fell into her stomach, though she didn't know why. She hadn't thought of Ison that way, not like she had Reid, and yet a part of her sought his companionship, whatever relationship they had. She needed it.

"I'm not good at...relationships," he finally said. "It's not what I want. Not right now." His voice shrank. His shoulders slumped. "For me, it was just...physical." His gray eyes met hers, desperate, worried.

Just physical.

Nodding, she said, "I understand."

Ison held his gaze on her. They remained there, staring at one another, until Juniper stole her eyes away from him.

"I think that's enough magic for one day," Ison whispered. His footsteps trailed through the sitting room and to the door. He mumbled a brief farewell to Reid and left.

Juniper sat in front of the hearth for several long moments, willing the horrible feeling in her stomach to quiet. She reclined onto the stone floor, just outside the sunlight's reach. She felt no determination to make a flame, not unless she could conjure one powerful enough to burn the entire city to the ground.

CHAPTER NINETEEN

Ison returned to his chambers with Juniper on his mind. He had ruined their friendship; he knew he had. He had crossed a line. Not that he hadn't enjoyed her—he had—but he couldn't stop thinking about Clara, about how she had pleaded his name as she became one of those...monsters.

He had seen the rejection on Juniper's face, heard it in her voice, felt it in her words. He had hurt her with those words, but he couldn't... He didn't want anything more than what they already had.

He'd gone to her at a horrible time. She still felt for Reid, and Ison had thought—selfishly—that he could erase Clara's memory with Juniper. Instead, he only found guilt and disgust at himself.

Ison sat down on his bed and lowered his head into his hands. A dull throb started.

Had Juniper thought to erase the memories of Reid with him? Juniper had whispered Reid's name, not Ison's.

How did you get yourself into this mess?

Ison let out a low chuckle. Gods only knew.

She won't let you in close again. Not when she still feels for the squire. He is a strong young man, built for a lady's pleasure. You're the scrawny mage with a future of imprisonment; it isn't hard to see why she would choose him over you.

Ison collapsed onto his bed. Scrawny mage. The blackness rose up in his chest, pulling him down, down, down, and making him feel like crawling underneath the bed and staying there until the world forgot about him. It wouldn't take long. He shouldn't have brought the matter of their relationship up at all. He'd only ruined what they'd built.

It was a mistake to teach her magic. You should have reported her. Save yourself from suspicion. Gain favor with the Order.

Should he have reported her as an apostate? She would have been accused of summoning those things. She likely would have been executed.

And no one would have looked twice at you, the mage who turned in the apostate.

Ison inhaled, held it, and let it out slowly. He willed the intoxicating nothingness of sleep to steal him away before his thoughts worsened.

MAGE IN THE UNDERCITY

Without taking off his boots, he curled into himself on top of the blankets. Half awake, half asleep, he let his lazy gaze drift to the window.

Slowly, the sun lowered, and the moon rose on the other side of the sky. Mason came and went in the other room. Ison heard the study door open and close, books being shuffled, then Mason's chambers opened and closed.

Night is her time. The ice mage is dangerous. She will turn on you. She will kill you so she can keep the squire.

Ison let out a breath of a laugh. What a stupid idea. Juniper would never try to kill him, not without a legitimate reason. And how would his death let her keep Reid? Ison didn't stand between them.

The squire knows you spent the night with her. Your death in his eyes would be a peace offering, a return of love.

Ison rolled onto his back. No, no, that's not right. Juniper would never—

You don't know the ice mage! screamed the hissing voice in his head.

Ison gasped at the realization. He shot up in bed, hands clutching either side of his head. Every part of him shook, every fiber of his being quivered. He should have noticed it sooner.

The apostate.

"No, no, no," he pleaded. "Not again. Not now. Get out! Get out of my head!"

What is wrong? The voice whispered, a caress of words against his skull. As kind as a blade. *Haven't you missed me? I've missed you.*

The door, the wall. Juniper had been right. The apostate was still in the castle.

I never left, hissed the voice. *You were foolish to think that the ice mage could do anything against me.*

"You have no use for me," Ison pleaded. He lifted his legs. Mason. He needed Mason. He would know what to do—his feet hit the floor, but his legs refused to respond. His body went limp; he collapsed on the floor.

Foolish boy. There is nothing you can do to stop me. There is nothing your ice mage can do. There is nothing your court magician can do, hissed the voice, spitting Mason's title with malice.

Ison lost his ability to speak, to think logically. He felt his body leave him behind. The floor felt far away, even as his hands pushed his body into his feet, even as he began to walk. He no longer belonged solely to himself.

The master had returned.

CHAPTER TWENTY

Juniper woke before dawn. With time before Reid arrived, she decided to work on her flame. She sat up, curled her legs underneath her, held her hand out, and focused. She felt the magic within her, charged from sleep, rejuvenated. She snapped.

Nothing happened.

She felt her magic, but she could feel something else. It was magic too. It was different. It was thinner than her magic and everywhere. Was this what Ison meant by unnatural magic?

She called to that unnatural magic, summoning it as if it were her own. She snapped. A tiny spark flashed on the tip of her thumb, a ghost of a flame, and it went out as quickly as it appeared.

Almost! Wouldn't Ison be in awe if she could produce a flame so soon? She tried again. The flame appeared but didn't last. She tried again, again, again, and again until at last, when her magic dwindled, when the sunlight had brightened, a flame burst to life on the tip of her thumb. It was no bigger than the candle burning on her bedside table, smaller even, but she had done it!

She let out a squeal of delight and set her fist onto her knee. The magic flame twitched—it jumped from her thumb to her knee. The flame licked the fabric, seeping through. At the sudden heat on her skin, her panic rose, and her magic surged; in reflex, a freezing mixture of ice and water sieged upon the unwanted flame. The flame went out instantly. The water soaked her knee, much of her thigh, and some of the bed underneath.

After a moment, she examined herself—she hadn't been burned. A pinprick of soot on her knee served as the only evidence. It had not burned through; it had not transferred to Adrian.

And yet she had conjured a flame and doused it with water. Her pride beamed.

Juniper scooted to the edge of the bed to change before Reid—

The main door opened, and Reid marched across the sitting room. As her bare feet touched the floor, he simultaneously knocked and let himself into her bedroom. He scowled, attention snagging on her wet pajamas.

"I spilled water," she said at once, not bothering with pretending innocence.

"I'm sure you did," he said, his words short and clipped. He knew what she had done. "Breakfast will be arriving soon. You'd best change."

Reid stalked back into the sitting room to wait for the servants, and Juniper went to her dressing room. She supposed that him thinking she had been practicing magic was better than him thinking her incontinent.

❋

Ison did not visit that afternoon, and Juniper filled her time with a simple workout for her body and reading her magic texts and library books. Marcy, one of the few servants allowed to see her, had brought a fresh stack of books and returned the others to the royal library. After dinner, Juniper reclined in bed, a romantic adventure propped open on her knees. Reid had business in the city, and Penet was stationed in the corridor.

The main character, a baker's son who joins the City Watch, is suspicious of smugglers within the city, but his captain, his companions, and people in the city give him conflicting information—and at the end of chapter five, Juniper set the book aside.

Ison and Mason had given her conflicting information. Mason didn't want her learning magic too fast or thinking about the apostate. Ison wanted to find the apostate, but Mason didn't want Juniper to talk to Ison about the apostate.

It was all...conflicting and confusing.

When she had wanted to hunt down the demons herself, Reid had obliged. Begrudgingly, but he had obliged. If she hadn't, if she had stayed in her cushioned prison, they wouldn't have found the sewers. They wouldn't have found that demon and ended it. It might have returned to do worse harm to her or Adrian. She had hunted down the demon on her own. She had fought the wechun—she didn't need permission to hunt down the damn apostate!

In a fit of righteousness, Juniper jumped off the bed. She marched to the door but paused halfway there. What did she hope to accomplish?

She sighed. Maybe she just needed a break from this prison. She returned to the bedroom for her robe and boots, then complained to Penet about the restlessness in her legs.

The squire frowned.

"Accompany me," she said, then added, "Unless you do not fear Reid's wrath."

Penet's expression changed slightly, and she knew she'd struck a nerve. Penet and Reid were both squires, and suggesting Reid held a higher station plucked a nerve in Penet. He held himself straighter, defiantly.

"No, I trust you to return in one piece," Penet said. "Just be back before dawn, or Reid will skin us both. And, if you need anything, just shout."

She offered him a warm smile of gratitude and set off down the corridor. Despite the warmer air outside, the castle corridors held a chill. She meandered, pausing to listen for moving stones or soft footsteps, but she heard none. She avoided guards and stuck to the shadows. She didn't see any mysterious doors in the stone or cloaked figures.

Had she expected the apostate to be wandering around the Royal Chambers? Suddenly, this entire endeavor felt foolish.

Not wanting to return to her chambers so soon, she meandered to the smaller courtyard. Her first step through the doors ushered in honeysuckle and lavender.

She took a deep breath. Through the archways that lined the courtyard, she could see a sliver of the Royal Grounds, dark woods thick with summer's lush vegetation. The Royal Grounds looked marvelous at night, the dark trees and brush and undergrowth mad with bugs and birds and shadows—like any magical creature could be hiding within. Maybe once, there had been. In the shadows of the courtyard, she felt her magic respond, grow stronger.

She thought of trying again to produce a flame, but she didn't want to draw attention to herself. She had promised Mason that she wouldn't use her magic foolishly.

She lingered in the moonlight for a while longer, then meandered back into the castle. She eased the courtyard doors closed, started to turn, and she heard them—footsteps. The shoes were not armored or heavy. It was not a knight or a guard. The footsteps were soft, someone not wanting to be heard.

Like an apostate.

Her heart thudded, and her thieving instincts kicked in. She kept to the shadows against the wall and listened. She couldn't tell which direction the footsteps were coming from. Above her or below? No...it sounded, strangely enough, to be coming from beside her. Inside the wall?

The footsteps came closer, and she slunk deeper into the shadows. She followed the steps as they made their way down the corridor. Then, the footsteps halted. She halted too and sucked in her breath.

Where had—

Stones began to shift, so quietly it sounded like a draft, in the corridor in front of her, just out of sight.

Her heart thumped wildly, and she started forward at a run.

Got you!

The apostate couldn't close his door so quickly. Juniper careened around the corner with speed on her side. There, she could see the blackness of the archway, the cloaked figure stepping through. She could catch him—she opened her mouth to shout at him, to distract him, when the toe of her boot struck something solid. She stumbled face-first to the floor. She twisted, throwing her arms to shield her face, and her shoulder took the brunt of the fall.

Looking up from her spot on the floor, through her mess of hair, she saw the stone knitting back together.

Gone.

"Damn it," she spat to no one.

She shoved herself back to her feet and dusted herself off. She turned to kick whatever had tripped her, but she found nothing. No stone or bucket or lost broom. But what had she tripped on? Her boot had hit something very solid and very real, yet she saw nothing that could plausibly be the culprit.

Of course, if this apostate could manipulate stone, he might have sent one of the stones of the floor up to trip her.

Bastard.

✳

Penet said nothing as Juniper slipped back inside her chambers. She worked on freezing a glass of water until she had drained her magic, and then she fell into a dreamless sleep. She woke to a rhythmic thudding, and her drowsy mind thought it the shifting of stones—the apostate had come for her.

She slid her hand under her pillow for the dagger she kept there, and when her hand fastened around the handle, she jumped into a sitting position, unsheathing it in a fluid motion. She held it out to defend against—

Reid stood at the foot of her bed, brows furrowed at the dagger pointed at him. He knocked his knuckles against the bedpost.

And she felt foolish. She retracted the dagger. "I-I'm sorry." She quickly sheathed it and returned it to its hiding place.

"Breakfast is ready," Reid barked.

"I am famished," she said absently. She scooted to the edge of the bed.

Reid moved too fast—he grabbed her arm and yanked her to her feet. A yelp escaped her throat. Reid's honey-brown eyes burned into hers.

She frowned. "Should I have kept the dagger?"

"What were you doing last night?" he demanded, grip tightening on her arm.

"Nothing?" Juniper tugged on her arm. "I didn't do anything. Release me." Her heart thudded. Had Penet tattled?

"Lies," Reid spat. He held her palm up and drew a line across her skin. "Adrian received a cut on his hand last night."

Juniper blanched, and Reid noticed. Had she injured herself? She blinked at her hand, to the invisible line Reid had drawn. She had fallen, but she didn't remember striking her hand on anything. She'd been too worried about the apostate getting away.

At her silence, Reid growled and released her hand. "You should not have left your chambers unattended. I've already spoken with Penet. He will not be tricked into letting you wander alone at night again."

Juniper cradled her hand. She could feel the ghost of Reid's touch on her palm. "I hope you weren't too hard on him." She grabbed her robe and slipped it over her shoulders. "He's a nice squire, unlike others."

He scoffed. "Adrian's wounds transfer to you, but yours still transfer to him. And, I will remind you, his life means more than yours." His words sunk deep.

"I do not need you to remind me of how worthless my life is," she said lowly.

She marched into the sitting room. Breakfast had been arranged for two. She took her seat and began to fill her plate. Reid sat across from her, but she kept her eyes on her food.

He asked, "What did you feel important enough to leave your chambers so late?"

"I went for a walk," she said dryly. "I fell. I hadn't realized I'd hurt myself."

"The cut wasn't deep. The healer fixed it in a blink."

"Then why make it sound as though I stabbed Adrian myself?"

Reid mirrored her frown. He poured himself a cup of tea and said, "I advise you to learn to walk properly. You are literally carrying Adrian's life around with you."

She stabbed her sausage hard enough to clink the china. *His life means more than yours.* Meaning hers carried little weight. Another reminder that if and when the apostate was found and the binding spell destroyed, she would be out of luck. She ate the rest of her breakfast listlessly.

"Juniper?"

Her name on his lips snagged her attention. She looked up from her plate to meet his eyes; the burning had subsided.

"Are you all right?" he asked.

She dug her fork into her eggs. "I'm perfectly fine. Nothing for you to worry about."

CHAPTER TWENTY-ONE

Ison came to on a cold floor. Bluish light flickered around him, sending ghostly shadows along the walls, up and up until the ceiling vanished into darkness. He didn't have to question his whereabouts. The smell. The forever flame. He knew exactly where he was.

He'd come back to the Death Chamber. No—he had been brought.

Don't you feel at home?

"Why?" Ison asked, his voice penetrating the still air of the cavern.

Why? The voice repeated. *You are the one who made everything possible. I should be thanking you.*

"But you're not."

The voice chuckled. It sounded like he remembered: cold, articulate, and ancient. He did not, however, remember being able to speak to it before.

"What do you want?"

I did not bring you here to discuss what I want. It is what you want, my boy.

"What is it you think I want?" Ison wanted to laugh. He knew enough to know that making deals with demons or such creatures only ended in disaster.

Freedom.

Ison blinked at the far ceiling. "Freedom?"

I can give it to you.

He laughed. "And how will you do that?"

I have my ways. I have my followers. I can get you out of the castle and into their hands. They can get you out of the city, out of Duvane.

"And what's in it for you?"

The voice chuckled. *Always the clever boy. You would be free, but I ask that you join me. Help me return the world to its rightful order, to free mages everywhere, to rule like we were meant to, instead of cowering from lesser humans. I want a world free from the Marca and the Order's foolish ideals.*

Ison closed his eyes and rubbed his head against the cool stone floor. It felt as though he'd sleep for days, but his mind wasn't as muddled or foggy as it had been before. The master's doing, no doubt.

Yet what the master said made sense. It spoke to the deeper distrust he felt for the knights, for the Marca, for the cage he had lived in since the knights had ripped him away from his family.

This kingdom has been tricked into thinking mages are the lesser humans. But we are not, are we? We are by far the superior beings, just look at what we can do! We can command nature! Those foolish humans fear us, so they want to lock us away and pretend they control us, but they are wrong.

But— "And if I decline your offer?"

The voice didn't speak for a moment. Then it said, *Then you will perish with the mage-haters and the knights. I will rule this kingdom, Ison. It is only a matter of time. Join me, or perish. You have done much for me. Join me, and I will make sure you live the rest of your life in luxury.*

Ison stayed silent for a moment.

The voice added, *You will not want. I will save the ice mage for you if that is what you desire. I can make her love you.*

"Why me?"

The voice went quiet. *Why you?*

"Why me, of all the mages in the city, of all your followers? Why did you pick me to carry out..." he couldn't bring himself to speak it. "Why did you make me do it?"

A matter of convenience, I'm afraid. No one would have suspected you, the quiet, kind mage. You, being a Marca mage, have never been taught mental resistance, and your mind was easy to slip into. Another thing the Order commands. They want mages to be weak. I will teach you to be strong like me. I can teach you magic that the Marca doesn't even know of.

"Why Clara?" Her name had not been spoken from his lips in weeks. Yet her face came to the front of his mind as easily as if she stood in front of him.

The voice did not answer.

Ison waited, but the voice remained silent. Thinking the master gone again, Ison sat up. No blinding pain, no staggering numbness. He waited for the confusion, but it didn't come. He started toward the mouth of the Death Chamber, down the lit hallway, and through the ruins.

Still, he could remember every word the master had said.

He had made it to the podium in the ruins, marked with runes that mirrored those on Mason's desk, when the voice spoke again.

Do you want to see her again?

Ison froze. Even the words sent ill tides of shivers down his spine and into his toes. "It's impossible."

Nothing is impossible.

Ison couldn't move. No force held him, but his own disbelief rooted him to the ground. Clara's voice fluted through his mind, sweet as song, kind as any girl could be. And she had been murdered by his own hand. Taken from him.

"How?"

The voice chuckled. *The magic is old, forbidden, but not impossible. For one such as me, it would be a simple matter. But first, I need you. There are things that need to be done that I cannot do without you. Do these things for me, Ison, and I will give you the girl you lost, and the two of you will remain safe. I will make sure of it.*

Ison balled his fists. Despite his trembling chest, his weak knees, and everything inside of him screaming at him to run and not look back, he asked, "What do you want me to do?"

CHAPTER TWENTY-TWO

After her evening with Mason, Juniper and Reid said little on the way back to her chambers. Ison had been absent. Mason said he had sent Ison out for a few ingredients, but he hadn't looked her in the eye when he said it.

"Does Ison's absence bother you?" Reid whispered when they had reached the privacy of her chambers. She let herself in, and he lingered in the doorway.

"Yes, it does," said Juniper, feeling a bit spiteful. "Does it bother you that it bothers me?"

Reid frowned. "Stop being childish."

"I'm not being childish. I asked you a question."

"I will not stoop to answer."

"Then I take your answer as a yes."

He frowned. "And why is that?"

Holding her chin high, she waved her hand dismissively toward him. "Because, otherwise, you would have said that it didn't bother you, but you hate lying, and to spare yourself from lying or admitting the truth, you avoided the question entirely."

He raised a brow, then asked, "You want it to bother me?"

"I didn't say I did."

"Yet your persistence with the topic implies otherwise."

She heaved a quick sigh. "Fine. Maybe a part of me enjoys seeing you fume and frown over Ison. Your jealousy gives me a tiny bit of satisfaction." She saw it—a glint in his eye. Before she could stop herself, she added, "It lets me know that you still care, even if it's a small amount."

That glint turned to a wildfire. Oh, she'd done it.

His fists curled, and he snapped, "I care nothing for you, mage." Reid stormed into the corridor with savage grace and slammed the chamber door behind him, leaving Juniper standing alone in her sitting room.

She stood, frozen. His words resounded in her mind, *I care nothing for you, mage*, spat with enough venom to turn her blood cold. It took a few long heartbeats to gather her strength and force her wooden legs to walk into the bedroom. She collapsed onto the bed. The pit in her stomach opened wide enough to swallow her whole.

❋

Juniper woke to a darkened bedroom. She had fallen asleep in her dress. She pushed herself off the bed and rubbed the sleep from her eyes. Moonlight streamed through the windows. Sleep felt too far away to return to.

She washed her hands and face in the darkened bathing room, then brought a cup of water into the moonlit bedroom. She set the glass on the table and focused on her magic. She listened to it, that gentle force deeper than her bones. The water frosted over. Tendrils of ice crept through it, feathering icicles without so much as a ripple. An inch of fragile ice, then two.

Before the ice reached halfway through the water, she felt the strain. Sweat beaded on her brow and neck, and her insides felt the incoming seize of her magic's depletion. She felt like a rag being twisted, wrung of its water, until she had no more to give. Before she seized, she released her magic.

The ice began to melt.

She leaned back, eyes on the ceiling of her bedroom.

I care nothing for you, mage.

The words punched a hole through her chest. She sucked in her next breath and released it slowly. He didn't care for her and never would again.

The farther away the past, the blurrier it would become.

She focused on the water, freezing it a little at a time until she couldn't any longer. She returned to bed and gave in to the exhaustion of magic drain.

❋

Juniper slept remarkably well and woke sometime after dawn. Reid hadn't arrived yet, nor had breakfast. She rolled out of bed and put herself through a few of her morning exercises. She was not as strong as she had once been, but she had retrieved a portion of her strength and stamina. And her magic use the night before had left her exhausted. They had better bring meat with breakfast.

After expelling all the energy she had left on her workout, she shut herself in the bathing room. While she washed, she heard the bedroom door open. She froze. She grabbed the handle of the back brush and held it like a club. Armored footsteps stalked inside, not trying to be quiet.

"Juniper?" Reid called, annoyance in his tone.

Her panic settled. She splashed the bathwater. "I'm in here."

His armored footsteps retreated to the sitting room, and in a few moments, she heard the distant clamor of dishes. Breakfast. She finished her bath, and when she walked into the sitting room wrapped in her robe, breakfast had been served. It smelled delightful—she caught the spicy scent of sausage, and her mouth watered. But she hesitated in the doorway; she didn't feel like sharing breakfast with Reid while wearing nothing more than her robe. In that hesitation, Reid's gaze lingered a moment too long. His honey-brown eyes traveled along her robe-draped frame. A feverish tremor settled in her stomach, not unlike the one he used to give her.

Her cheeks warmed, and he stole his eyes from her.

"You should get dressed," he barked.

"You're starting to sound like the captain." She retreated to the safety of her bedroom, and out of spite, left the door to the sitting room open. She tossed her robe with enough force that the plop would carry to Reid. She picked the first dress in her closet, a simple day dress of pink and gold.

Breakfast was silent and bitter. Reid finished his meal first but lingered in the room while she ate her fill. Gods, her magic and physical workout had left her ravenous. Luckily, Reid said nothing about her appetite. As a squire, no doubt, he knew how magic affected the body.

After she had eaten enough, she stood within the bedroom while the servants cleaned the table. Reid stood in the doorway to keep nosy servants from trying to glean a glimpse of the mysterious Veiled Lady.

"I don't understand why I have to hide like this," Juniper whispered.

Reid, because of the servants, didn't respond. He held his eyes on them.

"Most of the servants have already seen my face, and it's silly to hide me like some..." She stopped herself from saying *criminal*. "Half of the people in the castle have already guessed who I am by now." Like Penet.

Reid released a slow sigh.

"So many secrets," Juniper mused. "Another guest just so happens to arrive on the day Roslyn leaves? One who doesn't require the room to be cleaned or stocked or anything? It's suspicious, and anyone who has worked in the castle long enough is smart enough to put the pieces together."

The servants left, and the door closed. Reid spun into the bedroom so fast, she let out a gasp of surprise.

He spat, "You'd rather be thrown into a cell? That is still an option. We can change your housing arrangement if you think it would be more fitting."

She didn't say anything. No, she would not rather be in a cell.

Reid continued, "You are being treated as a guest of His Majesty, even though you deserve nothing short of the gallows."

His gaze bore into hers, and her knees felt like they might give in. She locked them into place.

Reid took a step into the bedroom, his voice low. "Would you rather be paraded about the castle and city where any intelligent assassin could put an arrow through your throat? Or where the apostate could easily get to you?"

She reached out to the wall. The stable, solid stone met her fingertips. She leaned into it, yearning for that sense of solidity. She wanted to tell him about the wall-moving apostate, but his rage stole the words from her throat.

"That damned binding spell is the only thing keeping you from execution," Reid spat. "You'd be wise to remember that."

The darkness oozed into her thoughts, into her limbs, into her being. She met Reid's burning eyes, the eyes she once sought after, eyes now full of hatred. Her voice came out small. "I apologize for being such a burden. When the binding spell is lifted, I'm sure you will get the execution you want."

His burning eyes softened. His hand lifted toward her, but she threw herself into the sitting room before he could touch her.

"Juniper!"

She ran to the door, into the corridor. He called her name again, but she didn't stop. She couldn't. She couldn't let him see what he'd done to her—she refused to cry in front of him. She ran through the corridors, away from Reid, away from her prison. She ran into her favorite courtyard and collapsed into the grass.

The courtyard, thankfully, was empty.

She let the sobs empty her chest. She clutched fistfuls of the sun-warmed grass. Tears trailed down her cheeks and fell into the dirt, vanishing.

Damn Reid, that altered spell, this castle, and everyone inside it!

She crawled into the thicker vegetation, where no one could easily spot her, and she cried until her body couldn't any longer. How long she sat between the birch tree and the honeysuckle, she didn't know.

She finally stood and started back toward her chambers to read, to stare at the ceiling, and to contemplate all the ways she could end her own life before she could be executed. A bitter voice suggesting hanging herself in Reid's chambers. A parting gift.

With that thought fresh in her mind, she nearly missed the subtle movement at the end of the corridor. She blinked and turned in time to see Ison vanish through an archway of pure black.

Her heart thumped. "Ison?"

He gave no notice that he'd heard her, and the blackness swallowed him. The archway began to close—the stones were stitching together. Juniper broke into a run, but the archway closed before she got there. She slammed her fists into the solid, unmovable stone.

"Ison!"

CHAPTER TWENTY-THREE

Juniper beat against the stone, but the archway didn't reopen.

Where would he have gone? Why Ison?

The apostate was controlling him again—it was the only answer. She had done right to not tell Ison anything that Mason had said. But she couldn't just stand by and let Ison do whatever horrible act the apostate had in mind. No! She had to find Ison and snap him out of it. Maybe if she slapped him, the apostate would feel it too.

But where...

She knew where, the only place: the Death Chamber.

Juniper slunk through the corridors of the Royal Chambers to the portrait room. She slipped inside, let her eyes adjust to the darkness, and then yanked open the secret door that led into the bowels. She ran, breath fleeting, watching for moving shadows or cloaked figures. If she met the apostate, she wouldn't let him walk out. Archmage or no—he couldn't have Ison. Not her only friend.

Tunnel after tunnel, she ran toward the Death Chamber. Breath ragged, she slowed her run through the ancient ruins. The door to the forever flame hall stood open, and she crept down it. Her heart thudded against her chest with each beat, with fear for what she might find on the other side.

And she hadn't grabbed a weapon.

All she had was her flimsy magic.

She found Ison kneeling before the rune, which, to her relief, was empty. No bodies begged and bled out in the center, no blood, no demon. No wechun. She tiptoed to the side, within Ison's peripheral. He gave no notice of her. He knelt over a pile of crushed herbs. He used small obsidian tools to arrange a mixture of herbs into a strange rune of whorls and lines.

"Ison?" she breathed.

Ison didn't move. He arranged a straight line of a strange white herb and then reached into his robes for a vial of blue-green liquid. He added three drops of the liquid on either side of the white herb.

Whatever he was doing, she didn't like it. She knelt beside him and set her hand on his shoulder. "Ison? Answer me."

His head turned toward her without surprise, but his steel eyes were not his own. The gray had turned a shade bluer, almost icy. They were not his eyes. Not at all. He looked at her, but the gaze was not piercing. Distant. "Ison?"

He blinked, but his blue eyes remained. Not Ison—the apostate. The one who moved the wall. The archmage. The one who had commanded the wechun, who had ordered Ison to slaughter all those people. The one who had turned those monsters on her and Adrian.

Her hand tightened on his shoulder, and she wanted to twist his neck—but she couldn't. Not while he used Ison.

He blinked. "You," a voice unlike Ison's said. Cold and ancient. Those blue eyes searched her face. Ison's face twisted into a grimace. "I knew you would be a problem."

"Ison," she pleaded, "come back to me."

Ison shoved her away and stood. She tumbled backward but regained her footing. She felt a strong wind rush her, shoving her backward, and she jumped away from it—a slice of air cut through the material of her skirt as easily as a sharpened blade.

The apostate possessing Ison sent another wave of air at her, but this time, something inside of her clicked. Her instincts. The wind came at her. Her magic listened—a wall of ice grew in front of her, quicker than a heartbeat. The wind bit into the ice, chipping it. Another blast of air hit it, then another, and another until the ice shattered.

"You are the one who defeated my wechun," said Ison—or the apostate. Their voices combined, but the apostate spoke stronger. He narrowed his eyes at her in disgust. "The ice mage."

She balled her fists. Her magic coursed underneath her skin, waiting to be called on, waiting for her command, her will. "What are you going to do about it? Let Ison go!"

Ison prepared to send another blast of air at her, but he hesitated. The hateful gleam in his eye turned into one of suspicion, curiosity. "Wait," he said, blue eyes searching her face. "I know you. I've seen you."

"Yes, you caught a glimpse," Juniper said, taking small steps to the side. Ison began to move with her, though his possessor walked with too much arrogance. "I saw you sneaking through the castle."

"In the Royal Chambers," Ison said, thoughts connecting behind those ice-blue eyes. Then he smiled, and it sent a chill down her spine. "Your face. Your voice." He laughed. "You're the one they paraded about as Roslyn

Derean, but you're not her, are you? No. And here I thought the rumors of Juniper Thimble in our castle were false, but it *was* you all along, wasn't it?"

Your face. *Your* voice. *Our* castle. The apostate had met her as Roslyn? He *was* in the castle. Right under the king's nose. Mason had been right to be suspicious.

"What about it?" she spat.

Ison laughed again, closing his eyes. Juniper made her move. She had been shortening the distance between them, gradually letting him get closer, and in the blink of an eye, she had him unconscious on the floor. A heartbeat passed, then another, and she rolled Ison onto his back. She lifted one of his eyelids. The blue had vanished, leaving his eyes the color of steel.

"Oh, Ison, I'm sorry," she whispered. She looked him over; he didn't look injured, nothing more than a few bruises from her attack. She knelt over him, hand on his chest. His heart beat underneath her palm, steady.

At last, his eyes fluttered open. Gray eyes found Juniper and blinked. "Jun?"

"Ison!"

He groaned and lifted a hand to his head. He blinked once, twice.

"Are you all right? What happened?" she asked.

Ison laid his hand flat against his temple. "What?"

"I saw you vanish into one of the apostate's archways," she said, her voice quivering. "I thought you might be on your way here, and when I found you, you weren't...you. I knocked you out."

She helped Ison to his feet. At first, he wobbled but then glanced around the Death Chamber. His gaze settled on the strange rune he had been making out of powders and herbs.

"Ison?" she asked. "Do you remember what he wanted?"

Ison met her gaze; he wore no easily read emotion. "I remember," he whispered. "And I fear I've made a mistake."

CHAPTER TWENTY-FOUR

Juniper helped Ison through the ruins, through the dark passages, and back into the Royal Chambers. Not until she turned the corner to her chambers did she think of Reid—but the doors to her chambers were unguarded. She opened the door cautiously, but no one waited to scold her on the other side. Reid had left, presumably to find her or alert the guard that she had fled.

It didn't matter. Reid didn't matter. Right now, Ison mattered.

She helped Ison into the sitting room, where he collapsed into the closest armchair. She fetched him a glass of water from the pitcher in the bedroom. As he drank, she knelt in front of him. "Ison, what happened?"

He drained the water and set the glass on the table. He shuddered. "I heard the voice. I heard it clearly." He held his gaze on his hands. "The apostate wanted me to help him. One last time, and then he would help me get out of here. Out of Duvane. Away from the Marca, where I could be a free mage. He promised to..."

She gawked. He would leave? Leave her behind? Her chest burned, but she pushed the feeling down. She asked softly, "What did he want you to do?"

Ison didn't answer at once. He considered her hands, then whispered, "He asked for ingredients to be brought to the rune. Which I did. I took some from the storeroom, and..." His eyes grew distant. "I took some from the kitchens, I think. I remember being in the kitchens, but it's blurry."

"You looked like you were making some sort of rune with the herbs," she said.

Fear flooded his eyes. "I-I was, wasn't I?" He looked at his hands, then curled his fingers into fists. "I remember gathering ingredients from the workroom as he asked, but then...when it came time to make the rune, I... He took over."

"And I interrupted," Juniper added. The rune had been left incomplete. Would he try to steal Ison again to finish it?

He met her gaze, then looked away. "Yes."

"Ison, It's not a good idea to listen to him. You can't trust him. He's using you, just like he did before." She wanted to smack him for even considering it.

"How do you know that?" Ison met her gaze, fierceness in his eyes. "Jun, I could finally get out. I could leave all this behind and just be me, a person, not a mage. No knights following me or hunting me down. I could go where I want, sleep in, wear what I want, without worrying about being discovered or reported or killed just for being a mage."

"I understand that, but do you think—"

"You understand?" Ison snapped. "You understand what it's like to be marked a monster and ripped from your family and locked away and watched every day of your life? You understand how that feels?"

Juniper hadn't the answer. She balled her fists in her dress, clutching the material for stability. She'd already lost Ison.

Ison leaned back and heaved a sigh. He ran a hand through his curls. "I'm sorry, Jun. I didn't..."

Bitterness bubbled up her throat like bile. Had she known he would only leave her, she would have left him in the Death Chamber. Let his new best friend carry him out. She stood. He reached for her, but she stepped out of his range. Her back hit the mantle.

Ison stood. He reached out to her but didn't come any closer. "Jun, I'm sorry. I shouldn't have lashed out at you. You didn't deserve that. I just... My mind is spinning right now." He dragged his shaking fingers through his hair and hoarsely whispered, "He said he could bring her back."

It took a moment for his confession to sink in. *Bring her back*—Clara.

"And you believed him?" Juniper whispered.

"I know," Ison spat, meeting her eyes. "I know it was stupid. You don't have to tell me. I just..." He heaved a sigh.

She wanted to smack him even harder. But she understood, to a degree. Ison felt a tremendous guilt for what he had done, and he had seen a glimmer of redemption. He had jumped on it, and she couldn't honestly say she would not have done the same. She had made enough bad decisions in her life for countless people.

"Is that even possible?" Juniper whispered.

"I don't know." A darkness passed over Ison's face.

"You really want to leave?"

Ison didn't answer immediately. "Yes. The thought that I could go somewhere without fearing the knights or being thought a monster because of my magic, that is the greatest appeal." His eyes searched hers. "Whatever the apostate has against the king here, it's none of my business. Why should I protect the kingdom that enslaved me?"

She had no answer for that either.

"They brought you here as a prisoner too." He took a step closer. "Sold you as a child. Enslaved you to the crown because their prince meant more to them than you. Locked you in here like an animal."

She leaned fully against the mantle.

"Jun," Ison said softly, a plea. "Come with me."

"You know I can't," she whispered.

He looked like he wanted to say something else, but didn't.

❄

Reid stalked back to Juniper's chambers. With any luck, she'd returned. Where in Hiada's Underworld had she run off to? The guards at each exit to the Royal Chambers wouldn't have let her out, and he had searched the Royal Chambers as thoroughly as possible without drawing suspicion to himself. He hadn't found her anywhere, and he was not about to inform the Royal Guard that he had lost Juniper Thimble inside the castle.

The king would have him hanged if something happened to her—to Adrian.

Reid made it back to her door in time to hear her soft voice speaking from within. The tightness in his chest released; then his anger returned. How dare she act like a child! But he released his anger in a short sigh. Part of the fault was his; he knew he shouldn't have said those things to her. He owed her an apology, like it or not.

He reached for the door handle, but a second voice from within her chambers made him stop cold.

"Just stay here for the night," said Juniper.

"Would it be all right?" came Ison's reply.

His heart burst, and he no longer felt it beat.

I care nothing for you, mage.

He had brought it upon himself. Why had he said those cursed words to her?

Nothing. There could be nothing between them. Not between an apostate and a squire. If the Order caught wind of it, she would be killed, and he would be stripped of his title.

He released the handle and took up his post in the corridor. They spoke too low for him to hear. Their voices drifted away—to the bedroom, he imagined. Heat flooded his veins, and he forced himself to keep his fists from clenching or his mind from imagining the ways in which to throw Ison from the castle.

Footsteps came to the door—bare footsteps. The door opened, and Juniper walked through. At the sight of Reid, she jumped. Her midnight eyes widened, and a subtle fear looked back at him. The last time she had looked at him, tears had lined her eyes.

"I'm glad to see you returned to your chambers," Reid said as calmly as he could. "I advise you to not wander off without supervision."

She frowned. "I advise you to not be an ass," she said quietly. "I came to inquire about lunch. Ison is here. I ask that he be brought something to eat as well."

"I will not be joining you," Reid said flatly. "There will be enough for two."

She looked like she might argue, but he didn't give her the chance. He looked away from her and schooled his face into neutrality.

After a heartbeat, Juniper shut the door. Her bare feet padded back to the bedroom.

CHAPTER TWENTY-FIVE

Reid pushed himself off the floor, his shoulders and back whining with the strain, again, again, and again until he didn't think he could do another. Then he heaved himself upward once more. He let himself down and rolled onto his back. The sweat between his shoulder blades soaked into his undershirt. He gave himself only a moment to rest, and then he hauled his elbows to his knees.

The sun had gone down, Penet had relieved Reid of his post, and Juniper was spending her night with Ison. Again.

It shouldn't bother him, but how could it not? Maybe his uncle had been right; maybe he should try to meet someone else. Plenty of the guardsmen had daughters that had been raised without the court-trained malice, and he could meet several at the upcoming Royal Guard's Ball.

A knock came to his door, a lighthearted, three-toned knock.

Reid pushed himself to his feet. He wasn't expecting any visitors, and who would be knocking this late in the evening? His mind surged through a number of horrible scenarios: his uncle, the king, the Order, Juniper, Adrian—

The knock came again, louder.

"I heard you," Reid called. He grabbed his overshirt from the bedpost and yanked it over his head.

"Well then hurry up," came Adrian's friendly voice from the other side.

Reid tensed; he'd spoken ill to the prince. He went immediately to the door. He had an apology ready on his lips, but Adrian didn't give him the chance to say it. As soon as the door opened, Adrian pushed his way inside. He wore simple but elegant clothes, fit for a prince lounging about his chambers. In his arms, he carried a simple basket covered with a pink cloth.

Destry lingered in the corridor. He knew he didn't need to follow Adrian into Reid's chambers. Adrian would be protected.

Reid nodded to the older knight and shut the door. "Is there a reason you're out so late?"

"Is there a reason you're sweaty this late?" Adrian set the basket on the table in the sitting room. "Don't you have to be up early? Wouldn't want our dear thief to eat alone."

Reid huffed and brought a hand to his temple. A throb had started after dinner, which he hadn't eaten.

"Oh, come on, Reid," Adrian said, throwing back the pink cloth. Inside the basket was a bottle of wine and a tin of what looked like cookies. Adrian had brought two glasses, which he sat on the table. "I don't see why you're so sore with her."

Reid heaved a sigh. "You know why."

"I thought you two were great together."

"I'm a squire, and she is an apostate." Reid lowered his voice. As much as the king trusted Destry, he didn't. "If we were found out, I would be exiled or killed, and she would be too. It's too much risk."

"My father wouldn't allow Fowler to order your death or exile," Adrian said. "He'd sooner exile that senile old man."

Reid didn't argue; he didn't know how much power the king had when rivaled with the knight commander, and he didn't want to be the one to bring it up. He walked to the table and joined Adrian.

His friend gave him a knowing look and said, "Are you sure that's the only reason?"

Reid raised a brow.

"I hear she's getting friendly with Ison." Adrian spoke in a sociable way, but his words were laced with concern.

Reid chose not to speak on the matter.

Adrian continued, "Or are you still mad that she hid her magic from you all that time?"

Reid refused to look at Adrian. He had the uncanny ability to read his thoughts, and he didn't like it. He didn't want Adrian to see what he felt, the misery Juniper had caused him, the misery he had brought upon himself by ever letting her get that close. He occupied his hands by opening the cookie tin.

"She kept a secret," Adrian said, uncorking the wine. A floral, fruity aroma filled the air. "Most people do. Maybe, if things hadn't gone like they had that night, she would have told you. Think of it from her point of view: you told her how you hated mages; that itself is a reason for her not to tell you. She was afraid."

"I didn't realize you knew her so well," Reid said a bit bitterly. Adrian could still walk into her chambers and receive a warm welcome. She either glared at Reid or pretended not to notice him at all. Not that he treated her any different.

Adrian shrugged.

"She is still a mage," Reid said.

"She is also a thief and a murderer," Adrian said. "She is also a friend of mine, and of yours, like it or not. She saved our lives. She knew that putting herself out there would result in this. She knew you might hate her for it, but she still did it. Or maybe she hoped she felt enough for her to see past it." Adrian raised his brows slightly, waiting for the argument against him.

Reid didn't have one.

Adrian nodded to the basket. "I came back from a meeting to find this jewel waiting for me in my chambers." He reached for a handwritten note. He opened it and read, "To Adrian, a friend I love and cherish, signed Juniper." He turned the note around to show Reid the quick, slanted handwriting.

He raised a brow. "She sent you wine?"

"And cookies. My favorites too." Adrian poured a healthy amount of the sweet wine into each glass. "Drink with me. We've earned a good drink these past few months. It's not the same as getting drunk in a tavern with a girl whose name you don't know on your lap, but it'll have to do for now. Just be aware, I will not sit on your lap in substitution."

Reid chuckled, and it jarred his chest. How long had it been since he'd laughed? "I would have to kick you out if you tried."

Adrian lifted his glass, a wide smile on his face, and for a moment, Reid believed everything to be as it had before the threats, before the demons, before Juniper. Reid lifted the second glass.

"To health," Adrian said, triumph on his tongue, "and luck."

Reid clinked his glass against Adrian's. "To health and luck."

With the clinking, the wine sloshed. Adrian brought his wine to his lips, and Reid mirrored his action but paused.

The sweet scent tickled his nose. Too sweet. Sickly sweet. Reid glanced into the wine but saw nothing amiss. Only wine. But something about that scent unsettled his stomach. Reid set his wine on the tray, untouched.

Adrian drained his glass in two gulps and set it on the table for a refill. He had the second glass halfway to his mouth—Reid grabbed his prince's arm. The wine sloshed out, splattering Adrian's tunic and the tablecloth.

Adrian blinked at the mess, then at Reid. His brows furrowed. "Yes?"

"Put it down."

Adrian's humor vanished. "Come now, Reid. I know it's late, but with all the blandness in the castle and the panic in the city, I thought—" He coughed. "A few drinks would liven things up a bit." He coughed again, harder. He set the glass down. "Father's got it in his mind that...it would be fitting for me...to...do a tour of the temples...and..."

Adrian swayed. His face grew paler with every blink. The color drained from his lips.

"Adrian?" Reid jumped to his feet.

"Shit." Adrian ran a hand through his hair. His hand shook. His face had moved from pale to ghostly. "You were right. I-I drank too fast." Adrian slumped onto the table.

Reid grabbed him by the shoulders and held him upright. "Adrian? Adrian! Stay with me!"

The door to his chamber burst open. Destry came running in, hand on his pommel. At the sight of Adrian, he paled. Destry returned to the corridor, shouting commands. Feet shuffled in response, but Reid didn't dare leave Adrian. He and Destry lifted Adrian, barely conscious, and set him into the bed.

The healer ran, breathless, into the room, a robe thrown over her nightdress. She took up a post on the bedside, chanting, humming, and running her hands over Adrian's body, using her magic in gods-only-knew ways. Adrian's breath came in quick huffs—struggling.

Reid stumbled backward. No, Adrian couldn't. He couldn't. Reid's gaze traveled to the basket, to the wine. Heat coursed through his chest, fire in his lungs, burning through his skin. He grabbed the note. Underneath the slanted words, her name.

"What happened?" gasped Destry.

Reid couldn't bring himself to speak. He gestured to the wine, to his untouched glass, and the glass that had spilled. The open bottle sat between them. Destry lifted Reid's untouched glass to his nose.

"Poisoned," spat the knight. "I should have been in here."

Reid felt the world shift underneath his feet. He had been there, and he had been too slow to stop it.

"I have a colleague who specializes in determining poisons when diluted in liquid," said the healer. "Bring me a scribe so I may send for him at once."

CHAPTER TWENTY-SIX

"Ison," Juniper started, then paused to rethink her question. "If the apostate is in your mind, then how did he not know me at first?"

He lay beside her in the bed, both of them clothed. She hadn't remotely felt desire, and he hadn't either. They hadn't even practiced magic. After dinner, they had gone straight in for a nap. Juniper, however, couldn't find comfort to sleep.

Mason had warned her about Ison, about his connection to the apostate—the apostate who now knew who she was.

He blinked. "What do you mean?"

"You know me, yet the apostate didn't recognize me at first."

Ison shrugged. "I don't know. I don't think he's that invasive. He knows my thoughts when he's speaking to me, but I don't know if he can access my memories like that."

It made sense. But the thing that had been troubling her the most—"Do you think that he found out about the binding spell through you?"

Ison turned his face away from her. His fingers twitched at his sides. "I can't say for sure. He might have." He paled. "That means that I am the one who altered the spell."

"Do you remember doing it?"

He shook his head. "No, but...it's not unfathomable that it was me. He didn't want me remembering, like whatever he had made me do in the kitchens. He didn't want me to know what I was doing."

An uncomfortable silence settled.

"Oh, I wanted to show you." Juniper lifted her hand safely away from the blankets and snapped—a small flame appeared on her thumb. It hovered here a heartbeat before it vanished. She released a shuddering breath. Holding a flame was much harder than freezing water.

"See?" Ison said. "You just needed practice."

"I only almost burned myself once."

Ison chuckled. "If you'd gone to the Marca, the knights would've been angry that you learned it so quickly. It's suspicious. They would likely throw you into the quiet rooms."

"Quiet rooms?"

His entire face darkened. "Rooms without windows or lights or sounds. It's a cell warded to prevent magic. They would toss mages in them to 'calm down' and think about what they'd done or said."

She didn't have to ask if he had gotten thrown into the quiet rooms. His face told her enough. He had, and he didn't want to think any more about the experience.

"Maddox's rule was law," she said. "Disobey him, and he'd deal out your punishment. What punishment he gave depended on his mood."

Ison's gaze darkened with caution. "You don't have to go back there, Juniper."

"I'm not sure I'll get the chance to go back. The king might keep me here as Adrian's shield and decide that he likes having an extra life protecting our future king."

Ison paled.

"Ison?"

He swallowed. "I, uh, have something to tell you. I was afraid to mention it before, but you need to know."

The fear in his voice triggered her own, and she sucked in her breath. "What?" she asked, her voice barely there.

Ison glanced at her, worry dancing in his wide eyes. "It happened last night, before you found me in the Death Chamber. I wasn't entirely myself, but I..."

"What happened?" Juniper whispered.

Ison swallowed; his throat bobbed. "We destroyed the binding spell." Juniper gaped at Ison, sure that she had misheard him. She sat up. Her voice came out as a wisp. "You did what?"

"I-I didn't do it by myself. He helped me. He told me what to do and how to... I'd never be able to do something like that on my own," Ison whispered.

She felt the blood drain from her face. "He wanted it out of the way."

Ison didn't argue. The apostate was done playing. She jumped off the bed, her bare feet landing hard on the stone.

"What are you doing?" Ison asked.

"We have to warn Adrian," Juniper gasped, tugging on her boots.

"Why?"

"Because his life is in danger." And even though hers wasn't, she couldn't leave him on his own—Adrian, who'd done nothing but make her feel welcome.

Ison slid to the floor and ran to the bedroom door. He threw his arms out, blocking her way into the sitting room. "Juniper, don't you realize what this means?"

She blinked at him. "It means someone could be trying to kill Adrian as we speak."

"It means you're free," he pleaded. "You have no obligation to stay here. You can leave, with me."

"Ison—"

"We will always be second-class citizens here. We will always be mages. We will always be looked at with distrust and hatred." Ison's voice shook. "We can leave all this behind, Jun, and start over where mages are welcomed."

Her hands trembled. She leaned against the sturdy bedpost and wrapped her hands around the dark wood. Free. Could it be that simple? Run away with Ison and never look back? Find a place where even Maddox couldn't find her?

A heavy hand fell on her chamber door. She and Ison both jumped. As she entered the sitting room, her chamber doors swung open, slamming against the walls hard enough to rattle the paintings and books. A fully armored knight marched inside, a man she had never seen before. His weathered face looked down at her with a cold, empty hatred, and the world shifted under her feet.

He knew.

Ison appeared at her side and placed a hand on her arm and another on her back. He stood defiantly in the knight's gaze.

A second knight strolled into the room, older than the first but no less intimidating. The two knights stood shoulder to shoulder, blocking her easy exit from the room. Both had a hand on the hilt of their Mage's Bane.

Ison stiffened, and his hand on her arm tightened in warning.

Wrong. Something was wrong.

Juniper straightened her shoulders. In her best lady's tone, she said, "Yes? I hope you have a good reason to intrude a lady's chamber without knocking or permission."

The older knight spat, "Juniper Thimble, it has come to the Order's attention that you are imbued with magical talent."

All else in the world ceased to be. All she knew were her shaking hands and the accusation now voiced. The imminent future, or lack of one. She couldn't breathe. Reid had told. Or Adrian. Or Mason.

Ison took a step away from her, but his hand remained on her arm.

Juniper held herself as steady as she could. "You've come to take me to the Marca?"

"No," spat the younger knight. He looked down his nose at her, his dark brown eyes cold and merciless. "The Marca is for the innocent. You are under arrest for the attempted assassination of Prince Adrian Bradburn and for participating in the recent Demon Crisis."

"What?" her voice cracked. Her knees buckled. If not for Ison's hand, she might have fallen. "That is preposterous! I would never lay a hand on Adrian!"

"Yet we have evidence that suggests otherwise," drawled the older knight. "It was discovered this evening that the binding spell connecting your life to Adrian's was destroyed, severing the connection. Not long after, poison mysteriously found its way into the prince's favorite wine, gifted to him by *you*."

The younger knight took a step closer, hand tightening on the hilt. "I doubt it was a coincidence. You were planning to kill him and run."

Beside her, Ison trembled. Juniper tried to mimic Reid's indomitable strength, but her knees quivered. She met the older knight's cold, snobbish gaze. "And yet here I am," she said, words trembling, "sleeping. If I had done any of that, I would not be sitting around waiting for you to come to me. I'm a smarter assassin than that."

The older knight scowled. "You are under arrest. I recommend you come quietly. The Knight Commander might show mercy if you—"

The younger knight stepped forward, a pair of small manacles in hand.

"No!" Ison threw himself between Juniper and the knights, hands outstretched. Before she could blink, the air in the room tickled with something like lightning—everything turned blue. The knights froze mid-step, mid-blink; the older knight's mouth hung open mid-word.

The very air around them had stopped.

Juniper's breath seemed to halt as it left her lips. "What?"

Ison shook her arm. "Come on, we don't have a choice now. We've got to get out of here. That will only hold them for a while."

She had to run. Now.

Juniper ran into her bedroom, and with hands that didn't feel quite like her own, she started to pack. She changed into a tunic and trousers and her favorite leather boots. She had spent hours and hours thinking of what she would do if she had to flee, and all those thoughts formed a quick plan.

She grabbed supplies and things she could easily sell in the Undercity and strapped Reid's dagger to her waist. She stuffed the book she had yet to finish into the bag.

Juniper slung the bag over her shoulder, and she and Ison left the frozen men in her sitting room and closed the door. The blue air didn't extend over the threshold. Juniper glanced up and down the corridor; she didn't see Penet. What had they done to him?

Ison started to run, but Juniper latched onto his arm. She whispered, "Don't run. It signals trouble. If no one else knows, we might be able to walk out of here."

He nodded. The two of them leisurely walked down the corridor. With every step, her panic subsided. Her fear remained, but her thief's instincts sharpened.

She couldn't stay here. Adrian didn't need her. Reid didn't want her. If she stayed, she would only meet her death, either at the hands of the knights or the gallows. She refused to bow to either, not when she could still run. Not when she still had a fighting chance. She could do this; she could flee under the cover of night. And she would.

Ison turned down one corridor, but she grabbed onto his arm.

"This way," she said, pulling him down another, toward the portrait room.

Ison nodded, but he looked guilty. Clearly, she'd have to give him some professional pointers on breaking the law. They walked casually for a while, passing unworried servants and busy guards, none of whom gave them a passing glance. It didn't look as though the Order had announced her supposed treachery yet.

She closed the door, and Ison brought his blue fire to life, casting them both in its eerie light. They climbed through the secret door, into the darkness beyond.

Chapter Twenty-Seven

Juniper pulled the secret door shut. Ison took the lead on the stairs. Neither of them spoke as they descended into the bowels of the castle. Again. His flame flickered over the stone walls, shadows jumping with each stair he took. His nerves reflected in his flame, for it jumped and shook as if it were afraid.

Juniper rallied her shaken thoughts. The apostate had destroyed the binding spell—had made Ison destroy the binding spell. He wanted her out of his way. The apostate had most likely been the one to inform the Order of her magical nature.

And the knight had accused her of an *attempted* assassination, as in *failed*. Which meant either Reid or Destry had been there to protect him. Despite her current situation, a burden lifted from her shoulders, knowing that Adrian had survived.

They reached the bottom of the stairs and Ison stopped. "Where are we going?" he asked flatly.

"These tunnels lead into the sewers," Juniper said, taking the lead. "We can either find a way into the city sewers or find a way out of here and into a different part of the castle and then into the city." She didn't know which way they would have to go. The tunnels were a maze.

"Juniper," he whispered.

She gave him her attention; he looked guilty and worried. The flame in his hand exaggerated the shadows on his face.

"It was me, wasn't it?" He looked up at her. "The apostate took me into the kitchens. It was me. I put the poison into the prince's wine. I know it was. That's what he didn't want me to remember, or I would have stopped it." He looked close to tears.

Juniper set her hand on his shoulder to steady him. "And it didn't work. It was an attempted assassination, not a successful one."

He nodded, and the tears didn't start.

"Adrian will be all right," she said. "Reid and Destry won't let anyone near him."

He inhaled, straightened his shoulders, and focused his gaze on the dark tunnel ahead. "You're right. We can't worry about him right now. We need to worry about us." He motioned forward with his empty hand. "Lead the way."

Juniper picked a tunnel and started forward. The two of them walked and walked and walked down tunnels with low ceilings, tunnels that had partially collapsed, and stairways that descended down into the inky darkness. Ison never complained. He never faltered. His flame evened out.

They reached the bottom of a steep staircase, and she said, "If you need to take a break, we can pause."

"I'd rather not be trapped in the dark."

"You won't be," she said softer. "I'll get us out."

He nodded, though he didn't look convinced. "Okay."

❋

They kept going, tunnel after tunnel, until she at last heard the dripping of water, the faraway gushing of pipes. She guided them toward it, if only for a change of scenery. The tunnel opened up to a walkway that ran alongside a wide underground river. A familiar stone bridge crossed the dark water. Down one side of the river, sewage cascaded from the sluice. On the other side, darkness.

"We're not going swimming, are we?" Ison cringed at the water. "I'm not a strong swimmer."

"No." Juniper shook her head. She'd rather not jump in that mystery water either. Gods only knew what lurked under the surface. "Reid and I stumbled onto an old part of the sewers that looked remarkably like the city sewers. I'd bet gold we could find something similar to that or even make a new exit if we had to. We will take the sewers into the Undercity or into the city. Either way, we are getting out of here." Even if she had to swim in a river of piss. Juniper straightened her shoulders. "From there, I don't know."

"East." The flame flickered in Ison's eyes. "There are mages to the east, in Collatia. If we can get to Collatia, we will be free."

In the north of Collatia, where rebel mages were rumored to be gathering. She didn't know if that was where she wanted to go, but she didn't have much choice. She started toward the bridge, toward the darkness on the other side. As they crossed the bridge, the same bridge that she, Adrian, and Reid had crossed that fateful night, she said, "I've never been outside of Rusdasin, let alone Duvane. I'm not good at anything besides thieving and..." Assassinations. "It's all I've ever done. We wouldn't have to go straight to Collatia. We could see what fortune could be had underground. I'm sure there are plenty of apothecaries in need of a skilled assistant."

Ison shook his head. "No. I won't stoop so low as to be hired by thugs and criminals. I want out of this city. I want out of this mage-hating kingdom. I want to live without the fear of knights hovering over me. Because of this"—he gestured between them—"I will be a dead man if I ever meet another knight."

Ison had signed his death warrant the moment he'd defended her against the knights. Now, Ison was an apostate. As was she.

"Okay," she said. "However, I think it wise we stock up on supplies before we flee the kingdom. Give me a week to get a few odd jobs done in the Undercity, stock up on gold. It will make the cross-country journey easier."

"That is acceptable," he said. "And, I suppose, since it is my idea to travel so far, I should try to shoulder the burden of work. I could make a few potions for shady customers if it would help us get out."

She chuckled and glanced back at him over her shoulder. "I think you'd make a better courtesan."

He gave her a sheepish smile. "Glad to know I have options." He pulled her to a stop. "Thank you, Juniper. I mean it."

The murky water below them burped, and the horrid stench of vomit and old sewer water magnified.

"Thank me when we are both alive and safely out of here. We should keep going. It's only a matter of time before the castle realizes what happened and sends every guard and knight looking for us. Reid and Adrian know that I know about these tunnels." She started toward the opposite side of the bridge. With Ison's flame lighting the shadows, it didn't look nearly as intimidating. "There's a so-called safe room up here. We should stock up on supplies if we can. I'm not sure how far we'll have to go to find our way out of here."

On the other side, it didn't take her long to locate the iron door to the safe room.

"It's warded." Ison glared at the iron. He demonstrated by holding his flame close to it. It sputtered and nearly died, bending away from the iron. "I won't be able to bring it inside."

"It's okay." She pulled the door open. She felt the ward work against her magic, but it did not dim her eyesight. She stepped over the threshold. "I can see in the dark."

Ison stood beyond the threshold, flame in hand, as she gathered supplies.

She found leather bags in the cabinet and stuffed them with whatever emergency supplies she found. She found enough supplies to keep them going for a while: dried meats, medicines, canteens of water, and a bag of coins, mostly bronze and silver. It wouldn't be enough to get them far, but it would do for now.

She tossed one bag over her shoulder, adjusting it over her other bag. She stepped over the threshold and felt the strange wards ease up on her magic; it felt like taking a breath after being underwater. She handed the second bag to Ison. "We'll be okay."

Ison nodded. "I believe you."

They started down the very corridor where she had faced the wechun. No ice or ash remained. She marched past the scene. Too late to dwell on it. With every step, that night became farther away. One day, she hoped it would be blurry.

CHAPTER TWENTY-EIGHT

Reid found sleep impossible that night. The scent of magic lingered from the royal healer, as did the sickly sweetness of the poisoned wine. A group of servants had delicately carried Adrian to his own chambers, under the supervision of Destry and Captain Sandpiper. Reid was still awake when a servant knocked on his door—the king was requesting his presence in the throne room immediately. Reid dressed quickly, grabbed his sword belt, and was buckling it as he hurried from his chambers. He met his uncle on the way; he had also hurriedly dressed. Neither said a word, but they shared a look of concern. The king would not have woken them up for good news.

Reid entered the throne room behind his uncle. Torches had been lit. The high, narrow windows were dark. King Bradburn sat on his throne, looking exhausted and haunted. The last few hours had not been kind to him. The lines of his face appeared deeper, his skin paler. He had refused all food and drink, except a strong glass of his favorite moonwater—which the king currently stared into a green bottle of.

Isaac and the court magician were already there, neither looking enthused or happy. Captain Sandpiper and Reid walked inside, and two of the king's trusted personal guards shut the door and stood beside it—listening for eavesdroppers in the corridor.

Reid felt a chill. This meeting reminded him of those before Juniper had been captured, dark and hushed and late at night.

"We are gathered," said Isaac.

"Your Majesty," said the captain. "What has happened?"

"An incident." The king's hand twisted on the bottle. "Fowler came to me a few hours ago, demanding an explanation for why I was harboring Juniper Thimble under my roof."

Captain Sandpiper spat a curse—one he had slapped Reid for saying years ago.

"Fowler refused to acknowledge how the information came to him," Isaac added.

Reid met the eyes of the knight; had Isaac been there for that meeting? Reid glanced to the court magician. He didn't seem surprised either. Reid had the feeling Isaac, Mason, and the king had shared words before he and his uncle had arrived.

"Fowler presented me with evidence that not only had Juniper Thimble been learning black magic and contributing to the Demon Crisis, but that she poisoned my son," the king said darkly, eyes on the moonwater.

Reid felt the blood drain from his face, but he schooled his features into neutrality. His uncle did the same.

"Fowler demanded justice, and I could not withhold it with the evidence as it was presented," said the king. "He forced my hand, and I authorized her arrest."

Reid's heart dropped. If the Order had already gotten to Juniper...

"However." The king glanced up from the bottle and met Reid's eyes. "Two knights were not enough. After being told the accusations, Ison cast some sort of spell over the room. Juniper and Ison have fled."

Reid fought to remain impassive at the news. The Order had not gotten to her. She had escaped. Had she been caught, she would have faced the bane.

"Ison is gone as well?" His uncle glanced at Mason.

Mason held the captain's stare. If he found the news of Ison's desertion uncanny, he held it in well. "There are those in the Order who believe Juniper caused or had a hand in the Demon Crisis," Mason said lowly. "And now, with this, Ison's name has been thrown into the fire as well."

"The evidence was there." Isaac frowned. "Juniper is a mage and has spent considerable time in the Undercity, a known market for black magic. She would certainly know her way around poisons. And now—" he sighed in exasperation "—she has attacked two knights of the Order. Fowler is calling for her death by Mage's Bane."

The hair on Reid's neck bristled.

"We cannot allow it," said Captain Sandpiper at once. "Adrian—"

"The binding spell has been broken," Mason added, his tone quiet but strong.

At this, a thick silence settled over the room.

Mason continued, "I found it this morning. Whoever, be it Juniper Thimble or another, planned this attack on Adrian to coincide with it's severing."

"The spell is broken?" Captain Sandpiper asked, unable to hide his astonishment. It was the same that Reid felt.

This way, Juniper could not harm Adrian from outside the castle. Still, the entire affair had settled like a stone in his stomach. Reid curled his fingers around the hilt of his sword.

"However," Isaac started, "We cannot say for certain who summoned the demons or controlled the wechun. Juniper's being an apostate does not warrant the Bane."

Reid agreed adamantly, but he couldn't force his mouth to work.

"And the Order found no trace of magic within the Royal Chambers," Mason said sternly, glancing at Reid.

Juniper had been practicing magic. Reid had felt the residual essence in her chambers, the faint floral scents left behind by natural magic, the hints of metallic left by unnatural magic—the strange mixture of her teaching herself and learning from Mason. But the essence had been centered in her bedroom and hadn't gone farther than the sitting room. He had stood in the corridor; he hadn't detected it there. And the magic had not been tainted. She had not resorted to black magic or demon summoning. Reid would have felt the difference. And he didn't think she would have poisoned Adrian, yet...the note that came with the wine suggested otherwise.

Had it been her plan all along? Had stealing the king's crown been a ruse to get inside the castle? Had she been so clever as to have fooled them all?

And... His heart skipped several beats. Isaac and Penet had both entered her chambers. They would have both felt the magic in the air.

Gods, Reid felt stupid for not warning Juniper.

"And, if I am not mistaken, the knights patrolled the Royal Chamber and found no trace of black magic," added Captain Sandpiper.

"I do not think Juniper had a role in the Demon Crisis," Isaac said. "She knew her life was tethered to Adrian's. Why would she summon demons, knowing the wounds would only transfer to herself? She suffered from the demon attacks. Why would she have done that to herself?"

Reid closed his eyes and put a hand to his temple. Gods, he needed rest. And a stiff drink. But not wine; he wouldn't go near another bottle of wine for a long while.

"...Fowler seemed adamant," Isaac was saying. "He even went so far as to throw your nephew into the argument."

Reid's attention returned to the meeting.

"For what?" Captain Sandpiper asked.

Isaac hesitated, then said calmly, "He accused him of keeping her bed warm, though he might have used more colorful language."

Reid's heart skipped several beats. His uncle had suspected his involvement with Juniper, and now he had another stone of proof. Reid avoided meeting his uncle's eye, furthering his own guilt. The air thickened. His uncle shifted his feet, giving Reid the chance to deny it. He didn't.

"Fowler also seems adamant of Ison's guilt," said Isaac, shifting the topic. Reid glanced up at the knight; their eyes briefly met. "He thinks Ison could have set the entire thing up to make Juniper look guilty."

"He accused Ison of thinking Juniper was indeed Roslyn Derean," Mason added. "Fowler suggested that Ison thought to trick Lady Derean into helping him so he could use her in some way, likely as a shield. I assure you, Ison is not that malicious or conniving."

Reid wanted to argue further—Ison knew exactly who Juniper was. For Fowler to suggest that implied that he did not know the relationship between Juniper and Ison. Whoever had told him about Juniper didn't either.

"Ison is smart," the court magician said. "He no doubt figured out the truth before he went to her. If I had to guess, he knew she was a mage before any of us."

"As is Juniper," Isaac added. "She is a strong-willed girl. She won't let a mage control her without putting up a fight."

Reid agreed.

"There is a chance," Isaac said lowly, "Ison and Juniper fled together because they are both mages. They fled after being accused of black magic. I suspect they fled for their lives, to escape a convicted mage's fate at the Bane, not because they are guilty."

"Two mages have a better chance of surviving than one," said Mason.

Reid didn't like this. Who had told Fowler about Juniper's magic? He hadn't breathed a word of it to anyone, and neither had Adrian. The only others who knew were Ison and Mason, neither of whom had anything to gain from exposing her. The king had not been surprised; neither had Isaac. They had either known or suspected her to be a mage. It wasn't beyond reason that someone else put the clues together and tattled to the knight commander.

King Bradburn heaved a heavy sigh. He set his weary eyes on Reid. "Squire Sandpiper," he said, commanding yet exhausted. "What is your opinion of all of this?"

Every pair of eyes shifted to Reid, but he didn't look at anyone but his king. He inhaled, stretching the aching in his chest. "Running does make her look guilty; however, I do not believe she poisoned Adrian, practiced black magic, or summoned demons. I would have detected it."

"Yet you knew of her magic," added the king.

Reid hesitated a heartbeat too long. The furrow in the king's brows deepened.

"Yes, Your Majesty," Reid confessed. "She used her magic to save Adrian and me from the wechun. She killed it, not I."

"And you kept the secret from the Order," the king added, neither disapproving nor disappointed.

Reid nodded. "I know Juniper is a criminal. I know she has killed before. But she and Adrian were friends, and I know she would not have hurt him intentionally."

"Could someone have poisoned her before the binding spell's destruction?" asked Captain Sandpiper.

"The timeline doesn't fit," said Mason. "The binding spell was destroyed hours before Adrian's poisoning."

"And Juniper is an untrained mage," said Isaac. "She would not have been able to break the binding spell on her own. Neither could Ison."

"I agree," said Mason.

Reid saw a flicker in the court magician's face, there and gone before he could identify it. He knew more than he said, like always.

"It doesn't matter if she poisoned Adrian or if she broke the binding spell," said King Bradburn, ending the discussion. "She is gone, and my son is dying. I want Juniper Thimble caught, not killed. I want to question her myself. If my son dies..." The king hesitated, his eyes seeking the bottle in his hand. "If my son dies, then she will die by the same poison, as she should have. Until then, Adrian is not to be unguarded." He looked to Reid and then to Isaac. "One of you will be by Adrian's side at all times, as well as Destry. I will inform him of the situation later today."

"What of the knight commander?" asked Captain Sandpiper.

"I will send word that I want her captured alive," said the king. "In the meantime, I will reevaluate my staff. I want no spies in my house."

Like that, the meeting ended. Reid was the first into the corridor. He did not stop to see if his uncle had words to say about Juniper or if he had a sour expression. Reid walked straight to Adrian's chambers, where the royal healer sat at the bedside, her green magic hard at work.

MAGE IN THE UNDERCITY

Adrian's skin had gone ashy and pale. His breaths were shallow. No matter how many blankets they piled over him, he couldn't keep warm. Sweat beaded on the healer's brow. Her eyes reflected her exhaustion.

Before he could ask, the healer mumbled, "No, the poison hasn't been identified."

The healer had sent for a poison specialist. He had not yet arrived, and the poison coursing through Adrian remained unknown. Without identifying the poison, she couldn't give him an antidote. Without the proper antidote... Reid didn't want to think about it.

With a nod to Destry, Reid left Adrian's room. He meandered; his thoughts were roiling. He thought of Adrian and Juniper, and found himself walking toward her chambers. Silently cursing himself, he steered himself to his own chambers. The sun had begun to rise, a steady pink glow. Reid sat on his bed and dropped his head into his hands. He didn't want to think about anything for a long while.

Damn her and every hair on her head.

CHAPTER TWENTY-NINE

Juniper and Ison wandered for hours. In her mad rush to get out of the castle, she hadn't anticipated there not being a way into the Undercity from the catacombs. They passed walls of carved runes and a language Ison suggested might be Iluvin; it looked like the characters from Mason's books. That suggested the ruins came from a time before Duvane, before the Great War, when the Iluvin people ruled much of the known world. The sheer age of it all startled her, and she felt more like an intruder than she had in all her stay in the castle above.

Still, they kept moving forward. Juniper led the way through tunnel after tunnel, crumbling corridors, up and down staircases in varying states of collapse, all with Ison's flame guiding the way. They barely spoke. She feared that Ison felt the same hopelessness she did, the fear of wandering forever and dying down here.

They came upon what looked to be an old communal area. A long-cold hearth was circled with stone benches. Time-worn ashes lingered in the hearth, along with what looked like bones.

"We rest here," Juniper said firmly.

Ison's flame had gradually shrunk. He did not protest, and he sat down on one of the remaining benches. His flame diminished a little more, becoming a glow in his hand.

"Rest," Juniper said, softer. "I'll be right here the whole time. I promise."

She saw it in his eyes—the fear of the dark, of the ruin, of the shadows lurking just beyond his light.

He let his magic rest, and plunged them both into darkness. It took a few heartbeats for Juniper's vision to adjust. The blackness became shades of blue and gray. She could almost see better without the flame. The room came into focus, the ceiling vaulted, carved with hundreds of stars. A chandelier had once hung, but it had long since rusted off. Dozens of corridors led off from it, connecting all the various chambers.

"Jun?" In the dark, Ison's eyes searched for her.

"I'm here." She shuffled her feet and sat beside him, close enough to feel him. Ruffling through her bag for something to eat, she talked to fill the darkness. "I didn't know the Iluvin were in Duvane." She pulled out a few dried meat strips and set one into Ison's hand. She took a bite. Chewy, old. "Do you think there are Iluvin ruins all over the kingdom or just here?"

And had the Bradburn king of the time conquered the Iluvin city and killed them all? Reid would know.

"The Iluvin stretched far and wide," Ison said. "The Marca doesn't teach much about them as a people, only that they existed and that they had powerful and dangerous magic. A lot of their knowledge and history was lost when the Order purged them from existence."

Juniper bit off a large chunk of dried meat. The Order had killed the Iluvin and buried their magic where no one could know about it. It struck her nerves and stirred her hatred for the Order.

"It's a maze down here," she said after a while. And it had a distinctly haunted feel that she did not like.

Ison nodded absently. "It's better than what's waiting for us aboveground."

He didn't have to say it: because of this, Mage's Bane would be waiting should they be caught. Juniper absently touched the pommel of her dagger, Reid's dagger. He had given it to her for her defense, and she would use it.

"We will find our way out of here," Juniper said. "I refuse to die in a sewer."

"What if we don't?" Ison whispered.

"There's always the swimming option, but I'd rather save that for life-or-death."

A faint twitch of his lips was all she received; then the blankness returned to his features. She wanted to say something to make him feel better, but she didn't know what. Ison had lived in the Marca most of his life, and he had never been on the run before.

After their rest, they continued. The ruins seemed endless, an entire city underneath the castle.

To reassure Ison, she said, "I refuse to believe that a ruin of this size doesn't have an entry point somewhere in the city. Judging by how long we've been walking, I'd say we left the confines of the castle grounds behind."

Ison gave a small grunt of agreement. "I'm starting to wish I'd stayed behind. I...I don't really like being underground."

Then, the Undercity wouldn't be the place for Ison.

They kept walking and walking and walking. They stopped for

another meal and a rest and then walked further still. The sheer size of the ruins astounded her. Hundreds of people could have lived in the underground city.

They walked and walked and walked.

And walked.

Several times, Ison had to let his flame go out. He refused to stop, so she held onto his hand as she navigated the dark tunnels.

And they walked and walked and walked.

Until, at long last, with exhaustion settling in, Juniper heard the sound of rushing water somewhere ahead. Her heart jumped into her throat. She whipped around to Ison, who mirrored her wide-eyed gaze. She followed the sound of water—underneath the rushing, she heard the sound of distant, drunken voices and laughter. Her heart slammed against her ribcage, and she walked a little faster. So did Ison. The ruins became an old sewer.

A thought struck her. The Undercity had been built into a part of the Iluvin ruins. She had never before questioned the underground space, the structures, or the logic of it all. Because the Undercity had always just been there.

Which meant—there! Not far into the sewer, she saw the most glorious thing: a sewer grate. Light shone through the bars, and laughter echoed on the other side. It didn't look as though the grate had been made for the hole it had been pushed into; it looked uneven, hammered flat, something of the Undercity.

"We made it," Ison breathed behind her.

They stepped through the puddles of water and piss and gods knew what else to the grate. Juniper put her hand on Ison's shoulder. "Let me go first."

He frowned but didn't object.

She climbed the old ladder to the grate, the rungs creaking and groaning, and pushed against the grate. It gave with little fuss. She didn't push it up too high. Instead, she listened. Men, four or five by the sounds, were somewhere on the other side. Could they see the grate? They were drunk and drinking by the riotous laughter, slurred speech, and sloshing. She pushed the grate up a little higher. No response came, no fluctuation in their drunkenness. She pushed it up a little higher, enough to peek out.

It looked like a cellar. A lantern lit the space with bright yellow light. Beyond the stacked barrels, bottles, and kegs, the cellar was empty. The sound of the men came from above them.

"It's the cellar of a tavern," she whispered.

She shoved the grate aside and crawled into the cellar. Ison crawled after. They crept to the steep wooden stairs on the far side of the cellar, and she took a deep breath.

"This might get a bit ugly," she whispered.

Ison frowned. He looked like someone who had never been to the Undercity.

"Just act like you're supposed to be here." Or he'd get eaten alive before he ever made it topside.

Ison inhaled, puffing out his narrow chest.

Juniper pulled open the cellar curtain and walked out like she knew exactly where she'd been and where she was going. Ison followed right behind. The grog-thick air hung heavy with body odor and cheap perfume. The bartender's back was turned as they passed. Through the drinking and drunk crowd, to the open door on the other side, closer, closer, closer—Juniper stepped out of the tavern. Behind her, Ison let out a heavy breath of relief.

The Undercity looked like it had when she had left: a city built into the ground, into the ageless Iluvin ruins under Rusdasin. Being underground, no sunlight filtered down; hundreds of lanterns, candles, and magelights kept the Undercity glowing. The streets were gray and reddish stone, the buildings were gray stone and wood, and little plant life survived. The plants that lived in the Undercity were cared for by magic.

Juniper and Ison had come out in the business side of the Undercity, and she could hear the hammering of metal from a nearby smithy, smell the leather from the tannery, and the hot iron from a foundry. Above it all was that musty dankness and salty mineral stink that belonged to the stone. Chatter filled the air. People wandered about the narrow streets: men, women, and children; thieves, assassins, whores, mages, and bakers. No one paid Juniper and Ison much mind, thankfully.

"It smells lovely," Ison mumbled.

She nudged him, grinning. She hadn't missed the smell either. Gods, she already missed the sweet scent of the castle.

"Come on, we both need a wash and a long nap," she said. She and Ison started through the streets. No one expected the Undercity to have order, yet it did.

The Undercity was laid out in a circle. In the center was the market, where stalls of smiths, bakers, enchanters, and anything one wanted could be found. The outer ring was mostly residences, spotted with less flashy businesses such as mercenaries, brothels, and guilds. Though, people lived anywhere they could in the Undercity, be it alleyways or tavern closets.

She guided Ison down a street of artisans and craftsmen. Blacksmiths, silversmiths, jewelers, weavers, painters—all manner of people and goods could be found in the Undercity. Ison took it all in, holding his amazement well.

"It feels so strange being back here after everything," Juniper mused to Ison as they passed a jewelry vendor. The man wore a ring on each finger, a dozen bracelets on each arm, and at least twenty necklaces of varying lengths. Sitting atop his head was an emerald diadem. Ison tilted his head at the man, and Juniper explained, "Harder to steal when they are on his person."

The market was alive with bartering, shouting, and drunks making their merry way to and from wherever they needed to be. Dice games were being played on upturned crates, cards on barrels, and the shops were beating to the regular rhythm that they always had. It felt the same but different.

It wasn't home anymore.

They started down a residential street lined with townhouses and condos, clubs and keeps.

"You," came a grumbled voice.

Juniper ignored it. A man stepped out from an alley, brandishing his sword at her. That, she couldn't ignore. She stopped.

"You ain't from around here," grumbled the voice behind her.

She half turned, keeping both men in her sight.

"Them's fancy clothes." Both were heavyset and built for bullying. Mercenaries on a slow week, looking for easy prey. She expected him to recognize her face and turn tail, but the man didn't move. He didn't even flinch. He spat onto the stone between her boots.

Oh, he wasn't going to walk away from this.

"You's from up top," said a third man from the alley. He sauntered out, a dagger in each hand.

"That's a nice belt," said a fourth man who sauntered from the opposite alley. He gestured to the leather belt around Ison's waist. "You think it'd fit me?"

"One way to find out," said the third man.

The man with two daggers came at her, and she had her dagger out before he could blink. They collided—her dagger broke his in two. Before he could react, she had him on the defense, and then her dagger crashed into the side of his throat.

The man stumbled backward, gagging on his own blood.

"That is no way to speak to a lady," Juniper said. Oh, that had felt good. She slashed her dagger through the air, spotting the ground in an arc of blood.

The other three men started to close in. She readied her dagger; Ison looked ready to pass out. She might be able to take them all, but if Ison helped—

"Hey," came a sharp, lyrical female voice. A lithe young woman sauntered out from one of the alleys, shiny twin daggers on her shoulders. "Go bother someone else, shitbags."

Juniper blinked; she couldn't believe it. The young woman had straight black hair cut just above her shoulders and pale olive skin. Her onyx eyes glittered with amusement as she regarded the men with cold humor. Her leather armor had been made not just for thieving, but to show a slice of her skin above her hipbones, her collarbone. Thief. Courtesan.

Amery.

CHAPTER THIRTY

"Beat it," Amery commanded.

"They's upsiders! And I want that belt!" one of the thugs complained.

Amery unsheathed a dagger from behind her back and gracefully twirled it in her fingers. She poised it to attack. "You want it bad enough to join your friend there?"

That friend had died.

The three remaining thugs hesitated, then scampered off to bother someone else, leaving their "friend" dead where he fell—while murmuring insults and threats.

Juniper wiped her dagger clean on the dead man's clothes, then sheathed it. The thug didn't look like he had much, but Juniper quickly rifled through his pockets. As she'd suspected, he had a few copper pieces. She pocketed them anyway.

"Where in Bera's name have you been?" Amery slid her dagger onto her back and set her hands on her hips.

Bera—Goddess of Shadow—supposedly thrived in the Undercity. Her miniature shrines dotted dark alleys and makeshift temples.

"It is a long story," Juniper said.

Amery held her arms out wide, and Juniper welcomed her friend's embrace. A part of her briefly anticipated something sharp in her back. Nothing poked her; both of Amery's hands flattened against her.

"No knife?" Juniper half laughed.

Amery shrugged. "I'm not killing you unless there's a major payout." She tugged Juniper toward the keep. "Come on, I've got time to hear this long story of yours." She hooked her arm through Juniper's, then glanced at Ison. Her gaze turned suspicious, though curious. "Your friend?"

"Ison," Juniper said. "This is Amery. Amery, this is Ison. He's with me."

Amery looked him up and down. Like Juniper, she had been taught to judge a man quickly by his dress, his stance, and the look in his eye. "Where'd you find him?"

"I'll explain everything," Juniper said, exhaustion pulling at her. "But only after a drink and a nap. I wouldn't say no to something to eat either."

"Oh, that means it's a good one," Amery said, smirking. She hooked her other arm through Ison's and started them both toward the keep.

The thought of a drink and a bed enticed Juniper, but the thought of facing Maddox after all this time filled her with a certain type of dread.

*

Amery led Juniper and Ison through the residential streets of the Undercity and to Maddox's keep. A nice house by any standards, the townhouse had a heavy iron gate and matching bronze statues in the small yard. No grass grew—only stone. Maddox's townhouse rose to the ceiling of the Undercity, four stories. Stone pillars and iron lattice protected the front stoop, along with a hefty assassin named Dornell.

Dornell nodded at Amery, blinked once at Juniper, and quickly memorized Ison. He didn't say anything as he opened one of the solid oak doors. Juniper held her chin high and walked into the foyer as if no time had passed at all. The stone walls of Maddox's keep had been warmed with wooden paneling, bookshelves, thick rugs, and scenic paintings. The foyer held two parlors: one open for guests, one closed for private meetings. The keep was surprisingly empty, but it wasn't abnormal for everyone to be out or somewhere else.

Amery took them to the third floor, to the bedroom that she and Juniper had shared. To Juniper's surprise, it looked just as she had left it. Her bed hadn't been touched. Someone had dusted her things, though. A single lantern lit the space, making the room glow gold.

The clock on the wall revealed it to be morning.

They'd been wandering all night.

Juniper meandered through the familiar room, the twin beds, the small sofa and bookshelf that held her assortment of books. She dropped her bags by her bed. Amery retrieved a spare blanket and a pillow for Ison and spread them on the couch.

"I'll leave you two to it," Amery said. "I've got a few quick jobs to finish up. I should be back in a few hours, and then you'll tell me what happened?"

Juniper nodded. "I'll tell you everything."

Amery left, and Juniper showed Ison to the small bathing room. After a quick wash, Ison collapsed on the couch, and Juniper curled up in her old bed—it didn't take long at all for sleep to claim her.

*

When Juniper woke, it was to a bottle being set on her bedside table. An unlabeled green bottle. Moonwater.

She blinked. Amery hopped onto her bed, folded her legs, and met Juniper's sleepy stare with wide, anxious eyes. For a moment, nothing had changed, and Juniper's months in Bradburn Castle were a dream. Then Ison snored from his place on the couch.

"So?" Amery whispered. "Come on, I promised you booze, and you promised me a story."

Juniper sat up and popped open the moonwater. She took a long swig of the cool drink, letting it flow down her throat and into every part of her body. It took a moment to place the taste. Chamomile. Then she took another.

"It started the night we went to steal the crown..." Juniper told Amery about that night, being caught, becoming the royal protector, the apostate, the demons, the ball—but she glazed over the wechun's defeat.

Amery tilted her head. "I'm guessing they didn't turn you into a courtier, or you wouldn't be here."

Juniper shook her head. "There's something else I should tell you."

Amery's curious gaze darkened.

"I'm a mage," Juniper whispered. She cupped her hands; flurries swirled together in a haze of bright blue. "I used my magic to fight off the demon and the wechun. Adrian and Reid told a different story to everyone else, but it didn't matter. The Order found out, and they've blamed everything on me."

Her magic was no longer secret, not if the Order knew. Her name would be among the apostates the Order vowed to hunt. Not that it made a difference. The City Watch had been hunting her down for years.

"Ah," came Amery's reply. The darkness vanished from her face. Instead, she wore surprise. "It makes sense now. You never wanted to go to the magic shows or spend any more time with mages than you had to. I thought magic just made you uncomfortable, but all this time, you've been a mage in denial." She smiled. "Don't worry, I love you just the same."

Ison shifted but didn't wake up.

"But what else happened?" Amery asked. "You and Reid seemed to be getting along before this wechun business." She raised one dark, finely plucked brow. "You know you can ask me any question about men. I've seen a lot."

Juniper blinked; had she let that slip? Of course, Amery could read people far better than Juniper could. Juniper's cheeks burned. She looked away from Amery's knowing expression and at anything else—the bookshelf, the window, Ison's sleeping form. When she dared to meet Amery's gaze, the other girl was frowning.

"What happened?" Amery asked in that big-sister tone of hers.

Juniper sighed and slumped forward. "We hated each other at first. Then...things changed. We were friends, and then we were together. I saved his life with my magic, and he turned against me."

Amery's curiosity softened. "And he broke your heart. You don't have to explain that to me."

He hadn't just broken her heart; he had shattered it.

"Life down here has been the same. Nothing worth mentioning," said Amery. "On the positive side, because our heist of the crown was secret, no one down here has heard about the fumble."

Juniper tried to look happy about it. "So, my reputation is still gold?"

Amery shrugged. "I don't know about that. Those thugs didn't even recognize you. I'd say you've got to prove yourself in some fights before people start to tremble at your name again."

Juniper half laughed and took a drink of the moonwater.

From the couch, Ison inhaled, groaned, and rolled onto his back. He blinked several times at the ceiling before he sat up. He regarded the two girls with sleepy confusion.

"Good morning, sunshine," Amery said, smiling. "Thirsty? There's some moonwater on the floor. Drink up. You need it."

Ison found the green bottle beside the couch, popped it open, and drank a third of it. After a beat, he belched.

"I like him," Amery said, watching Ison like a cat might eye a mouse. She looked back at Juniper, and her pretty face dropped all sense of humor. Her eyes held a seriousness that chilled Juniper. Amery leaned forward and whispered, "Listen, Jun, about that heist—"

Footsteps sounded on the staircase. Sure, confident steps. Boots. Leather laden with steel, hidden and not.

Both girls froze.

Juniper felt a knot form in her chest, one that expanded into her stomach, into her gut, into her legs, making her feel like one giant twisted ball. Her gaze landed on the closed bedroom door, as did Amery's, and Ison turned around to see what they saw.

A hand fell on the door, and a calm, smooth male voice said from the other side, "Amery, I hear you have a guest."

"It's unlocked," said Amery.

The handle turned, the door opened, and in the doorway stood Maddox Hawk.

CHAPTER THIRTY-ONE

Maddox's dark hair had grown out and was tied behind his head in a short tail. He wore a fitted tunic of dark gold and black trousers. Leather bracers hugged both of his arms, lined with daggers and throwing knives. His boots held daggers inside and out. He wore only the finest leather, carried the sharpest blades, and he could use each with deadly skill.

Her guild master took a precise step into the room, his presence commanding—one fitting the leader of one of the deadliest guilds of thieves and assassins in the Undercity, in Rusdasin, and possibly in Duvane. His brown eyes took in Juniper, and if he found her presence surprising, he held it in well. He took in her fine clothes, the leather bags at the foot of the bed, the moonwater. His eyes lingered on her boots—her expensive leather boots. He shifted that gaze to Ison, who didn't so much as flinch under it.

"I heard Juniper Thimble had returned, but I had to see her for myself," he said, his tone clear, commanding, but not urgent. His gaze drifted back to Juniper, and his smile became unfeeling, clinical. "You two"—Maddox motioned between Juniper and Ison—"come with me. We need to have a talk."

Juniper stood, glad to have rested. She felt much more confident about meeting Maddox than she had that morning. The moonwater had also helped.

Ison stood with her, though if he felt nervous about this meeting, he hid it as well as Maddox. His half-lidded eyes, his casual stance—Ison looked more bored than anything. And Juniper knew Maddox would find it either irritating or interesting. Hopefully, it was the latter. People who irritated Maddox tended to have bad luck—the deadly kind.

Amery remained in the bedroom while Juniper and Ison followed Maddox to the first floor, where several familiar faces lingered about. They watched with varying stares of astonishment and worry as Juniper descended the stairs. Maddox led them to his study—the one reserved for deals and clientele.

His stout bodyguard, Bulo, stood beside the door. At the sight of Maddox, Bulo swiftly pulled open the dark oak door. Maddox walked through first, and Bulo's curious gaze raked over Juniper and lingered on Ison, who gave no notice.

Ison's indifference made Juniper jealous. Her knees trembled, and she feared her unease radiated.

Bulo shut the door behind them. Maddox stood beside his grand desk, a masterwork of oak.

"Please, have a seat," Maddox said in his best gentleman's cadence, the one he used when reassuring clients of his guild's success.

Juniper sat in one of three leather chairs, and Ison slumped into the chair beside her. She tried to catch his eye, but he held his empty gaze on the desk. Maddox strolled around the desk and sat, dark eyes sizing them up in silence.

Maddox's office was clean, tidy, and held only the essentials for his deals: clean parchment, an elegant feather pen, black ink, a polished brass lamp. Everything in the office—the chairs, the desk, the sparse decorations—had been expertly crafted to reflect Maddox's wealth and status, as well as to ensure that his clients would be satisfied. The bookshelves held dusted volumes of literature, history, and poetry, none of which had been opened, so the spines remained unbroken, the covers flawless—books for show.

Maddox's real office connected to the fake office through a hidden door in the paneling. It stood directly behind his chair, nearly invisible unless one knew where to look. Juniper did. She'd been taken into that office to see maps of the city, detailed maps of buildings. Unlike this office, his real office was cluttered and dusty. It held scattered contracts, files and reports, and all manner of paperwork that Juniper found nauseatingly disorganized. A second hidden door led from his bedroom into his real office; another led from the real office to the topside of Rusdasin.

"So." Maddox leaned forward and folded his fingers together. His gaze moved between Ison and Juniper. "I hear these last few months have been wild for you."

Juniper had gone over what she would tell him and what she would not, and before Ison could speak, she told Maddox about the night she'd gotten caught, her role as royal protector, and the demon attacks that kept her forcibly employed. She did not mention her magic, what happened between her and Reid, or about Ison's involvement with the Demon Crisis. She skipped ahead to the accusation and their flight from the castle.

Maddox gave her a small smile. "Everyone's been talking about the

Demon Crisis. I had a few clients attend Bala's Ball. Most of them got out, but it's shaken the nobles. The king fears for his own life, they say."

"I can't confess how much the king fears for his life." Juniper fought to keep her hands uncurled in her lap. She wouldn't show her nervousness in front of Maddox. "But he feared for his son's life enough to hire a thief to protect him."

"And protect him you did," he said with a sigh on his tongue. "And he's rewarded you for your service by raising your bounty to fifty thousand gold."

Juniper gasped, and Ison's emotionless gaze shifted in surprise. "Fifty thousand?" her voice cracked. That amount would have the foolish and the brave coming after her head.

"Alive," Maddox added. "Dead, you're worth only twenty."

She slumped back in the chair. Fifty thousand gold, alive. The king wanted her alive, but he'd take her body as payment too. "For running?" she asked.

"For poisoning the prince," Maddox said.

She closed her eyes and leaned forward. She needed a longer nap and another bottle of moonwater. Maybe someone to punch.

The king thought she had poisoned Adrian too? Did Reid think her guilty? What did Adrian think? He couldn't think her guilty...but that knight said he had evidence against her, planted by the apostate, no doubt.

To get rid of her.

With a bounty of fifty thousand, she might as well paint a target on her back.

"Tell me, Juniper," Maddox crooned. "Did you try to murder the young Prince Adrian?"

"No," she said at once. She met his gaze, pleading him to see the truth. "Someone framed me. Someone wanted me out of the castle."

He raised his brows.

"The same person who summoned the demons," she clarified. She wanted to look at Ison to see his expression, but she didn't want to give Maddox a reason to bring him into the conversation.

Maddox's gaze drifted to Ison anyway, and Juniper tensed. "And you brought the court magician's apprentice with you?"

Ison met Maddox's curious gaze. He didn't blink. He didn't flinch. Juniper swallowed; men bigger and stronger than Ison had trembled under Maddox's gaze. Most knew what Maddox was capable of, the people he commanded. Ison knew a fraction of Maddox's control, but still he didn't

154

BEATRICE B. MORGAN

flinch. Maddox's brows furrowed in confusion or interest, and he shifted that gaze to Juniper.

"What is your plan now?" Maddox asked her, leaning back in his chair.

She took a deep breath, the anxiety of her request worming through her legs. "We need to leave the city."

Maddox didn't speak. He didn't need to. His gaze intensified. The silence within the office thickened. His stare and his silence weighed on her shoulders.

She sat up straighter. "With fifty thousand gold on my head, everyone will be on the lookout for me. I need to get out, at least until my name loses its heat." She glanced at Ison. "And I promised I would help Ison get out of the kingdom."

Maddox held her gaze. "I can't let you simply walk out. You know that."

She knew. She owed him too much. "It won't be forever. A year, maybe two."

He didn't answer. Her lie tasted sour on her tongue, and he knew as well as she did that if she left, she wouldn't come back.

"It will be near impossible to go anywhere with the Royal Guard and the City Watch looking for me, not to mention every fool in need of gold. Then there's the bounty hunters." She'd dealt with bounty hunters a few times, and she hated the lot of them. "I won't be of use to anyone if I can't even walk through the market without getting attacked." She waved her hand toward the window. "If I can't work, I'll be useless to you."

Maddox took in her argument and steepled his fingers. Thoughts moved behind his eyes, churning his angle, his counteroffer. Juniper steeled herself for whatever he wanted of her.

Finally, Maddox lowered his hands to the desk. He had made his decision. His hard gaze settled on Juniper. "One last job."

She nodded.

"Do this for me, and I will help you get out of the city," Maddox said carefully. He glanced at Ison. "Your friend too if that is what he wants."

Ison looked up at Maddox "It is what I want."

Maddox looked to Juniper, his face a mask.

"What do you need me to do?" she asked, her confidence returning. No bank had vaults strong enough to keep her out; no house could withstand her. Not when she had the secret power of her magic on her side. She would steal fifty thousand gold worth of loot if he asked; one hundred thousand, even. Anything to get them out of the city.

Maddox held her gaze. He had always made her feel small. "It's a contract I've had for a few weeks. No one else has been able to fulfill it."

She sat up straighter.

"Assassinate Leif Tinnly, Captain of the City Watch."

CHAPTER THIRTY-TWO

Juniper stared at Maddox, sure that she had misheard. When he did not relent, did not admit the joke, she gawked at him. Had Maddox lost his mind?

She shook her head. "The Captain of the City Watch?"

Ison glanced between Maddox and Juniper, his eyes widening by a fraction. Either by her surprise or by the request itself, Ison understood the gravity of the contract.

Maddox nodded, amused by her reaction. He'd expected it. "Someone doesn't like the captain and has agreed to pay dearly for his removal from the Watch. It's an open request, and the first assassin who kills him wins. However, no one has yet to complete the assassination."

Because it's impossible, Juniper wanted to say. Captain Leif Tinnly was an inhuman force. He had lasted longer than most in his position. Like Captain Sandpiper, he did not put up with nonsense—not from lawbreakers nor his own men. Under his command, the City Watch had put a serious dent in the city's crime, as well as strangled a few of the black market shops and dealers, limiting the guilds and keeps of ill repute to the Undercity.

To assassinate him would bring back the crime lords that he had put an end to. For other assassins to have tried and failed... She knew why Maddox would ask it of her. Because he knew the odds of her success. He knew it was nearly impossible. She would either not be able to complete the job or die trying. Either way, she would not have his blessing to leave.

She knew that, and yet she sat up straight, met Maddox's gaze, and said, "Consider him dead."

Maddox's smile turned a shade darker. "I've missed your confidence."

She hadn't missed his. "Is there a time limit?"

"No," he said. "But there are stipulations. First, bring back his dagger with the Watch's signet. It's passed down from captain to captain and worth a fortune. Our client is also asking for his head for confirmation."

Juniper treated it just like any other assassination contract, any other heist. She wouldn't let Maddox see her doubt. Assassinating Captain Tinnly sounded as farfetched as assassinating Captain Sandpiper. A few months ago, she would have relished the challenge, but now, her knees trembled.

Maddox hadn't asked her out of his confidence of her skill, but out of his desire not to let her leave.

But, if it would get her and Ison out of Rusdasin, she'd do it.

"I'm overjoyed," Maddox stood, signaling the end of their meeting.

Juniper stood with him, and Ison followed her lead. Maddox held his hand out to her. She took it, and his long fingers wrapped around hers.

"Welcome home, Juniper. Considering you've had a long few months, take the next few days off and relax. Readjust to the Undercity. I'm sure the castle has left you missing its luxuries?" He smiled. "I'll escort Ison to a guest room."

Ison gave no implication he heard Maddox, but when Maddox started up the stairs, Ison followed a step behind, which left Juniper standing in the hall.

"Look who's back," came a drawling male voice. "I've missed you, sister."

She turned to meet Xavier's blue-gray stare. He didn't wear the head-to-toe black that he had the last time she had met him. He wore a dark tunic and pants and a dark green jacket. Daggers lined the inside of his bracers, his waist, and his boots. Without his hood, his smooth dark brown skin gave away his youth, not a month older than Juniper.

"Brother," Juniper said in greeting.

Xavier and Juniper had been kidnapped and sold by the same bandits. As tradition went, that made them siblings. The last time they met came to the front of her mind; Xavier had snuck into the castle and used her as a human shield to escape. She drove her fist into Xavier's jaw.

His eyes widened only a fraction before the impact. He stumbled back, hand on his jaw, looking at her with a mixture of anger and amusement. "I suppose I deserved that."

"I thought you did," she said.

She and Xavier stared at once another a moment longer, his blue-gray eyes calculating his chances of a counterattack. His somber expression turned into a sly grin, and he opened his arms. She stepped into his embrace and hugged him back. As she had suspected, he had several blades hidden under his jacket.

A tiny part of her had missed him.

"I hear you're worth fifty thousand gold," Xavier said as he let her go.

She chuckled, though she scanned his hands for weapons.

He laughed. "I don't need the gold, sister. But there are those that do." His smile faded. His eyes, which were so often cold and unfeeling, held sincerity. "If you leave the keep, take me with you. I don't want to break into the castle dungeon to find you. The first time was hard enough."

She nodded. "I'll hold you to that."

With a nod of parting, Xavier headed toward the hall that led to the basement—Maddox kept training equipment there, sparring rings and practice weapons. A part of her wanted to follow Xavier down there and see how far she'd fallen from her once masterful skills, but her mind drifted to Ison, alone upstairs with Maddox Hawk.

A handful of thieves and assassins stood in the main room, watching her. She ignored them and jogged back up the stairs. She found Maddox and Ison standing outside a guest room, and at the sight of her, whatever conversation they had been having ended. Neither looked worried or annoyed; if anything, they shared a frightening similarity of indifference.

Maddox patted Ison on the shoulder and retreated down the stairs. Ison's guest room held the essentials, a bed, water basin, and small nightstand.

Ison dropped onto the bed and set his head into his hands. "I never thought I'd be here, the Undercity."

"It's not as bad as it seems. We'll take you on a tour if you'd like, Amery and Xavier and me." Because she'd need both of them with a fifty thousand gold bounty on her head.

"That sounds nice," Ison said, eyes closed. "But, later. Right now, I just want to rest." He curled up on the bed.

Juniper wanted desperately to say something encouraging, something fruitful that would make him smile, but she didn't have anything. She stepped out of his room and closed the door behind her. She took a step toward her room, toward the moonwater she hadn't finished, but stopped mid-step. Maddox leaned against the banister.

"He's a nice boy," Maddox said, searching Juniper for anything to read.

"He's had a hard few weeks," Juniper said.

Maddox shoved off the banister and closed the space between them. He stood several inches taller than her, and he had a good many pounds of muscle on her; she had always felt a certain fear in his shadow. His dark eyes searched hers, thoughtful and curious, but that familiar sense of insignificance didn't come. She looked back into his eyes without fear.

Maddox no longer held her future in his hands.

She owed him, but if he tried anything, she could freeze him solid. She had never held that kind of power before, and knowing that she had magic as a last resort stiffened her resolve.

Still, if Maddox had heard the rumors of her flight from the castle, then he might have heard the rumors of her magic too. He would then know she had hidden it from him all this time. She waited for the confirmation, the questions, but he remained silent.

"I've missed you," Maddox said softly. He brushed hair away from her face. "It's not been the same here without you. I was starting to worry that something had happened to you, something that would take you away."

She blinked, and he flattened his hand against her cheek. His calloused fingers felt cool. He ran his thumb along her cheekbone, the subtle pressure warning her not to move. He pulled her into an embrace, and she gingerly snaked her arms around his middle, above the dagger sheaths that crisscrossed his lower back.

He leaned away just enough to press a dry kiss to her temple.

With his lips lingering against her, she whispered, "Would you have killed me that night?"

He hummed a questioning note. He knew the night she mentioned, when she had run after the assassin, thinking him the apostate, only to find Maddox. He had held a dagger to her throat, but he hadn't cut her.

"I came to check on you," he whispered back. "Xavier's report didn't settle well with me, and I wanted to see it for myself. Then you followed me, and I thought I could lure you into the forest and save you, but then..." He leaned away. His clinical gaze wandered along her midsection, where Adrian's wounds had transferred to her. "I thought you would die," Maddox whispered. "That was the binding spell's doing, I take it? I've seen lesser wounds kill a man twice your size." His hand roamed up and down her back in soothing motions. "Then, to my relief and rage, I watched that squire carry you back into the castle."

She swallowed; he hadn't answered her question, but he knew about the binding spell and he would have known slicing her throat would have killed Adrian, not her. And if he thought she had defected, he would have killed her without hesitation. Yet he hadn't. Had he realized that something else kept her at the castle? She searched Maddox's dark eyes for the answer, but found nothing.

If Reid hadn't appeared, she would have died that night. She almost had.

Maddox pressed another kiss to her temple, and said, his breath hot against her skin, "I am glad you're back, Juniper. Even if it's not for very long."

He released her, and by his sweet tone, his sweet smile—he didn't think she could kill the captain. He knew she would never leave, and she knew, then, that she would prove him wrong. One way or another. She would get out of Rusdasin, she would take Ison with her, and she would go somewhere that Maddox couldn't find her.

CHAPTER THIRTY-THREE

Juniper let herself into her bedroom, and Amery jumped to her feet. "What did he say? Where's your friend?"

Juniper let out a heavy sigh and sank onto the couch. "I told Maddox what happened, minus a few personal details. I told him I wanted out of the city until the heat around my name goes down."

"Fifty thousand," Amery said. "Everyone's heard about it by now. It would be smart on your part to keep a low profile."

"I know," Juniper said. "With all the guards and bounty hunters looking for me, I won't be able to walk through the city, up there or down here. But he wants me to assassinate the Captain of the City Watch first; then he'll help me and Ison get out."

Amery chuckled darkly. "That's impossible. A dozen assassins have already tried, and failed. By failed, I mean they're dead."

Juniper slumped onto her knees. "I know. He doesn't think I can do it. He doesn't want me to succeed."

"He wants you to stay here." Amery hummed a disapproving tone. Her face softened. "Although, I can't argue with him about wanting to keep you here. I've missed you. And you just got back. It's too soon for you to leave again."

Juniper gave Amery a pleading look.

The other girl sighed. "I know. I can't keep you here." Amery came to sit beside her. "You'll figure something out. You're you. In the meantime, think of the hell we can raise."

Juniper tried to laugh. "But let's do that later. I've got loot from the castle I'd like to sell." Her eyes drifted to the leather bags. "If I'm not going to be able to get any odd jobs around the Undercity, I'll have to do what I can for coin."

Amery smiled wickedly. "We could turn you in, collect the bounty, and then break you out again. We could split the gold. I could use twenty-five thousand gold. Or we could turn you in, pretending you're dead, then steal you from the morgue. Ten thousand is better than nothing."

Juniper forced a laugh. "Maybe. But later. I need a good bath and a strong drink." She stood and grabbed the bottle of moonwater. She took a long drink.

"You do smell a bit like a sewer," Amery said, hand on her chin.

Juniper laughed. She would tell Amery all about the journey through the sewer later too. Right now, she took her moonwater and fresh clothes and locked herself in the bathing room for a warm bath.

✳

Clean and dressed in fresh clothes, Juniper returned to her bedroom. Amery had gone. With the room to herself, she sorted her satchels into two piles: things to sell and things to keep. The pile of things to sell ended up being larger. She'd never been one to keep things. She didn't see the point in keepsakes. She hadn't had much room for things either.

She put her unfinished book on her bedside table—she wouldn't be returning to the Royal Library anytime soon—and returned the sellables to one of the satchels. With that task finished, she flopped onto the bed and sought the comfort of the pillow, the blankets. She laid on her back, closed her eyes, pictured the wooden canopy of her bed in Bradburn Castle.

She took a deep breath of the keep. It smelled of stone, candles, and underground musk. Bradburn Castle and all those inside it were a finished chapter of her life; she would not see them again, and hopefully, she could put Reid behind her.

She would assassinate the captain, get out of Rusdasin, and find a new place to live where she wouldn't have to worry about any of this anymore.

She tried to sleep, but her mind refused. Finally, she gave up. She pulled on her boots, a dark jacket from her old closet, and secured Reid's dagger—*her* dagger—around her waist. He had given it to her. It was no longer Reid's. It belonged to her now. A part of her wanted to sell it and be rid of it, but she knew she wouldn't find the same quality steel in the Undercity, not without a hefty price. No, the logical solution was to keep it.

She heaved the bag of things to sell over her shoulder and found Amery coming up the stairs. She blinked at the bag on Juniper's shoulder, and then nodded. The two girls made their way out of the keep and to the street. They started toward the market, and Juniper felt eyes following her, more than usual. Curious eyes. Hungry Eyes. Eyes that saw the bounty. Eyes that were desperate enough to try. She spotted them too, looking at her from alleys, between stalls, and from tavern doorways. None looked like real threats—not to her, anyway.

They made it to the market stalls without a fuss, and Juniper couldn't decide if she felt more disappointment or relief. Amery guarded her back while Juniper haggled. She sold her castle items one at a time, filling up her coin pouch a little at a time. At last, when the bag had been emptied, she had coin that would last her a good while in the Undercity.

She felt the familiar sense of relief and triumph that came after a night of bedlam—the relief of selling off her stolen goods, the comfort of a full coin purse, and the knowledge that she would be able to eat for a while longer.

"Got anything in mind you want to buy?" Amery asked.

"No." Juniper glanced at the weapons stalls as they passed but withheld her desire to stop. "I'll need to budget if I can't work."

Amery nodded, and the two of them started back toward Maddox's keep at a leisurely pace. Just because Juniper hadn't a desire to spend money, that didn't mean Amery didn't. They stopped at a few clothing stalls, and she stroked silks and velvets and admired delicates with hidden weapon slots.

"Look, Collie, two whores looking to expand their wardrobes," came a drawling female voice. A hulking woman with a man's haircut stood a few steps behind them, looking down her crooked nose at Juniper and Amery. She wore thick leather armor, and the dented pommel of her sword had what looked like bloodstains in the creases.

Collie, her companion, looked to have bought his leather armor from the same shop. He had three scars on his jaw, spaced like claws. He let out a gruff laugh. "Where you're going, you won't need silks."

A third man in similar armor appeared on their other side, and a woman with red braids appeared on the other. Surrounded.

"You'd best come with us," said the hulking woman to Juniper. "I'd rather deliver you in one piece. Though, the bounty only required you to be alive, not whole."

The man behind her laughed.

Amery let out an annoyed sigh and dropped the corset she had been admiring. "So tiresome. A girl can't even shop," she whined.

Juniper set her hand on her dagger, wishing she had come more prepared for a fight.

"Ha!" The hulking woman pulled her sword from her side. "You'd fight me with that puny blade?"

Amery glanced at Juniper, curious—to fight or flee? Juniper held her gaze steady. She had already formed a plan in her head. The blade the bounty hunter carried was Undercity steel.

"I bet," Juniper said playfully, "I can break your sword in half before you can lay a scratch on me."

The woman laughed, and her companions laughed with her. When she stopped, they stopped. The woman stepped closer.

"If I do, you'll leave," Juniper said. "And if I don't, I'll go willingly."

Amery shot her a warning glare, and the bounty hunters looked like they couldn't believe it. The hulking woman looked Juniper up and down, trying to find the trick.

"Fine." She adjusted her sword.

Juniper unsheathed *her* dagger. She readied herself, feeling, listening, commanding. All around them, the market had come to a halt. All eyes were on her, save for a few who looked elsewhere—clever thieves taking advantage of the event.

Good. Let them see Juniper Thimble in action.

The hulking woman came at her with the ferocity of a bear. She held her eyes on Juniper, not on her sword as the slivers of frost appeared, as the ice penetrated deep into the cheap steel. The hulking woman came at her, swung, and Juniper met the incoming blade with her own. Her dagger, a splinter compared to the size of the sword, shattered the larger sword into a dozen pieces.

The woman's eyes went wide. She carried the hilt through the swing. As the broken pieces clattered to the ground, a ghost of a smile appeared on her lips.

And then, a searing pain struck Juniper's shoulder.

CHAPTER THIRTY-FOUR

Before the cry left Juniper's throat, Amery's dagger flew over her shoulder with a sickening wet swoosh. The bounty hunter with the red braids grunted in pain.

Juniper reached for the slender knife lodged in her shoulder. Pain radiated from the wound, but nothing vital had been struck. She pulled it out, trying to keep her pain off her face.

Amery had a dagger in one hand and a throwing knife in the other, giving the remaining bounty hunters a daring glare.

At the sight of her blood on the knife, Juniper's instincts kicked in—something deep in her bones snapped. The hulking woman started toward Juniper, pulling a dagger from her side. She had halved the distance to Juniper, and her wicked grin faltered. Her next breath became a white puff; her eyes widened.

But Juniper couldn't keep it up. Her magic wavered. She couldn't rely on it.

The woman stumbled back, and the knife with Juniper's blood found its new home in the hulking woman's throat.

Her magic squeezed, and Juniper pulled it back before her body could seize. Amery dispatched the other two bounty hunters, and just like that, the fight ended. Juniper cursed silently; she had wanted to impale that woman with an ice spike, but all she had done was turn the air cold.

And the Undercity returned to business as usual. Juniper slid her dagger back into the sheath. Her shoulder cried in pain.

"You'll need a healer." Amery examined the wound and confirmed her original statement. "Sooner rather than later too."

Amery pulled Juniper's good arm and started toward the opposite end of the market, away from the clothing and weapons, to where the mages sold their wares, potions, and services. The crowd parted for them, and Juniper ran her eyes over every person who dared to meet her gaze, daring them to try their hand at the bounty.

Through the crowd, Juniper met the eyes of a man in a blue cloak. He didn't look away. He smiled. A second man in a blue cloak appeared beside the first, and he too gazed at Juniper. The second man didn't smile, but curiosity piqued in his cruel eyes.

"Who are they?" Juniper asked Amery. "The blue cloaks?"

Amery groaned. "The Dual Fangs. Weirdos."

"Who?"

"Right, they moved in while you were gone," Amery said. "Don't make eye contact. I don't want them to think they can talk to me."

They walked out of eyesight of the Dual Fangs. The colorful stalls of the mages came into view. Potions, ingredients, enchantments, runes—the mages' market held anything magical one could want. Amery navigated her to a healer's stall, one run by a local guild of mages. Green fabric of all shades had been sewn together to make a large tent, hung off the stone ceiling of the Undercity. Inside, three stories of stone rooms held the sick and injured. Magelights hung in the air, spreading glittering cool light like daylight.

Juniper sat down on an unoccupied table. Several healers worked on sickly looking people, some conscious, some not. The healers' hands glowed with magic in all shades of green, blue, and yellow. The entire tent smelled like flowers and freshly cut wood but also faintly metallic.

"What do we have here?" an older healer asked Juniper. She didn't wear the robes of mages; most of the Undercity mages didn't. She wore a simple tunic and trousers and cloak. A green sash identified her as an advanced healer.

"She got into a fight," Amery explained quickly.

"Hmm." The healer took a look at Juniper's wounded shoulder. The healer's magic grazed the wound, a tickle of warmth. "Doesn't look like the blade was enchanted or poisoned."

Juniper sat on the table while the healer magically cut away her ruined tunic. Amery turned on her heel and vanished through the tent's flap.

"It missed the vitals," murmured the healer. "You're lucky."

Juniper tried not to twitch; the feeling of her skin knitting itself back together felt like an insect crawling over her skin, and she fought the urge to swat at the healer's hands.

Amery reappeared with a fresh tunic in her hands. "Unless you'd rather walk back without one," she said, smirking.

"Thank you," Juniper said.

"There were two of those Dual Fangs watching the fight," Amery said to the healer.

The healer let out a huff.

"Who are they?" Juniper asked.

"Mages but not the good kind," said the healer. The tingling of her skin slowed, then stopped. The healer stepped away. "The Dual Fangs represent the kind of mages the Order wishes to eradicate."

Juniper took the fresh tunic from Amery and pulled it over her head. Rebel mages in the Undercity—she remembered Adrian talking about them. Juniper jumped off the table and moved her shoulder up and down. "Thank you." She pulled payment from her coin purse. "It feels like it didn't even happen."

The healer accepted it and tucked it into her tunic. "As a good healing should," she said with a smile. "But, a warning, stay away from the Dual Fangs. They're aren't here to make friends."

✳

Juniper kept one hand on her dagger as she and Amery made their way back to Maddox's keep. No one else tried to jump them, but Juniper didn't let go of her paranoia. There were plenty of stupid people in the Undercity.

"You froze that blade," Amery said, frowning. "You weren't joking about being a mage."

"I wasn't." Juniper brought one hand out and summoned a few flurries; she tried to solidify it, but the flurries and ice pellets only twitched.

They passed a bakery, and Amery yanked Juniper into the narrow alley between it and the seamstress next door.

"Jun," Amery whispered, her tone urgent. "I want to talk to you about the heist."

"What about it?"

Amery cast her black eyes to the mouth of the alley. She spoke so low that even if someone stood eavesdropping, they wouldn't be able to hear. "I've been thinking about it a lot. How easy it was to get in. How there were no guards. I think it was a setup."

A gaggle of drunk men walked by, laughing as one of them continued a lewd joke.

"I think you're right." Juniper had thought about it too, but she'd had so many other things to think about, she had pushed it to the back of her mind.

"Those guards were talking about something happening that night, but they didn't know what," Amery said. "The whole time, I kept asking myself where all the guards were. And then, when I was in the king's dressing room, I heard footsteps. Quiet footsteps of someone trying not to be heard, but I knew it wasn't you. I heard a man say he saw the thief go in through the queen's dressing room, and that the captain was already inside. So I waited where I was. I thought I'd let your capture be a distraction so I could get the crown and then get you out of trouble." Amery gave her a soft smile. "Then I heard the jewel room door open, and you were ambushed."

"The captain jumped me," Juniper added.

"But I didn't see anyone in the Royal Chambers," Amery said. "Which means the captain was in the jewel room the whole time."

"Waiting for us." Juniper let out a groan; she felt foolish for not putting the thoughts together that night. She had been too concerned with getting the crown first, with showing Amery up, with being Maddox's favorite.

Amery continued, "They *knew* someone would be in *that* room at *that* time. They knew someone was going to steal the crown, and they were waiting."

"Because they needed a criminal," Juniper said, thinking of that meeting in the dungeons. "The king would have gone through as many criminals as he needed to find someone to be his royal protector."

Amery took a step closer so that her breath brushed against Juniper's cheek. "Maddox is the one who planned that heist," Amery whispered. "He is the one who said it was top secret, but he never told us who the client was or how he got the blueprints for the Royal Chambers. The whole thing was planned."

"There was no client," Juniper spat. Her feeling of foolishness swallowed her whole. "How did I not see that!"

Amery nodded. "When I came back alone that night, I thought he'd be furious. But he wasn't. I thought it was strange that he didn't ask more questions about what happened to you and where the crown was. He didn't ask for a detailed report of the failure, because it wasn't a failure. He knew one of us wouldn't make it back. But, when days passed with no word about you, he started getting irritated. When I told him I saw you with the prince on the way to Bala's Temple, he got that look of cold fury that he gets when someone's duped him."

"And Xavier came to find out what I was doing," Juniper added darkly. And Maddox had found the rest out for himself. He'd already known about the binding spell.

Maddox had sold her, hadn't he?

Juniper slumped against the wall of the bakery. She wanted to break something, to feel bones breaking. A setup. The whole thing. A trick to get her to the castle where Captain Sandpiper could ambush her.

She didn't need to ask Amery who she thought did it. She knew immediately. The same desperation that had led the king to hire her had led him to contact Maddox Hawk. The king had had Juniper delivered to his doorstep.

CHAPTER THIRTY-FIVE

Juniper focused—slivering tendrils of ice spread through the water. Her ice slowed near the bottom of the glass. Her breath came in gasps, beads of sweat trailed down her neck, and she felt the squeezing of her empty well. It threatened to seize, but she pushed her ice further. Only when those tendrils of ice reached the bottom of the glass did she release her magic. Gasping, she slouched against the bed. She sat on the floor, in a square of Undercity light that came in from the window. The mostly frozen glass of water sat before her.

Amery had gone out to inquire about a possible job that afternoon, which left Juniper to her own devices. She had knocked on Ison's door; a grunt had been her only response. She had invited him on a tour, but he hadn't answered.

Poor Ison. She didn't know what to do for him. He wanted to get out of the city, and now he was stuck until she killed Captain Tinnly. According to the grapevines, Ison had not only been labeled an apostate and a criminal, but he now had a bounty of twenty thousand gold on his head.

After several breaths, Juniper focused on her ice. Thawing it came harder than freezing; she had to work her magic backward, and her focus kept slipping. It felt like writing with her left hand. She gradually shrank the ice by a third. That space inside of her started to quiver again, and she released her magic.

She hadn't eaten enough to support this much focus.

When her breath caught up with her, she dumped the water and the small ice ball into the water basin. The ice clinked against the copper. She hadn't been able to thaw ice a week ago. Feeling triumphant, she went into the hall to give Ison the good news. He needed good news. She knocked on his door, but no response came.

She knocked again. "Ison, it's me. Can I come in?"

He grunted.

She didn't know if that meant yes or no. She opened the door anyway.

Ison lay on the bed in nearly the exact same spot as when she had last seen him. He wore the same clothes, but he'd removed his boots.

Juniper sat on the bedside and told him about the water she had frozen and almost thawed.

"That's great," Ison said listlessly, his voice muffled by the pillow.

"Are you all right?" She knew the answer, but she wanted to hear it from him.

He didn't answer.

A shadow appeared in the door. Xavier leaned against the doorframe, taking in the scene before him. "There you two are. Dinner is served. Might want to head down before it's gone."

Juniper stood, and she didn't give Ison the chance to decline the invitation. She grabbed him by the arm and hauled him to his feet—he gave little resistance and tugged on his boots. She hooked her arm with his and led him down the stairs and to the dining room on the first floor.

The dining room could sit twenty but often sat ten or twelve. Tonight nine pairs of greedy, hungry eyes watched Juniper walk inside but she ignored them. She sat Ison next to her, and Xavier sat on his other side. Amery appeared not long after and sat beside Juniper. The chair at the head of the table—Maddox's seat—remained empty. He wouldn't be joining then.

"Well, look who's back from the dead." A thin-shouldered thief glowered at Juniper, then eyeballed Ison. "And you brought back a souvenir?"

The thief and a few others chuckled, and Ison looked up. His cold steel eyes met the thief's. A beat paused, and the thief's smile faded. He looked away and didn't look back. Ison blinked; Juniper added food to his plate, then her own.

The food, while all right, paled in comparison to what she'd eaten at the castle.

She began to eat, one ear on the talk at the other end, one ear beside her as Xavier asked Ison, "You're a mage, right?"

Ison nodded. "Yes."

Xavier leaned in closer. "From what I hear, you're the court magician's apprentice."

Silence gripped the table. Chatter stopped. Silverware stilled. All eyes shifted to Ison.

"You're shitting me?" One thief who did more assassinating than thievery narrowed his eyes at Ison. "You're the court magician's apprentice?"

Ison regarded the room with a coldness that put Juniper on edge. Xavier glanced past Ison to her, his brow furrowed.

172

Finally, Ison answered, "I used to be."

"That means you're an apostate now," said a thief at the far end of the table.

Ison seemed to slump.

"Just like every mage in the Undercity," added Xavier, glaring at the thief; most knew him to be one such apostate. The thief looked away and found his creamed corn much more interesting.

"Xavier, you might take Ison to see Josephine," said Amery.

Ison glanced at Juniper, his gaze holding a dose more hopelessness that it had before.

She explained, "Josephine is the matriarch of a guild of mages."

"*A* guild? There's more than one?" Ison winced.

"Hers is the best." Xavier pointed at Juniper with his knife. "You should come too. Most of the Undercity has heard about your spat with the bounty hunters. Froze her blade solid. Still took a hit to the shoulder."

"I heard about that," said one of the older thieves. He had always been jealous of Juniper's skill and notoriety. "I bet that's how you've been getting all those jobs done. You've been cheating with magic?"

Juniper shrugged. "Does it matter?"

Xavier leaned forward to hear the thief's answer.

He frowned and didn't respond.

"I hear you've taken the job of assassinating the Captain of the City Watch." One of the assassins laughed. He used to be a watchman until he was caught stealing gold. He escaped prison and ended up in the Undercity. "Good luck with that."

Juniper smirked at him. "I suppose that means you cowered out of it?"

He chuckled. "I'm not an idiot. I'm not going after that job. It's a death sentence."

"I guess that means you pissed off Maddox just enough," said one of the thieves. "He didn't kill you outright, which means he wasn't totally pissed, but enough to send you to your own death. That's why I like him."

Juniper didn't engage. She knew the thieves well enough to know when they were fishing for information. Her eyes found a younger thief, maybe thirteen, a few seats down the table. He hadn't said anything so far, but he'd kept his blue eyes on Juniper.

"That's Ven," said Amery. "He's been with us for about a month and a half."

Ven gave Juniper a nod.

"He's a bit of an awkward kid," Amery said, loud enough that Ven heard, but he didn't engage. "But he's not gotten arrogant like the others. Keeps his mouth shut. I like him."

Ven's tan cheeks blushed.

❋

After dinner, Ison went back up to his room. Juniper followed him, but he shut himself into the guest room without a word.

"Is he all right?" came Xavier's voice. He climbed up the last of the stairs. "He seems a bit off."

"He's had a rough few months. He lost someone close to him, and with the Demon Crisis, a lot of people in the castle were wary of him." Juniper said no more; Ison's story wasn't hers to tell.

"Ah." Xavier sauntered a step closer. "Are you sure about Captain Tinnly?"

Juniper sighed. "No, but what other choice do I have?" If she just left, Maddox would hunt her down. "Besides, maybe no one else has been able to finish the job because no one else is as good as me."

Xavier chuckled. "I've missed you." His smile faded. "But, honestly, do you think you can handle it?"

Juniper shrugged. "Yes. For one thing, I've got my magic now. And secondly, I'm Juniper Thimble."

Xavier smirked, and Amery laughed as she came up the staircase.

"Give me a few days to get it together, and then you'll see," Juniper said.

Xavier went to his room at the end of the hall, and Juniper and Amery went into theirs. In a few days' time, she would have a plan of how she was going to assassinate the captain. She would prove to them all that Juniper Thimble had returned, remind the king of whom he had played with, and remind the whole damn city who she was and what she could do—nothing was impossible for her.

CHAPTER THIRTY-SIX

Juniper crumpled another piece of parchment and threw it into the trash can on the other side of the room. It bounced off the wall and landed inside, atop the other five letters she had failed to write.

"Want to tell me what you're trying to say?" Amery hadn't yet gotten out of bed. Juniper had started before dawn.

"No," Juniper said flatly. She started to write the sixth draft of the letter.

Amery rolled onto her side. "I've been told I'm great with words," she said, voice dripping with a courtesan's honey.

"No, thank you," Juniper said, though she mumbled. Amery had always been better with words than her, but this letter needed to be from Juniper, no one else.

She paused her quill a moment too long, and ink dripped onto the parchment. She let out a grievous sigh but kept going. She would likely throw this one away too. She scribbled her thoughts, one after another, but it didn't sound right. It sounded better than her first letter, but it still sounded stupid.

The sixth draft soon joined the others.

"Maybe you should try again later." Amery sat up and leaned onto her knees. Her black hair looked a wild mess, and her dark eyes were soft from sleep. One of her nightdress's straps fell down her shoulder, and Juniper had little wonder why she had been picked for the courtesan route; she oozed with that particular kind of sensual grace.

"How did your job hunt go?" Juniper asked, changing the subject.

Amery sighed through her nose. "Maddox has raised my price, and the clients are becoming fewer. I still have my faithful clients, but Maddox says I don't need any new ones. He keeps giving me thievery jobs instead."

"Hmm," Juniper said as she mulled over the blank parchment that would become her seventh draft. She decided that Amery was right and set aside her quill and corked the ink. She shouldn't waste paper. She would think about her letter and then come back with a fresh mind.

"Who are you writing to?" Amery asked.

Juniper pretended not to hear her and carefully arranged the supplies on the shelf.

Amery hummed. "You don't want me to know? Or are you embarrassed to say?" she asked, her voice low and clever. "Is it someone at the castle?"

Juniper felt her cheeks heat, and she kept her gaze on the parchment.

Amery stretched her arms over her head. "It's fine. If you change your mind about my help, let me know."

The two girls started the old morning routine. Because there was one bathing room on the third floor and everyone had to share it, Juniper and Amery had grown up using it at the same time. With the toilet curtained off from the wide vanity and the bath and shower behind another, two people could maneuver without stepping on each other. Amery washed up in the shower while Juniper washed her hands and face in the sink; her skin didn't feel up to a full bath, not without the soothing tonics and salts she had gotten used to.

"You've got a lot more scars now than you used to," Amery said.

Juniper's gaze fell to her reflection, to the scar that started on her collarbone and curved between her breasts and to her side, to the ten dot-like scars on her torso left by a demon's talons.

"They look wicked," Amery said. "In a good way."

"I won't disagree with you." Juniper dried her face and arms on a rough towel and pulled her tunic back on. "I'm pale enough that they're nearly invisible."

"Want to start moonbathing?"

"Moonbathing?"

"Yeah, it's like sunbathing but at night," Amery said. "For girls not used to the sun. The moonlight is less harsh on the skin than sunlight."

Juniper didn't give her a definite answer.

They found Xavier leaning against the wall outside, waiting.

He wore his pajamas and had clean clothes slung over his shoulder. Amery held the door open for him.

"Remember to keep your hair out of the drain," Xavier taunted as he walked inside. "I'm not unclogging it again."

The bathing room door closed, water gurgled through the pipes, and as Juniper and Amery headed toward the stairs, it felt like nothing had changed.

But it had. Juniper glanced to Ison's door. Still closed.

*

Juniper spent the day sleeping on and off. Amery came and went. Juniper left her bed only to visit the bathroom or the kitchen or to attempt another letter. The magelights faded into the dim indigo of night, and when Juniper opened her eyes again, buttery early morning light draped across the room.

"Good morning, sunshine," Amery said, yawning, as she tied her boots.

Juniper mirrored her yawn. Gods, she felt remarkably better.

Breakfast rarely happened at the keep, mostly because thieves and assassins kept late hours. Most wouldn't get out of bed until near midday. She and Amery walked downstairs for tea and found Maddox sitting alone at the dining table.

"Good morning," he said pleasantly. A cup of steaming tea sat in front of him. He was looking over reports. "Come, sit with me. It's not every day I'm joined for breakfast." He called one of the servants for another pot of tea.

The older woman nodded and scurried back into the kitchens.

"What is your plan for the day, Juniper?" Maddox asked casually, eyes on the reports.

"Xavier wants to take Ison to see Josephine, and he wants me to go with them," Juniper said.

Maddox's gaze slid from the report to her. "Because you're a mage?"

His gaze prickled against her skin. He'd heard about the incident with the bounty hunters then. No sense hiding it from him. She added, "I want her to teach me more about my magic. We all know that I'm better at sneaking and stealing, not...whatever it is mages do. Ison, on the other hand, is a masterful potion maker."

He considered her words.

The tea arrived, a steaming pot with two additional cups. No honey; it was an expense that Maddox didn't see as profitable. Juniper didn't complain; she drank the warm, soothing tea without sweetener. Though bitter, it warmed her insides.

"I want to see you in the basement this morning," Maddox said at last, returning to his reports. "I want to make sure you haven't gone soft since you left."

Left, as if she'd had a choice. She reminded herself who had sold her to the castle in the first place. She swallowed a gulp of the tea and nodded. "Ah, I see. You miss having a decent sparring partner?"

Maddox smirked. "I have missed that mouth of yours."

"Is mine not smart enough?" Amery asked, brow cocked.

"Yours is sweet, not smart." Maddox tipped his tea toward her. "Keep it that way, please."

Amery held Maddox's gaze, and Juniper felt something pass between them. Suddenly, she felt like an intruder on their breakfast.

Maddox has raised my price, and the clients are becoming fewer. Maddox says I don't need any new ones. He keeps giving me thievery jobs instead.

Juniper sipped her tea to hide her curious smile.

❋

Ison woke to a pounding. It took him a moment to realize it was not in his head, but at his door. He pushed himself onto his elbows, then swung his legs over the bedside. Gods, his body felt like wood.

The knocker got impatient, and the door swung open. The assassin—Xavier—stalked into the room, scowling. "Get up. We're leaving in an hour. You should wash." Xavier dropped a bundle onto the foot of the bed. Fresh clothes. "I'm not taking you anywhere looking like that."

Ison stood, picked up the bundle, and followed Xavier's pointed dagger to the bathing room. The steam welcomed him; someone else had used this room recently. Floral soaps lingered in the air. Hair lingered in the sink's drain. Ison set the clothes on the counter, shut the door, and ran himself a cold bath.

He saw himself in the mirror, a ragged, scrawny mage.

No, not a mage anymore. An apostate.

He would never be welcome in the castle again or the Marca. He would be killed on the spot. He would have knights hunting him down for the rest of his life. Without mercy. Without a trial.

Unless the apostate got his way first and dismantled the Order.

No, that was a horrible way of thinking. Out—Ison needed to get out of Duvane. But he couldn't do anything until Juniper killed that captain, and he couldn't leave without her. He could, but he knew he wouldn't make it very far. He had no mind for survival, and he couldn't leave his only friend behind, not after all she had done for him.

Ison turned away from his reflection and stripped. The cold water felt rejuvenating, though in the back of his mind, he thought to drown himself.

He didn't. He washed, dried, and donned the clothes that Xavier had brought him: a simple blue tunic, gray trousers, clean socks.

Ison finger-combed his dark brown curls. He needed his hair cut unless he grew it out and tied it back like he had seen other men do, but his hair never cooperated. It wanted to grow out instead of down.

He returned to the hall to find Xavier leaning against the door of his guest room. Guarding it.

"That's better," Xavier said, looking Ison up and down with those blue-gray eyes of his.

Ison bristled. Xavier's eyes unsettled him. It felt like he was peeling back his skin.

"Now, let's go. Josephine's an early riser, and she's more understanding in the morning." Xavier started toward the stairs and, with a graceful flick of his wrist, motioned for Ison to follow.

Ison glanced at Juniper's door as they passed; it was closed.

"Jun isn't coming with us," Xavier explained. "She'll be by later. She has something else to do first."

Ison didn't question it, though a knot in his chest tightened. He didn't like the idea of going into the Undercity without Juniper and with a stranger. Xavier was an assassin, a murderer. Then again, Ison reminded himself, he was a murderer too.

Xavier led Ison out of the keep and onto the street. This time, being well-rested, Ison could see it clearly. He walked a step behind Xavier, not letting the assassin out of his sight, but took in as much of the fabled Undercity as he dared.

He didn't know how he felt about it. He had always pictured the Undercity with dirty streets, shaded alleys, and lopsided market stalls—not a literal city underneath Rusdasin. He'd pictured the denizens as cutthroats and thugs, which he saw, but he also spotted normal people. Children. The Undercity wasn't as horrible as he had imagined.

He spotted the lawlessness, the drunk thugs and whores and black market stalls, but he felt the societal structure that had been built within that lawlessness. The City Watch couldn't get into the Undercity, but the Undercity didn't need the City Watch; it took care of itself.

Maybe the Undercity was nothing like Rusdasin. He didn't really know. He hadn't spent much time in the city at all. His experience with the city was limited to the apothecaries and greenhouses where Mason had sent him for ingredients.

Darkness crept over him at the memory.

Xavier led him onto a street lined with businesses and shops: bakeries wafted delicious breads and sweets; another shop sold teas and coffee beans; and half a dozen taverns roared with laughter and drunken song. The stench of piss, grog, coffee, and bread merged together into a strangely harmonious odor.

People lingered in open courtyards beside the taverns, drunk and sober, laughing, talking, shouting, and singing—unbiased and free. Was this what it would have been like had he grown up free of the Marca? Would he have been able to walk about the streets at his leisure?

Was this the world the apostate had in mind? A world without the Order.

They went down another street, narrower than the other, and it took Ison a moment to realize that the homely, cozy establishments on either side were brothels. Women and men of every age, hair color, skin color, and body size—so blatantly displayed, so blatantly enjoyed. Windows had been left open, doors were propped, and laughing and pleasure oozed through the air, along with a stench that Ison didn't want to think about.

Xavier fell back to walk beside Ison. "I take it you've not seen that many whorehouses?" His wicked, knowing smile made Ison feel foolish. "I thought you Marca mages were supposed to be easy about this sort of thing?"

They walked past a courtyard of silk pillows and throws, where barely-dressed girls and well-toned men chatted and flirted with clients.

Ison cleared his throat. "It's not that. I've never seen it so displayed before. So accepted."

"Ah, that's right. The upsiders like to pretend that they are more sophisticated than to partake in a whore's company. Most of them do. I've seen a few of the lists the madams keep." Xavier let out a low whistle. "You'd be surprised."

Ison had little doubt that he would, but he didn't inquire.

They continued through the business district. Ison hadn't realized how large the Undercity was. There were so many people living in the Undercity. He saw entire families, young people, old people, and everyone in between.

This was where Juniper had grown up. If he had grown up in the Undercity, what would have happened to him? Would he have grown into an assassin like Xavier? A courtesan like Amery? A thief? Between the three of them, he would be best at being a whore.

He'd always heard how unintelligent the people from the Undercity were, how they were rude, ruthless, and worthless, addicts and killers, and yet none of the people around him seemed the worst of Rusdasin. None seemed anything of the sort. He spotted some who did, the people sunk in alleys, bleary-eyed and hopeless, but for the most part, the Undercity was just another thriving part of Rusdasin.

Seeing it all loosened something in his chest, something that he hadn't realized had been so tight, so deafening.

The people here were just that—people.

CHAPTER THIRTY-SEVEN

A cloud of despair had descended on Castle Bradburn. It filtered through every window and draft, dampening even the skies outside. Summer rain had kept the courtyards and grounds muddy and humid. Rain splattered against the walls in uneven spurts. The wind howled and whined.

Reid stood on guard in Adrian's bedroom.

One of the royal healer's apprentices worked on Adrian. He held his hands over Adrian's body, pale green magic glowing from his palms. The poison lurked within Adrian, and without an antidote, all the healers could do was stop it from reaching his head and his heart. A healer stood at his bedside day and night, keeping the poison back, while the royal healer and the poison expert worked tirelessly to identify the poison. Once he identified it, an antidote could be made.

Adrian, while deathly pale, looked as though he slept. His chest rose and fell gently. As Reid approached the bedside, the healer gave no mind. He worked on, concentration never faltering. Reid looked at the face of his prince, his friend, and his chest tightened at the thought of his death—a death Reid should have prevented. If something happened to Adrian, if no cure could be found—if no cure was found in time—it would be Reid's fault.

Voices sounded in the corridor. The door opened and closed, and armored footsteps made their way across the sitting room and to the bedroom. Destry appeared in the doorway and nodded to Reid. "Any change?" Destry whispered.

"No," Reid replied.

Destry came to stand beside Reid and looked upon his prince. Guilt darkened his eyes—he blamed himself for not being there when it happened. Reid understood. He felt the same guilt; only, he had been there, and he had not stopped it.

"You are relieved," said Destry.

Reid nodded. He had taken the early morning shift of Adrian's guard; Destry had the afternoons and evenings. Isaac stood guard at night. Between the three of them and a dozen Royal Guard, no one would get to Adrian.

"Thank you," Reid said. He made his way back to his chambers. He had more studying to do. His wards were still weak.

If Adrian didn't make it—

No. Reid couldn't think like that. The healer would find a solution. Adrian would recover, and the assassin behind it would be hanged.

His heart squeezed tighter. Had Juniper honestly tried to kill him? His gut told him no, yet the evidence looked him in the eye. Her name signed the note. The binding spell had been broken, Adrian had been poisoned, and Fowler had discovered Juniper's magic—all within the same day. He refused to believe those three events mere coincidence. Someone had planned it. Not just someone—their mysterious apostate.

Or had Ison been the apostate all along? Had he used this to finally free himself? But, if Ison had done it, why had he waited around for the knights to find him? The knights had found Ison and Juniper in her chambers. It made sense, yet it didn't.

A thought slammed into his chest—that night she had fallen and a cut on her hand had transferred to Adrian, what had she been doing? Had she slipped something into a bottle of his favorite wine?

"Reid!"

He halted. Penet ran down the corridor, his youthful face full of panic and fear. At once, Reid's panic rose.

"What is it?" he demanded. Adrian?

Penet reached him and bent over, hands on his knees. "The king asked me to fetch you," Penet gasped between breaths. "You're needed in the throne room."

Reid clasped his fingers around the hilt of his sword on reflex. Wanted in the throne room? "Has something gone wrong?"

Penet gasped, his eyes wide. "They've arrested Juniper Thimble."

The ground underneath his feet shifted.

He walked as fast as he could without running. Blood rushed through his ears. He saw the corridor in front of him—all else faded from his vision. He arrived at the massive doors to the throne room, typically open, now closed. The fully armored Royal Guard who stood on either side of the door looked him over in their unfeeling, silent assessment, just like his uncle taught them. They opened the doors for him. Reid stepped through, heart in his throat.

A number of City Watch and Royal Guard stood inside the throne room. They stood in a semicircle around a girl. Between the armored bodies, he spotted auburn hair and slumped shoulders. She'd been chained. Reid stood back from the main horde; he took a stance among the Royal Guard along the wall. Penet arrived shortly after him and stood by him.

Reid couldn't take his eyes off the girl. Her baggy clothes hid her body. Her slumped posture and wild hair made it hard to see anything past her pale skin.

The door behind the throne opened, and King Bradburn stepped through with enough authority for the guards beside Reid to take a breath and straighten their shoulders. The king had lost weight and sleep these past few days. Shadows lined his eyes, though he powdered his face to try to hide them. His cheeks had thinned.

King Bradburn looked to the girl on the floor, then to Reid. The girl didn't so much as flinch.

"Squire Sandpiper," said the king, "come."

All eyes in the room shifted to Reid. He held himself properly as he started toward the king. His heart thumped louder with each step. He didn't dare look at the girl.

She would be a dead girl this time. No offer. No chance of redemption. The king would send her to the gallows, and she would be dead before sundown. He didn't know if he had it in him to watch.

Reid came to a stop before the king.

"Tell me," said the king, his voice as commanding as it had ever been. "You know her better than I. Is this her?" He motioned toward the girl. "I will let you identify or dismiss her."

His heart fell. King Bradburn was deferring to him—to either let her go or send her to her death. The king knew Juniper well enough to pick her out of a crowd, yet he had given Reid the task. A test of loyalty? The king knew what had happened between Juniper and him; everyone in the castle knew by now.

His foolish heart felt ashamed. Reid schooled his face into calm neutrality. He steeled himself against unruly emotions unbecoming of a knight. He turned and set his gaze on the girl.

His heart heaved a heavy sigh of relief, though he didn't show it. The girl kneeling on the floor had coppery brown hair, pale skin, and blue eyes, but she was not Juniper Thimble. Her pale blue eyes lacked Juniper's cleverness; her skin was gaunt and shallow where Juniper's was supple; her posture gleamed hopelessness, not Juniper's arrogant swagger.

"It is not her," Reid said. And the king would have known immediately.

The king nodded. He said to the room, "It is not her, dismiss her."

Two watchmen hauled the girl to her feet, chains clinking, and half dragged her out of the throne room. Within the chaos of sudden sound, the king whispered to Reid, "Stay behind."

Reid stood as the City Watch left, as the Royal Guard followed behind, and as Penet lingered, then left.

"Follow me." The king led Reid into the king's meeting room behind the throne room. Unlike the others, it hadn't been luxuriously adorned. The stone walls were bare, the wooden table plain, the chairs sturdy. Once inside, the king asked, "Are you relieved or frustrated?"

Reid hesitated to answer. "Both, Your Majesty. Relieved that I do not have to watch her execution and frustrated that she is still out there."

The king folded his arms behind his back. "I understand. However, she must be found and made to answer for what has happened. I cannot grant her a pardon when the city believes her to be an assassin. I would have riots of shopkeepers and councilors and gods know who else. The council is already up in arms that I kept her in the castle without their knowledge." He scoffed. "I can't even invite a guest into my own house."

Reid nodded.

After Adrian had fallen ill, rumors that Juniper Thimble had tried to assassinate him had flown through the city. Her fifty thousand gold bounty had helped those rumors along considerably.

King Bradburn took a seat at the table. He sighed, and his age became more apparent. His voice softened but rang with urgency. "Reid, this is not the only reason I asked you here. There is something else I must ask of you."

"Of course, Your Majesty." Then Reid's heart leaped into his throat. A king's quest?

"I want you to accompany my new royal herbalist to the Royal Greenhouses. Adrian is in need of tonics, and I don't want anything to happen. Word has spread about his illness, and I do not want anyone to disturb the healing process."

Reid tried his best not to let his disappointment show. Not a king's quest, a king's *request*. Still, he couldn't refuse. "Of course, Your Majesty. I will make sure nothing happens to the herbalist."

"Good. Go to the Alchemist's chambers an hour after midday. He will be waiting for you." The king stood and set his hand on Reid's shoulder. "I told him I would find the best guard I had, and I believe you are among the best, Reid."

But not good enough for a quest, Reid thought bitterly. He bowed his head. "Thank you, Your Majesty."

CHAPTER THIRTY-EIGHT

Ison followed Xavier through the business district of the Undercity and into the market. He gawked as they passed stalls of jewelry, food, enchanted items, books, clothes, trinkets—anything he could possibly want or need had a place somewhere in the market. *Black market*, he reminded himself.

"Ison," came Xavier's growl, and he snapped to attention, thinking he had done something wrong. Xavier held his piercing blue-gray stare on him, then said plainly, "I have a few questions for you."

Ison nodded. "Okay."

"About the Marca."

Ison's skin pricked at the mention, but he nodded. "Okay."

Xavier began his interrogation about the Marca, the magic learned there, the classes, the teachers, the knights. Ison answered his questions simply and honestly; he had nothing to hide. Xavier seemed eager to learn anything about the Marca. His cruel eyes glittered with each question and answer.

"They teach everyone the same for a while," Ison told him. "We learn the basics of control, the laws of the Marca, the elements of magic, but we also learn what any other student would learn: history, art, literature, mathematics. After a mage has cleared the first level of learning, they can focus on their element. After they clear the second level of learning, they can focus more on an industry of their choosing. I chose potion making and herbalism."

"What do the others study?"

"There's plenty," Ison said. "A mage can study to become a librarian or historian within the archives, enchanters, teachers, healers. Some train to become battlemages in the king's army."

Question after question came about magic, and then Xavier broke the pattern. "So, tell me." His drawl fit his leisurely, predatorial stroll. "You and Jun are friends?"

"Yes."

"Have you fucked her?"

Ison blinked, sure that he had misheard. Xavier repeated the question. A glint flashed in his blue-gray eyes, and Ison had the feeling that Xavier would know if he lied.

So he didn't. "Yes," he answered.

Xavier's hand twitched to his side, toward a hidden dagger, Ison assumed.

Ison added, "Just once. It was more of a spur of the moment." Should he have counted the first time? He hadn't touched her then. He decided not to tell Xavier about it. "I apologize if there was something between the two of you."

Xavier let out a dark chuckle. "Nonsense. She's my sister."

Ison blinked; Xavier and Juniper were siblings? They looked nothing alike. Juniper had the pale complexion of the north, whereas Xavier had dark skin and dust brown hair.

The assassin chuckled, but the glint in his eye didn't go away. "We're not related by blood. Jun and I were in the same crop of children sold in the market." He pointed his thumb toward the other side of the Undercity. "It's tradition that children brought in together are considered siblings."

The child market. Ison shuddered. Juniper had mentioned it only once, and he hadn't pressed her for details. He didn't ask Xavier about it either, not because Ison didn't want to bring up unpleasant memories for the assassin, but because he didn't want to know any more about it than he already did. He had enough of his own horrors to deal with.

Xavier continued, "Tell me, what happened while Jun was enslaved to the crown? Did they treat her well?"

"As far as I know, they did," Ison answered. "She had spacious rooms in the Royal Chambers and had plenty of food."

"Did they use her as a whore?" Xavier growled.

Ison met Xavier's stare, and he saw it: a protectiveness for his sister. Ison admired that about the assassin. He was not just an assassin and a mage and a thief, but also a brother looking out for his sister.

"No, they did not. The prince, as far as Juniper has told me, had a lover. Juniper disguised herself as his lover to fool others. He didn't pursue a relationship." Ison hesitated, and Xavier's eyes narrowed. "The squire, however..."

Xavier growled at the news.

"They fell in love," Ison admitted. "But he is a squire in the Order. When he found out about her magic, it ended." Badly, but Xavier didn't need to know that.

"And it would never work out," Xavier finished for him. "That's why she's so..." He hummed the word he didn't have.

Ison supplied, "Heartbroken."

Xavier nodded.

Ison understood. He had pushed off the word as long as he could, but...he felt it too—for Clara—not because he had loved her, but because she had trusted him, and he had killed her. He felt it for all the people he'd killed, for all the families he had torn apart, for all the hearts he had broken with his deeds.

"You got into the castle to see her," Ison said. He hadn't been there, but he had heard about the assassin who had broken into the prince's chambers.

"I did," Xavier said proudly. "Maddox wanted to know what Jun was up to, and he sent me. He knew I'd get inside without trouble. He had expected her back before then, and he was getting worried. Oh, and it pissed her off too." He grinned wickedly.

The rest of the walk through the market was filled with questions about the Marca, the castle, and Juniper's stay there. Ison answered them all as well as he could, leaving out the details that he would rather let Juniper explain, like Reid. The stalls shrank from sturdy counters to flimsy boards perched over barrels. The clever-eyed merchants became beady-eyed and hunched. The items became less legal, their purpose and worth more and more obscured. They had entered a dangerous part of the market.

They passed a quiet stall run by a strange little woman. Bottles lined the wooden shelves and were stacked on the floor. Some held swirling dark smoke, some were full of what looked like mud, and others held nothing at all yet were corked.

"Back so soon?" the little woman asked, her voice thin and chirpy. Her wrinkled mouth turned upward into the most hideous grin Ison had ever seen.

"Not today," Xavier said calmly, and he walked past without another word.

The little woman's grin fell into an equally hideous frown.

Once past, Xavier whispered to Ison, "Best poison dealer in the Undercity but mad as hell. She also makes this drink that will have you floating."

Ison walked with Xavier through the strange corner of the market, and they finally came out to the other side, into a neighborhood of stone buildings and courtyards that looked the same as the one where Maddox lived—the other side of the Undercity.

"There are a few guilds of mages here." Xavier gestured down the stone street. "The best is run by a woman named Josephine. She is one of the few mages who escaped the Marca."

"What does a guild of mages do?" Ison thought of the guild Juniper and Xavier came from that stole and killed.

"It depends on the guild," Xavier answered.

They passed three shady broad-shouldered men. Each wore an assortment of leather armor. One of them sneered at Ison, and the other two followed suit. Xavier casually put his hand on the hilt of his exposed dagger and shifted his jacket in the process, revealing the plethora of weapons on his person. The men glanced at him, then away.

"Mercenaries," Xavier spat, "looking for easy prey. That's why you don't walk the Undercity alone unless you're prepared."

"And I suppose I'm the easy prey?"

Xavier lifted a brow, then shifted his gaze over Ison. "Yes, you are. You walk like you expect to get robbed. Don't slouch so. Walk like you're supposed to be here and you'll slit the throat of anyone who says otherwise."

Ison thought of all the people he had seen; he hadn't seen many walking alone. He nodded and tried to mimic the way that Xavier walked, but when Xavier let out a humorous chuckle, he returned to his slouched posture.

"Just don't go outside without someone with you," Xavier said. "But, like I was saying, some guilds sell their magic; others use it to keep themselves sustained and out of the way. Some operate just like Maddox's guild and are willing to accept payment for stolen goods, assassinations, mercenary work, and other odd jobs that people don't want other people to know about. Some sell spotty enchanted blades and questionable runes."

"Really?" Ison asked.

"Is that surprising?"

"Enchantments and runes are heavily monitored by the Order." The Marca knew about every enchanted weapon that had been made within the past five hundred years, knew the buyer, the current owner, and location.

Xavier scoffed. "Of course they do. Wouldn't want someone to slip through their control, would we?"

"In order for a mage to sell anything, they have to be approved by the Order and then the Market Association and then reapply for a license every year." Enchanting weapons and items was highly guarded and scrutinized, and only a select few mages would be allowed to do it. Even the potions he had sold were marked and noted, each one accounted for.

Xavier grumbled, "Market Association. What foolishness. The upsiders are so concerned with rules and order, it makes me a bit sick. They're so worried about missing out on a few copper pieces. Come on, Josephine's guild isn't that much farther. With luck, she'll invite us for breakfast."

They turned onto a quaint street, and Ison forced himself to ask the question that had been rolling around in his head since that morning. "Xavier, why are you helping me?"

"Because you're Jun's friend," he said simply. He turned toward Ison, chin proud, gait easy with grace. The magelights gleamed in his strange eyes. "That is how the Undercity runs. We protect our own. If someone messes with Jun, they mess with the whole guild. Same goes for me, and the same goes for you now."

"But—"

"You're one of us, Ison. Like it or not."

Whatever argument Ison had, vanished at Xavier's matter-of-fact tone. The assassin paused and lifted a brow at him, daring him to try. Ison didn't know what to think. Xavier, who had only known him for two days, was willing to include him into the folds of friendship? That soon? That easily?

"And," Xavier said, "I expect you to do the same for any of us."

Ison deflated. "I'm not a strong fighter," he confessed.

"Then brew them a potion, and make sure they choke on it," Xavier said, as if it were the easiest thing in the world. "Jun mentioned you were brilliant with potions. I take that to mean you're also decent with poisons?"

Ison hesitated, then nodded.

Xavier gave him a wicked, knowing grin.

Ison followed the assassin down a well-kept street lined with townhouses of gray stone. Most were homes. Many had been decorated with wooden shutters, shingled awnings, and porches. If not for the rocky ceiling, Ison might have thought them walking down a street on the surface. Xavier took Ison to a mansion-like house with real grass and bushes. Magelights lit up the yard like tiny suns, four of them flooding the yard and much of the street with a cool blue light.

"They're enchanted to mirror the light from above ground," Xavier said. "Looks like it's still early enough for breakfast."

A gentle hum came from the house: hushed voices, the clatter of pots and pans, and giggling. It reminded him, strangely enough, of the Marca. A wooden fence lined the property, but as Xavier and Ison approached the gate, he felt something else—not just a fence, but a ward.

Xavier paused at the open fence gate. "Feel that?" he asked.

Ison nodded. "It's warded."

"Anyone with ill-intent would burst into flames the moment they touched the ward," Xavier explained. "And Jo's got a list of people that aren't allowed in. Luckily, I'm not one of them."

Did Ison harbor ill-intent? He didn't think so. Still, as Xavier started through the barrier, Ison's stomach dropped. He followed Xavier through—a sizzle started on his foot, and as he moved through the ward, it zapped upward along his skin, his bones, his hair. It took him a moment to shake it off.

"Got me the first time too." Xavier grinned wide, showing his white teeth.

He tugged Ison toward the porch. On this side of the ward, Ison could smell the dirt of the yard, the dew on the grass, the warmth of the vegetation. He had the urge to throw himself into the grass just to feel it on his skin.

Halfway up the walkway, the double doors to the house opened. A woman with gray-streaked black hair and dark skin stood in the doorway. She wore robes of yellow and green, and she regarded Ison with a matronly stare. She placed one hand on her hip; her right sleeve hung flat against her, straight from the shoulder.

Ison's heart skipped a beat, then another. Xavier's words rang in his head, *She's one of the few who escaped the Marca.* Everyone in the Marca had heard the legend of the Jantian mage who had cut off her own arm to escape. The knights had nicked the back of her hand with Mage's Bane—her offense varied from story to story—and when the knights thought her dead, she cut off her arm.

Ison gawked at the one-armed Jantian mage before him. Could it possibly be the same woman from the stories?

"Josephine." Xavier nudged Ison. "Look who I found."

The older woman looked Ison up and down. The lines on her face suggested she frowned more than she smiled. After a moment, she let out a stiff grunt. "He looks like a Marca mage," she said, her voice velvety and stern, "trained to be passive and useless."

Ison nodded. "That sounds about right."

Josephine's lips twitched upward. "You passed the ward, and you're not a pile of ashes, so that means you're decent. All right, come in."

She stepped back into the house, and Xavier pushed Ison forward. He stumbled up the steps and into the foyer. His eyes adjusted, and he gasped—every bit of wall space in the foyer had been taken up by bookshelves, and every single shelf was packed with books. The air smelled of a flower garden in spring, like pollen and nectar.

"This way," came Josephine's voice.

Xavier pulled Ison out of his reverie and said, "Stop gawking, you're making me look bad."

Ison stumbled into a cozy parlor. A teapot sat on the table, along with three cups and a plate of cookies. Xavier followed him inside. With a wave of her hand, Josephine closed the parlor doors and took a seat in a well-used plush chair. She motioned to the chairs across from her. Ison sat down and Xavier slouched in the chair next to him. The teapot lifted itself and poured an equal amount in three cups.

"Sugar?" Josephine asked.

"A small amount," Ison answered.

"No, thank you," said Xavier.

The little spoon in the sugar bowl lifted itself and dumped its contents into one of the cups. The two cups lifted off the tray and floated to Ison and Xavier. A third floated to Josephine.

"Thank you, ma'am," Ison said, the warmth surging into his fingers from the china.

Josephine laughed, a blast of sound. She repeated, "'Ma'am.' You can drop the formalities, mage. You're not in the Marca anymore." She sipped her tea and held her dark brown eyes on Ison. "By the look on your face, I take it you know who I am."

Ison nodded, and his guilt increased.

"That's fine," she said. "But I want to know who you are. What in Bala's name has forced the court magician's apprentice into the Undercity?"

He gawked at her.

She hummed. "Word gets around. I've plenty of ears in the Undercity. Now, tell me everything. Don't leave out the dirty details."

Ison looked down into his tea. "It's not entirely my story to tell."

"Then tell me your side of it."

She wouldn't relent. He saw the determination in her eyes, not unlike the way Mason used to stare at him, like he already knew the answer. So Ison told the one-armed woman everything.

CHAPTER THIRTY-NINE

Juniper collapsed to the training ring's wooden floor, panting. Sweat trickled along her scalp, down her spine. She rolled onto her hands and knees and gasped for breath. Maddox panted, but not as heavily as she. He broke his stance and leaned against the wall of the training ring, wooden sword held lazily at his side. Lucky for her, he had wanted to practice with wood, not steel.

"You're not as rusty as I thought you might be," Maddox said after a while, his tone bored.

"I trained." She wobbled back to her feet.

"They allowed you to train?" Maddox asked, brow raised.

She nodded. "Under supervision. Otherwise, I was trapped in my room. I might have lost my mind had I not had access to the Royal Library."

He smirked. "I suppose I shouldn't be too hard on you. It's not every day one gets a free vacation in the castle. I hear the food is exceptional."

"It was." A vacation. Is that what he thought of it? It had been, she supposed—a break from herself, from constant jobs, from the Undercity.

Of course, she didn't know how much of her stay Maddox knew about. What had the king told him in order to get him to agree to send two of his best thieves to the castle? How much had the king paid?

Juniper picked up her practice sword—Maddox had thrown it across the ring with a clever disarming maneuver. She straightened, and her eyes drifted to the far side of the basement, where Maddox kept his small furnace; above it, on the wall, hung the brand.

A hand touched her back—she jumped. Maddox's hand. She hadn't even heard him move. His hand slid down to the brand, his brand, that he had seared into her flesh when she was twelve. The day she had given him her life and become part of his guild.

Reid had promised to keep her at the castle, to not let her return to Maddox. A lie.

Maddox's hand flattened against the brand, warm and steady.

"And now you're fighting with magic," Maddox said, a tilt in his tone. "I hear those mercenaries were on their way back to a client to collect payment. That client sent me a thank you note and half of what they would've paid the mercenaries."

"I didn't know," she said.

"And you still exceed," he said warmly. "It's more than enough to handle room and board for you while you plan your assassination of the captain."

Ah, there it was—his angle.

"You've been a mage the whole time," he said, that same tilt, curiosity lined with anger.

"I didn't want to be a mage," she said, her voice small. His hand remained on her back.

"But you want to learn it now?"

"It's a part of me, always has been," Juniper said. "I want to control it like Xavier can. It is a powerful tool at my disposal, and I've been ignoring it. I want to hone it."

Maddox hummed affectionately. His finger stroked the jagged spiral of his brand, a barely-there pressure on the deadened skin. "That's my girl, always thinking ahead."

"I was thinking more of daggers made entirely of ice," she said. "Gone when I don't need the extra weight or visible weapons, there when I need something sharp, and nonexistent when the Watch is looking for murder weapons."

He laughed; it echoed off the stone walls. "That's my girl." He stepped halfway in front of her. This close, she could see the finer lines around his mouth and eyes. "I have a favor to ask of you, Juniper."

Her chest squeezed; was this a test? She held in her surprise. "Oh?"

"I have a few errands to run this morning, and I want you to accompany me." His words were simple, but she saw something else in his eyes, heard it underneath his words.

"Okay," she said.

His smile grew wider. "Freshen up. We leave in half an hour."

✳

Juniper's anxiety grew as she washed the sweat from her skin and braided her damp hair over her shoulder. What could Maddox want from her? The only time Maddox personally took her anywhere was to find new weapons, fit her for better armor, or meet a client. She needed no new weapons or armor, and he wasn't giving her any jobs until she assassinated the captain. So what could he possibly want with her?

As she dressed and made her way down to his office, she ran through the only logical option. It had to have something to do with the captain or a way to kill him. Maybe he wanted her to have the best weapons when she did it.

Maddox was standing in the foyer, talking to Ven, the young thief. At the sight of Juniper, Ven's cheeks reddened. Maddox didn't say anything about it until he and Juniper were on the street.

"Ven is taken with you," he said.

"I noticed. He's a bit young for me, don't you think?"

Maddox laughed. "When I brought him to the keep, the first words out of his mouth were, 'You're Juniper Thimble's guild master.' I admit, I was flattered. I knew you would be too."

Juniper allowed a smile. "I am."

Maddox guided her toward the market. "I caught him trying to sneak up to your room yesterday," he said casually. "The others have told him that I nearly had you trained as a courtesan. Poor boy was blushing like fire."

The conversation remained light as they made their way through the market. Juniper kept an eye out for their reason, and as they made their way deeper into the market, to the far side, the ugly truth started to form.

They were headed to the child market.

Her legs started to shake. Her hands started to tremble. Maddox, if he noticed, pretended not to. The child market was nothing special—a narrow wooden scaffold they used as a stage and a few buildings to house the children before and after. Maddox guided her around the empty stage where the children would stand and be auctioned off like cattle, to the building behind it.

"What's going on?" Juniper finally asked. Despite her churning unease, she teased, "Are you sending me back?"

"Of course not," Maddox said. "I've been invited to a private meeting."

Of the guild masters.

Juniper held herself as steady as she could and followed Maddox into the building. They entered a small foyer lit by a single lantern. The stone walls were empty. A man in mismatched leather and daggers lounged against the wall. At the sight of Maddox, a grim smile stretched over his lips, and he pushed off the wall.

A bandit, a child seller. Juniper folded her arms over her chest to hide her shaking hands.

"Maddox, welcome," said the slaver. "It's a pleasure."

Maddox held his face passive, bored. "I've come to see the new stock."

"Right this way." The slaver eagerly gestured them onto the next room.

Maddox followed him, and Juniper kept a step behind. She could think of a hundred places she'd rather be. They entered a long hall. Tables and chairs had been pushed to the sides, and at the far end stood three children. Another slaver stood by them, a switch in his hands. Juniper felt the beginnings of a dark tunnel surround her. She remembered the switch, the sting across her shoulders.

Maddox sauntered over to the children, Juniper a step behind. One boy was pale, one boy was tan, and the girl had the dark skin of Janti. Her curly hair fell to her shoulders, tangled and matted in places. She had been crying. She met Juniper's stare, and her dark eyes shone with terror—no doubt she had heard what happens to girls like her.

And then Juniper knew why Maddox had asked her to come: to remind her where she had come from, of who had pulled her out of the lineup.

To remind her that he owned her.

"Juniper," Maddox asked, his voice clear. "Any of the crop strike your interest?"

She blinked at him, then at the children. All three were staring at her. The pale boy looked like he might try to bite her. The tan boy looked weary, confused. The girl held her face expressionless, curious, yet underlined with fear.

"You're asking me?" Juniper said.

He nodded. "It's been a while since I added to the guild, and I could use more hands like yours."

Did he mean once she had left? He wanted her to pick out her own replacement?

Her eyes returned to the girl. Her face hadn't changed.

"I wanted to ask you first, of course," came the slaver's sickly-sweet tone from the other side of the room. "I'm afraid there's a limit of one per customer today."

"Which one?" Maddox asked Juniper.

She swallowed. Three lives stood in front of her. Three futures—and she was to choose the future for one of these children. The pale boy looked mad. The tan boy had the shoulders of a brute. She met the dark eyes of the girl. There, under the fear, something like relentlessness looked back at her.

"You girl," Juniper said, "What's your name?"

"Blythe," said the girl, her voice small but powerful.

Maddox glanced at Juniper. "Your choice?"

"Her," Juniper said.

"We'll take the girl," Maddox said to the slaver.

"Excellent choice," came the slaver's greedy chime.

Juniper held the girl's gaze, and as Maddox stepped aside to work out the payment, she extended her hand to the girl. Blythe gingerly stepped forward and placed her small, delicate hand into Juniper's. Another guild master came in, and another slaver started over the same greeting.

Juniper led Blythe back to the open air of the Undercity. "How old are you, Blythe?"

"Nine."

"Where are you from?"

"Nowhere."

"Nowhere?" Juniper asked.

"My father owed bad people money," Blythe said. "He sold me because we were poor."

"He sold you?"

"He had four sons and three daughters," she said. "My sisters were prettier and could find husbands, he said. My brothers could work the fields. I was the extra mouth."

Juniper hummed her disapproval at the parenting. "Tell me, Blythe, what do you think happens next?"

"Are you going to teach me how to be a whore?"

"No," Juniper said.

Blythe's brows twitched; the only sign of emotion on her youthful face.

Juniper bent to look the girl in the eye. "I'm going to teach you how to defend yourself, how to fight, and how to make sure that people don't take advantage of you anymore."

"You're Juniper Thimble," said Blythe.

"I am."

"Those men were talking about you, saying how you're the best the Undercity has."

Juniper shrugged. "I might be that too."

"And you're going to teach me to be like you?"

"No," Juniper said.

Blythe blinked.

"I'm going to teach you to be better."

CHAPTER FORTY

Josephine didn't say a word as Ison spoke. He told her everything that had happened between when he became the court magician's apprentice and his escape into the Undercity with Juniper Thimble. He hadn't anticipated telling her everything, but the words started, and he couldn't stop. They tumbled from his lips, his mind, his heart—his guilt and his shame. Everything that he had done, everyone he had butchered, he confessed to Josephine.

He held his gaze on his trembling hands, afraid to see her thoughts in her eyes. Beside him, Xavier sat still as stone.

Ison could feel the assassin's blue-gray stare, its coldness, its ruthlessness. Ison couldn't bring himself to look at Xavier in fear that he would find sympathy or, worse, pity. Xavier had killed—maybe more than Ison—and he didn't want to be told what he felt was ignorant or foolish. In the corner of his vision, he could see his dark hands, hands that had killed. They looked no different than Ison's hands. That terrified him.

When he finished, the room's silence pressed in on him, drowning him. He gathered the shattered bits of his courage and met Josephine's gaze. The older woman beheld him, her deep brown gaze not betraying any emotion.

Xavier remained still.

Ison felt tears pushing on his eyes, but he refused to cry in front of two strangers. He sought that darkness within, that calming nothingness, and the urge to cry evaporated. He cupped his hands around his teacup and took a drink; it hadn't cooled. Magic. His fingers grazed a rune carved into the bottom of the teacup. Without the knights and overseers, what other sort of applications did these Undercity mages use magic for?

Xavier shifted in the chair beside him, but Ison kept his eyes on the tea.

"That is interesting," Josephine said, her voice strong and curious. "You say this apostate spoke to you and used your body as a puppet?"

Ison nodded.

Josephine leaned forward and set her arm across her knees. She frowned, and the lines beside her mouth deepened. "That is dark magic. It is not a magic we use here in my keep or in the Marca. For good reason. To enter another's mind without permission is strictly forbidden, has been for thousands of years. Even the Iluvin forbade it."

Ison knew that, yet he had let it happen. If he had done something sooner, told Mason or someone—even if it would have gotten him killed by the Order, he might have saved those people.

Or, as Juniper had said, the apostate would have used someone else. Those people would have died one way or another. But that didn't make him feel any better.

Xavier leaned forward and whispered. "Do you think it could be connected to those Dual Fangs?"

Josephine's stare shifted; the look in her eye became one of calculation, and it made Ison feel small. It reminded him of Mason's clinical, wizened stare. "It's possible," she whispered back.

Ison wanted to ask who or what these Dual Fangs were, but he hadn't the energy. He wanted to return to his guest room at Maddox's keep and lie there until the numbness went away, until it didn't hurt so bad to think about things.

"Ison," Josephine said. "You are welcome to stay here rather than with Maddox. All mages are welcome under my roof as long as they follow my rules. I know how much of a busybody Maddox is, and he'll have you working for him before sundown tomorrow to earn your room and board. Gods only know what he'll dig up for you to do."

"And if I stay here?" Ison met her gaze with that reckless fearlessness the darkness gave him.

Her brown eyes softened into something motherly but no less strict. "Mages under my roof are expected to earn their keep but by chores: cleaning, cooking, potion brewing, tending to the gardens, that sort of thing. I would have you using your skills to teach. You're a noted herbalist, I've heard. I might have you working with the potions we sell. Your knowledge in the art could be useful."

He swallowed. "I'm not a good teacher."

"You specialize in herbs and potions, and we haven't had anyone with your level of knowledge in a decade. You would be valuable to us, Ison." She stood. Her empty sleeve swung forward and back. "I will not make you stay, but I will provide a room for you. Now, if you boys will excuse me, I've got a few chores to tend to myself."

She left them sitting in the parlor, and through the open doors, Ison heard the chattering of the keep—voices, footsteps, and doors. The hum of life. Not unlike the Marca, only less clanking.

"I recommend you stay here and take her up on that offer," Xavier said lazily. He sat sideways and slung his arm over the back of the chair, his leg over the arm. He looked like a cat assessing his prey, considering the best time to pounce. "She's right about Maddox. I can guarantee he's already got a few jobs lined up for you to earn your keep as he'll call it. It could be anything from running errands, poison making, courtesan work, or an assassination. If you're not feeling up to any of those, take Josephine's offer. Maddox won't hold it against you."

"I thought Maddox was supposed to be possessive?" Ison asked.

Xavier's brow twitched.

"Jun said Maddox would send someone after her if we left without his permission."

Understanding smoothed Xavier's face. "That's because he owns Jun. He hasn't branded you or invested in your career. You can do what you'd like."

"He owns you too?"

Xavier hesitated, a subtle crinkle formed in his brow, and then he nodded. "Yes." Meaning a brand marked his back too.

Ison let out a long sigh, tossing his options over in his mind. "It doesn't matter. I'm barely good at anything. I'd mess up any job either one gave me."

Xavier chuckled and sat forward with deadly grace. "Yet you're good enough to become the court magician's apprentice." His piercing gaze became serious. "Mages end up in the Undercity because they fear the Marca. Some come here on their own, some escape, some are freed by other mages. Some are brought down here as children to be sold, and Josephine buys them. They're from all over the kingdom, from all walks of life, but they are all mages who want freedom."

Ison didn't have the words; the intensity of Xavier's stare stole his breath. He looked like he might strangle Ison then and there.

"The mages who grow up in the Undercity have no formal training other than what we learn from ourselves," Xavier said. "Josephine runs a few stalls in the market for healers and health potions. There will always be sick people and injured people coming to her for help. The better those potions are, the better they work, correct?"

Ison nodded.

"Josephine is without a potion master. You are a potion master without a job," Xavier said, his tone pointed. "The answer is obvious and simple."

Ison sat there underneath Xavier's glare for a long moment, letting those words seep into his thoughts. He stole his attention from the assassin and looked to the doorway Josephine had left open. Beyond it, he stared at the towering bookshelves, thick with tomes, some so old and faded, they looked held together by magic.

After a moment of silence, Ison turned his gaze back to Xavier. "Why are you with Maddox instead of here? Aren't you a mage?"

Xavier shrugged. "Because Maddox bought me. I work for him, but I spend time here too. Josephine doesn't buy people to own them like the other guilds. She welcomes runaway mages. This is a home, not a business." Xavier swung his legs to the floor and stood with the swift grace of an assassin. "Come on."

Ison stood on wooden legs and followed Xavier deeper in the house. The sounds of life filled the house—dozens of voices were talking and laughing; feet crossed floorboards and stone, thundering and padding and running; pots and pans signaled the beginnings of lunch; and someone on a higher floor was singing. Magelights lit the entire house, glittering like tiny suns along sconces and from within lanterns.

Xavier took Ison down a hallway near the back of the house and into what looked like a playroom. Four children, none older than five, played with building blocks of faintly painted wood. An older girl, maybe fifteen, sat on the far side of the room with a book open on her lap. Ison recognized the cover; it was a mid-level book for teaching air mages. The children glanced toward the door, but none of them gave much mind.

The girl looked up and let the book fall into her lap. "Xavier?" She frowned. "Oh no, has someone finally decided the world would be better off without me?"

Xavier chuckled. "We know there isn't a soul who'd think that. And if there were, it would be their body in the gutter, not yours."

She gave him a small smile—one of gratitude but also of fear. She knew he meant those words.

"Selene, this is Ison. He's visiting."

"Greetings, Ison," she said, nodding.

"Hello," he said in return.

Xavier said, "Selene, be a dear, and tell Ison how you came to be here."

Selene's calm smile flattened into a straight line. Her gaze flickered to Ison, then to the children, then back to Ison. "I was ten. I was working in the market stalls outside the Marca. We sold bracelets that we'd made. It had been raining, and I dropped one of the baskets, and the bracelets fell into the mud. Ruined. All of them. The overseer beat me for it because I'd lost them a whole basket's profit." Selene absently tugged at her sleeve. "The others were too afraid to step in, but then one of Josephine's friends saw and saved me. We fled the Marca, and he led me here. Took me three days of healings to be able to walk again." She tapped her feet. "I've been here since."

Ison averted his gaze from Selene's. He had known the knights and overseers to get violent from time to time.

Selene said, "Your name sounds familiar. Have we met?"

"Until about a year ago, I lived at the Marca. I spent most of my life there," Ison said. He would have been in the advanced classes and the older dormitory. He glanced at her book. "We might have shared a few classes."

She brightened, though her cheeks turned a shade of pink. "You're an air mage?"

He nodded.

Her brows came together. "Ison?" Her eyes went wide. "Wait, you're the court magician's apprentice."

Guilt yanked on his shoulders, and he wanted to fall through the floor and into the stone of the earth. He said quietly, "I was."

Selene opened her mouth, but Xavier cut her off. "He's one of us now." He set his hand on Ison's shoulder. "An apostate."

Ison deflated at the word. He was.

"It's better down here," Selene said. "At least I think it is. Fewer beatings for mistakes. Josephine's strict but forgiving."

Xavier took Ison through the house, introducing him to a number of mages of varying ages, including a girl near his age—Nera—who made most of the potions for the stalls. Her short brown hair was tied back, and at the news of a potion master, her entire face lit up. She had the bronze skin of the south, paled to a golden beige by years spent underground.

"Oh, that is wonderful," Nera said of Ison. "I only know a bit from my mom—she was an apothecary—and from whatever I've been able to read. I know I'm doing things wrong. It will be great to have someone to show me the advanced potions!"

Xavier took Ison throughout the house, meeting everyone who had a spare moment. They all had similar stories of escaping the Marca or escaping the knights. A few, like Nera, had heard about the guild and came searching for it on their own. None seemed like vile monsters, not at all like the dreadful apostates the Order made them out to be. They were mages like him, like those in the Marca.

After the tour, Xavier walked Ison back down to the parlor. Josephine stood beside a girl of maybe ten or eleven. The girl hovered her hand over a cup of what looked like rocks. An earth mage.

"Concentrate," Josephine said to the girl. "Feel your magic working, feel it connect with each stone. Feel your magic respond."

The young girl pulled her bottom lip between her teeth. She focused hard on the rocks, and the rock on top began to move. It lifted out of the cup, hovered for a short time, and fell back into the others. The girl let out a disappointed sigh.

"Keep trying." Josephine spotted Ison and Xavier. She said to the discouraged girl, "Keep trying, and one day you'll be able to move entire boulders with a thought."

The girl picked up the cup of rocks and walked deeper into the house, not giving Ison or Xavier a glance. As she passed, the strong scent of roses wafted.

"She's another fledgling mage trying to gain a hold on her powers." Josephine rested her gaze on Ison. "Have you thought about my offer?"

Ison, for the first time in a long time, felt sure about something. "Yes, I have. I would like to stay here while I'm in the Undercity."

Josephine gave him a small, motherly smile. "While you're here? You plan to leave us?"

He didn't have a sure answer. "I had hoped to get out of Rusdasin for a while," he said meekly. "Maybe out of Duvane."

Her motherly grin faltered. "Out there is a dangerous world for mages, especially with the Order."

"The Order?" Ison blinked. "They don't extend beyond the borders of Duvane."

"The Order knows no bounds," Josephine said. "An apostate is an apostate, and if Knight Commander Fowler had his way, the Order would overshadow any king. But, it is not just the Order that lurks beyond these halls."

Ison felt a tremor in his chest. "What do you mean?"

Her eyes narrowed, and he saw a glimmer of fear pass over them. "I fear you may have already encountered it."

The voice. The apostate who could control people and walk through walls and hide from the Order and fool the king. His very bones trembled.

"The ritual you described is old magic, dark magic," she whispered. "That sort of magic has been lost to time for a very good reason, and no decent mage would willingly partake. Magic like that can easily corrode the mind and blacken a soul."

"Old magic," Ison whispered. Mason had often called it such too. Until now, the answer seemed unreachable. With Josephine in front of him, somehow he grasped it. "Do you mean the Iluvin?"

Josephine's lack of an answer gave him her answer.

She suspected the apostate to be an Iluvin mage? Ison's hands started to shake, and he grabbed fistfuls of his shirt to stop it. "But...that's impossible."

"Nothing is impossible. There is a darkness gathering, a darkness that threatens to tear apart the world we have so carefully built for ourselves here. There are mages who think that darkness is for the better, but do not let them fool you. Stay away from those mages, Ison."

His stomach soured. "How am I to know which mage to trust and which not to?"

Josephine stepped closer to him. "Let your magic decide—if not your magic, then your gut. I have taken great care to build a safe haven for mages to learn and live without the oppression of the Order, and I do not need these wicked mages thinking that magic will solve the world's problems."

Ison nodded, his stomach roiling. He felt the truth radiate through his being. He knew, somehow, that she was right. "Damn," he muttered.

"That's a copper for the jar," Xavier said, a smile in his tone.

Ison glanced at him.

The assassin *was* smiling, as if the revelation that an Iluvin mage was causing trouble were no more than common street gossip.

Josephine added kindly, "We have a clean speech policy. Each foul word is a copper in the jar. Speaking of, you owe it about three gold, Xavier."

He shrugged. "I'll bring it up next time Maddox pays me."

She sighed through her nose, and Ison suspected she knew that Xavier wouldn't cough up three gold. Ison wasn't going to scrounge for a copper either. Not when he had barely a handful of coppers to his name.

A burst of laughter from a room upstairs shattered the grave air.

"Will the two of you be staying for lunch?" Josephine asked.

"I promised Maddox I would be back before lunch," Xavier said. "He's got some job he wants to discuss. And I don't want Juniper thinking I left her friend in the gutter somewhere."

Josephine let out a disapproving huff but didn't push. She started down the hall toward the kitchens. "Don't be strangers."

"We won't," chimed Xavier, and he guided Ison out of the guild.

Once on the other side of the ward, Ison asked, "What does she mean, 'a darkness'?"

Xavier didn't answer right away. His blue-gray eyes were scanning the street before them. Ison had seen Juniper do the same—taking in everything, exits, people, possible threats. "I don't know. She's a healer by trade, and her magic feels things like that."

Ison asked no more; he didn't want to know.

He and Xavier started through the market toward Maddox's keep. They rounded the first corner of stalls, and the hair on the back of Ison's neck prickled. It didn't take him long to find the source—three sets of eyes were staring in his direction. All three strangers wore dark blue cloaks fastened with silver brooches. The tallest of the three held Ison's stare, and his dark gaze unsettled the small peace that he had found.

CHAPTER FORTY-ONE

Reid donned his armor, secured his sword and two daggers—one at his side and one in his boot—and started toward the royal alchemist's chambers. Although he didn't anticipate much trouble through the Royal Grounds, he would not be caught off guard. The previous royal alchemist had died some years before. They hadn't the need to replace him until Ison fled, leaving the castle without an herbalist and potion master. Rather than hire another mage, they found an herbalist.

The royal alchemist lived in the western tower, known formally as the Alchemy Tower. Reid reached the door just past midday. He knocked. No answer came. He knocked again, louder. This time, quick footsteps padded across the stone floor. The door swung open.

A young man blinked at Reid, no older than eighteen. His large eyes and high eyebrows gave him a perpetually frightened look. He stood of average height and carried more than the average weight on his middle; however, Reid would not call him large. He wore his long brown hair tied behind his head.

"You are the herbalist?" Reid said, straightening his shoulders.

"Yes," he squeaked.

Reid put a hand over his heart. "Squire Reid Sandpiper. I am here to escort you to the Royal Greenhouses."

The young man's eyes widened. "Wow, a squire? That's wonderful." He gave a quick nod. "I'm Graison Alyun. It is a pleasure to meet you, Squire Sandpiper. Please, give me a moment. I'm nearly ready."

Graison left the chamber door open and vanished through a door on the other side of the sitting room. Reid took a step inside. White sheets still covered most of the furniture, and the hearth had long since been used. Boxes and bags were piled by the door into the office, and several more were stacked against another door. The herbalist hadn't been employed but a day or two, and the bare stone walls, cold torches, and cloudy windows showed it. The space smelled of dust and stale air. It reminded Reid of the tunnels under the castle.

Graison came back wearing a traveling cloak and a leather satchel for the herbs. "I am ready."

Reid walked Graison to the stables—the herbalist admitted he didn't know his way around the castle, and he'd already gotten lost twice—where horses had been prepared for them. The two of them started off across the grounds to the Royal Greenhouses. Reid's eyes wandered over the grassy fields to the pale green specs in the distance. Juniper had often stared out at the greenhouses. She said they had reminded her of the home she barely remembered, the home she had been stolen from.

"Have you been a squire long?" asked Graison, his voice awkward and unsure, unused to casual chitchat.

"I became a squire at eighteen," Reid said. "A little more than a year ago."

Graison then confessed to his twenty-two years. Reid held in his surprise. The herbalist's youthful face made him appear several years younger. Graison didn't comment, and they trotted through the waving grasses and flowering bushes; bugs and birds chirped high in the trees and underneath the greenery—everywhere.

"The castle has been a marvelous place," said Graison. "Have you been here long?"

"I've lived in the castle since I was a boy," Reid answered shortly, hoping his tone didn't imply any further questions as to why.

"Your name is Sandpiper. Any relation to the captain?"

"He is my uncle."

Graison nodded, then became silent for a short while.

A hawk shrieked, a bluebird flashed through the green boughs of an oak, and wild dogs were barking.

"My mother wanted me to grow up to be a knight." Graison's brow creased, and his shoulders slumped forward. "I tried to be brave, but I'm not fit. I prefer books to swords and can't wield one to save my life." He sighed and patted the satchel. "But I make up for my lack of strength with knowledge. And when I told my mother I had been asked to become the Royal Herbalist, she cried. It's not knighthood, but it is a job worth bragging about to her friends."

"There is more to being a knight than bravery," said Reid. "A knight must be intelligent, cunning, and have a good heart."

Graison gave him a sheepish smile. "Well, I've got one of those at least. Or I'd like to think so."

Reid didn't ask which one.

The horses trekked along the stomped path, through the spotted forests and grasses, toward the greenhouses. The wildflowers grew in dense patches between the trees, bright splotches of purple and yellow and blue. The previously rain-soaked air smelled of the dense wildlife, the flowers and soil, the animals and game. It didn't take long for Graison to start talking again of the drafts in the castle, of the change from an open herb garden to a stone-walled bedroom, of the food he'd eaten—on and on he went. Reid kept his eyes open for any and all threats, be it a man with ill-intent or a threatening beast.

In a way, Graison's awe at the castle's luxury reminded him of Juniper, how she had been surprised by everything given to her, from the food to the bath salts. He had found her prattling annoying at first, but the absence of her voice had left a strange hollowness where that annoyance had once lived.

And he feared that hollowness would never leave him.

The path forked: one path headed toward the game fields; the other led to the Royal Greenhouses. As they came closer, the air ripened with scents of blooming fruit and vibrant herbs. The gates of the greenhouses were massive structures of wood and iron, connected to a wooden wall that stood just beyond jumping height for a grown man.

A man ducked out of the gatehouse. His clothes were dirty and stained, he wore a straw hat with frayed edges, and his feet were bare and coated in dirt.

"Hello there, Mikel," said Graison. "We've come on official business from the king."

Mikel smiled wide. Reid had expected him to be missing teeth, but he had them all—off-white but all of them. Mikel said, "I knew you wouldn't be able to stay away. Let me get the gate. Welcome back, Graison."

Mikel unlocked the front gate and hauled one side open. The horses trotted through, and Mikel closed the gate behind them. Reid guided his horse to the post just inside. Beside him, Graison did the same—albeit he slid off the horse a bit ungracefully.

In all the years that Reid had lived in the castle, he hadn't once been to the greenhouses. He'd never had the need to. The air was thick with soil and humidity. Each of the five greenhouses took up as much space as a city block, all pale green glass. Magelights illuminated the greenhouses day and night, giving the plants inside perpetual sunlight. The plants inside appeared as dark shadows against the clouded glass. In the gardens, bushes, trees, and all manner of herbs grew in neat rows—not a weed in sight. Reid spotted at least twenty hats like the one Mikel wore, tending, weeding, watering, picking. On the other side, he spotted a little resting house for the workers to get out of the summer sun.

Graison, having tried several times to tie off his horse, finally succeeded. He led Reid to the far side of the garden. Not far from the resting house, a moderate cottage with white stone walls and pale wooden shutters had been tucked away in the shade of an old oak, cozy in every sense of the word.

"Mikel knows you by name," Reid said casually.

"Yes," Graison said, nodding. He cleared his throat. "I worked for the Calverts before the king recruited me."

The Calverts ran the Royal Greenhouses, husband and wife. He was an apothecary; she was an herbalist. Reid had never met them, but he had heard the name in passing. From what he gathered, they were quiet and liked the outdoors.

They started down the stone path to the cottage. Halfway to the door, it opened. A man stepped out. He wore the sun well on his tanned skin, and his blond hair had been bleached nearly white by the sun. The man's surprise faded quickly into a smile.

"Graison." The man walked out to meet them. "The king's order is nearly ready. Mal is finishing it in Greenhouse One as we speak." He shifted his gaze to Reid, to his armor. "You're either a knight or a well-paid bodyguard."

"A squire," Reid said. "Squire Sandpiper."

"Ah, I see." The man held out his hand. Dirt caked underneath his short fingernails. "I'm Barnum Calvert, the chief apothecary here. My wife, Malen, is the chief herbalist."

Reid shook his hand. "It is a pleasure to finally meet you."

"I'll take you to Mal, this way," said Barnum.

They reached Greenhouse One, and Barnum led them through a propped-open door. Inside, it felt like a different world. The plants were thick and exotic; Reid saw leaves pale as moonlight, others bright as daylilies, and some black as ink. Water misted from somewhere above, thickening the air with oppressive humidity. The glass walls intensified the sunlight. Reid felt sweat gathering on his neck, down his back, and across his chest; his armor became a personal oven.

Barnum led them into a small workroom at the back of the greenhouse. A thin woman stood at a worktable, her dark brown hair tied back into a messy bun, her baggy pants spotted with dirt, and tools stuck out of every available pocket on her leather belt. She was looking through a bronze scope at a plate, on which sat one of the smallest leaves that Reid had ever seen, smaller than a newborn's fingernail.

At first, Reid didn't think she noticed their entrance. Barnum stood patiently, and Reid took a better look. The woman held silver tools with fine heads, and she moved with a slow, almost imperceptible precision. She dropped what appeared to be thin white hairs into a vial, one after another—from the leaf.

Graison watched her with wide, awestruck eyes.

Then, at last, Malen Calvert straightened, corked the vial, and turned around to her visitors without surprise. "I'm finished," she said shortly and handed the vial to her husband. Her brown eyes drifted listlessly over Graison and Reid.

Barnum quickly introduced her and Reid, but her sullen expression didn't change. Then, suddenly, she snapped at Reid, "Did you touch anything?"

"No, I haven't." Reid held his words calm.

"You're far too wide to be in here," she barked, motioning to the width of his armored shoulders. She pushed past him and into the main space of the greenhouse, inspecting the plants along the row they had come. "Some of these plants are very sensitive to light, to sound, to touch. One wrong breath could cause us seasons of work."

Her tantrum and the heat gathering in his armor were not working well together, but he held in his retort. A knight had endless patience, he told himself.

"Don't worry, Mal," her husband pleaded. "I was watching them both."

She made it to the end of the row and stormed back. She huffed. "Fine. You've got your herbs. You've no other reason to be in here. Shoo."

She returned to the workroom, and Barnum led them back into the gardens. Reid relished the cool breeze on his neck.

"Don't take it personally. She doesn't do well with strangers in her space. She doesn't like the workers in there either." Barnum's brows shot upward, and he snapped his fingers at Graison. "Before you go, come back to the cottage. I've got a box of strawberries for you."

Graison smiled. "Fantastic."

At the cottage, Reid waited outside while Graison followed Barnum inside for the strawberries. Reid meandered to the thicker shade of the oak. The ground gently sloped, and he could see the sky's reflection in a small pond between the resting house and the cottage. Perfect for swimming on hot summer days.

Reid was looking at the glassy surface of the water, thinking of dunking himself in cold water, when he caught a whiff of something sweet and familiar. Curious, he stepped around the corner of the house and spotted the cause of the smell: sprouts of lavender grew alongside the house, underneath the two windows. Honeysuckle had climbed onto an old patch of lattice.

The breeze ushered the mixed smell to him, and it took a moment to place it. It smelled like the bathing room after Juniper had used it. She favored the lavender and honeysuckle scents.

His heart skipped a beat, then another. A cold sweat broke out over his skin, despite the heat still trapped in his armor.

I remember there being greenhouses... There were honeysuckle and lavender outside my bedroom window. I'd leave the shutters open at night just to wake up and smell them.

Reid leaned against the cottage. And she had so often stared out at the greenhouses.

Gods.

The door to the cottage opened. Reid gathered what strength he had and returned to the path.

"Thank you, again," Graison said, stepping out of the cottage. He held a box of freshly picked berries.

"Don't wait for an order to stop by," said Barnum.

Reid searched the man's face; he brought Malen's face to mind. Neither looked outwardly like Juniper. Neither had her midnight blue eyes or auburn hair. The girl the Watch had brought in had resembled her more.

There were dozens of greenhouses scattered around Rusdasin, hundreds, even. The odds of a greenhouse growing lavender and honeysuckle were high. So he remained silent.

Graison and Reid returned to the horses, but he felt a world away from his body. Graison was talking about strawberries and desserts, but Reid wasn't listening. He was searching the gardens for any clues, anything that might trigger a memory of something else she had said—then he saw it. Nestled in a corner of the garden, away from the other plants, was a scraggly tree. A juniper tree.

They passed through the gates and started back across the grounds toward the castle, vital herbs safely tucked in Graison's satchel. Mikel shouted a goodbye as he closed the gates.

"They are a nice couple," Graison said, sorrow in his voice. "But, as you saw, he is nicer than she is. She was always that way, harsh, hard to speak to. She loses herself in her work, and she is one of the best herbalists I've ever met."

"Perhaps that is why she's hard to get along with," Reid said. A trait she might share with her daughter. "She spends too much time with her plants."

"No, that's not entirely it," Graison said. He looked a bit guilty as he said, "She's had a rough life. It was hard for her to conceive, and both children that she had nearly killed her, and she lost both of them."

Reid's chest tightened at the word, at the information he hadn't even asked for. For the first time since he met Graison, he was glad for his chattiness.

"Stillborn?" Reid found himself asking, though he knew the subject sensitive. He had never felt such a desire to dig for gossip.

"The first was," Graison said.

"I understand," Reid said. "My aunt hadn't been able to conceive. The only child she carried had made her deathly sick, and she lost it." Every time she spoke about it, or someone losing children, she got a glossy look in her eye.

"I-I never asked what happened to the second child," Graison said, looking guilty. "She died, I think, but I don't know how. I never felt right in asking about it. She was older, though, several years older."

Reid fought to push Graison for information. A rock had formed in his stomach; he had the sickening feeling he knew exactly what had happened to the second child.

CHAPTER FORTY-TWO

After getting Blythe situated in her new room at the keep, Juniper took her into the basement for a general skills assessment. Maddox had once done the same for her and Xavier. Juniper stood at the side while she guided Blythe through a short obstacle course and asked her questions of basic mathematics and history as she jumped, ducked, and rolled.

Blythe was nimble and flexible, and she could think while she acted—a dangerous combination in the Undercity. The young girl kept her chin up, and when Juniper gave her a quick run-down of her new life in Maddox's keep, she didn't flinch or fret.

Juniper had cried. Maddox had told her that he owned her, and she would work for him, and she had cried. She'd begged Maddox to take her home, that her parents would pay him back. He didn't. He had let her cry herself into a stupor, then carried her up to her new room with her new roommate. He'd whispered, "You'll be safe here."

And she had been, mostly. She told Blythe the same. "With some training, you'll be one of the best fighters in the Undercity. Your guild family will have your back, and you'll have theirs."

"I fought with my brothers and my nephew." Blythe wiped the back of her hand across her mouth. "I'm not afraid to fight dirty."

"That's good," Juniper said. "Don't be afraid to throw the first punch, or the last."

Blythe nodded.

"If you need anything and I'm not around, Amery and Xavier are trustworthy," Juniper explained.

Blythe nodded, her expression solemn, her dark eyes soaking in the information.

After the assessment and tour of the keep, Blythe followed Juniper up to the third floor and sat on the couch while Amery rubbed dark dye into Juniper's hair. With the whole city on the lookout for Juniper Thimble, she couldn't wander Rusdasin without something of a disguise. Amery added highlights and shadows to make her face seem fuller than it was.

"It's not bad," Amery said, shrugging. "You still look like you but not as much."

"It'll throw off people who don't know me." Juniper dug baggy clothes out of her closet to hide her frame. With her makeup, hair, and clothes, she'd be able to slip in and out of crowds easily.

With a quick goodbye, Juniper left the keep. She wandered to one of the dozens of access points that led from the Undercity to the backrooms of shady taverns, shoddy black market shops, slum alleys, and brothels. The one she chose led to the vacant backroom of the Empty Tankard, a near useless tavern with a few sleazy patrons who doubled as Undercity lookouts. She slipped out the backdoor without a sound.

The mid-afternoon greeted her with a vicious brightness, reflecting off puddles that lined the streets and alleys. It stung her eyes, and she blinked until they adjusted. The city reeked of humid stink.

She stood in a narrow alley in the slums. A street over, children were playing; the sound of sticks smacking against sticks echoed off the stone. On the other side, she heard a few vendors calling out their wares, wines and specialty drinks that would make hair grow a different color, that would add luck to the drinker's day.

Juniper took in a deep breath. She knew her chances of finding Captain Tinnly today were slim; she'd just needed to get out of the Undercity for a while, get some fresh air.

She made her way through the slums, through the clusters of houses and buildings packed so close together that the alleys were barely wide enough for one person, through alleys with washing strung out between balconies and windows, and between shoddy stalls of the poor trying to make something of a living selling handmade bracelets, bread, and questionable goods.

It all felt so familiar and yet like a different world.

Had living in the castle changed her that much?

She crisscrossed her way out of the slums and into the middle-class neighborhood. She paused as two city watchmen meandered along the street, their horses stately and groomed. The Captain of the City Watch wouldn't stay in one place; he would move throughout the city during the day, and that left her with an area far too large to search blindly.

The City Watch had five Towers: Central, West, East, Southeast, and Southwest. The captain lived in the Central Watch Tower, a stake of gray and white stone just off Royal Avenue, within sight and walking distance of the castle. The Central Tower would be the best place to start.

Juniper wound through Rusdasin, avoiding crowded streets and oddly empty ones. The further east she traveled, the wider the streets became, the clearer the alleys, the nicer the shops, and the more law-abiding the people. The shops sold better crafted and legally obtained items, and the air itself seemed to be perfumed. She made it to Royal Avenue, the main street that divided Rusdasin in two.

Juniper meandered down Royal Avenue, pretending to take in the boutiques of clothes and jewelry, the sweet shops, the bookstores—while keeping an eye on Central Tower. The monolithic stone tower rose above the buildings around it by several floors, giving the captain an unobstructed view of Royal Avenue. Juniper bought a bag of sweets and a bottle of wine, then wandered into one of her favorite bookstores in the city. New book in hand, she went up to the third floor courtyard and took a seat in one of the several wooden chairs arranged for pleasure reading. She sat where she could see the tower and its entrance.

She snacked, drank, and read while keeping one eye on the Central Tower. She noted who entered, who left, and how often—Captain Tinnly did not show. The sun sank lower, staining the air a shade more golden with every passing minute. Juniper continued her vigil of the tower.

Sweets gone, crowd in the courtyard thinning, the smell of dinner wafting throughout the city, Juniper shut her book in defeat. She tapped her fingertips against the nearly empty bottle of wine. She could feel the water within, feel her magic respond to it.

No one was looking.

She focused, cooling the wine that had grown warm. She cooled it until it started to frost and her magic started to protest. Releasing her hold on the wine, she leaned back, let it warm up on its own, then cooled it once more. Her magic tensed at the use; her insides threatened to seize.

When cooling such a small amount of wine took so much out of her, she found it hard to believe that she might one day move entire lakes.

Still, the captain hadn't appeared—though plenty of watchmen had, their dark iron armor blinking in and out of crowds.

She let her magic replenish. She took a swig of the cooled wine. Then she focused. Underneath her fingertips, the cool wine reacted. She focused harder. *Warm.*

The wine began to grow warm, warming the glass under her fingertips. It took more magic, more focus, and more stamina—she had to stop before she fell out of her chair. She took her breaths slowly so as to not draw attention to her sudden breathlessness.

Still, she had done it!

She took a drink of the warm wine, too delighted in her own skill to mind the warmth on her tongue. Juniper turned slightly and returned to her book so that the tower's door was above her thumb, within easy sight without moving her eyes too far.

She waited, read, waited, read, drank, and waited. The sun tilted down; her pages moved from right to left; then, at last, with twilight not far off, with the city lamps sparking to life, Captain Tinnly arrived at the Central Tower. He wore the same iron armor as the Watch, only his breastplate was adorned with white and gold accents, as was his helmet. He returned to the tower with four watchmen, their armor worn and well-fought.

He did not go immediately into the tower.

Juniper casually closed her book, stood, stretched, and headed down to the street. She followed Captain Tinnly down Royal Avenue, through the bustling market, to where he stopped with a handful of his men for a bite to eat. Everyone greeted the captain as a regular, several people shook his hand, and everyone wanted to speak to him. She sat in a shadowed corner, out of sight, nursing wine that continuously moved between cool and warm.

Tinnly wasn't an overly handsome man, but he had the ruggedness of a soldier. His short blond hair had taken on the shape of his helmet, and his complexion had taken the summer sun well. He laughed with his men, talked with them, and listened as they spoke.

The bartender didn't want to take the captain's gold, but Tinnly refused to not pay for his food.

When the captain started back to the tower, a few bright stars twinkled.

Halfway to the tower, a young watchman ran out from an alley. "Captain!"

"Barkley?" answered the captain, his voice smooth, fatherly, but stern. She'd heard him shout and threaten. He could be menacing when he wanted to. "What's the trouble?"

"We caught a thief trying to steal bread in the market."

"Ah, a thief. Let's see about him then."

Juniper followed at a cautious pace but close enough to hear. It would seem that the young watchman was not a watchman yet, and he could not legally make decisions on his own. A scout, they were called—like squires but instead of becoming knights, they joined the City Watch.

Juniper followed the captain and the scout to an alley just off the market street, where the majority of the shops had already closed. Another scout stood at the mouth of the alley. Juniper wouldn't be able to get in that way. Instead, she slipped into the next alley and climbed onto the roof. She crept over to the alley to listen.

Footsteps walked into the alley, two sets of them: captain and scout.

"My men tell me you're a thief," said the captain.

The thief trembled. His voice spilled out in a series of gasps and whimpers. Crying.

Some thief, Juniper silently scoffed.

"Explain yourself," said the captain.

"I-I stole a loaf of bread," whimpered the boy, who didn't sound older than fifteen. "But I only did it because we've nothing to eat!"

One of the scouts huffed. "Likely story."

"Simon," said the captain. "Does this boy look like a thief by trade?"

A beat of silence. "No, sir."

"Why not?"

Another beat.

The captain said, "You say you've nothing to eat?"

"Yes, sir," said the thief, his voice trembling. "My sister and I live alone. Our parents died this winter, and I-I haven't been able to find work. Everyone tells me I'm too young. I-I don't want my sister to whore herself out just to be able to eat. We are starving. Please, sir, have mercy."

He didn't sound like a liar, but she had met very good liars. She wished she could peek over the edge and see this thief, but she didn't want to risk being seen.

"I see," said the captain. "I will let this offense go."

A shuffle of armor—one of the scouts disagreeing, no doubt.

The captain continued, "Barkley, I want you to take this young man to the bindery. Ask for Harold. I know he is in need of strong hands. See if he will hire him, and maybe his sister too."

The thief let out a shuddering gasp. "Oh, thank you!"

Armored feet shuffled toward the street. Juniper risked a peek over the edge. The scout had been right. The young man did not look like a thief. He wore baggy clothes and looked unwashed, and he had the jittery look of terror. The not-thief followed the scout out of the alley with a look of hope in his eye.

Juniper leaned away from the edge. The captain had handled that fairly, presenting a good example to the young scouts. Would he have been so lenient if it had been her they had caught?

Of course, they wouldn't have caught her stealing in the first place.

Juniper returned to the street and nonchalantly resumed her tracking of the captain. Rather than continue to the tower, Tinnly stopped in the middle of the street to speak with two watchmen, one of whom lifted his gaze the moment Juniper walked out of the alley.

Their gazes met, and though her heart leaped into her throat, she turned calmly into the second stall, a counter full of jewelry made from seashells. She marveled at a ring whose pearl centerpiece had been artfully surrounded by tiny seashells. She pretended to admire the tiny shells while keeping her eyes on the watchmen behind her. The captain moved on, but the two watchmen remained.

Had he recognized her?

She carefully set the ring back on the counter, much to the dismay of the vendor. Another potential customer stopped at the counter; the vendor's attention shifted; with a flick of Juniper's wrist, the ring fell into her pocket. She turned from the vendor and started away.

A good thief didn't steal bread; a good thief stole something smaller and more valuable that would later buy bread. She tucked that lesson away for Blythe.

Juniper turned down another street, one lined with jewelry vendors. Some had already closed for the evening, but some had stayed open—unlike the food stalls, the general goods stalls remained open longer.

A watchman followed.

She strolled along the stalls, looking and looking, but never picking up. She turned down another street, and the watchman followed. She walked a maze through the market stalls, winding this way and that without looking suspicious. If she broke into a run too soon, it would signal panic and more watchmen.

She turned down an alley that would take her away from the market and onto the maze of streets and alleys where she had lost a number of City Watch, and then a commanding male voice said, "Hey."

Pretending to think he had spoken to someone else, Juniper continued. She was only a few steps into the alley before he repeated his command, anger on his tongue.

She glanced casually over her shoulder.

The watchman followed, eyes on her. "Stop."

She made it to the end of the alley and broke into a run.

"Hey!" he shouted, his armored feet clanking on the stone street.

She ran through one alley and then another, but the watchman persisted. To her dismay, a second pair of armored feet joined him.

Quickening her pace, she slid out of one alley and onto a street—right into the path of a watchman. At the sight of her, his brow furrowed, and his gaze turned suspicious. At the sound of armored steps chasing her, he reached for his sword. "Halt," he commanded.

Heart pounding, Juniper kept going. She barely avoided the grabbing hand of the watchman—his fingers grazed the edge of her hair. A few strands ripped from her scalp. Ignoring the sting, she ran down alleys, one after another, but the three watchmen stayed close on her tail. They divided—armored footsteps sounded to her right and left and behind her. They planned to trap her.

She came out of one alley and slid onto the street. Right in front of her stood the Temple of Blugo, God of Winter, a blue and quartz masterpiece of a building. She didn't have time to think about repercussions or sacrilege; she dashed toward the temple gates.

Being the patron of lost and weary souls, Blugo's temple doors were always open. This time of evening, no priestesses or monks lingered in the courtyard or on the steps, and Juniper dashed through the doors and into the darkness beyond. Her eyes quickly adjusted, and she slid through the shadows as quietly and as quickly as she could. The armored steps of the watchmen followed behind her.

She knew of only one room where they might not follow. She followed the main corridor all the way to the back of the temple, then down a spiral stone staircase, and into the offering chamber, the holiest of rooms. Behind her, the watchmen's footsteps had slowed. All other sounds of the city had been muted by the stone.

Blugo's statue had been carved from bluish quartz, depicting him in long, fur-trimmed robes. He held his hands together in a fur muff. Snowflakes dotted his robes. At his feet was a silver offering plate. On either side, blue flames burned—forever flames. Below the offering plate, wooden sticks had been artfully arranged in a basket, to burn one's offering.

Juniper looked up into the stone eyes of Blugo. Having been born when his stars crowned the sky, Blugo was her patron. She had never before set foot inside his temple. She had been afraid to.

From above, she heard the calm murmur of a priestess; the guards had alerted her.

"A criminal fled into this temple," one of the watchmen said.

"Blugo's hearth is home to all," a priestess responded. A hint of bitterness made it into her voice. "Please, allow them to pray before you drag them out."

Juniper knelt in front of the offering plate. *Please*, she silently said. *If they catch me, they'll kill me. If not, they'll drag me to the knights and let me die by Mage's Bane.*

An offering... She thought of the stolen ring in her pocket but hesitated. Would a stolen ring appease the god of winter? *Winter.* Juniper brought her hands together and summoned her ice. Flurries appeared, more and more of them, and she set a small pile of snow into Blugo's offering dish.

Please, she begged. *Send them away. Give me another chance to fix this. I want to find the bastard responsible and end him before I go.*

Somewhere in the temple, someone laughed. An eerie, melodic laugh that seemed to come from within the stone itself.

The armored footsteps started to descend the stairs into the offering chamber. Juniper crawled to the other side of Blugo, hand clasped over her mouth to halt her breathing. Those stairs were the only way in or out.

One pair of footsteps made it to the bottom. The second halted.

"Don't be a coward," barked the watchman in the chamber.

"I'd rather be a coward than offend the gods," said the other, farther up the stairs.

The watchman in the offering chamber huffed. He walked up to the statue. Juniper's heart stopped—she had left her snow in the offering dish. The watchman would see it.

Then, through some form of grace, the watchmen retreated up the stairs. Juniper slumped against Blugo's statue, heart rampant. When the armored footsteps faded, she crawled out from behind him with wobbly limbs.

The snow had vanished from the offering dish; it wasn't even wet.

She inched up the stairs, wary of hiding watchmen and lingering priestesses. One of the watchmen stood at the temple doors, talking to a young priestess in her ice-blue robes. Juniper slipped out a side door of the temple, ran across the courtyard of snowberries, and jumped the stone fence to the street beyond.

CHAPTER FORTY-THREE

Ison rolled onto his back. The magelights outside Josephine's keep glowed with the pale blue light of early dawn. He had slept well, considering the new bed, new room, and the new smells and sounds. He had slept well in comparison to the last few weeks.

Judging by the lack of noise in the keep, no one else had woken.

Underneath the silence, the distant sounds of the Undercity faded into screams, the same screams of pain and torture that he had heard every night for weeks, months. A dull throb. He knew the screams weren't there; he was imagining them—no matter how many times he told himself so, he still heard them.

When the magelight had gotten slightly brighter, Ison got up. He couldn't handle the silence anymore. He washed his face and hands in cold water, then retreated to the empty kitchen on the first floor.

But it wasn't empty.

Xavier sat at the small wooden table in the corner. A brown-haired girl sat beside him. It took Ison a moment to place her—Nera, the current potion maker. Ison knew at once something was off. Xavier didn't look as confident as he usually did. His blue-gray eyes were lidded and glossy; his cheeks were flushed. Xavier lifted a goblet to his mouth and drank greedily, with his eyes settled on Ison.

Ison blinked between the two of them, feeling like an intruder. "Sorry, I'll just—"

"Sit down," Xavier commanded, pointing to the third chair at the table. Drunk. Xavier was drunk.

"No, I'll just be—"

"Sit down," Xavier said, each word hard. A threat.

Nera stood. "I should get something started for breakfast." She moved quickly to the other side of the room and set a fire underneath the stove, then set a large kettle on top of it. She found something to do in the next room.

Ison took each step with caution, and with each step, Xavier's cold eyes watched him. He sat and folded his hands in his lap. "You're drinking," Ison said flatly.

BEATRICE B. MORGAN

Xavier didn't blink. "I had a job last night," he slurred. A job—assassination. "Sometimes, it's a quick in and out, and they're dead, but sometimes it's not. Sometimes they're waiting. Sometimes they're ready for someone to come at them, and they fight back. This one fought back."

Ison held his breath; the victim had fought back. They hadn't wanted to die.

"Now he's dead," Xavier said. "He got it worse than if he had just taken it from the start."

Ison swallowed. There had been a fight, a struggle. Underneath the glossy drunkenness in Xavier's eyes, Ison saw something else, something eerily familiar—darkness.

"You've killed people." Xavier leaned back in the chair. His drunken air charged his predatory stare; it became reckless, and it gave Ison a chill. "Butchered, as you called it. You didn't want to do it." Xavier chuckled. "You feel guilty about it, but it wasn't your fault. The people I kill, I know what I'm doing. I'm very aware of what I'm doing, where I'm going when I leave the Undercity. The blood on my hands is my doing. No one commands me."

Ison couldn't look away from the reckless darkness in Xavier's eyes. The job he had done, the drinking—Ison felt guilty. He opened his mouth to admit it, when the kettle started to boil. Its shriek shattered the air. Nera appeared, and without looking at Ison or Xavier, she poured three pots of tea.

Xavier stood, strangely in control of his drunken grace, and sauntered out the kitchen door. Ison felt both relieved and anxious to be without his harsh gaze.

"I'm sorry," Nera said quickly. She artfully arranged teacups on three separate trays. "He showed up drunk this morning. I-I made him tea to calm him down."

"Did it work?" Ison asked.

"Well, considering he couldn't walk straight when he fell through the door," Nera said, motioning to the kitchen door, "I would say it worked."

Footsteps sounded on the floor above, and morning chatter filled the air, warm, welcoming, and cheery.

Nera took a deep breath. "Help me carry these trays into the dining room."

✳

After a breakfast of fruit, porridge, and toast, the mages scattered. Ison returned to the kitchen to help clean up, and then Nera pulled him into the workroom off the kitchen.

"This is where we make our tonics and potions," she said.

His chest squeezed at the disarray: unorganized shelves, cluttered cabinets, stacked jars of poorly labeled ingredients, and unmarked vials and metal containers. Without Nera's permission, he started to sort through the closest rack of ingredients. Most of the herbs weren't stored properly; minerals were in the wrong container, and he spotted several that hadn't been thoroughly processed. A few of the herbs had even started to wilt!

"I know it's not the best," Nera said, absently picking at her nails. "It's just been me for a while now, and I haven't had much to go on except for a few books." She motioned to one of the shelves. A few outdated volumes of herbs sat there, spines broken, leather covers stained and tattered.

"Well, first we need to organize this mess." Ison started to go through the ingredients one by one. He tossed the useless herbs and minerals into a bin. Those that could still be used, he set aside to arrange later. As he worked, something in his chest clicked; the part of him that needed to do something, to make progress, warmed at the sensation of organizing.

Ison spent the morning with Nera. He went through all the ingredients and examined them. He explained why they were good or bad, and she soaked in everything he said without question. He explained how certain herbs and minerals needed to be stored in particular containers, various metals or colored glass; some needed to be stored in sunny locations, and others, in darkness; some needed clear crystal, while others needed fresh air. He explained how to properly dry the herbs, how to crush herbs and powder minerals, and how to tell unicorn hair from horse hair.

"See this?" Ison held supposed unicorn hair against the magelight. He pulled it taut. "Unicorn hair shimmers. This is horse hair."

Nera cursed under her breath. "I thought that merchant looked shady. Would you like to go with me to replenish the supplies? I could use an eye like yours."

"I did most of the shopping for the court magician," Ison said.

Nera's eyes went wide at that.

They arranged the ingredients Ison had deemed fit to use and made a list of essential ingredients that needed to be replaced. By midday, Ison felt better than he had in a while. He had spent much of the morning talking potions and tonics, things that he knew, and things that Nera wanted to know; he felt useful.

As Nera helped prepare lunch, Ison went through the potion books and made notes and corrections. He made a mental note to leave a list of books for Nera to buy if she could find them. Ison joined the mages for lunch, and then he and Nera set out to the market.

It took a few stalls to find quality ingredients, nothing like the stalls above ground, and Ison could tell that Nera felt inadequate.

"It's all right," Ison said to her as they left a stall with decent mint leaves.

"No, it's not," she said. "I've been in charge of gathering ingredients for three years, and I don't know what I'm doing."

"But you can learn," Ison said as they came up to the next stall, whose vendor gladly reached for the glass jar of unicorn hair. Ison performed his trick in the light, and as he suspected, he'd been handed horse hair. He handed it back to the vendor, who didn't appreciate it. It took nearly a dozen different hairs before he finally found a genuine unicorn hair, and Nera gasped when he held it in the light. The pure white hair shimmered.

Unicorn hair safely tucked in her satchel, Nera led him to the next stall. As she paid for the salmon bones, Ison had the strangest feeling of eyes on the back of his neck. He turned, and his gaze settled on a blonde girl in a blue cloak. A Dual Fang. When his eyes met her pale ones, she gave him a small smile. Ison turned his attention away, thankful that Nera hadn't noticed. She tucked the bones into her bag, and they continued on.

But the sensation of being watched didn't go away.

At the next stall, he glanced and found the pale-eyed Dual Fang. She had followed him.

By the time Ison and Nera had found all of the ingredients on the list, Ison had a much better layout of the market. It wasn't so chaotic after all; he could find his way to Josephine's and his way to Maddox's. At the center of it all was a fountain that stole its water from above ground where the Weslie River and the Ruby River met.

Nera meandered through the market and guided Ison into the colorful stalls of jewelry and clothing. She came to a stop at a stall of men's clothing.

Ison blinked at her. "What do we need here?"

"Not *we*. You." She motioned at the men's clothes.

The vendor watched calmly, eagerly.

"Josephine wants you to buy something else to wear."

"What's wrong with this?" Ison looked down at his wrinkled clothes.

"You wore them yesterday, and she said you need at least three days' worth of clothing." Nera motioned toward the stall. "So go. I'll wait out here."

"You can go on home," came a drawling voice. Xavier, dressed in common clothes of dark grays and blacks, leaned against the side of the stall. "I can babysit."

Nera hesitated. She looked Xavier up and down.

"I'm sober, hungover as hell but sober." Xavier smiled mischievously at her. "Your teas work wonders, Nera."

Nera's lips pressed together. "Make sure he's back by dinner." She turned on her heel and started back toward Josephine's with the ingredients.

"Is it safe for her to walk alone?" Ison asked.

Xavier chuckled. "Everyone down here knows that messing with one mage will bring the wrath of the others, and,"—he grinned wider—"Nera is good at setting things on fire. Now, come on, finish your shopping."

Ison shuffled through the tunics and trousers and picked a few that looked like they would fit. The vendor shoved him into the curtained-off dressing room. After Ison picked three days' worth of clothes, the vendor folded them up and tied them together with string.

"I-I don't have coin." Ison realized, feeling utterly foolish.

The vendor waved him off. "I'll send Josephine the bill."

"Good, now let's go." Xavier grabbed Ison by the arm and pulled him away. "We have a talk to resume."

"We do?"

Xavier laughed, and Ison didn't think he liked the sound of it. The assassin walked leisurely. "This morning, I was trying to tell you a story, but in my state, it didn't come out very well."

"It did lack coherence."

Xavier didn't smile. "I wanted to tell you, when I was first dragged down here and sold like livestock, I hated it. I hated the people who sold me, I hated the man who bought me, and I hated myself for letting it happen. Ripped from my family, my home, because I wandered away from my mother at a market. I was alone. Then, one day, I met a shopkeeper on the surface, a man from Janti like me. He reminded me of my father, and I kept going back to see him. We became friends, as much as a grown man and a twelve-year-old can."

Ison didn't ask questions. He could see the darkness in Xavier's stormy eyes, the disquiet.

"And then that shopkeeper became my first target," Xavier said, his voice quiet and hard. "My first friend, my only friend, and I was sent to kill him."

Ison swallowed against the lump in his throat.

"And I killed him." Xavier met Ison's stare. His eyes hardened. "I haven't made friends outside the keep since, because I couldn't go through that again. I refuse to. I would rather be alone in this world than murder a friend, to see the light leave their eyes." The darkness ebbed, and something unfamiliar took its place. "I understand what it feels like to kill someone you care about, someone who trusted you, and how it feels to carry that guilt for the rest of your life. It doesn't go away."

Ison didn't have the words. He felt foolish, but he felt something else; Xavier had opened up to him, shared something personal, to make Ison feel better. He opened his mouth to thank him, to say something, but Xavier started to march away.

"I'll take you back to Josephine's," he said quickly.

Ison had to jog several steps to catch up with him.

Xavier did not follow Ison into Josephine's, but Ison didn't have time to dwell on it. Josephine called him into one of the study rooms. The walls were bare stone. A single magelight twinkled against the ceiling.

"Nera tells me you have done wonders for the potion room." Josephine sat in one of the few chairs crammed into the space. She motioned for Ison to sit across from her.

"We did," Ison said, sitting. "Nera helped."

"Good. Now, Ison, I have something to teach you. It is a serious matter." Josephine's dark eyes bore into his. "The Marca does not teach mental resistance, but it is something that all mages need to know. There are mages out there who do not heed the laws of magic and nature, like your apostate. You need to be able to defend yourself should he try again to break into your mind."

Ison swallowed. "Okay."

"I am going to try and slip into your thoughts," Josephine said. "You are to block my entry."

Ison paled. "You know such magic?"

Josephine's stoic expression betrayed nothing. "I have prepared myself against such magic, and I prepare my mages against such magic. In order to do so, I have to understand such magic."

He understood, but he felt vulnerable. This felt too much like the black magic the Marca warned against.

"Are you ready?"

No. "Yes." Ison steeled himself.

Josephine's gaze intensified. He felt a blurriness, a heaviness, like a bout of drowsiness.

You need to be strong. You need to resist.

Ison tried, but he didn't know how. He felt something that should not be—it felt strangely like the apostate, the extra presence within him, a fragment of life that did not belong to himself. He pushed against it. It did not budge. He pushed harder. The world started to fade. Pressure built behind his eyes, between his ears. His heart skipped a beat.

Josephine removed herself from his thoughts, and Ison released a shuddering breath.

"Good, but you need practice," she said. "We will continue this every day until you can block unwanted influences."

Ison nodded, though he hadn't been given a choice, not that he would have declined.

CHAPTER FORTY-FOUR

Amery had taken Blythe out of the keep to teach her how to people-watch, leaving Juniper a moment alone. She ran her hand over a fresh piece of parchment but hesitated before starting another letter. Why was this so hard? She knew what she wanted to say, but when it came to putting those thoughts into ink, she fumbled. She had started the letter a dozen different ways, but none felt right.

A knock interrupted her thoughts, and she shoved the paper and ink aside, grateful for the distraction.

"It's open," she called.

Maddox entered, looking casual and calm. His brown eyes scanned the room—the empty beds, the empty sofa—and then he closed the door behind him. At the click of the door's mechanism, her skin prickled. Maddox strolled over to Amery's bed and sat, elbows on his knees and fingers laced together. "How did yesterday go?" He meant her hunt for the captain.

"Like I expected." Juniper sat on her bed, across from him. "He's well-armed, well-trained, and generally surrounded by watchmen."

Maddox took in her words, and she felt a bubble of anxiety. He hadn't personally come to check on her missions in years. Had he lost that much faith in her?

She cleared her throat. "He lives in Central Tower's top floor with his wife. He has a study on the floor below, and he likes to keep the window open." Luckily, she had gone back to Central Tower before returning to the Undercity last night, or she would have missed that important detail.

Maddox lifted a brow.

"I'll have to keep watching until I find my entry," she said. "The tower is heavily guarded day and night."

"One wrong move and you'll have a horde of watchmen after you," he said.

She nodded. "Another reason to take it slow."

He smiled. "Glad to see that confidence of yours working again," he said, standing. "I'm ashamed to say that I had my doubts when you agreed to assassinate the captain, but if anyone can do it, you can."

Her pride swelled, and at the same time, her heart deflated.

Maddox started back toward the door, and she saw her chance—she swallowed that pride and jumped to her feet, startling Maddox to a halt. He pinned his brown eyes on her, alert and wary.

"Maddox," she asked, her voice low, "what do you know about the Dual Fangs?"

His face betrayed no emotion. "They're mages. They're also fanatics. Why?" He tilted his head. "Thinking of joining their cause?"

"No," she said at once. "What cause do they have?"

"To make mages the superior beings." He stuffed his hands into his jacket pockets. "They've collected quite a few mages from the Undercity, all thirsty for change, hungry for something to believe in other than the Marca." His gaze became one of warning.

"I'm not thinking about joining them," she said. "Honest. I don't like them. They give me the creeps. Every time I've gone to the market, I've seen them watching me."

"And?" he asked.

"And...what?" She blinked at him.

Maddox closed the space between them in a few graceful steps. He lifted one hand from his jacket and pinched her chin, tilting her face. "There's more to it than curiosity," he whispered. "I know you better than that, Juniper."

He didn't release her, and she knew it would be foolish to lie to him now.

"I want to know if they know the apostate from the castle," she whispered, not wanting anyone else to hear it.

Maddox lifted a brow. "And if they do?"

"I will hunt him down," she said flatly. The truth. "I want him to pay for what he did to me." And for what he had done to Ison, to Clara, to all those servants, and to everyone else in the castle.

Maddox smiled wide. "That's the Juniper I know and love. You've got a personal vendetta against this apostate, and it is a beautiful sight." He leaned forward and placed a dry kiss on her forehead. His lips lingered a moment too long, and her heart skipped a beat. A wave of heat and panic rushed from his lips to her fingertips and toes; it radiated in the small space between them. She thought of Reid's kiss, of Ison's kiss, and the impulsive, sudden thought of Maddox on top of her sent a wave of strange anxiety through her bones.

Maddox leaned away, gave her a warm, fatherly grin, then left. Juniper slumped back to the floor, heart thumping more than she would like. Her letter sounded even more impossible than it had a moment ago.

✳

Ison and Nera spent the rest of the afternoon in the workroom. He showed her the proper way to boil, heat, simmer, and prepare the herbs and minerals using the flasks and burners; how to crush, mince, and powder with the mortar and pestle; and how to store and seal the different types of minerals and herbs to best protect them from time and air. By the time the dinner bell sounded, Nera looked ready to give up, but she took notes, didn't complain, and never questioned his judgment.

"Got all that?" Ison nudged Nera's arm.

She gave a humorless laugh. "It's a lot to take in at once."

Ison reduced the heat underneath a basic health potion. They had made several potions to sell the following day at market. "I understand. I've had years to learn all of this. I took classes just to learn the herbs and another on using the lab equipment and yet another on processing herbs. The classes got more advanced each time, adding new herbs, showing more complicated potions, delicate recipes."

"I've heard that some potions can only be brewed in the dark." Nera pointed to the potion book that Ison had made notes in. "And there's one near the end of the book that requires the breath of the maker."

"Ah." Ison nodded. He'd seen that potion. He'd marked it out. "Old calming tonics required the breath of the maker, assuming that the maker was calm while brewing the potion. They've gone out of style. We've found new herbs and mixtures of herbs that produce the same effect. Don't ask me how the breath thing worked, because even though it's been explained to me, I don't really understand it. Something about the emotional state of the person being contained in their breath. That's a good example of when magic gets complicated."

Ison worked with Nera to make a total of ten potions, all of them slight variations of a basic health potion, meant to ward disease, ease pain, and stop common sicknesses. With the potions packed and ready for market, Ison and Nera joined the other mages for dinner.

✳

After breakfast the following morning, Nera and Ison took the stock of health potions to one of Josephine's market stalls. The market buzzed with activity, the chatter of haggling, the laughter of drunks, and the shouting of goods for sale. Ison stood by while Nera haggled prices with customers. She didn't trade only for coin, but also for things; she traded one potion for a wolf pelt, another for a sack of potatoes, one for a bottle of ink and a few feather quills.

It felt so different from the market stalls in front of the Marca. Topside—Undercity slang for the city above ground—people were wary of mages and of the glowering knights. No one lingered longer than they had to at the Marca's stalls. The potions had a set price, no haggling, coin only. But, as Nera explained, when she traded for quills and ink, someone else didn't have to go hunt for ink and quills. It saved time for everyone.

The rush of the market slowed. They had three potions left.

Nera bent to store the bartered goods in a chest in the back of the stall, guarded by two younger mages, each with a short sword at their side. They were among the few who trained for combat, something else the Order highly regulated—battlemages.

An old man staggered to the counter, his watery eyes on the potions. A dry cough lashed at his throat and shook his thin chest, something more than a simple head cold.

"Potion, sir?" Ison said, the same tone and words he had used in front of the Marca so many times.

He twisted his hands together. He pulled three bronze pieces out of his pocket.

Nera appeared at Ison's side. "One silver," she said flatly. "Unless you've got trading."

The old man looked in his other pocket, then his shabby jacket. He produced a total of five bronze pieces. "Please. I might not wake up tomorrow without it."

Nera held no sympathy on her face, and the old man turned his attention to Ison. If he turned the old man away, he would die. Another life on his hands.

"Five bronze it is," Ison said.

Nera frowned; the old man looked relieved. He handed Ison all of his bronze coins, Ison handed him the health potion, and the old man staggered away, mumbling thanks under his breath.

"That wasn't smart." Nera crossed her arms, looking at the two remaining potions. "Now everyone is going to want cheap potions."

"He looked desperate," Ison said.

The old man still staggered down the street.

"Most people in the Undercity are desperate." She let out a sigh. "There are a lot of people who will take advantage of your kindness."

He felt a weight fall into his knees. "I'm sorry."

"It's fine," she said, though she didn't sound convincing.

Within the hour, the final two potions were traded for a crate of empty glass bottles—for future potion making—and a few herbs that they could use. Finished, Ison, Nera, and the two battlemages hauled their goods back to Josephine's. They neared the house, and Ison's heart jumped at the sight of deep auburn hair.

Juniper was leaning against the warded fence, talking to Xavier. At the sight of Ison, their conversation ended. They both regarded him with cool indifference, learned in their profession, no doubt.

"Hey you," Juniper said to Ison. "Feel like a walk?"

CHAPTER FORTY-FIVE

Juniper guided Ison toward the park at the center of the Undercity. It felt strange to be apart after spending so much time at the castle together. Something about Ison had changed since their flight—his eyes no longer carried the deadweight of guilt and dread.

They meandered through the market and into the park made by pieces of pipe and crisscrossing metal contraptions. Children played games on the bars and chased one another through the pipes. The chatter of the market, gushing of the fountain, and gurgle of the pipes cloaked any conversation—which Juniper had counted on. She led Ison to a part of the garden where children weren't playing and motioned to a puddle on the ground.

"I've been practicing while trailing the captain." She showed him how she could heat water to near boiling.

Ison smiled a genuine smile. "That's good."

Juniper released her hold on the puddle and straightened. "Is Josephine treating you well?" she asked, though she knew the answer.

"Yes." Ison told her about all that he had done, the potions he had been making with Nera, how they had arranged the storeroom, and how he had watched the younger mages learn. He spoke with the energy she remembered him having before.

As he spoke, a tightness in her chest loosened; Ison was enjoying himself, whether he knew it or not. Xavier had chosen right in sending him to Josephine. Ison had made friends, found a place of usefulness. As the tightness deflated, something uglier took its place: jealousy. Ison had come out of his mood, yet she lingered in hers.

Despite that, she knew she should be happy for Ison, and she was. She listened to him speak, felt the happiness in his voice, and tried to soak it in for herself. But the iron of the City Watch reminded her of Reid's silver armor. The captain's honor and sense of duty reminded her of Reid. The rumors she heard about herself made her sick—that she had poisoned Adrian, that she had situated herself in the castle and fooled them all. The people loved Adrian, and now the people hated her with renewed vigor.

And she had heard the rumors of Adrian. He wasn't doing well.

"What about you?" Ison asked.

Juniper faked a grin. "This job is proving harder than I first thought but not impossible."

"Jun," Ison whispered, brow furrowed. "I have a strange feeling about the Dual Fang mages."

She nodded. "I don't like them either. Why? Did they do something to you?"

He sighed, then told her about how they had been watching him in the market. Just like they had been watching her.

"They're looking to recruit," she said. "According to Maddox, that is."

Ison's smile faded, and he glanced toward the fountain. "And then..." Ison whispered about his first meeting with Josephine, how he had told her everything that he had done and heard. Juniper held in her disbelief that he had told the woman all of it, but she didn't disapprove. Josephine was a wise woman, if not strict and secretive.

And then he told her what Josephine had said about a darkness gathering.

Her heart skipped a beat.

Ison folded his arms across his chest. "Do you think she was talking about the apostate?" he whispered.

The Iluvin archmage apostate, Juniper thought, the ancient mage who could control the wechun, who had slaughtered innocents to create monsters, who had taken control of Ison. She thought of the growing threat in the north of Collatia that had the king worried, the rebel mages in the Undercity.

Yes, she did.

"I can't say." She didn't want to think about it, but anxiety clawed up her spine.

"Speaking of apostates," Ison said lightheartedly, "Josephine asked me how you were doing."

"With what?"

"With your magic."

Juniper rolled her eyes. "I'm fine." She motioned to the puddle. "You saw the extent of it. I don't have time to sit and practice anymore. Between this job and training the new kid, I'm busy."

"New kid?"

"Blythe," Juniper corrected. She told Ison about going with Maddox to the market. "He did it to remind me that he owns me."

"You bought her?" Ison asked, disbelief and disgust on his face.

"Maddox would have picked one regardless. And this way, I know she's not going to become a whore. She reminds me of me, a little." Blythe had proven herself to be cunning and a quick learner. She'd already stolen a pouch of gold from a noble.

Ison frowned but didn't push the issue. "Josephine wants to see you."

Juniper cringed.

"She wants to see how your magic is progressing," he clarified.

"Maddox doesn't like me fraternizing with other guilds." It was the truth, though he hadn't argued against her learning about her magic. In truth, the idea of walking into a guild of mages terrified her.

"It's not fraternizing... It's socializing."

She gave a hollow laugh. "Fine."

They left the fountain and started toward Josephine's.

"I didn't realize the mages down here lived so...normally," Ison admitted. "I feel foolish for thinking so in the first place."

"That's because the Order wants everyone to think of apostates as these horrible, despicable creatures, and the City Watch wants everyone to think of the Undercity as a hole for the worst of humanity to hide in," she said bitterly, "neither of which is true." Juniper motioned to one of the hundreds of magelights that dotted the Undercity. "Mages have made this place hospitable. They gave us light, a way to grow food, and a way to keep the water clean. Trust me when I say life has improved greatly since the mages moved in. Sure, there will always be the scum of society, thugs, thieves, and murderers, but it is what it is."

"How long have they been down here?"

Juniper pretended to think about it. "When did the Order form?"

They laughed.

"I don't know how long they've been here, but I've heard how horrible this place used to be without them," Juniper said. "Mostly stories passed down. Before the mages, this really was a hole in the ground for the worst of humanity, which is why no one rats out the mages. Everyone knows how much we rely on them for food and water."

She motioned toward one of the many water spigots in the Undercity. Three mages pulled water from the spigot and then pulled the guck and muck and whatever else from the water—purifying it. They then ushered the clean water into the waiting container of whomever stood in line. No one pushed in that line, and many were children; they knew they would all get water.

She glanced again at the three mages. Water mages. They were several years younger than her, maybe ten or twelve years old, and they had a much better handle on their magic than she did.

A bitterness settled into her bones.

They turned a corner in the market, and Juniper started to speak, when she noticed Ison's attention drift over her shoulder. His steel eyes focused on something and then quickly looked away. He paled.

Juniper glanced to see what he had seen, and sure enough, a taller boy in a dark blue cloak was looking in their direction. At Ison.

A Dual Fang.

Juniper groaned loudly and pulled Ison a step in another direction. She hooked her arm with his. "You okay?"

"I..." Ison swallowed. "It's like they know."

"Know what?"

"Know about me," he whispered. "Know what I've done."

"Nonsense," she said, waving his concern away with her free hand. "They weren't there, nor do they know you."

"Unless the apostate is one of them," he said darkly.

She guided them around a corner, and the tall Dual Fang met them mid-turn, blocking their path with a fluidity that she did not like.

"Move," snapped Juniper.

The Dual Fang didn't move. He stood several inches taller than Juniper, and he looked down his nose at her. He sneered, and his green eyes were full of self-importance.

She balled her fists. A few months ago, if Juniper Thimble had told someone to move, he would have moved.

The green-eyed Dual Fang shifted his gaze. "You're Ison." His calm voice held the lilt of an accent, but she couldn't place it. He held out his hand to Ison. His short fingernails were immaculate. "My name is Clive, and I—"

"And you're in the way," Juniper snapped. She guided Ison to step around Clive, but he sidestepped, blocking their path again. She twisted her hand to her side, and her fingers closed around the hilt of one of the daggers she had borrowed from Xavier.

"My master has told me about you," Clive said to Ison.

Ison stiffened.

Juniper pulled the dagger with a delicate swish and held it against Clive's neck. "And if you wish to speak to anyone ever again, you'll stay put."

Clive's green eyes slid to Juniper, and a sudden dull ache squeezed against her head. Something wanted in, but she didn't let it. Clive's eyes widened, but the flicker of surprise became a smirk. She pressed the dagger further into his neck—he stepped back. The blade had left a small cut, nonlethal. Clive brought a hand up to his throat, and his fingers came away with spots of red; he frowned.

Juniper pulled Ison away from the Dual Fang, and this time, Clive stayed put.

When they arrived at Josephine's, Xavier met them in the foyer. He took one look at Juniper and asked, "What happened?"

Juniper glanced at the handful of mages in the room, most of whom were reading. Xavier caught her meaning, and he led them into the closest empty room. In a few breaths, Juniper related their encounter with the Dual Fang, Clive.

Xavier had the reaction she thought he would: his fists clenched, and his eyes grew murderous. "And you didn't slice his throat?"

"If he had tried to follow, I would have," she said, shrugging. "I told him not to, and he didn't, so he's alive."

"For now," Xavier murmured.

✳

Ison stood to the side as Juniper showed Josephine the extent of her powers. She demonstrated her ability to create ice, which came easiest, and how she had learned to melt the ice, heat the water, and then refreeze it. When Josephine set a marble on the counter and told Juniper to move it with her raw magic, Juniper blinked.

"Manipulating water is one thing," Josephine explained. "But harnessing your raw, natural magic is another. This is what the Order does not want mages to learn, because it gives them a fierce weapon."

"But what is it?" Juniper asked. "How do I get to it?"

"Feel the magic within yourself, the force of it, the strength of it, and visualize it as something tangible, something capable of moving a marble." Josephine gestured to the still marble.

Juniper stared at something unseen, something within herself, concentration fogging her eyes. She held her hand toward the marble, and after a long moment, a flickering tendril of bright blue appeared before her palm. It smacked the marble and sent it flying—it thudded against the wall and rolled under the table.

Juniper's tendril of magic flickered out, and as it did so, she gave a shuddering breath.

"Hmm," Josephine had said, eyes on where the marble had vanished. "I've seen better, and I've seen worse. Keep practicing, but keep your raw magic in mind. It's beyond useful."

Juniper and Xavier left for Maddox's, whispering between each other—about the Dual Fangs, Ison assumed. He tried not to mull about the encounter with Clive and helped Nera and a few others prepare lunch. The midday meal was not as formal as the evening meal, and mages came and went from the dining hall. Ison offered to help with the cleanup, but they refused. He had done enough already, they said. He tried to relax in the library, but he couldn't focus. His mind kept wandering to the Dual Fangs.

Ison rolled his neck over his shoulders, and then he heard the cough from a floor above. Another followed it. Curious, he got up and found the source—a child, sick. Josephine leaned over him, a boy no older than seven, pale and green.

"Nothing serious," Josephine said to the two mages with her. She met Ison's gaze. "Nothing a quick lung tonic wouldn't fix."

Ison didn't need further instruction. He quickly estimated the weight of the boy, headed straight to the potion room, and readied the ingredients. They did not have a supply of fog essence—not surprising. It was expensive and hard to work with, and only the most daring and experienced apothecaries carried it. He hadn't seen a single flask of it in the market when he and Nera had gone out.

No matter, he could find a substitute. He gathered a few coins from the herbal fund and slipped out through the side door without anyone noticing. It would be quicker to go on his own.

The midafternoon crowd in the market teemed with chatter. Ison had tucked his coin purse inside his jacket like Xavier had said—harder to steal. He meandered through the mage sector of the market until he finally found an apothecary that carried his ideal substitute for fog essence. He haggled and won a lower deal, much to his surprise, and tucked the flask into his pocket.

He started back toward Josephine's, feeling better than he had in a while. The flask in his pocket mattered; the potion that he would make with it mattered; the boy's health mattered, and Ison could do something to help him.

Ison was going over the other ingredients in the lung tonic when he turned a corner and nearly walked into someone. He stumbled back a step and muttered a quick apology, but then he got a better look at the girl he'd nearly walked into. She wore the blue cloak of the Dual Fangs and had pale skin and glassy faint blue eyes. She was the same girl he'd seen before, watching him.

Ison started to step around her, intent on pretending she didn't exist.

"I was waiting for you," she said, her voice soft, dreamy. Her glassy eyes shifted over him but did not look directly at him, and it gave him a shiver of unease. "You are Ison."

He stopped mid-step. She hadn't said it as a question. He swallowed. Unlike Clive, this girl didn't seem like a threat. He glanced around; no one watched. "I am. And you are?"

"My name is Bois."

"You're a Dual Fang?" Ison motioned toward the brooch that held her cloak together. It was a silver cast of two fangs, one slightly larger than the other, like the side view of the Collatian mosscat, whose four fangs could grow as long as a grown man's forearm. "What do you want?"

"Only to talk."

"You're doing a fine job so far," Ison said bitterly.

A subtle, almost imperceptible emotion reflected in her eyes. "I will not force you to, but if you would like to speak with me, I will be waiting by the fountain in two hours."

Ison tensed. "Why would I want to speak with you?"

She blinked, but her eyes did not move. Her stare remained on something far over his shoulder, unfocused and glassy. Ison glanced behind him but saw nothing.

Bois spoke softly, "The master has told me about you. He told me the court magician's apprentice ran from the castle and might be in trouble. He told me to help you if I could."

Ison's blood ran cold. The master. The apostate. "He speaks to you?" he whispered.

"Yes," Bois said. "And he has spoken to you. We are connected, like it or not. The master has chosen us both."

Ison felt the market around him vanish. Bois knew about the apostate, the master. The Dual Fangs knew about the apostate. They would have answers that no one else did. And he could get them.

His hands began to shake, and he stuffed them into his pockets to hide it.

Bois stood calmly before him, waiting for his answer.

Finally, Ison said, "I will consider it."

"I will be there," she said, a small smile on her pale lips. "Bring your friend along if you'd like. I will be alone."

Bois walked away. Ison stood there, watching her, waiting for the double cross, the arrow through the throat, the bag over his head, but it didn't come. Bois turned a corner, gone. Ison started back toward Josephine's with shaky legs and trembling hands. His mind raced back and forth, unsure of what to think about first.

When he arrived in the potion room, he pushed all other other thoughts out of his mind and focused on the potion for the sick boy.

CHAPTER FORTY-SIX

"Jun, your friend is here," came Xavier's chime from the top of the basement stairs.

Juniper's training session with Blythe came to a halt.

Amery, who had been leaning against the training ring, straightened. "You have friends?" Amery asked in mock shock.

Juniper left Amery and Blythe to train without her and headed upstairs. Xavier didn't look happy, and it took a moment to realize why. Ison stood in the foyer, the thieves and assassins eyeballing him. He looked out of breath and worried, and when his gray eyes settled on Juniper, that look intensified.

"He arrived by himself a few minutes ago," Xavier said lowly.

By himself. Ison had somehow made his way through the twilit magelights and darkened lanterns of the Undercity, all the way from Josephine's keep to Maddox's. She scanned him quickly; he didn't appear hurt, only worried.

Juniper moved through the foyer, grabbed Ison's arm, and led him out onto the porch, away from the house, and into an alley where no one could listen in without being seen.

"Are you all right? Is something wrong?" Juniper asked.

In a single breath, he told her that he had met a girl named Bois, a Dual Fang who wanted to meet him by the fountain that evening.

"Are you crazy?" Juniper asked.

Breathlessly, he said, "I want you to go with me."

She sighed and ran a hand down her braided hair. They had a chance to find out more about this apostate, and she had promised Blugo that she would find the bastard before she died.

Ison's gaze turned pleading.

"Yes," she said, nodding. "I'll go. Where and when?"

"Near the fountain," he said. "Soon."

❄

On the way to the fountain, through the darkened lights that mimicked the grays and blues of the night, Juniper scolded Ison for going so far by himself. They passed a street lamp that had gone out, leaving a sizeable puddle of darkness below it. Though Juniper could see that nothing lurked within, she guided Ison around it.

Ison chuckled nervously. "I, uh, did blast a few thugs out of the way."

She frowned, and his smile turned sheepish. "What happened?"

"They approached, but I was in a hurry, so before they could finish their threats, I swept them out of the way," Ison said, talking with his hands. She felt a brush of wind against her front. "Josephine told me not to be afraid of using my magic defensively."

Juniper put a hand over her heart. "It warms my soul to know that I'm rubbing off on you," she said, smiling wickedly.

Ison offered her a smile in response.

Most of the market stalls and shops had closed for the night, their goods locked away or gone entirely. A few of the nicer shops paid thugs to stand guard until the shop opened in the morning. Only the worst of the stalls remained open, those that sold things that made her skin crawl: one stall advertised real human hair, eyes, and teeth; another sold trinkets marked with runes, a few of which were human-shaped.

"I'm glad you agreed to come with me," Ison said, eyeing a hunched woman standing in a stall of steaming potions. Her eyes and cheeks had sunk, giving her a skeletal appearance.

"I promised Blugo I would stop the apostate," she told him.

He raised a brow at her, and she told him about the chase and how she had ended up in the temple's offering chamber.

Ison chuckled, and the sound alleviated a growing pressure in her chest. "That's a bold thing to say."

"I don't always think ahead when I'm panicked and cornered." She adjusted the hilt of the dagger at her side. She had gotten used to her own, and Xavier's spares didn't feel right on her person. She might have to spend the extra coin for a few new pieces since the best of her collection had been confiscated by the Royal Guard. "But it's done. I say we meet with this Bois, poke her for answers, and see if we can't kill the apostate before whatever darkness he's bringing comes our way."

Ison nodded.

Juniper kept her hands within reach of her daggers on the way to the fountain. She watched each shadow for threats. She listened for extra footsteps. If Bois had tricked Ison into walking into a trap, Juniper would make sure it was the last thing she would ever do.

The fountain came into view, illuminated by magelights. The churning waters reflected the blues and grays. A blonde girl stood in full view beside it. She wore her blue cloak over plain clothes and had pinned half of her hair up with what looked like bones. The magelight reflected off her silver brooch. Bois watched them approach, her misty and unfocused eyes unsettling.

Juniper and Ison stopped a safe distance away. Juniper felt the water in the fountain, felt its submissive presence. She couldn't explain it—she knew the water would answer if she called upon it, knew it would listen to her.

Bois greeted them with a soft, feminine smile. "I'm glad you came." She had a soft voice that courtesans would kill for. "We haven't had the pleasure of meeting. I am Bois."

The Dual Fang extended her hand toward Juniper. She looked Bois over but saw no immediate weapons or sheaths. Of course, a mage wouldn't need weapons. Juniper cautiously took Bois's soft hand. "Juniper," she said in greeting.

Bois gave no hint that she knew Juniper's name or reputation. Her sweet face remained neutral, her pale pink lips slightly turned upward, giving her a pleasant countenance. She looked no different than a lord's daughter out on a stroll, but Juniper knew better than to assume much from one's outward appearance. She had fooled plenty of shopkeepers into thinking her a starving, desperate girl stealing to survive.

"Juniper," Bois repeated. "The master has told me a little of you."

Ison tensed, and Juniper's fingers twitched toward her daggers. No one jumped from the shadows; no ambush came. Juniper kept calm. Answers, she needed answers.

Juniper said, "Your master knows my name?"

Bois nodded. "Yes."

"Does your master have a name?" Juniper asked.

Ison shot her a quick glance; clearly his idea of poking for information differed from hers.

Bois gave her a small smile. "Yes, but I do not know it."

Juniper raised a brow. "You don't know it?"

"That is correct. He doesn't want to be known. Not yet." Bois's glassy eyes shifted toward Ison. "Our master offers you a place. He offers you a chance to be in the new world, where mages will be free."

Juniper glanced at Ison. He looked as skeptical as she felt.

Bois's pale cheeks flushed pink. She laced her fingers together in front of her and said softly, "I'm not the best with this sort of thing. If you would like to hear more, please, come with me to the keep. Clive is better at explaining things than me."

"You want us to follow you into a den of strange mages?" Juniper asked, and Bois's cheeks flushed brighter. And to Clive, of all people. "Sounds like the perfect plan to murder two unsuspecting people," she drawled, tapping her thumb on the pommel of her dagger. "From what I've heard about this master of yours, he seems the sort to try it."

Bois's shoulders slumped. "It does, but I promise you it's not."

Those misty eyes darted over to Juniper, and she felt a strange wave of energized air—magic. She caught a whiff of tulips.

"And I believe you are capable of walking away from a fight." Bois gave her a knowing smile.

Juniper looked again into Bois's misty eyes—her eyes, the magic. "You're blind?" she blurted.

Ison let out a small gasp of surprise.

Bois nodded. "Yes. With my magic, I can see, just not in the same way that you can see. It's something the master taught me. Please, all I ask is that you hear us out. The master has told us about you, that we are to help you."

Juniper glanced at Ison, and a silent agreement passed between them. As horrible of an idea as it sounded, if they wanted to find out more about the apostate, they would have to wander into enemy territory.

"All right," said Ison. "We'll hear you out. Lead the way."

Against her better judgment, Juniper and Ison followed Bois toward the residential district. Bois maneuvered well considering her lack of sight; she must have used magic to map out the world, avoiding stalls and other people as if she could see them with her eyes.

The Dual Fangs lived in a modest, if not slightly rundown, townhouse a few blocks from Josephine's keep. No ward protected the perimeter. No garden grew. The single magelight lingered in a cage on the front porch, shining with moonlight.

Bois led them to the porch, then paused. She knocked on the door twice, once, waited a beat, then knocked once more.

The door opened instantly. Despite the gloom outside, magelights lit the insides. The walls were mostly bare, save for a few bookshelves and paintings and junky furniture. Two mages sat in the foyer, a game of cards between them—they had upturned a barrel for a table. They paid little attention to their visitors.

Bois led them into a parlor off the main room. Two bookshelves hugged a painting of the countryside. More books were piled on the floor; they had more books than shelf space. Seating was arranged around a low table where three candles burned. Two boys stood on the other side of the parlor, by a window that looked over the street; they had watched Juniper and Ison approach.

The taller of the two was Clive. He wore his blue cloak but kept the hood up. He ran his green eyes over Juniper, then Ison. "So they both came after all," he sneered.

"You owe me a silver," said the second boy. He stood a head shorter than Clive. He slid his dark eyes over the visitors; all the while, his wicked grin grew wider—not the grin of an assassin, the grin of a madman. Juniper knew at once she disliked him.

"You have met Clive," Bois said, motioning to him. She motioned to the other. "This is Dyn."

Beside her, Ison shifted.

"We are in charge of the Dual Fangs," said Clive in a tone that indicated that *he* was in charge. "And our master wants us to talk to you—both of you, apparently. So, please have a seat."

Ison and Juniper sat on a lopsided sofa. Her bottom sank farther than she expected, and she heard the creaking of wood underneath. Thirdhand furniture, maybe fourth. Clive sat in the largest and best chair; Dyn and Bois sat on either side of him.

Clive held his chin and shoulders proudly—a boy not used to being in charge but a boy who craved to be in charge. "Our master wants to shut down the Order of the Knighthood. He wants to destroy the Marca and set mages free. We'll be able to live where we want, marry who we want, and have whatever jobs we want, without the Order breathing down our necks. Without the Marca, we will be able to use our gods-given magic how we please and learn however we wish." Clive slammed his fists onto the arm of his chair. "We will not be locked up and imprisoned."

"Our master will make the world better for mages," Bois added, her voice soft compared to Clive's.

Dyn added, "But he can't do it alone."

"That is why we are here," Clive said. "We are his eyes, his ears, and his hands in Rusdasin."

Juniper met Clive's vicious gaze. *In Rusdasin.* That meant their master had other followers elsewhere doing his bidding. She ran her finger along the hilt of her blade.

246

"Your master sees fit to slaughter innocent people for his goals?" Ison asked, his voice cold and unforgiving.

Clive frowned. "If that is what it takes to change the world, so be it," he spat.

"Or he'll stomp out those who disagree?" Juniper closed her fingers around the hilt but didn't make a motion to pull it out. She doubted a dagger would do much against three mages, plus those lingering in the room beyond.

"As would any leader," Clive said. "Victories are not easily obtained. People die in war. Leaders must keep a hold on their people."

"And in order to change the world," Ison continued, "your master is willing to build himself a ladder of bodies to reach the top. Do you know what all he did to the people in the castle?"

None of them spoke. Clive's frown deepened.

"He used me to butcher innocent people, servants of the castle, people who had no reason to be slaughtered," Ison said, and Juniper felt her skin prickle; she had never heard him speak so coldly. "He used them, their souls, their blood, in order to create a handful of beasts with no other purpose than to cause havoc in the castle. You tell me that you want that madman in charge of this world?"

The silence settled in around them, and Juniper wished that she had told Xavier where they had gone; Josephine could have had an army of mages ready to get them out of here if this turned ugly.

"He is not a madman," Bois said softly.

Ison started to disagree, but Juniper nudged his knee with her own. She cast as subtle of a warning as she could; they were supposed to be gathering information, not pissing them off.

"Even if he is," said Clive, burning eyes on Ison, "The Order and the Marca are broken systems. They must be torn down if mages hope for anything better. Our master wants a world where mages are free, and we can't have free mages while there are knights who think otherwise."

"Not that I disagree with removing the Marca and dismantling the Order," said Juniper, "I disagree with destroying those in the way and those who disagree. I dislike the slaughter of innocents."

Clive focused his eyes on her.

She held her voice steady. "However, I would rather see the Marca torn down than be forced into it."

And the tension eased slightly.

Ison cleared his throat and met Clive's stare. "Have you met this master of yours?" he asked.

No one answered. Something silent passed between Dyn and Clive, and Juniper saw her chance. "If you've not seen him, how do you know he's even real?" she asked softly, pretending intrigue.

"Because he speaks to us," Clive said, eyes pinned on Ison. "He spoke to you, right? You know what it feels like."

Ison paled.

Clive continued, "He is real, as real as I am sitting here. He has extended an offer of friendship to you, Ison." His gaze slid over to Juniper, then back to Ison, excluding her from that offer. "But it won't stay open for long. Choose your side wisely."

Clive stood, the parlor doors opened on their own, and just like that, the meeting was over. Clive stormed off and out of sight. Dyn lingered by the doorway, leaning against it with small zaps of lightning dancing between his fingers. Bois escorted Juniper and Ison outside and to the street. Once they passed the fence, Bois let out a heavy sigh.

"It's rubbish," Juniper said.

"It's not," Bois said, pouting like a child.

"And you're certain of this?" Juniper asked, doubtful. The Dual Fangs were fanatics, just like Maddox said, a cult for mages who wanted extreme justification.

Bois flushed; she looked close to tears. "I lost my sight as a child because of Mage's Bane." She fisted her dainty hands in her cloak. "Then I was hauled across the kingdom to the Marca, always in the dark. The knights didn't care. They told me mages were nothing, taunted me, said I belonged in the Marca. Then, the master spoke to me. He was kind. He said he would help me escape a horrible fate and that I would be free, like mages should be. The master saved me and taught me how to use my magic to see." Bois remained still, but the same energized air flushed over Juniper, and by Ison's small gasp, he had felt it as well. "I can feel the world and everything in it, like how far away you are standing, how often you rolled your eyes at me," she said to Juniper, "and how many daggers you have on your person. I count five."

Juniper shifted; she indeed wore five daggers, two of which were visible.

Bois continued, her voice small and wet, "He helped me get here, to the Undercity, and told me that he wanted to end the Order's reign of terror on mages. He would restore my sight because it was wrongly taken from me." Bois's grip on her robes turned white-knuckled. "The master promised that when he returns to power, he will restore my sight entirely."

"Returns to power?" Juniper repeated.

Bois froze. The rosy tint on her cheeks paled. Her cloudy eyes widened. She had said too much.

Juniper stepped closer. Obviously, if they were going to get information, it would be from Bois. "Who?" she whispered.

"I-I..." Bois swallowed. She stumbled back toward the house. "I should get back."

Bois half ran back to the house. Juniper and Ison shared a knowing glance; they had uncovered something. They started away from the Dual Fangs, and Juniper tried out Bois's trick. She sent her magic out in a net of detection. She couldn't feel the world enough to close her eyes but felt the stalls and the shops. She could feel the empty space behind them. No one followed, at least not closely. She couldn't hold the net out for long; it drained her quickly.

Neither of them spoke on the way to Josephine's. They paused before the ward.

"Returns to power," Ison repeated. "Gathering darkness."

"I don't like it," she whispered.

"Neither do I." He glanced toward Josephine's closed doors. "Jun, maybe we should tell Josephine about all this. She might know something."

Juniper bit her lip. She remembered Mason's warning. She wanted to tell Ison everything he had said. She didn't want to be the secretkeeper anymore. "Maybe, but let's wait. I want to think about it myself a little longer."

Ison's frown deepened. He started to say something, then stopped. He searched her face, then whispered, "Jun, are you hiding something?"

She swallowed. "Why would you ask?"

"You didn't answer the question," Ison said quickly, and she had the sinking suspicion that Xavier had taught him that trick—avoidance, and how to spot it.

"I'm keeping things from a lot of people," she said.

His eyes narrowed. "But are you keeping things from me?"

She didn't answer, and she could see the anger in his eyes, not just anger but disappointment and betrayal.

"It's not because I don't want to tell you everything," she said, desperate for him not to look at her like that. "I promised him I wouldn't."

"Him?" Ison said quickly. The thoughts connected behind his eyes. "Mason?"

She tried to think of a lie, but she wasn't fast enough.

Ison let out a groan and took several steps back. "I knew he was keeping things from me. I knew it. And he told you something, didn't he? About me?"

"Not just about you," she whispered, the truth on the tip of her tongue.

Ison didn't believe her. He looked her over like a stranger, and she felt the rift between them, felt something fracture.

"Ison."

"Josephine wants you to come by tomorrow for lunch," he said flatly, business-like. "She wants to test you on your magic."

Ison stepped through the ward, and Juniper stood rooted to the street. She forced her legs to head back to Maddox's guild.

Why hadn't she just told him about Mason's Iluvin suspicions? Why couldn't she have just blurted it out?

She knew why.

If there was still a chance that Ison had a connection to the apostate, she didn't want the apostate to find out what they knew. Still, as she trudged through the sparse market, her heart settled somewhere low, and that old familiar darkness opened wide to swallow her whole.

CHAPTER FORTY-SEVEN

Reid returned to his chambers. He had spent his morning watching over Adrian and his afternoon studying and training, and he felt like his body hadn't slept in weeks. He shut himself in the bathing room. He wanted nothing more than to rest, but he had promised his aunt he would come by for dinner.

He washed his face in cool water and had the towel against his skin when a hurried knock sounded on his door. Reid groaned into the towel. What now?

"Reid?" came a voice he knew—Squire Henry Julian.

Reid tensed. He and Henry had been studying together that day. Had something happened? A series of worst-case scenarios played through his mind as he rushed to the door. Henry stood on the other side. Henry's hair was damp from a bath, and he hadn't donned his armor.

"Yes?" Reid asked.

"A summons," Henry said. "The king has called a meeting in the throne room. We're invited."

"Adrian?" Reid asked, his heart quickening.

"I don't know," Henry said quickly.

Reid hurried into the corridor, and the two of them started toward the throne room. Reid's fear went to Adrian first, then to another Juniper Thimble impostor; the Watch had been dragging girls in by the dozens, each hoping for the reward. Reid had seen enough of those, as had the king, and he wouldn't call a sudden meeting for another one.

No, something else had happened. Something *wrong*.

They arrived at the throne room. The crowd surprised him. His uncle and aunt were present, neither letting their worry show, as well as several knights, upper staff, and a handful of stone-faced nobles. The air was thick and somber, and Reid did not like it. Despite what he felt, he held himself straight—like a knight. The king stood before his throne, flanked by the court magician and Rourke Hendle. Ron Hendle stood to the side of his father, chin held at an arrogant angle. He surveyed the crowd before him as if he were king. Reid bristled but held it in.

The king held up his hand, and the chatter in the room died at once.

"Thank you all for coming on short notice," said the king. "I have grievous news. My trusted advisor, Destin Ulgan, passed this afternoon."

A murmur went through the crowd, and relief washed over Reid. No one looked surprised. Ulgan had been deathly ill.

The king continued, "There will be a funeral for him in three days on the Royal Grounds. Before he passed, Ulgan recommended I appoint Ronald Hendle to replace him in the event of his death because, in Ulgan's words, Ron has a good head on his shoulders." The king looked to where Ron stood beside his father. "And with my approval, Ronald Hendle is now advisor to the king."

A quiet applause followed. Reid clapped for Ron, but he didn't like the idea of a father and son advising the king. Though, if Ulgan supported Ron, then Ron and his father must not see eye to eye. The king would know that.

The crowd dispersed, and Reid felt a weight lift from his shoulders. He knew he shouldn't feel such in the wake of Ulgan's death, but he had never been fond of the man. His passing didn't affect him in the slightest. He and Henry made their way toward the throne to congratulate Ron—Reid did feel glad for his friend.

Ron greeted them with a cool, proud gaze.

"Congratulations, friend." Reid held his hand out to Ron.

Ron hesitated just a beat too long, skimming over Reid with appraisal. Then he gripped his hand. "Thank you, Reid."

Henry held out his next. "You've had this coming."

Ron looked at Henry—for a brief moment, he did not look at Henry as one looks at a friend, but as one sizing up an enemy. "Thank you." Ron spoke evenly, in the voice of a trained politician. He did not smile; he held himself stern and proper.

Did he already think himself above them?

Reid said, "It looks like Ulgan may have rubbed off on you."

"A little too much," added Henry. "You're standing stiffer than a man in a whorehouse."

Ron tensed. His gaze went between Reid and Henry, and then he let out a charming laugh. He smiled, and he looked more like himself, but something seemed off. Reid couldn't place it. Ron had weaseled his way into the king's inner circle and likely inherited Ulgan's chain of spies and scouts, and it seemed the new position had given him a strong sense of pride and status.

Henry and Reid stepped away from Ron. Two nobles replaced them, blubbering congratulations and compliments.

Once out of the throne room, Reid asked, "Did he seem off to you?"

"Yes," Henry answered without hesitation. "He's got a bigger head now than he did this morning. It'll only get bigger."

Reid sighed through his nose. He agreed. However, maybe having Ron as an advisor would not be all bad. He and Adrian were friends, after all, and the transition seemed natural. Reid bid farewell to Henry and pushed out the thoughts of the evening. He didn't want to think until morning.

CHAPTER FORTY-EIGHT

The next morning, Juniper started toward Josephine's with a sickening feeling in her stomach. She had repeated the words "returns to power" and "gathering darkness" to herself over and over until she had fallen into an uneasy sleep. Her lack of quality sleep had ripened her mood, and the bright yellow of the magelights didn't help.

She inhaled the stench of the Undercity and decided that she would tell Ison at least part of Mason's suspicions; she would tell him that their apostate was likely Iluvin. She would leave out the archmage bit. She still had a hard time believing that one. She had a hard enough time believing that anyone alive today could be Iluvin when the Order supposedly wiped them out a thousand years ago. Of course, the apostate had proven himself a master of hiding himself in plain sight, under the Order's nose.

She didn't know what to think. She would rather their apostate be some scrawny man hiding in a broom closet of the castle, someone with a nose she could break.

Juniper was halfway to Josephine's when Xavier joined her, but he didn't look happy.

"I hear you and Ison went to see the Dual Fangs." When she didn't deny it, Xavier's mouth turned downward. "You know how horrible of an idea that was?"

"Nothing happened," Juniper said, waving his concern aside.

"They are a cult," Xavier said to Juniper. "They'd sooner skin you alive than speak the truth. If that's what you want, come back to Maddox's. He's in a mood today."

Juniper harrumphed.

Xavier leaned forward, his eyes searching. "What's gotten to you this early, hmm? The baker skimp the sugar on your sweet roll?"

"Ison's mad at me," she said plainly.

Xavier straightened. "Oh. What did you do?"

She sighed. "I kept things from him. I *am* keeping things."

"We all have secrets," Xavier said.

"Yeah, but he thinks I'm not telling him because I don't trust him."

"Do you?"

254

She didn't answer, and Xavier nodded. After a moment, he added, "He knows this is the Undercity, right? Trust is one of those commodities we don't operate on. Trust in the Undercity is worth more than gold."

"I know that," she said.

They arrived at the ward. Josephine was standing on the porch, a deep frown on her face, hand on her hip.

"Looks like she knows about your date last night," Xavier muttered.

Juniper took a deep breath and stepped through the ward. The magical net tingled against her skin, but nothing happened—not that she had expected to burst into flames. Xavier came in behind her.

Josephine didn't say a word until they reached the porch, then ordered them into the parlor. Ison was standing by the window, pretending not to notice their entrance.

Juniper sat across from Josephine and showed her the lack of progress she had made. She could whisk flurries around her cupped hands, form those flurries into ice pellets, and form those ice pellets into a lumpy ice ball. She concentrated hard to melt the ice ball without water spilling, and then harder to boil the water. She felt the strain as she refroze the water—it did not freeze solid. Water sloshed around in the middle. For her pitiful finale, she strained her magic to form a tendril of bright blue—it grew out of her palm like a wicked weed, bent and unyielding, then flashed out of sight like lightning. Exhausted, Juniper dropped the ice ball into a bowl. She felt the squeeze in her arms and legs, and she reclined back into the chair.

"You have made progress," Josephine said, to Juniper's surprise. "Small to some, but you have gotten quicker between freezing and heating. It takes some water mages years to get that fast." Josephine stood. "Have you eaten yet today?"

"No," Juniper said.

Josephine hummed her disapproval. "Sit tight. I will fetch you something before you collapse."

Josephine left, and Juniper sighed. "I've frozen and heated and refrozen water before," she whined. "Why can't I do it now?"

"She's watching," Xavier said plainly. He leaned in, hot breath tickling her ear, "She makes me nervous too."

"And you honestly haven't eaten today?" Ison asked, frowning.

Juniper met his steely gaze, and guilt pulled her shoulders down.

"Maddox doesn't do breakfast." Xavier glanced to the doors. "She's not watching now."

Juniper leaned over the bowl. Without Josephine, with just Ison and Xavier, a calm came over her. She froze the ball solid.

"Melt it," Ison said from her side, his voice soft and soothing.

She did as he instructed, melting the ice into a ball of water.

"Boil it," he said.

The water grew warmer, warmer, warmer. It steamed, and a few boiling bubbles twitched their way to the surface.

"Freeze it," Ison said.

Her magic wavered—it started to seize within her, but she refused to stop. She commanded the boiling water. And it froze solid.

"I'll be damned," said Xavier.

"That's a tip for the jar," came Josephine's voice.

They all three jumped; Juniper dropped her ball of ice. It hit the side of the bowl and bounced out and landed on the floor.

Josephine stood in the doorway, tea tray in her hand, a grand smile on her face. "I knew you had it in you."

Juniper grabbed the ice ball with her bare hand and set it within the bowl.

"Your well of power has grown, too," said Ison.

Josephine set the tea tray on the coffee table. Xavier sat in one of the chairs, and Ison sat beside Juniper on the sofa.

While Xavier and Josephine were talking, Juniper whispered to Ison, "I'm sorry."

"It's okay," he said. "I understand. I just was frustrated with everything."

"Friends?" she asked.

"Of course," Ison said. "You think I'd toss you to the side because of one little fight? You don't know me that well."

Ison joined the talk of magic, and Juniper tried to follow. Xavier and Ison knew more about magic than she did, and she found her attention drifting. The tea warmed her in a way that normal tea could not, and the cookies replenished something inside of her—her well of magic.

She had progressed greatly in the past few weeks, but it wasn't enough. She wanted more. She wanted the power she had unleashed upon the demon. She wanted the ice that could freeze a creature solid in the blink of an eye. She wanted to feel that rush of power, to feel like she could command the entire ocean.

Josephine and Ison were talking potions and herbs, and Juniper's already fragile attention traveled into the main room, over the towering bookshelves, to the thousands of books. So much magical knowledge in one room.

It was strange to think that only a few months ago, she had nothing to read but Reid's boring history book.

A history book.

Her heart skipped a beat, and she dropped her half-eaten cookie to the floor. Thoughts in her mind connected faster than she could speak, and she stumbled to her feet and into the main room.

"Jun?" came Ison's voice.

She paid them no mind, no time. She had to find that book. She scanned the shelves, but all she found were magical texts. What was the title of that book? Something about knights and the Order and history... *History of the Knights of the Order.*

Xavier grabbed her arm. "What are you doing?"

"Looking for a book," she said quickly.

Xavier didn't release her. His blue-gray eyes carried worry. It gave her pause; she had rarely seen Xavier worried.

"Jun?" Ison asked, standing beside Xavier.

"I'm looking for *The History of the Knights of the Order.*" She turned her gaze toward Josephine, who observed the scene with motherly interest. "Do you have it here?"

Ison frowned. "Why are you looking for that book?"

Juniper wiggled her arm out of Xavier's grip. "Because there was a passage in the beginning about an Iluvin mage falling from power."

Ison realized her meaning; his face paled.

"I can't remember the details. I was half-delirious at the time, but it was during the Great War. I read about it. It was why the Order was formed—or something—to defeat this Iluvin mage."

"You are talking about Nexon," Josephine said sternly. She stood in the door to the parlor, looking at Juniper like she had uttered the worst possible word, and no amount of gold for the jar would undo it.

The name sounded familiar. "Who is that?" Juniper asked.

Josephine didn't answer. She stared down at the three of them, her dark eyes pinned on Juniper. After a long moment, she said, "Sit. Drink up. Eat something more, the three of you." Not a request. An order.

Juniper, Xavier, and Ison returned to the parlor, and this time, Josephine closed the doors. She waited until they each took a seat and a bite of a cookie, then said, "Nexon was an Iluvin mage who lived a thousand years ago. He and his army conquered most of the known world. A force rose up against him, one that would become the Order. The Great War began. The world divided. It seemed that the Order would not prevail; however, when Iluvin mages began to side with the Order to defeat Nexon, the tide turned. And then, in the Battle of Blackwood, Nexon fell, and his reign ended."

The room grew silent. Juniper held onto her tea. Her hands shook, and gentle ripples wiggled along the amber surface.

"Why would you be interested in a story like that?" Josephine looked thoughtfully at Ison and then at Juniper. "Would it have anything to do with your new friends?"

Juniper wanted to shrink from the older mage's glare.

"Don't think I don't know about your excursion last night," Josephine said, and beside her, Ison flushed. "So, go on, explain yourselves."

Ison explained his meeting with Bois, and they took turns explaining their meeting with the Dual Fangs.

"Bois mentioned that their master will return to power," Ison said at last, meeting Josephine's furious gaze. "What does it mean?"

"It's nonsense," Josephine said quickly.

"The king didn't think it nonsense." Juniper met Josephine's dark and angry eyes. "He worried about the mages in the north of Collatia. They were gathering power, but he didn't know for what or who could be organizing them. But...could it honestly be Nexon?"

"He'd be over a thousand years old," Ison said.

Josephine didn't answer. Her one hand was balled tightly into a fist.

"It is possible," Juniper said for her. She remembered what Mason had told her about the Iluvin. "The Iluvin live longer than we do."

"Perhaps it is better if you return to Maddox for lunch instead," Josephine said, each word a threat.

Juniper felt the words like a punch to the chest. Guilt and defiance warred within her. She had only been to Josephine's twice, and she'd already gotten kicked out. Great. Juniper finished her tea in two gulps, then stood. Ison walked with her and Xavier to the ward.

"She looked pissed," Xavier whispered. He wore disapproval but intrigue. "Are you sure about this?"

"Not in the slightest, but what if it is Nexon?" Ison asked. Xavier opened his mouth to argue, but Ison continued, "Every time I close my eyes, I see someone dead because of me. I can't sleep. I can't think. I can barely get through each day as it is. Even if I have a small chance of finding the mage who did this to me, who killed all of those people, I have to take it."

Xavier glanced at her. "You feel the same, Jun?"

She nodded. "If I don't do anything else with my life, I can say I stopped whatever tide of darkness Nexon is trying to bring. Then I can say I lived a life worth living." She smirked. "Besides, I've got a few right hooks for that bastard's face."

Gods. How was she supposed to hunt down and exact revenge on a one-thousand-year-old mage?

Ison tried to give her an encouraging smile, but it faltered. He bid them both a farewell and returned to Josephine's keep, leaving Juniper and Xavier standing on the other side of the ward.

"Some problem you two have uncovered." Xavier sighed, then nudged her. "Do you think you'll burst into flames if you try to go in again?"

She eyed the ward. "I'd rather not test it."

CHAPTER FORTY-NINE

Juniper picked through her lunch. She tried to push Nexon out of her mind, but he kept resurfacing.

Amery found a muddy brown wig that smelled strongly of cheap perfume and helped Juniper pin her hair back. With her disguise, Juniper resumed her stalking of Captain Tinnly. She meandered through the bustling market stalls and shops along Royal Avenue, keeping Central Watch Tower in her sights. An hour after midday, the captain left the tower with a few of his men; they took their horses on a patrol through the city.

She couldn't get him while he rode through the streets, not without alerting half the Watch and causing mass panic. If she did, then she wouldn't be able to fetch his dagger or his head. So, rather than exhausting herself by following him, Juniper slunk into the shadows of an alley. She climbed to the roof of a dress boutique and sat behind a wide chimney to hide her from the tower and the street.

The captain would be back. Until then, she flexed her magic, summoning ice, heating it, cooling it, moving it about the air, and using her raw magic like an extended hand. She flexed it out like she imagined Bois did and closed her eyes to feel the world. She could feel, but it was not the same as seeing. Her magic felt along the stone of the roof, the loose pebbles, the edge, the drainage pipe, the stones of the chimney. If she focused, she could feel the seams between the stones.

She pulled her magic back before she tired herself out.

And waited.

And waited.

And waited.

The sun gradually sank, the light turned molten, and the first few stars dotted the eastern sky. She watched the stars blink to life as the sun went to sleep, and she felt her magic respond in kind to the night—her time.

She reached out with her magic. She could go farther than she could before, feel more. Her magic well had deepened.

The sound of hooves drew her attention back to the ground, to the mission. Captain Tinnly and his men rode back to the tower. They led the horses into the stables, where the stable hands took them, and the men entered the tower. Shadows of men and their voices came from windows of the second, third, and fourth floors—the barracks. The first floor was the main office; underneath were the cells. She knew that from experience.

She jumped onto the next rooftop and the next after that. With the night thickening all around her, her shadow wouldn't stand out against the others.

A light came to life on the fifth floor—the flicker of a candle. It traveled through the fifth floor—the captain's study—to his quarters on the sixth, the top floor. The captain had returned home.

Juniper crouched, waiting. The captain certainly closed any easy way to get him alone without putting herself in mortal danger.

She waited.

The last of the light faded from the sky.

And then, a light flickered on the fifth floor. Juniper readied herself for her chance. The light grew brighter as the captain lit more candles. The shutters opened, and Captain Tinnly appeared, helmet gone, hair a mess. He gazed out at the street below him, then retreated into his study.

Juniper's heart jumped into her throat, but she dared to go no further.

The captain had conveniently left the window open, a window to a room where he stood presumably alone, as if welcoming assassins to try their hand.

Many assassins had tried to kill him and failed. Captain Tinnly would know about the contract on his life, and yet he left his window open?

No. Juniper's instincts told her to stay away. A trap.

Watchmen stood at the tower's doors. Dozens slept in the barracks. If she tried to scale the tower and jump in through the window, he would see her coming. He would alert the Watch. She would be caught.

She would find a better way in.

❄

Juniper returned to the market the following afternoon, her hair hidden under a blonde wig. She followed Captain Tinnly for a while; she sipped tea in one café, wine in another, and read in the courtyard of the bookstore. She watched the watchmen come and go, studied their rotations. While the watchmen had a routine they followed, it didn't appear that their captain did.

She read all she could and then took to meandering the market. She soaked in the warm summer sun, so refreshing after staying in the Undercity, while she also soaked in the market gossip.

Girls with copper-brown hair and blue eyes were being taken to the castle in hopes they were Juniper Thimble, all because of that fifty thousand gold bounty. Dozens every day. Poor things.

The king's advisor, Ulgan, had died the night before last—sickness. She couldn't say she felt sorry for him; she hadn't known him.

"It's right this way. The next street," came a pleasant male voice from the street behind her.

A second replied, "We could have taken a carriage, Ron, not bothered with the crowds."

Whatever solace she had found in the sunlight shattered at the sound of that smooth, articulate male voice—his voice—so close behind her. Her magic shivered in response. She turned her back to the voices, pretending to be more interested in the stall of scarves.

"Yes, but the people need to see the new advisor. It makes me look personable." The young man gave a friendly laugh. "You could take a few notes, Reid."

"I'm supposed to look intimidating," came Reid's reply. "It deters threats. Which is why I'm here."

Reid and his friend walked past her—right behind her. Reid wore his silver armor. He walked with one hand on the pommel of his blade, the other loose and ready to act. Beside him walked a young man she had never seen before, who wore the clothes of a noble. He turned to wave at someone—he wore the sneer of a noble too.

Reid turned his head in the same direction, and she turned her attention back to the scarves, angling her face so that he wouldn't see her. It didn't matter; her cheeks burned, her chest squeezed her breath out of her lungs, and her entire body trembled.

"Are you all right, dear?" asked the vendor.

"Yes. Too much sun," Juniper lied. She meandered to the next stall, away from Reid. She paused at the engraved bowls and cups, then glanced over her shoulder.

Reid and his friend had continued onward.

He hadn't seen her.

And then, someone behind her dropped a very loud, very rude curse, and the chitchat along the street ebbed.

Reid turned, typical scowl on his bronze face, honey-brown eyes searching for the offending mouth. His gaze flashed over her head. Then, within a single heartbeat, those eyes dropped to her.

Her heart seemed to stop altogether.

Reid's brows came together in realization, and his lips started to move, started to form her name.

A couple passed in front of her; she dashed through the gap between two stalls, her wooden legs wobbly and not as nimble as she would have liked. She crisscrossed to the other side of the market but didn't stop. She put as much space between her and Reid as she could and didn't stop until she put three streets between them. She ducked into an alley and bent over, hands on her knees.

Her stomach threatened to undo her lunch.

No armored footsteps raced after her. No footsteps at all.

Reid hadn't followed.

Juniper slid to the ground, hand over her racing heart. When it slowed, she pulled the letter out of her pocket. She had finished it that morning, thinking she would mail it that day. With a shaking hand, she produced a small flame on the tip of her thumb. She set fire to the corner of the letter and let it flutter to the ground. She watched the flame grow and consume the entire letter, all of the words, until it was a pile of ash.

She would have to start over.

CHAPTER FIFTY

For the next five days, Juniper trained Blythe in the morning and stalked Captain Tinnly until he vanished into his Tower in the evening. She kept out of sight, meandered the markets, shops, and stores. She kept her eyes open for Reid and his friend, but she didn't see them again.

She also heard rumors of mages. Everyone worried about the rebel mages from Collatia, whispering about how they had infiltrated the city and worked their evil magic from the Undercity. The rebel mages were blamed for all manner of things, from house fires to insomnia to lost socks. Maybe they should educate non-mages about magic too. She smiled at the thought of mages and non-mages sitting side by side in a classroom, learning how magic worked and what it could do and what it could not.

Juniper rewrote her letter several times each day. She got tired of using Maddox's supplies, so she stole ink from one store, a quill from another, and paper from yet another—stealing all three from one store would be suspicious. She burned the failed letters. In between attempts to write, she practiced her magic. Beside each pile of ash, she left a pile of snow. It gave her practice switching between natural magic and unnatural magic. Snow and ice came easier than the flame, but she would get better.

Captain Tinnly left the tower early each morning and returned near sunset. Sometimes he went to his apartment on the top, and sometimes he went to his study to brood.

On the fifth day of her stalking, she followed the smells of sizzling meat, sweet spices, and butter to the market. She bought a chunk of pork speared on a wooden stick and ate it as she walked. She missed the food at the castle. She missed the free food that came delivered to her door. And her silk pajamas. And her large cloud-like bed.

She caught snippets of gossip as she meandered; she caught her own name several times, the girl who eluded the Watch.

"They should string that bitch up for poisoning the prince," came a sharp female voice from a fruit stand. A woman was slicing pineapple, the blade moving easily. "Or, better yet, they should tie her to a post outside the castle gates and let the people at her." The woman waggled her knife at another woman. "I'd show her what I think of her."

Juniper caught the woman's eye and gave her an innocent smile.

The woman gave her a friendly smile in return. "Pineapple dear? Fresh in this morning."

"I would love some, but I don't have much coin." Juniper fished out a few bronze pieces.

"No worries. Good thing about fruit is it slices in more ways than one." The woman who had threatened to show Juniper Thimble what she thought handed her a small skewer with a few pieces of pineapple, three bronze pieces' worth.

"Thank you, ma'am." Juniper took a bite and started away.

"Sweet girl," said the woman. "I wish more were like her. The world might not be as messed up as it is."

Juniper smiled to herself.

✻

Refreshed and in a good mood, Juniper threw caution to the wind and rewrote her letter one last time, using her last piece of clean parchment. She tucked it into her belt and headed for the Undercity to find a courier. She weaved through the crowd, trying not to look in a hurry. She didn't need any extra attention.

She took a shortcut through a small park and immediately regretted it. Couples lingered in the park, watching small children play, holding hands, and a few exchanged those sickening love stricken glances—it made Juniper half-sick. She stuffed her hands into her pockets and avoided as many people as she could, not that anyone in the park paid attention to her.

Reid's face came to mind, the quick glance he had given her. He had recognized her, and in that moment, he'd seemed surprised. He had found her, a wanted criminal, but he hadn't chased her down or sounded the alarm.

He'd let her go.

He had wanted her gone, and she had left.

She took a deep breath. Reid had always been beyond her reach. As a squire from a respectable family, he had a future. As an Undercity rat, an orphan, she had nothing. Whatever game they had played at the castle, it had been doomed from the start. She had been foolish to think otherwise.

Juniper gladly left the lovesick park behind and made her way through an alley shortcut to the next street. Stalls lined the sides, and people flocked back and forth. She had meandered through to the next alley when a gruff male voice cut through the chatter, "You think I believe you?"

It was a watchman. At his shout, the crowd stilled and hushed. Most stopped to watch. His dark silver armor had been well-used, nicks and scratches marring the breastplate. He glowered at a mousy-haired young woman who clutched a pearl and gold bracelet in her hands.

The woman mumbled something too low to hear.

The watchman bellowed, "You're dressed in those rags, and you expect me to believe you had the gold to pay for that?"

Tears lined the woman's eyes. She clutched the bracelet tighter. "I bought it, I swear!"

The watchman advanced a step, putting a hand on his pommel. The woman retreated a step, her back hitting the post of a stonework stall—the vendor had turned a ghostly shade of white. The woman looked around desperately for help, but no one did a thing.

"I-I saved up for months to buy it," the woman said, her voice cracking. Tears started to run down her cheeks. She sidestepped toward the alley, away from the crowd and away from the watchman.

The watchman's hand tightened on the hilt.

Juniper swallowed—silently begging the woman not to run, not to move. Her heart thudded in her chest, threatening to pop out.

The woman took another step, and Juniper saw the change in the watchman—the intent to strike. Juniper couldn't stand by. She took a step forward to distract him, to call him a liar, to give the maybe-thief time to get away. But a booming male voice halted her actions.

"Chynce!" shouted Captain Tinnly.

His horse trotted down the street, and Juniper quickly stepped out of his way and out of his immediate view; thankfully, most were looking at the watchman and the woman who clutched the bracelet to her chest. The captain stopped his horse a short way from the alley's mouth.

"This girl's a thief, sir," said Watchman Chynce.

She trembled. "I bought it!" she said, her voice barely there.

"Did you see her steal?" replied Tinnly calmly.

"No, but—"

"Was the theft reported to you?"

"No, I—"

"Then how do you know for certain that she is a thief?"

Watchman Chynce swallowed. The woman had sunk into the wall of the alley. "That bracelet's worth more gold that she looks like she has," he said.

"Ah," said Tinnly. "Because she looks poor, she must be poor, and thus she shouldn't have any gold. Is that right?"

Chynce went a shade pale.

"Young lady," Tinnly said, and Juniper felt every hair on her body raise, even though he did not address her. "Can you tell me where you purchased your bracelet?"

The girl quickly, albeit shakily, rattled off one of the finer jewelers in the market, how much she had paid for it, and how long she had been saving up to buy it for her sister as a wedding present.

"Thank you. Forgive my watchman for his assumptions. Here." The captain handed her a few coins. "For your troubles."

She accepted them with a shaking hand. She mumbled her thanks, and before anyone could take it back, she fled the scene. Then the captain turned his attention to his watchman, and his kind face turned into one of displeasure.

"I'm sorry, sir, but she looked—"

"It is not your place to assume who has money and who does not," snapped the captain, and the street grew quiet around him. "As a man of the City Watch, it is your duty to protect the people of Rusdasin, not accuse them and flaunt your title above them. A watchman does not flaunt, brag, or bully. A watchman is honorable, wise, and just. Your duty is to the people, not to yourself. Understand?"

A beat, then Chynce nodded. His face had gone red. "Understood, Captain."

"Make sure we do not have this talk again, for it will be your last." With that, the captain turned and guided his horse away.

Everyone on the street suddenly found something else to look at.

The scolded watchman turned with the sour expression of a man humiliated in public, and though Juniper had been watching the captain's retreating back, her eyes snagged on those of the watchman—a beat passed. His brow scrunched, and his mouth flickered downward. Recognition. His lips began to part.

She turned away from him, pretending not to have witnessed his scolding while trying to calm her thumping heart.

"Hey, wait." The watchman grabbed Juniper's arm.

"Let go," Juniper said in a voice higher than her own. "I've done nothing wrong."

A few people around the street paused, gawking at the watchman who would be so foolish twice in one day, but he gave no notice. He studied her face, and she got a closer look at him—he looked very familiar. The thin scar underneath his left eye had been from one of her daggers—she had thrown it as a distraction.

And he remembered it.

Caught.

To make matters worse, from over the watchman's shoulder, she spotted the captain's horse coming back.

CHAPTER FIFTY-ONE

Juniper didn't have time for a better plan. With her free hand, she flicked a dagger from her side and sliced it across the leather glove of the watchman. It barely went through the leather, but he jumped back and released her.

She bolted.

She zigzagged through the streets, hoping the captain hadn't seen the struggle. Juniper ran faster than the watchman, and it didn't sound as though anyone else had joined him in his chase. She didn't hear the pounding of hooves, at least.

She ran down one alley, then another, and then casually strolled onto the street. She meandered down the sidewalk, along the shops and boutiques, and none of the other people along the street gave her notice. She meandered to a shop that specialized in women's underthings, and as the watchman skidded out of the alleyway, she stepped through the shop's door.

The little bell on the door chimed, and the perfumed interior greeted Juniper with hints of roses and sandalwood. The first floor of the shop held traditional lingerie in all manner of style and color. Juniper went upstairs, where the shop kept its erotic underthings.

Juniper slipped behind a wide display of sheer, lacy off-white underdresses.

"Oh, no, not that color," chimed a feminine voice. A head of bright blonde hair appeared out of Juniper's peripheral. The young woman underneath it wore a practiced smile on her red-painted lips and a dress that accentuated her curvy figure, particularly her breasts. "You would look marvelous in red."

"Helena," Juniper breathed in relief.

Helena Thimble's smile flickered, but then recognition warmed her face. "Jun? I barely recognized you with that hair. You look better with dark hair."

The bell downstairs signaled another customer.

"What can I do for you?" purred a woman's voice.

"Someone came in here, a girl, just now," came the watchman's voice.

"I didn't see anyone," the woman said innocently.

Helena nudged Juniper's hip. "You got a man you need to lose?"

Juniper nodded.

"Get out of my way," spat the watchman. He started up the stairs.

Helena's plucked brows rose, and her lips puckered in distaste. She grabbed Juniper and pulled her to the back of the store and through a curtain. Helena clicked her tongue at an older woman who stood at the worktable, delicate pink lace in her hands.

"We've got a troublesome customer," Helena murmured.

The older woman got up without question and walked through the curtain. Juniper barely heard her say, "What could I interest you in today? Got a lady you need a little something special for?"

Helena pulled open a secret panel in the wall that revealed a steep, narrow staircase. Juniper moved as fast as she dared. The stairs led into a small dark storage room. Helena followed her down, closing the panel behind her.

Juniper released a sigh of relief and leaned against a stack of crates.

"What is going on?" Helena crossed her arms and pursed her lips. "You've been gone for months, and then your bounty shoots to the sky, and everyone's saying you tried to kill the prince. Don't tell me that's true."

"It's not," Juniper said.

"Good," Helena said. "I like the prince. He used to be a favorite customer. He hasn't been out and about as much."

"He found himself a lady."

"Oh," Helena said with a sigh, then shrugged. "That doesn't stop most men."

"Adrian's different."

She smiled. "You bet he is." Her smile vanished. "Tell me, what happened?"

"Someone poisoned the prince and made it look like I did it. Now everyone is looking for me." Juniper didn't tell her about the captain. Helena didn't need to know.

"Don't you worry about the watchman," she said. "Go out the back. It leads to the alley."

Juniper jumped to her feet. "Thank you, Helena. I mean it."

Helena waved her off. "Don't mention it. You've gotten me out of worse situations. We're far from even."

Helena's madam had hired Maddox more than a few times to get rid of unsavory and troublesome clients, mostly the violent type. Juniper had hunted down a few of them herself.

"Don't forget to stop by once in a while," Helena said as she started back upstairs. "I might start to think you don't like me anymore."

"I would never do that to my sister," Juniper said. She let herself out of the shop and into the alley.

✳

Juniper slid back into the Undercity. She made her way to the market and to the only courier she trusted.

On one side of the rose-colored building, Madam Denise Maren ran a profitable brothel. On the other side, she ran a courier business. As part of their training, the younger girls and boys worked in the courier office. For a price, one could get a letter to anywhere in the city without worry of guards or unwanted hands or eyes.

Juniper walked into the brothel's front doors with equal amounts relief and dread. The heavy scent of perfume stung her nose, and the heavy drapes and curtains of red and gold felt suffocating. The woman standing at the podium sized up Juniper in a fraction of a heartbeat.

"How can we serve you this day?" the girl purred.

"I have need of a courier." Juniper showed the girl the sealed letter.

The girl nodded. She motioned to a door to the side of the podium that led away from the main brothel. It led into a calm office space with pale red walls and no seating. A man stood at a desk, a few letters sorted into piles. On a cushion by the desk, a young boy sat. Both of them had the natural grace of a courtesan and handsome faces.

"Well now, what's this?" asked the older man in a smooth tenor. He looked Juniper up and down. "What is it you need, dear?"

"I have a letter." She pulled her final letter from her belt. "To be delivered as discreetly as possible."

"Oh?" He took the letter but did not open it. "To whom?"

Juniper half laughed. "That's the tricky part."

The man looked up at her, his green eyes smiling. "Oh, I do love a challenge."

"Good," Juniper said. "Then you're going to love this one."

CHAPTER FIFTY-TWO

Ison lowered the flame on a potion until a gentle steam rolled off the calm surface. Nera had gone to help prepare dinner for the keep, and Ison had offered to finish the potions they were working on. With everyone gone, the potion room felt quiet, secluded. It reminded him of the workroom in the castle, only...warmer.

He hadn't dreamed the night before. No screams had pierced his sleep, no blood had threatened to drown him, and he hadn't visited the Death Chamber.

He still felt the guilt, and he would make Nexon pay for what he had done. He would never be able to make it right, but he would avenge those he had helped kill.

Ison glanced into the small side yard of the keep. Without anyone there to join him, he let himself out. He needed to move. He needed to think through all the things he'd learned.

He wandered through the stalls, toward the fountain. He felt better than he had when he first arrived in the Undercity. He understood why so many mages preferred to live here instead of the Marca. The freedom. The peace of mind. He enjoyed his potion lessons with Nera, his magic lessons with the other mages, and his training with Josephine. It gave him purpose. It gave him something to wake up to.

"What are you doing wandering around alone?" Xavier slid up beside Ison. The assassin hadn't made any more noise than a shadow.

Ison jumped, but as soon as the panic flared, it receded. "I'm taking a walk."

"I can see that." Xavier fell into step beside him, his footsteps silent. "You've become popular with the guild, I hear. Nera's never been so excited to work."

Ison let out a small laugh. "She's eager to learn, and she's learning fast."

"She's not had someone who knows as much as you—at least, not someone willing to share his knowledge."

Ison shrugged.

"She's a sweet girl," Xavier said. "Smart too. The two of you share a love of potion making."

Ison felt something terribly like guilt twist his gut into knots. "And we've become friends."

Xavier lifted a brow.

"Not like that," Ison said.

"I'm sure she doesn't bite."

The knot in his stomach tremored. "It's not that, I just..." He sighed, and Clara's sweet face floated to the front of his mind. "I'm not ready for that kind of...relationship."

Xavier didn't say anything. They continued to walk. The magelights gradually grew a shade more molten. They reached the fountain. The water gurgled into the many pipes. Without the children playing, it felt terribly lonesome.

"Who was she?" Xavier asked after a while.

"Who?"

"The girl you're heartbroken about."

Ison looked down at the ground. "I don't know if it's that or not. I had someone, but she...she was among those I killed." He met Xavier's eyes. He knew the assassin understood. "I don't know if I loved her or not or if it was just the excitement of having someone notice me in a castle where I was invisible. I feel horrible for what I did to her, but I don't know if it's the same thing that Jun feels. It's...guilt, I think."

"It's best that people in my line of work stay out of that mess," Xavier said. "I've heard too many stories of assassins whose lovers are killed in revenge or become their target."

"You've never..."

"I've never had a lover, so no," Xavier admitted lowly.

Ison blinked at him. "You've never had...relations?"

Xavier gave him a mirthless smirk. "That is what the brothels are for, dear Ison." He allowed himself a small chuckle.

The two of them stood at the fountain a long moment. Then Xavier asked, "Has Jun told you what she's been doing in the afternoons?"

Ison stole his attention from the water to Xavier, whose eyes bore a frightening resemblance to the water. "Is something wrong? Is she in trouble?"

"No, not necessarily. Maddox put on her on the trail of Captain Tinnly of the City Watch."

Ison nodded. "I remember that."

"It's a suicide mission." Xavier balled his hands into fists. "Jun is good at what she does, but no one is that good. The prince was easier to get to."

"I can't talk her out of it," Ison said. He didn't even want to try.

Xavier laughed. "No one can. Is there any magic you can teach her that might help her survive? Can you help her gather the shadows like I do?" Xavier held out his hand between them. Snake-like tendrils of shadows slithered around his dark fingers.

"No," Ison said. "At least, not that I know. You're not gathering actual shadow; you're an energy mage. Your magic takes on the appearance of shadows. Jun is a water mage."

"Ah." Xavier's charcoal colored magic faded from his hand.

Ison opened his mouth, but the sound of running footsteps cut him off. Xavier moved in a smooth motion; he withdrew a dagger from his waist, sidestepped in front of Ison, and somehow a second dagger appeared in his other hand. Ison gasped at the quickness of it all and then realized that Xavier had stepped in front of him to protect him.

But the footsteps, to Ison's disbelief, came from an older man. He clutched a folded red something in his hands and made his way toward Ison. "I thought I would find you at the stall," said the old man.

Ison blinked, and then he realized—the old man from the potion stall, the one he had sold a potion to for five bronze. The man's voice was stronger than it had been, considerably so.

Xavier lowered his protective stance but did not put away his daggers.

"I saw you walk by and..." The old man held out the bundle to Ison. He cautiously took it, each action monitored by Xavier. It unfolded easily; it was a knitted scarf.

"For me?" Ison blinked at the old man.

He nodded. "I don't have coin, but I had some yarn left over. I used to knit when I lived up top, you see. And that potion saved my life."

"It's lovely," Ison said, wrapping the scarf around his neck. And warm. "Thank you."

The old man beamed.

❇

Ison continued to work through dinner, and after the magelights had faded into dark blues of night, he set the last cleaned flask into the cabinet. A few potions still simmered and would until dawn.

He rolled his head over his shoulders and flexed his fingers; his hands ached from writing potion recipes, marking through outdated recipes in the old books, correcting them, and trying to keep it all organized. He took a deep breath of the workroom air. It smelled of herbs, minerals, the faint smoke of the burners, and the subtle entwined mixtures as the potions brewed. It smelled like home.

The workroom at the Marca had been his haven. The workroom at the castle had been his refuge. The workroom here at Josephine's had become his sanctum, his place in the world, his reason to get out of bed, his reason to exist. Outside, the magelights had turned a lovely shade of pale silver moonlight, glowing through the workroom windows and glinting off the metal containers and glass flasks.

A half-moon, if he had to guess. He didn't know; he hadn't been above ground since he and Juniper had fled the castle. How long ago had that been? A few weeks?

What did Mason think? Did he understand? Did he blame Ison? Had he found a replacement yet? Maybe one day, he would be able to explain himself.

Ison stood, stretched his tired arms over his head, and meandered to the workroom door. At least when he worked himself ragged, he slept soundly. He had earned himself a rest.

Something flashed by the window.

Ison froze, hand on the workroom door. He blinked at the window, but nothing else interrupted the moonlight. He stepped closer to the window, scanning the small backyard. He didn't see anyone.

"Ison?" came a muffled voice from outside. It sounded like Juniper.

Had something happened? Ison let himself into the backroom, undid the dozen locks on the door, and stepped into the small yard. The soft grass hushed his footsteps.

"Jun?" he whispered.

"Ison," she said.

Her voice came from the direction of the garden shed. He crept toward it. The hairs on his neck stood on end, and his gut quivered. Why the secrecy? Had something happened? Had she uncovered something else? His thoughts went to Nexon, to Mason, to the captain she was following. With every step toward the shed, his heart beat faster until it felt like it might burst out of his chest.

A footstep sounded behind him, and he turned—

Something hit him between the shoulder blades, sending him face-first to the ground. Before he could shout, a black cloth swished over his face, his whole head—a hood. Hands yanked his wrists behind him, fastened them together, and another set of hands did the same to his knees.

No matter how hard he screamed, his voice did not carry.

A mute charm.

Several pairs of silent hands hoisted him into the air. The hood carried a metallic scent that filled his mouth and nose. With every breath, his thoughts and struggles became sluggish. Before he felt the zing of the ward, darkness swallowed him whole.

CHAPTER FIFTY-THREE

Juniper woke to rough hands yanking her arm. She had her other hand halfway to the dagger under her pillow when a firm hand grasped her wrist.

"Juniper," hissed Xavier.

She blinked—Xavier stood above her. He held her wrist with one hand and her arm with the other, and he did not look happy. The magelights' version of moonlight cast his dark face in shadows but illuminated his blue-gray eyes. She blinked again. Amery was awake and pulling clothes from the dresser.

Xavier pulled her into a sitting position, then released her.

"What time—"

"Ison's gone," Xavier spat.

"*What?*" Juniper shook her head. Was she having one of those rare lucid dreams? She swung her legs over the bedside and stifled a yawn. She wanted to fall back into the pillow.

No, not a dream. She had never been tired in her dreams.

Xavier reached into his jacket pocket and took out a folded piece of unlined parchment. He wiggled it at Juniper. She took it. Holding it in the moonlight, she could barely make out the neat, slanted handwriting.

"What's this?" Juniper asked.

"Courier dropped this off. It's from Nera. The Dual Fangs took Ison."

"What?" she snapped, accidentally crinkling the letter.

"Nera saw it from her window." Panic underlined Xavier's words. "They ambushed him in the yard and carried him out like a hog."

"They kidnapped him?" Juniper stood. Any sleepiness she felt vanished. Her hand shook; the letter trembled in her grasp. "I thought that ward was supposed to prevent things like this?"

"It is," Xavier spat. "I don't know how, all right? They just did. Black magic shit." Xavier clenched and unclenched his fists. He shifted his weight from one foot to the other. He looked to have gotten dressed in a rush: his jacket was wrinkled; his trousers had a spot of dirt on the knees.

"No," Juniper argued, willing it to be a dream. "Why would they? He didn't do anything to them."

Juniper jumped out of bed and stalked to the window. The Undercity was quiet. She started to pace. Ison. Why Ison? Was it his connection to their Iluvin master? His refusal of their offer? They knew the Iluvin master had spoken to Ison, and they might find him useful, or they might want to silence him. Or the Iluvin master himself wanted him.

"Jun?" Xavier asked, his voice barely containing his rage.

Maybe Ison had something they needed. Maybe he knew more than their master wanted him to. Maybe he had dug too deep; but then, so had she. Why take him and leave her?

"Juniper?" Xavier asked, his voice demanding, urgent.

"We're going." She balled her fists and inadvertently crumpled the letter.

Xavier nodded. No argument.

"No time to waste, then." Amery tossed Juniper's clothes onto the bed, dark clothes for sneaking and hiding blades.

Xavier stood outside while Juniper and Amery quickly dressed. A strange calm came over Juniper as she situated the short knives and daggers on her person, both hidden and not. Something familiar. She knew this. This is what she had been taught, what she excelled at, and the Dual Fangs would find that out the hard way.

Ready, Juniper and Amery met Xavier in the hall, but he wasn't alone.

Blythe stood there, her lips in a straight line, her dark eyes curious, knowing, and clever. "You're going out."

"Yes, we've got a friend to rescue," Juniper said. No point in sugarcoating it.

"Do you need help?" Blythe asked.

"How are you against pissy mages?" Xavier asked calmly.

"I deal with you just fine," Blythe said.

Xavier's brows furrowed, and Amery bit her lip to keep her laughter quiet.

"She's right," said Amery. "Come on, B, you're with me. You two go on ahead. It's time for some real-world experience."

Juniper and Xavier didn't argue. A part of her wanted to keep Blythe safe in the keep, but she knew that for the girl to learn, she would have to dive in headfirst. She would learn to survive, or she wouldn't make it.

The two of them hit the darkened street and headed silently toward the other side of the Undercity. She could feel Xavier's anxiety, or her magic could. It radiated off him like smoke, fuming with each heated breath he took, each rapid step.

Halfway there, she said, "We'll get him out."

"Or we'll slaughter every single one of them," he growled.

She nodded. If they harmed Ison, if they killed him—none of the Dual Fangs would live.

With every step, Juniper's heart thumped harder. A warning. Anything that befell Ison would be her fault. She had dragged him out of the castle and brought him into this mess. If it weren't for her, he would still be working as the court magician's apprentice.

They passed through the quiet market and started through the residential neighborhood; they passed closed doors and dark windows, one house after another, until the Dual Fangs' townhouse came into view. She stopped short beside a narrow alley that led behind the houses, just out of sight.

"They'll be—" she started.

"Watching," finished Xavier.

They glanced at one another and, without another word, vanished into the alley. Slick as shadows, they raced silently through the alley. Juniper paused behind the Dual Fangs' place. Xavier summoned his shadows and hid them both from view, and they inched closer. Most of the windows were dark, the curtains pulled. On the third floor, one of the windows held the flickering light of a candle. On the first floor, one of the kitchen windows had been left open.

She glanced at Xavier.

The Dual Fangs had left them a trap.

She held up her hand and cast a focused net of magic toward the open window. She felt two people standing just inside, waiting to ambush them.

"Two," she whispered. "I can take them."

She focused. She felt her raw magic, felt the ice of it, felt its presence. A tendril of bright blue slithered through the open window and split in two. Faster than the two Dual Fangs could blink, she wrapped her magic around their throats. Silently, they struggled. She felt them fall unconscious, and though a part of her wanted to squeeze them until they popped, she released them and gently laid them on the stone floor.

Juniper and Xavier, hidden by his shadows, crept to the kitchen window and slipped inside. The two men she had knocked out were strangers, and before she could speak, Xavier slit their throats. He wiped off his dagger on their clothes.

279

At the closed kitchen door, she met Xavier's stare. Together, they could do this. She felt her magic curling underneath her skin, clawing with the rage she felt toward the Dual Fangs. She would save Ison.

And, she reminded herself proudly, she didn't need her magic—she was Juniper Thimble.

❄

Ison came to, and the world was dark and full of whispers. It took several heartbeats and gasping breaths for him to recall the last few moments. The bag, the mute charm. An ache in his head told him he'd lost consciousness. With every breath, it eased.

Magically subdued.

Enchanted ropes held his shoulders against a high-backed chair and secured his wrists together. Panic quickly flooded his veins, replacing the calmness of the darkness.

"He's waking," came a voice from the whispers.

"About time," said another.

"I told you we could have waited until morning."

"And if he woke up and left?"

"I didn't say not to tie him."

"Stop it, you two. Just get on with it."

Footsteps, and then someone yanked the bag off his head. Ison blinked; magelights near the ceiling shone with cool light. In front of him stood three Dual Fangs in their blue cloaks. More lingered about the edges of the room, leaning against the walls, sitting on the floor, all waiting, all watching.

One of the Dual Fangs came closer, and the light graced his face enough for his sneering features to show. Clive. Behind him stood Dyn and Bois.

"Our master is interested in you," said Clive. When Ison didn't respond, he continued, "He told me to help you if I could, if you needed me to. He said you would be lost. He said that your world came crashing down when you ran from the castle. He said to welcome you because you helped him."

"He used me," Ison said, his voice raspy.

"He offered you a chance to be part of the revolution," Clive corrected.

"He took control of my body and used me to murder innocent people," Ison said through gritted teeth.

Clive frowned. At those words, a whisper went through the room.

"Your master used me," Ison said louder. "He used me to kill someone I cared about. What makes you think he won't do the same to you?"

Clive straightened. "An unforeseen complication."

"An unforgivable violation," Ison said.

"Our master is willing to do whatever it takes to change the world," Clive said. "And he is extending to you the chance to be a part of it, Ison Rolin. I highly suggest you take it. Our master has warned us; he will not accept no for an answer."

"Your master is going to destroy everything he touches," Ison spat.

Clive's frown turned into a sneer. "You are declining?"

Dyn's lips twisted into a maniacal smile that sent a chill down Ison's spine. Dyn took slow steps to stand beside Clive, eager and waiting.

"Yes," Ison said firmly. "As you should."

Clive let out a dramatic, grievous sigh. He stepped aside, and Dyn took his place in front of Ison. Dyn reached into his cloak and withdrew a dagger with an elaborately jeweled golden handle. The steel reflected the magelight, and at first, Ison thought it just the light; then he realized—the darkness of the blade, the feathery red. Mage's Bane.

His breath fell from his lips in a gasp. They were going to kill him with Mage's Bane.

"I am sorry to hear you say that," Clive said, hand over his heart, sorrow on his tongue, and wicked humor glinting in his eyes.

Dyn lifted the dagger to slice Ison's arm. Ison tried to move, but the ropes bound him. Dyn moved; Bois shut her sightless eyes and covered her mouth; Ison cringed, waiting for the blow; and then Dyn let out a grunt of pain. Ison opened his eyes to see Dyn drop the dagger.

Ison blinked—the tip of a throwing knife stuck out of Dyn's throat. The hilt stuck out the opposite side.

The Mage's Bane dagger struck the side of the chair—missing Ison by a hair—and clattered to the ground.

Four shadows descended. It became a blur of shadows, ice, and steel. The Dual Fangs shook their surprise and fought back. Fire and lightning, bolts of blasted magic in reds, blues, greens, and whites—magic brightened the room like daylight with each collision.

A petite figure appeared at Ison's chair. Black eyes looked out at him from within a dark hood, and small hands adeptly cut the ropes that bound him. Two Dual Fangs came up behind the girl, and Ison sent a wave of wind into the chest of one. The little girl aimed a knife at the heart of the other, and her aim was true.

Some Dual Fangs fought, but to Ison's surprise, most fled. They cowered with their hands over their heads, ran to the doors and curtained windows, and begged for mercy. Bois sat against the far wall, eyes wide, a gash on her temple.

The battle slowed. Juniper, Amery, and Xavier stood among the Dual Fangs, who were either begging for their lives, dead, or dying. The tang of fresh blood soaked the air, into the rugs that softened the stone floor, and it was all Ison could smell.

He returned to the Death Chamber. The rune ran full of blood. Bodies piled. Ison stumbled forward, and Xavier grabbed him by the shoulders and shook him. The Death Chamber dissolved, and the Undercity returned.

These people had tried to kill him, he told himself. They would have used Mage's Bane on him had the others not intervened.

"What are you doing?" Ison gasped.

"It looks like we're saving your ass." Juniper held a dagger in one hand and a tendril of magic like a whip in the other.

Ison stepped over the body of Dyn, the Mage's Bane abandoned on the ground. Amery bent to pick it up.

"It's pretty," she said, turning the jeweled hilt in the magelight.

"And it's deadly to mages," Juniper said. "So, consider it yours."

Amery smiled and tucked the dagger into one of the empty sheaths on her person.

They made it through the house with little opposition. Any Dual Fangs left cowered. Juniper kicked down the front door, splintering the wood. She charged out of the house first, but their triumphant rescue halted—a rock the size of a human head came barreling toward her.

She barely had time to shield herself with ice. The rock crashed into the ice shield, cracking it into a million pieces. The ice and the rock fell to the stone walkway and tumbled down the stairs.

"Well, you're not completely useless in your magic," came the sniveling voice of Clive. He stood at the end of the walkway, in the street. He'd lowered his hood. He had the same symbol tattooed on either side of his head, and a vision clouded over Ison's sight; he had seen that symbol before. In the rune in the Death Chamber.

CHAPTER FIFTY-FOUR

Juniper sauntered down the walk, frost slithering over the stones. She cracked her neck to the side and brandished her dagger and tendril of magic. "You going to keep talking, or are you going to fight me?"

Clive laughed. He didn't seem worried about her at all. If anything, his sneer widened.

Juniper sauntered toward Clive, who stood ready in the middle of the street. Halfway down the walk, Juniper flung her dagger through the air, splattering fresh blood onto the paving stones—Dual Fang blood.

The magic came alive at her will, swirling an ice storm underneath her skin, between her bones, and pulling at her reserves. Clive summoned several fist-sized stones from the ground around him, and they circled in front of him. An earth mage.

From the windows along the street, the ruckus had stirred the neighbors. Faces peeked from between shutters, from behind doors, and through curtains.

She passed through the open gate and onto the stone of the street; she felt the subtle change in the ground a moment before it broke apart. She jumped; the ground underneath her feet collapsed into a hole deeper than she was tall. She commanded, and ice formed over the top. That ice cracked when her weight came back down but held.

The ground cracked and groaned, and she threw herself to the side as the earth opened wider, shattering her ice and part of the fence. The ground split, and the crack raged toward her, thundering and shaking. Juniper sharpened a dozen ice pellets and sent them flying toward Clive. He brought a shield of earth to block her attack, and he blocked most of the pellets, but one sank into his shoulder.

Juniper fixed her focus on that one ice pellet. She reshaped it into a dozen tiny slivers of ice, and Clive let out a howl of pain as those slivers dug into his flesh, his muscles. He bent forward, blood running freely from his wounded shoulder.

With that distraction, Juniper used her ice to propel her over the crack in the ground and within dagger range. She felt her magic sizzle under her skin, ready, waiting—ice gathered at Clive's feet, raced up his ankles, his knees, his thighs, his waist. He yelped as the ice crept up his torso. He sent nugget-sized rocks flying at her, but she easily blocked them with an ice shield.

She felt it, the power within the ice. Within her. Unstoppable. Undeniable. Infinite. She felt Clive's magic, dwindling, pitiful in comparison to hers.

Ice crept up Clive's chest and shoulders. It secured his arms, one holding the wound on his shoulder, the other trying desperately to use magic against her. One last pebble, aimed at her head, met its end at her ice shield.

Only his face remained uncovered.

Juniper held in her triumph; she had covered him in ice just as she had done the demon. All the power of that moment came back to her, the infinity of it. Hers.

"Shit," Clive spat. His teeth chattered, and his breath fogged.

Juniper took purposeful steps toward Clive. She felt every bit of the ice. Every eye on the street watched her. Waiting.

"So," she said to Clive. "Here we are. Who is a useless mage? Hmm?"

He seethed. The skin of his face reddened where the ice touched him.

"Listen, Clive; I'll make a deal with you," she said. "You answer some questions for me, and I'll consider letting you go. Sound fair?"

His teeth clattered. To make him understand, she withdrew her ice from his neck.

"Fine," he spat.

"Good." She felt her control tilt; the temperature around her dropped, and she quickly regained her concentration. "First, I want to know more about your master."

Clive narrowed his stare.

"Where can I find dear old Nexon?"

His sneer cracked, and fear widened his eyes. He had known his master's identity. When he didn't answer, she inched her ice back up his neck and tightened it around his chest. An exhale tumbled from his mouth in a cough. She loosened the ice around his chest.

"I-I don't know," Clive said through chattering teeth.

"You don't know?" Juniper scoffed.

"I-I really don't know," Clive repeated. "No one does. It's part of his plan, he said, so that none of us could betray him."

"He thought wisely, then, I suppose." Even if it was backfiring on her plan. She sighed and allowed her magic to creep further up his neck and head until only his face was visible.

"Wait!" Clive gasped. His teeth chattered hard, the clank painful. "I-I don't know where he is. But I know his second in command is a woman named Lora. In the settlement, Baxion. If you want answers, go there. See her. Ask her."

Juniper memorized those words, the name. "You suggest that I wander into a rebel mage settlement all on my own? That's foolish."

"Your attempts to stop him are foolish," Clive said. "You may annoy us today, but soon our master will rid this kingdom of scum like you. You will be the slaves!"

Juniper held her ice around Clive, threading other things to ask him, to prod out of him. Anger and spite had replaced the fear in his eyes.

"Lora must be well-connected to have obtained her position as second in command," Juniper said casually. "Is she Iluvin too?"

"I don't know," Clive spat. "She would have to be. I've heard about her. Powerful. She would crush you like the worthless bugs you are." He started to struggle. "I gave you answers. Now, let me go, you bitch!"

"I said I would consider it," she said sharply.

She allowed her ice to shrink slowly away, and relief spread across his ugly features. Then, as the ice retreated from his shoulders, he sneered. She felt his magic flinch with killing intent—hers responded in less than a heartbeat—her ice surged over Clive's body, freezing him solid. Her magic encased him, and she felt his heartbeat slow, slow, and stop. His magic ebbed and died with him.

Juniper released a slow, calming breath. At her command, the ice shattered—pieces of ice and pieces of Clive clattered to the street, water and blood and fluid draining into the cracks he had made.

The magic inside of her squeezed hard, and she fought to keep standing. She flexed her stiff fingers and took a wobbly step away from the mess on the street.

She turned back to the house. Amery, Blythe, Xavier, and Ison stood on the porch. A few of the Dual Fangs had made their way to the porch, but no one made a move to fight. Bois stood in the doorway to the house, her glassy eyes unfocused.

People started to clamor onto the street from the other houses, through the alleys, and whispers started like smoke. They gathered with every breath.

Juniper pointed back to the Dual Fangs' house. "Anyone else feeling lucky?" she announced, her voice reckless in her exhaustion.

No one answered. The Dual Fangs remained silent and still.

"Your leader is dead," she said. "You've got two choices. Beat it, or learn to live without your master. Because this is my city, and he's not welcome on my streets. You cross Juniper Thimble"—the whispers tremored at her name—"this is what happens."

No one argued. No one stepped forward.

Juniper started up the walkway to the house with the grace of exhaustion. She picked up her bloodied dagger and stopped just shy of the porch, with Amery and Blythe on one side and Xavier and Ison on her other. "What now, Dual Fangs?" she asked.

Bois took a shaky step forward. Though she looked utterly terrified, her voice came out strong, "Leave them to me."

None of the remaining Dual Fangs argued.

"You've been lied to," Juniper told them. "You were lured with the promise of power. There is no power for you under Nexon's rule. He will use each one of you to further himself. Gather yourselves and stand against him. That doesn't mean you have to stand in favor of the Marca or the Order, but you stand against Nexon's tyranny."

Bois nodded. She put a hand to the brooch on her blood-stained cloak. "What you say is true, and I don't want a place in the type of world that Nexon wants to build." Several others came to stand with her, nodding. "The dual-fanged mosscat is a magnificent creature of resilience and fortitude and cunning. Like it, we will survive this change of pace. We will survive this lie we've been following."

"I highly recommend speaking with Josephine about an alliance between guilds," Ison said, his voice stronger than Juniper's.

Bois nodded, and a small smile stretched across her pale pink lips. "I will."

✻

With the spectacle over, the Dual Fangs started the cleanup. Earth mages fixed the cracks and holes in the street. Water and air mages cleaned the blood from the interior. Juniper, Ison, Xavier, Amery, and Blythe started toward Josephine's keep to report what had happened before the gossip got to her first.

"You handled yourself marvelously," Juniper told Blythe. "Were you nervous?"

Blythe looked at Juniper. The others stood a few steps behind, talking about the Dual Fangs.

"Yes," Blythe admitted, her voice small. She reached for one of the daggers she carried and fastened her small hand around the hilt. The dagger looked comically large on her petite frame. "I was scared that I wouldn't make it, or that one of you wouldn't make it, or that your friend the mage wouldn't make it." The faintest of emotions came over the young girl's face. Her lips turned downward, her eyebrows came together, and she looked, for once, like a child.

"I'm proud of you," Juniper said.

Blythe's eyes widened a fraction in surprise, then disbelief.

"You are quick on your feet, smart, cunning, and brave."

Blythe's eyes never left Juniper's.

"You have a future ahead of you, whether it's down here with the scum like me or up top running a shop or adventuring into the unknown corners of the world."

Blythe nodded, disbelief bright in her dark eyes. "My father said I would never amount to anything," she said softly. "He said of all his children, he could afford to sell me. So he did."

Ah, the realization hit Juniper. As the youngest child of a poor man, she had grown up thinking herself a burden. And Juniper had given her the very words she desperately needed to hear.

"You have a place here," Juniper said. "Friends to watch your back. A guild that's supposed to be something like a family. It's good enough, anyway. With some time and practice, you'll be the best of them all."

"What about you?" Blythe asked. "I thought you were the best?"

Juniper shrugged. "I have no qualms about retiring early and handing my title to another."

Blythe smiled, and her pretty face became beautiful.

CHAPTER FIFTY-FIVE

Nestled in a parlor, Ison and Xavier took turns explaining the events to Josephine. The older mage took it all in, thinking, while Juniper kept her gaze averted. She had never felt so drained; her limbs felt like wet sand, and she wanted nothing more than to sink into her bed. After the story, Josephine went to hurry the tea and cookies from the kitchen and find something better for Juniper's spent magic. They sat for a while in silence, digesting the events of the morning, waiting on the tea and cookies. Slowly, the magelights brightened.

Footsteps, quiet as a mouse, approached the parlor's open doorway. Juniper glanced up; it was the brown-haired mage. She carried an ancient book that weighed as much as she did. She looked grim.

"Nera?" Ison asked.

"I heard you come by." Nera stepped into the room. She wore sleepless bags under her eyes. "I...I've been looking through the library for information on Nexon and the Iluvin."

"And you've found something?" Ison asked.

A small smile flickered over Nera's face, then vanished. She came forward and set the book on the table.

"And it's not good?" Ison added.

"Here." Nera opened the book to a page she had marked with a thin strip of cloth. The old page was clotted with tiny print. Nera read aloud, "Though Nexon was presumed dead after the Battle of Blackwood, some speculate he survived. It has been suggested that he took precautions to secure his survival after one of his most trusted soothsayers predicted his fall and the end of the war. His allies were questioned, but none knew what precautions Nexon might have taken, if any."

"So..." Juniper said, eyeing the tiny print and how much there was of it. "We already know that he survived."

"This guy you're talking about is the same guy from that book?" Amery pointed a manicured nail to the thick tome. "I find that hard to believe. He would be ancient."

BEATRICE B. MORGAN

"There is more," Nera said dismissively. She skipped a few paragraphs down and began to read again, "These speculations include the legends and lore that also suggest Nexon to be one of the five Iluvin archmages."

A silence fell over the sitting area.

"Archmage?" Ison repeated, his voice thin in disbelief. "Nexon was an archmage? Ridiculous. There's no such thing."

"According to the Order," came Josephine's dark tone from the doorway. Their collective breath stilled at the sight of the older mage. Her one hand clutched her empty sleeve. Her eyes settled on the book, then on Nera.

From around Josephine, a younger mage brought in a tray of cookies. Another carried a tray of tea. When the two had left, Josephine closed the parlor doors. She set her gaze on Nera.

"You found that book in my private library, didn't you, Nera?"

Nera's cheeks went red.

Josephine let out a grievous sigh and for once looked her age.

"Wait." Ison's voice trembled. "Are you saying archmages were real?"

"Oh, they were real," Josephine said. "They were real, and they were dangerous."

"But what—" Ison started, but Josephine held up her hand. She motioned to the tray.

Once each of them had made a cup of tea and taken at least one cookie, Josephine said, "Legend tells that the gods bestowed magic onto five humans." She held up her five fingers. "The five elements. That magic gave way to the magic we use today. It is said that the gods-given magic traveled the bloodline. There would always be one archmage for each element to represent that element for humanity. Archmages had more power than any other mage, the power of one thousand, they said.

"More than a thousand years ago, one of the archmages, Nexon, set out to conquer the world. And he did, most of it. Those were dark days: war in every city, refugees fleeing in every direction. Then, the Order formed, and the war truly began. It seemed that Nexon would win, and he might have, had not the other four archmages sided with Order to defeat him in the Battle of Blackwood."

"And the magic spent tainted the earth," Ison said, eyes wide in disbelief. "And the Blackwood Wylds were formed."

Josephine nodded. "A land tainted by magic beyond repair."

"But..." Ison started, "history says most of the Iluvin people were destroyed."

"They were," Josephine said darkly. "Either by the Order before the war or by prejudice after the war. The archmages could only staunch the violence so much. There were only four of them and thousands of Iluvin mages, and even more people terrified of magic who hungered for revenge."

"What happened to the other four archmages?" Juniper whispered.

Josephine fixed her stare on her. "They survived the war. What happened to them after that is lost to time. With the purging of the Iluvin people and their knowledge, we may never know."

"But if the archmage magic travels the bloodline," Juniper said, thinking back to what Mason had said about the laws of inheritance. "Then even if those archmages are gone, there are new archmages. The descendants of the original archmages."

"They could literally be anyone," Xavier said flatly.

Josephine nodded. "Five archmages, and only two are known."

"Nexon," Ison said.

"And the Royal Mage to King Crespin Balendin, Delmont Thacket, although most know him only to be Iluvin. He is the Archmage of Fire, if I'm correct," said Josephine. "And Nexon has waited until his rivals are as good as gone before attempting to regain his power. It wouldn't surprise me if he has been working to get rid of them for the past one thousand years. He knows the archmages are the only threat to his power. But, before death, his soothsayer predicted another thing." She looked down at Nera. "Did you find the prophecy yet?"

Nera's blush deepened, and she nodded. "Yes."

"Might as well read it too."

Nera turned several pages and placed her finger underneath a small line of text. She read aloud, "The conqueror will again rise, but his fall will be repeated by the princess who returns."

Silence again showered the room.

"The only one who will be able to stop him is a princess?" Juniper asked.

"The only princess is Myrisha Balendin," Ison said.

"And her brother is thinking of making her queen," Juniper said, suddenly remembering Adrian speaking about it.

"She'll return to the throne," Ison said.

Juniper took a calming breath; she didn't know what to think about first. "It's the best thing we've got. If we are going to stop Nexon, then we have to go see Myrisha. And then find out who Lora is and where Baxion is."

Juniper looked to Josephine for input, but the older mage shook her head.

"And Myrisha would be able to connect you with the other archmage," Xavier chimed in.

Ison nodded. "He's right."

"And if Nexon's followers are primarily in the north of Collatia, she would have a reason to send her army up there and dispatch them," Juniper added.

"It is possible that Thacket is in contact with the other archmages," Josephine suggested.

Juniper nodded. If word got out that the Balendin crown had more than one archmage in their court, every other kingdom would be on edge. It would be best to keep that information secret.

"What's our next move?" Ison asked darkly. He already knew.

"We're going to Collatia," Juniper said. "And we're going to talk to Myrisha. We're going to stop Nexon."

"You make it sound easy," Ison said, a chuckle on his tongue.

She shrugged. "If I made it sound as hard as it will likely be, then I might not want to do it myself."

"But, before you make any history-altering moves, finish this plate and the tea. You'll need your strength for the journey." Josephine reached for one of the cookies and took a hefty bite.

Juniper obliged. They had a plan of action. They just needed to get out of Rusdasin first.

CHAPTER FIFTY-SIX

Juniper trudged back to Maddox's keep and slept soundly through the rest of the day and into the next. She woke up around midday, her magic replenished, her appetite ravenous. Amery and Xavier were training with Blythe and Ven, the two of whom had started to get along rather well. Juniper put herself through her morning exercises, took a long bath, and by the time she went topside, the golden streaks of evening feathered across the cloudy sky.

The market was full of ripe fruit—strawberries, peaches, watermelons—and countless sweets and breads. Could she squeeze in a few passes of the market to smell them one last time before she left the city behind forever? Gods only knew what she would find in Collatia. She might never return.

She ate her fill, and as the night rolled in, thick clouds muted the moonlight, all of it. It didn't matter; Juniper had a plan. Before the captain returned to his tower, she took up a perch on the topmost floor, behind a gargoyle. She felt her magic respond to the setting sun, to the growing night. It grew; it reacted. Her magic was most powerful in the dark, at night, and that was how she knew she would make it out of this assassination. That was what made her better than the others the captain had defeated.

Because none of them had been her. Because Juniper Thimble wasn't just any assassin.

She listened as the captain returned home. He spoke to his wife, complained about the boring meetings, Juniper Thimble still being loose in the city, and the rumors that she had taken down a guild of mages in the Undercity. Juniper knew the captain had eyes in the Undercity, and he would have gotten the news of her announcement, that Rusdasin was hers.

Juniper smiled. Word traveled fast in Rusdasin.

She heard footsteps in the bedroom, the groan of feet on floorboards, and the swish of clothing. A candle came to life, and footsteps started out of the room. Calm, silent footsteps.

Her heart thundered. Finally.

292

With the shadows hiding her, she slid down the tower to the gargoyle closest to the window the captain would open upon reaching his private office. Down below, the nighttime market buzzed; watchmen stood tall and proud outside the tower's well-lit base.

Light flickered to life within the office; it glittered between the wooden shutters of the window. She waited. Those footsteps approached. The heavy latch clicked, the shutters swung outward, and Captain Tinnly took a deep breath. He stood in the window for a short moment, long enough for a skilled assassin to make her move, but Juniper waited.

Not yet.

He retreated back into his office. She climbed down the stonework, no more than a shadow, her magic helping her to find the handholds, hiding her sounds, showing her the way. A tendril of her magic slid into the open window. When the captain's back turned, she crawled through the window and landed silently.

Captain Tinnly wore a housecoat over pajamas and leaned over the table in the middle of the room. No one else occupied the room. The only door was closed.

She straightened, keeping the window behind her. She rested her hand on her dagger, the dagger that she had borrowed from Maddox, and clicked the hilt slightly out of the sheath.

At the sound, the captain spun, reaching for the sword at his waist that wasn't there. His brows rose nearly to his hair.

Juniper didn't move. There lay enough space between them that she couldn't hurt him, and he could still react. A safe distance.

The captain straightened. His surprise waned. "Are you here to kill me?"

She steeled herself. Her decision had been made days ago. "Yes."

He tilted his head toward her, and his eyes glanced to where his sword rested against the wall. Too far.

"I came here to kill you because someone is willing to pay a hefty price for your head. I don't know who. I am only the assassin," she said calmly.

Tinnly didn't move.

"I've been following you. Watching you."

"I remember you," he said. "The market. One of my men said he chased Juniper Thimble into a lingerie store."

"He did."

His knuckles tightened on the edge of the table. "You're her, then? All my time spent hunting you down, and you come to me?" He bit back a laugh. Exhaustion tugged on his eyelids. "You're wanted for the attempted assassination of Prince Adrian Bradburn."

"I did not and would never harm Adrian," she seethed. "Someone far worse than me is plotting against this kingdom, against the crown, and they used me as a scapegoat. You've been in the Watch long enough to know how I deal with revenge."

He nodded. "I've heard."

"But you aren't on that list." She slid her dagger back into the sheath. His eyes followed the motion, and glanced again at his sword. "You are a good man, Captain, one of the few. The people love you. The Watch respects you. Your men are well-trained. You instill your sense of duty and honor in them. You are fair. You belong in this position. Rusdasin needs you."

The captain, eyes on her, stepped to his sword. She didn't move. He grabbed the hilt but hesitated.

"And I would like to ask something of you, Captain," she said calmly, "in lieu of your assassination."

He unsheathed the blade.

Taking a deep breath, she set her hand on the hilt of her dagger.

CHAPTER FIFTY-SEVEN

Reid adjusted his new dagger. It was heavier than the one he had given Juniper. He closed his hand on the shiny pommel. Had she used his to kill yet? He shoved thoughts of her aside and schooled his face into a stoic mask, which became easier every day.

He started toward the Royal Chambers. He had been summoned by the king to the Lavender Lounge, and he couldn't afford to look tired or stressed, though he was. Adrian had not improved.

Halfway there, a voice called him. "Reid?" Penet stumbled in his rush to get to Reid, breathless and red-cheeked. The younger squire doubled, hands on his knees, panting for breath. "Reid...I hoped to reach you first."

"What happened?" His heart jumped into his throat.

"It's Juniper Thimble," Penet said between breaths. He glanced up at Reid, panic in his wide eyes as he said, "She's dead. Killed by the Captain of the City Watch."

Reid stared at Penet, unsure if he had heard correctly. Penet repeated himself, his voice distant, like he stood at the end of a tunnel, but Reid understood.

Juniper—killed. Dead. While attempting to assassinate the Captain of the City Watch.

His chest squeezed painfully. Each heartbeat felt an eternity.

"Reid?" Penet asked, hand landing on Reid's shoulder. "Reid? Do you need anything? A strong drink? You look sick."

He found his voice, "No." He brushed Penet's hand from his shoulder. "I have a meeting to get to. Thank you for telling me."

Reid left Penet standing in the corridor. His legs carried him toward the Royal Chambers, through the dark mahogany doors, and to the Lavender Lounge. Despite feeling as though the world under his feet had dissolved, despite feeling like drinking himself into oblivion, he continued. A squire shouldn't need anything to be strong. Against anything.

Juniper was a thief, a murderer, a liar, and she deserved the end she received.

But if that were true, then why did it feel like his chest might cave in? Each heartbeat shuddered through his entire being.

He paused before the doors to the Lavender Lounge, guarded on either side by expressionless Royal Guard. Reid schooled his face into the same expressionless mask, and the guard let him into the lounge. The Lavender Lounge got its name from the pale purple walls. Elegant oak furniture angled around a circular table. The grand hearth was cold. Tall windows let copious sunlight flood into the somber room.

The room was empty, save for the king standing on the far side. He had lost weight. A guard shut the door behind him.

"Sit down, son," said the king.

Reid obeyed. He hadn't realized how woozy he had felt until he sat. The king walked over, hands behind his back, eyes on the map laid out on the table.

"I wanted to speak with you alone, Reid."

"Yes, Your Majesty." His own voice sounded distant.

"Have you heard the news of Juniper Thimble?"

Reid nodded. "Yes, Your Majesty." *Dead.*

"Captain Tinnly came to me early this morning and explained that she had tried to assassinate him last night," said the king. "He brought in her head."

A cold clamminess crawled over his skin. Her eyes floated into his mind, bright and clever and then dead and lifeless. He swallowed.

The king stopped pacing and set a hand on Reid's shoulder. His tone softened. "I am sorry, son. I know you felt for the girl, even if it was a passing fling. Do you need time to collect yourself?"

"No," Reid said firmly. The king hesitated, and Reid swallowed. He repeated himself, "No, Your Majesty."

The hand on his shoulder remained a moment longer; then the king began to pace again. "Very well. Reid, you've become an asset to me over these past few months. You are a skilled warrior, a brave soul, and a true friend to my son. You are loyal without a doubt, and I fear I must put your loyalty and bravery to the test." The king stopped on the other side of the table, his hazel eyes pinned on Reid's.

Reid nodded. "Of course, Your Majesty."

The king held himself straight, although his face was dire. "The royal healer and her associate, the poison expert, have successfully identified the poison used on my son."

Reid held himself ready to hunt down the assassin, the vendor who had made the poison, anything to protect Adrian.

The king said, "The poison itself is common; however, it has been cursed with black magic, which is why it has taken so long and why healing magic can only do so much. According to the healer, there is no cure."

Reid's heart sank further than he thought it could.

"My son will die from this."

Reid found it hard to breathe. First Juniper, now Adrian. No, he couldn't handle losing them both.

"But," said the king, a note of hope in his voice, "there are legends of a plant in the far north, planted by Boxel himself, in a garden of the gods, that is said to cure any illness or curse."

The floor beneath his feet shifted. A legend, the far north...could it be?

The king straightened his shoulders. "I have already spoken to Knight Commander Fowler, and he has given his approval."

Reid blinked. A quest.

"Squire Reid Sandpiper," the king said. "This is a task of dire importance, one I can only entrust to a small number of people. Will you accept this quest, fetch the plant, and bring it back in order to cure my son?"

Reid stood. His feet felt like wood. He bent forward, hand over his heart. "Yes, Your Majesty. I accept."

"Good," the king said, nodding. "I knew you would. But, there is more."

Reid straightened.

"The plant itself must remain secret. I am not sending you alone. Only Sir Isaac Pinul and the herbalist Graison Alyun know the true mission I ask of you. The others will be told they are to dispatch a murderous mage in the Galamond mountains." The king took a deep breath. "Only inform them of the mission's truth when you have to. I don't want anyone else to know."

Reid nodded. "I understand."

With that, a knock came to the door.

"Enter," said the king.

Isaac entered, looking grim, and Graison followed a step behind, looking terrified. "The herbalist," said Isaac.

Graison blanched and looked like he might be sick.

"Sit," the king said. "Time isn't on our side."

Reid remained standing while the king explained their secret mission to retrieve Boxel's Grace, a legendary plant. At the mention, Graison's eyes widened.

"Do you understand your role?" the king asked him.

Graison nodded. "To identify this plant and keep it safe," he said softly.

The king looked to the three of them in turn. "The kingdom is resting on your shoulders, as is my son's life, and the Bradburn line."

Another knock sounded on the door; this time Squires Berwick and Julian entered. The king acted as though nothing had been said and told them the tale of a troublesome apostate in the north and that the time had come for his three best squires to prove their mettle at last. Penet and Henry accepted the quest with the dignity and grace of future knights.

"You are to leave at dawn tomorrow," the king announced. "Horses will be ready, supplies packed. Say your goodbyes tonight, and be at the stables at sunrise."

With that, they left.

"Can you believe it," asked Penet as they walked back toward the barracks. "A quest, at last! And we get to travel this one together. I couldn't have asked for a better quest. I feared I'd have to go alone."

Reid nodded. "I feel the same."

"Oh, don't give me that, Reid." Penet nudged his arm. "Don't tell me you don't feel a pinch of pride at not having your own quest. I know you too well to think that."

Reid shrugged. He did, in a way, have his own quest. "I suppose there is a small pinching of pride."

Penet laughed, more jubilant than Reid had ever seen the quiet young man.

✳

Reid made his way to Adrian's chamber. The evening had been restless; his uncle and aunt had arranged a dinner for him, Henry, and Penet, and the entire barracks had joined in the celebration. If only Reid felt like celebrating; his heart needed a rest. With night settling over the castle, Reid needed to say his most important goodbye—to his best friend, whose life depended on his quest.

The royal healer tended to Adrian, her bony hands moving along his torso with a greenish glow.

Destry stood by the wall. At the sight of Reid, he made his way into the sitting room but stood where he could see Adrian.

"I have heard about your quest," Destry said. "Congratulations. There is little advice I can offer you against an apostate that you don't already know. I have faith that you will return victorious. When you return, we will be brothers in arms."

"Thank you."

Reid had looked forward to this day for years, treasured it, fantasized about it to lull him to sleep, and yet he had never dreamed that he would feel as troubled as he did. He glanced down to Adrian's calm, dreamless face. If Reid ever wanted to see those eyes open again, he had to return. And he would.

❄

Reid returned to his own chambers, torn between exhaustion for what lay ahead and the giddiness of finally receiving his king-given quest, the quest that would make him a knight.

Sir Reid.

He stepped into his bedroom, mind on a bath, when his eyes caught on a letter on his bed. He reached for it and turned the parchment over. No address. No name. Not even an envelope. He tore open the unfamiliar wax seal and flipped the parchment open.

A delicate, slightly scrawled hand wrote:

Reid,

I don't know where I'll be when you get this. I might be dead. I know you think the worst of me. Most people do. I promise you that I did not poison Adrian. I would never deliberately harm him. I know who poisoned him, but I fear that telling you would put you in danger. It would put everyone in the castle in danger.

There is a darkness gathering, and it is moving this way. I plan to do what I can to stop it before it starts, before it kills anyone else. Ison is helping me. He is no more guilty than I am. I can't tell you where I am or where I am going, only that you should be careful of who you trust. There is someone far more dangerous than a common apostate in the castle.

Be careful, Reid.

Also, I kept your dagger. It's far better than anything I've ever owned. It's the only thing I have that was yours. I wish I had something of mine to leave you, but I don't. I don't have anything to give you, except for my heart, but you've already got it. You always will.

I love you.

Juniper

He read it twice. The letter rippled in his shaky grip. He could hear her voice speaking to him, her smooth tone, her playful seriousness. Reid crumpled to the floor, unable to hold back the sobs that crashed through his chest. Damn her. Damn every hair on her head!

I love you.

Dead. *He brought in her head.*

He wanted to burn the letter, burn her memory, but he couldn't. He couldn't get rid of one of the few things he had of her.

Gods...if he had just...if he hadn't pushed her away, she would be alive. She would be here, with him.

Somehow, Reid pushed himself to his feet and staggered into the bathing room. He washed his face and hands in cold water. He took a cold bath and pulled on the first thing he grabbed from his closet. He sat on the edge of his bed, water between his shoulder blades soaking into his shirt, and he pulled Juniper's letter to himself.

He read it again.

I love you.

He had loved her too. He folded the letter and tucked it into his bedside table. His future was what he needed to focus on—his prince, his friend, not the past. Not the girl who had left him in tatters, not the apostates who had left him orphaned. He needed to focus on the things that still mattered. He would become a knight, and he would do his duty to the crown, to his kingdom.

He would save the prince's life before the poison took him.

Reid stared into the quiet hearth, the words of her letter repeating relentlessly. And then, thoughts came together. Juniper's letter to him had been from her, without question.

He held a piece of her writing.

Her signature.

The world tilted. He jumped to his feet, seized her letter from the nightstand, and flattened it against his bedspread. He could see the note that had come with the poisoned wine clearly; he had memorized it.

The signatures were not the same. The notes had not been written by the same hand.

Shaking, Reid rushed to the corridor. The king needed to know of this at once—but Reid paused at the door. He stood there, in his bare feet and undershirt.

It didn't matter. He could clear Juniper's name, but it didn't matter.

Dead. She was dead.

Reid stood there a long moment. Then he returned the letter to his bedside table and collapsed on his bed. He needed sleep; he had a long day ahead of him, but sleep felt further away than it ever had been before.

CHAPTER FIFTY-EIGHT

Ison woke up early to check on the simmering potions, all of which had brewed perfectly, and he had just walked into the kitchen to let Nera know, when a commotion came from the main room—the front door bursting open, running footsteps, a skin-tingling silence.

"What's that?" Nera whispered, clutching a wooden spoon like a sword.

Ison started toward the main room at a run, whip-like tendrils of magic at the ready. Nera ran behind, soup dripping from the spoon and fire dancing at her fingertips. Ison ran into the main room and skidded to a halt. Josephine's hand rested on Xavier's arm. The assassin was panting; sweat lined his brow and glistened on his neck. His blue-gray eyes met Ison's, and he felt a chill—Xavier wore terror and grief.

"What happened?" Ison asked at once, disbanding his magic. He grabbed Xavier by the shoulders. When Xavier hesitated, Ison shook him. "What?"

"Juniper," Xavier whispered, his voice hoarse.

Ice wormed through Ison's chest, stilling his heart. He met Xavier's eyes, the grief there, and Ison stumbled back. He held firmly onto Xavier's shoulders. He mouthed, "No," though it didn't make any sound.

"They say she's dead," Xavier whispered.

Ison felt the very ground move beneath his feet, but when he looked, the stone remained solid. His knees turned to water, and if not for Xavier, he would have collapsed. He fell forward, and he held onto the stability that Xavier offered.

"No," Ison said into Xavier's shoulder. Tears blurred his vision. "No. It's not possible. She said she knew what she was doing!"

Xavier stayed silent for a long moment, then said, "Amery went topside to see what she could find out. She should be back any minute."

Ison couldn't feel his legs. Xavier pulled him through the house, down the walk, and through the ward. They ran through the Undercity, but it all blurred. The vendors, the hushed talk, the worried faces; the news of

Juniper Thimble's death had surged too fast, unnaturally fast, and Ison wanted nothing more than to empty his stomach onto the stone.

He didn't. He kept his eyes on Xavier's brown hair and followed.

❄

Word spread faster than she expected. The Undercity was ripe with rabid, worried whispers about Juniper Thimble's untimely death. Several even claimed to have seen Captain Tinnly carry her head through the castle gates!

Oh, how delightful a thing to watch! She crouched in the shadows of the Undercity, observing, listening, committing the scene to memory. And yet it was strange to hear all these things. All the whispers about Juniper Thimble, the worry and grief, as if the people actually loved her and would indeed miss her presence.

The ousting of the bully mages had helped that.

With everyone preoccupied with gossip and grief, no one looked at her; no one spent more than a glance in her direction. She kept the hood of her short cloak up. Her new robes of sky blue and gold would have been out of place any other day, and maybe in a few days, the people of the Undercity would comment on the strange visitor who kept her face hidden, who appeared in the Undercity and then vanished again.

Or maybe she had been reading too much.

She walked with purpose toward the keep, each step a fight not to break out in a run. She got in the secret way, the way she had discovered years ago and had used to come and go without any of the others knowing. She hadn't told anyone about it.

Back in her room, she gathered what she had. It didn't take long. From the window, she saw Ison and Xavier run to the keep, and her heart sank.

She wouldn't be able to collect Ison from Josephine's and slip out without a word. She hadn't a heartbeat to rethink her plan, for the door to the room burst open. She turned to find Maddox standing in the doorway, and he did not look happy to see her.

And the ruse of her death ended.

"My office," he commanded, his voice low and cool. Underneath it, rage. "Now."

Juniper tugged the leather bag over her shoulder, a gesture that did not escape Maddox's notice. He stood and held the door open for her, eyes burning. She followed him down the stairs to his office.

This would not be a clean getaway.

They stepped onto the main floor of the keep. Most of the thieves and assassins had gathered to hear the gossip. Ison stood among Xavier, Amery, and Blythe. The younger girl hid her emotions better than the others. As Juniper descended the last stair, a heavy silence fell over the room, engulfing the entire house.

Ison's gray eyes looked her up and down. Puffy. His eyes were puffy. He had been crying. Her heart clenched in her chest. She met his gaze, and a stout anger pushed his worry aside. Xavier looked livid.

"You, mage," Maddox spat, pointing at Ison. "My office."

Her heart clenched tighter. Ison hadn't done anything—but he obeyed. Xavier's arm twitched, and he looked like he might argue but held his tongue.

Bulo shut the door behind them.

Maddox walked to the other side of the desk, his steps light and quick. His restraint exposed the little lines on either side of his mouth. He leaned forward on the desk, hands flat and fingers splayed. "What the hell are you doing?" Maddox seethed, his voice lithe with anger.

She suddenly felt glad for the wide desk between them, although she knew if he wanted to hurt her, the desk wouldn't matter. "Assassinating a man who can't be assassinated," Juniper answered plainly.

Maddox glared. He took in her new clothes, the bag on her shoulder, and her remarkably unscathed status for having been killed. And he put the pieces together himself. "You were going to run," he said coldly.

Juniper didn't argue. That had been the plan, simple as it was. "It is part of my plan. Captain Tinnly is very well aware of the price on his head, and he has taken every precaution. I got into the tower, he caught me, and there wasn't a way to kill him and get out without a fight that would most likely kill me. So, I struck a deal with him instead to fake my death. I pretend to leave, and then tonight, when he thinks he is safe, I go back in and finish the job."

"And you're readying to leave?" Maddox pointed to her bag.

"I would drop his head off before I left," Juniper said, pretending to be horrified that he would think any less of her.

Maddox straightened. His brown eyes bore into Juniper's. He didn't believe her. He gracefully stepped around the desk, hands behind his back. "Are you sure that was your plan? Are you sure you didn't fake your death so that I wouldn't come looking for you when you left me without completing your bargain?" He stepped closer and fingered the strap of her bag.

Juniper swallowed. "I told you I would assassinate the captain."

"And you've lied before," he whispered.

She frowned. "Like you haven't," she seethed. Before he could comment, she continued, "You sent me to the castle as bait. You knew one of us wouldn't come back. You sold me."

Maddox narrowed his eyes, but he did not deny it.

A part of her had wanted him to—that same part that claimed his keep as home wanted him to explain his reasons, to explain how much gold he had made in that deal. Maddox remained silent.

"The king asked for my best," Maddox whispered. "And I sent him my best."

Her hands shook.

"And look at all that you got to do," he whispered, taking the smallest of steps closer. "A guest of the king, a companion of the prince. You were treated like a princess, fed like one, dressed up like one, envied like one. You even found a knight in shining armor."

At that, her heart clenched tight enough to steal her breath. "I have to get out of the city. Something is happening out there, and I need to stop it."

Maddox shifted, a barely-there movement that anyone else would have not seen, but she, his student, did. A knife slid from his sleeve, and her magic reacted. He thrust the dagger toward her, and she summoned a shield of ice between them.

She felt the slightest of pokes. Her ice had formed around the blade, barely halting its thrust. She stumbled back. The dagger would have gone through her ribs, upward into her heart—a killing blow.

Maddox growled and yanked the dagger from the ice. She melted the ice and pulled it back, hovering it in front of her. The candlelight reflected on the undulating water, sending ripples of light across Maddox's face, where pure rage twisted his features.

"I own you, Juniper," he said.

"I own myself," she countered.

Maddox readied to throw his dagger, his fingers flexed—the room flashed. Maddox froze, and the very air stilled. Her own breath puffed against her lips. A moment of panic, and then she recognized it: when Ison had frozen the air around the knights.

"Ison?" Juniper asked.

305

"You don't want to kill him," Ison whispered. "He doesn't want to kill you."

And he was preventing them both from the act.

She nodded at him, thankful but unable to form the words. She dismissed her water. A rumbling came from outside the door. A shadow underneath the door hesitated.

Listening.

She put her finger to her lips and motioned Ison to follow. She tiptoed to the wall behind the desk, between two bookcases, and pushed. The lock gave, and she and Ison walked into Maddox's real office. Compared to the other, it was a mess. Papers were strewn about the desk, the bookshelves uneven and undusted. She secured the secret door back in place.

"What about the others?" Ison whispered.

Xavier and Amery and Blythe.

"I left Amery a note," Juniper said. "She'll know what to do."

She ushered him to the other side of the room, to the secret door in the paneling that would take them topside. She felt along a few panels before she found it—she knew that it existed, not where it existed. The locking mechanism popped and released. It slid outward to reveal a narrow hole and a simple wooden ladder. It went up, up, up, out of sight, to the surface. Maddox's private entrance.

She went first, and Ison came a few steps behind. She heard the door click back into place. They didn't have much time; Maddox would know exactly where she had gone when he unfroze.

CHAPTER FIFTY-NINE

The ladder led into the backroom of a print shop, and she and Ison slipped up and closed the trapdoor behind them. The rhythmic *thwap, thwap, thwap* of the print machine filled the air, copying page after page. The air reeked of bitter ink. She and Ison slipped through a side door between two crates of supplies and into a wide alley bathed in the early morning light of Rusdasin.

"Okay," Juniper said calmly. "We need to get out of the city. There should be a boat waiting for us on the Weslie. We get out, we head west for a while, then north, skirting Rusdasin as much as we can, then head east toward Collatia."

Ison didn't argue. He looked sick.

Juniper guided the way toward the Weslie, crisscrossing the city through alleyways, keeping clear of busy streets and the Watch, just in case.

After a while of walking, Ison spoke. "Jun?"

"Hmm?"

"What really happened with the captain?"

"We made a deal that I would leave the city, and he would say he killed me."

"He agreed? Just like that?"

Juniper bit her lip. "Not exactly. I told him how to get into the Undercity."

Ison paled. "You what? But...what about everyone down there?"

"I told him that the people who didn't fight back should be spared," Juniper explained. "I also explained to him that something was happening, something horrible. I didn't use Nexon's name, but he seemed to understand. I told him I was going to go do something to stop it before it got worse, and I tasked him with taking care of the city while I was gone."

Ison let out a humorless chuckle. "Why didn't you tell me about this plan?"

She heard the disappointment in his voice. "My original plan was to return to the Undercity before the news spread, find you, and we would get out. But, as you saw, the news reached the Undercity first." She sighed; she didn't like discussing the ways in which her plan had failed. "Xavier seemed upset."

"He was," Ison said darkly. "He was worried about you. So was I."

Juniper sighed. She spotted the glistening of the Weslie through the alleys before them. She stopped and turned, halting Ison. "You can go back if you want," she said, staring into his gray eyes.

He considered; hesitation turned his eyes cold. "No. I can't go back. Not now. Maddox will have it out for me and you."

"I'm sorry," she blurted. "I keep ripping you out of places."

He didn't argue. He closed his eyes, inhaled, and then met her eyes. His softened. "It's okay, Jun. I've already seen more of the world than I thought I would. I used to pray for adventure, and it looks like those prayers are being answered at last."

She tried to give him a warm smile, but it felt forced.

"Where are you going?"

They both jumped. Amery strolled into the alley, hood pulled over her dark hair. Blythe walked a step behind. Xavier, daggers out, lagged.

"You got my note?" Juniper asked, though Amery's presence was answer enough.

"I did," Amery said. "Are you coming back?"

Juniper didn't answer. She looked to Blythe, met her dark eyes. "You'll listen to Amery, won't you?"

Blythe nodded. "You're going to stop Nexon from coming back, aren't you?"

Juniper nodded, unsure how true her answer was. She didn't know. She might not even make it to Collatia.

"Maddox will have it out for you after this." Amery met Juniper's eyes. Not just for leaving, but for selling out the Undercity too.

"Are you ready?" Juniper asked.

Amery waved Juniper's concern aside. "I had my plan ready ages ago." Her humor vanished. "Don't worry about us."

"Good," Juniper said.

"When you get back," Amery said, "give me a shout."

"I will." Juniper's gaze slid to Blythe, who stood a little taller. "You'll be strong and brave, right?"

Blythe nodded. "The strongest and bravest."

And Juniper believed her.

Juniper looked to Xavier. He stood stone still, eyes uncertain, his fists clenched. His usually cool demeanor had been disrupted.

Amery turned to look at him too, a smile on her lips. "Do you have anything you would like to say, Xavier?" she asked knowingly.

He let out a short sigh through his nose. "I'm not the best with words," he said, taking steps to stand beside Amery.

"A hug would suffice," Juniper said, and she opened her arms.

Xavier huffed, started toward her, but walked to Ison instead. He grabbed him and kissed him full on the mouth.

Amery looked to Juniper and winked.

The boys parted, and a deep red had engulfed Ison's cheeks. Even Xavier looked a bit flushed.

A shout came from a few streets over.

"That sounds like Bulo," Amery said, frowning.

"Maddox did threaten you," Xavier said to Juniper. "Creatively too."

"Then we need to disappear," Juniper said.

"We'll head them off," Amery said.

Juniper grabbed Ison and started toward the glistening speck of the Weslie as the other three dashed in the opposite direction. They came to the river and wandered to the leather shop Captain Tinnly had told her about, and indeed, a small unmanned boat floated in front of it. The shop owner sat in a chair outside, smoking a sweet-smelling pipe.

Juniper climbed down into the boat, Ison followed, and the shop owner gave her a quick nod of his head.

To Ison's confusion, she whispered, "A gift from the captain."

Complete with supplies tucked underneath the seat as he had promised. Between the two of them, they untied the boat and started downriver, westward. She sat beside Ison and let the sunlight brush her skin.

"We'll find him," Juniper said, to herself, to Ison, to the gods. "We will find him and make him pay for what he's done. We'll stop him before he can do anything else. Nexon won't return to power."

Ison nodded. "We will."

Their little boat glided along the Weslie. On either side, shops were opening, bakeries were fanning their fresh scents out of windows and doors, and children were playing in the shallow streams of the flood channels. The sun rose steadily, their boat glided on, and soon, Rusdasin was a towering pile of stone on the eastern horizon. The forests and fields grew along the banks, alive with summer bugs, spotted with patches of blooming wildflowers.

Soon, she told herself, she would take her revenge on Nexon. Then, all the world would again fear the name of Juniper Thimble.

AVAILABLE NOW

Dreams in the Snow

STARS AND BONES BOOK III

BOOKS2READ.COM/DREAMSINTHESNOW

ACKNOWLEDGMENTS

It never ceases to amaze me just how much work goes into producing a book. It takes a great deal of time, and it also takes a great deal of teamwork. I have been blessed with an amazing home team that gives me the perfect blend of constructive criticism and blind encouragement.

First, I have to thank the incredible girls at Authors 4 Authors for giving me and Juniper a chance, for continuing to believe that I produced a story worth telling, and for putting up with me through the process.

Second, to Laurel and Ryan for being constant friends through thick and thin. You've celebrated every highlight, regardless of how small, and have been there to help me get over every self-doubt blockage. Sometimes, all I need is someone to point out how ridiculous all my worries are, and ya'll are my go-to.

And Stephanie, you keep me grounded when I get too far gone in these crazy stories of mine. There's nothing like a good craft beer to shake the routine! Also Travis for reminding me that it's okay to get lost in my own fantasy worlds and that it's okay to stay up until dawn playing Skyrim.

And most importantly, to you, dear reader. Each and every one of you make this dream worthwhile.

ABOUT THE AUTHOR

Beatrice B. Morgan lives in southern Illinois. When she isn't reading or writing, she is most likely playing a video game. She is a night owl, caffeine addict, yoga enthusiast, dog person, hopeless romantic, optimistic, and a shameless Ravenclaw.

Follow her online:

www.bbmorgan.com
Twitter: @BBMorgan_W
Facebook: @BBMorganBooks

Authors 4 Authors Publishing

A publishing company for authors, run by authors, blending the best of traditional and independent publishing

We specialize in speculative fiction: science fiction, fantasy, paranormal, and romance. Get lost in another world!

Check out our collection at https://books2read.com/rl/a4a or visit Authors4AuthorsPublishing.com/books

For updates, scan the QR code or visit our website to join our semi-monthly newsletter!

Want more female-led fantasy? We recommend:

Exile
by Melion Traverse

After killing a paladin in revenge for her family, Squire Bryn is cast out by order of the god Avgorath himself. Now she seeks atonement with the father of the dead paladin. But machinations far greater than a disgraced squire are at play. Unicorn riders—believed to be only legend—ride through the land. A young sorcerer needs help in finding his father, and a mystery brews that could hold the fate of two worlds.

books2read.com/exile